Sanctum

Jason Dean spent much of his professional life as a graphic designer before deciding what he really wanted to do was write the kind of international thrillers he's always loved reading. The James Bishop series was the result. He is now working on the next book in the Korso series. Jason lives in the Far East with his wife and their dog.

Also by Jason Dean

Korso Thrillers

Tracer
Sanctum

SANCTUM

JASON DEAN

CANELO

First published in the United Kingdom in 2022 by

Canelo
Unit 9, 5th Floor
Cargo Works, 1-2 Hatfields
London, SE1 9PG
United Kingdom

A CIP catalogue record for this book is available from the British Library.

Print ISBN 978 1 80032 570 8
Ebook ISBN 978 1 80032 569 2

Printed and bound in Great Britain by Clays Ltd, Elcograf S.p.A.

1

For Karanjit Rai,

who knows why

ONE

When the cop demanded to see his ID, Korso pulled a wallet from his jacket pocket and passed it through the service gap of the security cage.

The card and badge identified him as Detective John Nosalle of the Atlanta Police Department. Complete with genuine holographic overlay, the ID had cost plenty, but it was a necessary expense. He might even use it again sometime. The duty officer compared the photo with the unremarkable face in front of him before keying the name and badge number into his terminal.

Korso stifled a yawn, as though this was yet another mundane task in a long day full of them. He gazed around the small basement room in a casual manner, making careful note of everything, especially the CCTV in one corner of the low ceiling, next to the stairwell just behind him. He made sure to stand at an angle, so it only picked up part of his profile or the back of his head. There was nobody else in the room. He saw a cork bulletin board on one wall with a few pinned notices on it, a water cooler and a coffee machine with an 'out of order' card taped over the coin slot. The St Petersburg Police Department clearly didn't want to encourage casual visitors to this section of the precinct.

He turned back to the steel security cage. It ran the whole width of the room. There was a mesh door on the left of the cage, with no handle on the outside. Korso saw another door inside the cop's cubby hole, with a keypad next to it. The large duty officer was frowning at something on his screen.

The name on his shirt badge read Dassinger. There was a large pizza box open on the table, next to the monitor. Despite the air conditioning, the pungent aroma of pepperoni and cheese filled the room.

'So are we good?' Korso asked, taking back his wallet.

'Just checking the email your people sent over yesterday,' Dassinger said. 'Says you need to check on a piece of evidence in the Tomblin illegal firearms case?'

'Correct.'

'That's a local case. Kind of out of your jurisdiction.'

'There are similarities to another illegal possession case I'm working on.' Korso shrugged. 'When I get a lead, I have to follow it up. You know how it works.'

'Uh huh. Well, I guess you better come on in, Detective.'

He waddled over, unlocked the steel door and pulled it open. Korso stepped through and waited while Dassinger relocked the door. The officer turned and keyed in an eight-digit code on the keypad next to the other door. Korso memorised it out of habit. You never knew. There was a loud buzz, and the cop pushed the door open and stepped through. He pressed a wall switch and harsh fluorescents lit up the interior.

Korso followed him inside.

Despite the air-conditioning, the evidence room smelled musty, with an undercurrent of lubricant oil. The concrete floor was dirty with old stains. Steel storage cages lined the walls, while additional freestanding units took up the rest of the room. Korso saw cardboard boxes and cartons in almost every cage. A few looked new, but most looked tattered and well-used. Attached to the exterior of each box were a barcode and an itemised inventory. Each cage was identified by a sticker containing a five-digit code. Korso turned to his right and spotted another CCTV in the corner, close to the ceiling. It was currently panning left to right, away from him.

'What you want's down this way,' Dassinger said over his shoulder as he entered the leftmost aisle.

While the camera was still pointing away from him, Korso reached into his pocket and pulled out a one-inch-square cube-shaped device. He flicked a switch on the underside, crouched and slid the item along the concrete floor until it ended up under the evidence cage lining the entire right-hand wall. As the security camera began its return sweep, he quickly got up and joined Dassinger in the other aisle.

'You get many visitors down here?' Korso said, pulling a smart phone from his pocket. He pressed a single button and put it back in his pocket.

'Some.' Dassinger was checking the locker labels on the right side of the aisle. 'Not many from out of town. You're the first this month.'

Korso could hear faint but noticeable squeaks and scuffling sounds coming from the other side of the room. He made no mention of them.

'Here you go,' Dassinger said, tapping a cage at waist level. It contained a single cardboard box, one of the newer ones. 'E-7231. Tomblin.'

He grabbed the box, slid it out and handed it to Korso. It was heavy. Korso placed it on the floor.

'I have to wait while you check whatever it is you need to check,' Dassinger said. 'Rules, you know?'

'Understood.'

Korso removed the box lid. Inside he saw a multitude of items in clear polyethylene zip-lock bags, each one tagged with a printed label and another barcode. He pulled one bag out. It contained an empty handgun magazine. Korso looked at it, turning it around as though it might hold the answer he wanted. He waited patiently.

Finally, Dassinger said, 'Hey, you hear that?'

Korso looked up, his brow furrowed. He listened to the same squeaking sounds as before and nodded. 'Sounds like rodents. They probably came for your pizza.'

'Shit. Wait here.' Dassinger pulled a flashlight from his utility belt and shambled off in the direction from which they'd come. He turned left at the end of the aisle and disappeared from sight.

Dropping the gun magazine, Korso jumped to his feet and scanned the labels on the left-hand side of the aisle. He found the one marked D-1224 almost immediately. The cage contained four large cardboard boxes. He pulled the first one out, opened the lid and saw a stack of files and paperwork inside. Placing it on the floor, he opened the next box. This one contained more evidence bags. He rummaged through the contents quickly. When he didn't find what he wanted, he replaced the lid and put the box on top of the other one on the floor. He figured maybe twenty seconds had passed since Dassinger had left him. He didn't have many more to play with. The cop could return at any moment.

Korso opened the third carton.

This one held more baggies. He quickly rooted around with both hands, searching by feel alone, immediately discarding the larger items, and focusing on the smallest. He was just moving a bag containing a watch out of the way when his fingers came into contact with the exact shape he'd been hoping for.

He pulled out the evidence bag in question. The ring contained within looked like a men's silver band. It was intricately embroidered with Celtic imagery, similar to the ring Korso currently wore. Except this one was far too heavy to be silver. He checked the inner band and saw the 950 hallmark, identifying the ring as ninety-five per cent pure platinum. When he saw the series of engraved numbers and letters opposite the hallmark, Korso smiled to himself.

This was the one. Finally.

Unzipping the bag, Korso removed the silver band from his left ring finger and replaced it with the platinum ring. It was a little loose, but it would hold. He stuck the baggie in the bottom of the box, closed the lid and put the carton back where he'd found it. He picked up the other evidence box from the floor and was placing this back in the cage when he heard footsteps coming back his way. Korso grabbed the last carton and practically threw it into the cage, then crouched down in front of the Tomblin evidence again just as the footsteps became more distinct.

Without turning round, Korso said casually, 'Find anything?'

'It's coming from under one of the wall units over there, but I can't see nothing with the flashlight.' He sighed. 'Goddamn rats, they get everywhere.'

'Just call in the exterminators. End of problem.'

'I'll file a request, see where that gets me. What about you? Find what you needed?'

'I'm not sure.' Korso pulled out his phone and snapped a shot of the gun magazine he'd been looking at before. 'Same make and model. Ukrainian. It looks promising, but I won't know till I get back to the precinct and do some cross-referencing.'

Korso dropped the bag into the box and closed the lid. He hefted up the carton and placed it back into the right cage.

'That all you wanted?' Dassinger asked.

'That's it. I appreciate your help with this.'

'No problem.' The cop turned and began walking back down the aisle.

Korso followed a few feet behind. Just before he reached the end, he stopped and poked part of his head out to check the CCTV to his left. It was pointed right his way. He pulled back out of shot and knelt down to fiddle with his shoelace.

Dassinger had already reached the door. He turned back and frowned when he saw Korso was still in the aisle. 'You okay over there?'

'Hold on,' Korso said, retying his shoelace. Three seconds later, he stood up and walked out of the aisle, one hand to his face as he scratched his left cheek. Out the corner of his eye, he saw the camera was now panning right again, away from him. He dropped his hand and quickly joined Dassinger in his cubby hole.

As the cop let him out the steel-mesh door, Korso kept his head lowered as he pretended to do something on his phone. Once he was past the security camera, he climbed the stairs, and in less than a minute he was out of the building altogether.

TWO

The blazing midday sun and extreme humidity had Korso sweating the moment he left the police station. Florida in late June was like stepping into an oven. Walking across the official car park adjoining the precinct, he pressed his key fob and his rented Infiniti flashed its side lights at him. Taking off his sports jacket, he got in, started the engine and set the aircon to the highest setting.

He removed the platinum ring from his finger, pulled out his phone and took two snapshots. He made sure to show only part of the code on the inner band. He already knew what the numbers and letters signified, that they were the real reason he'd been tasked with recovering the ring, and he wasn't about to give away the whole store before being paid. He attached the shots to a brief text message.

Recovered. Awaiting Payment

He then sent it to the number he'd been given weeks before. He also disabled the mp3 recording of the rats, not that it mattered much. Since he was now out of WiFi range, the micro speaker he'd placed in the evidence room would remain silent for as long as the building remained upright. It had served its purpose.

Exiting the parking lot, Korso turned right onto 1st Avenue North, and began the twenty-minute journey back to his hotel in Dunedin. As he drove, he switched the DAB radio to one of the classical stations and nodded to himself when a J. S. Bach piano piece filled the car interior. It was as good a way as any to mark the culmination of a successful assignment.

Six weeks earlier, he'd received an email requesting the use of his salvage skills to locate and recover a piece of stolen property. The client was a Yemeni entrepreneur who explained at their only face-to-face meeting that, four years previously, an expensive platinum ring had been stolen from his then vacant Manhattan townhouse, along with a number of more valuable items. Thanks to a tip-off from the NYPD, officers from the St Petersburg Police Department apprehended the three burglars five days later at a small bungalow on Stimie Avenue that belonged to the sister of one of the suspects. They also found all the stolen valuables.

Unfortunately, things became more complicated from that moment on. It turned out that the burglars had paid a visit to another townhouse in the same neighbourhood on the same night and had caused the elderly owner to suffer a fatal heart attack when he discovered the intruders in his home. Thus the charges went from simple burglary to involuntary manslaughter. And with all three suspects retaining separate lawyers, each with their own complex agenda, the case quickly became entangled in a never-ending series of motions to postpone or dismiss, based on numerous petty technicalities, or to move the eventual trial to a different state because of perceived prejudices in the jury selection.

This was how it still stood. The wonders of the US legal system. The client had been patient through it all, knowing that his possessions were stuck in an evidence room somewhere but that he'd get them all back eventually. That was until three months ago, when his father died. The platinum ring had been a gift to his son, although he never explained what the letters and numbers on the inner band signified. After his death, the father's long-term personal assistant informed the son that they were the second part of a password needed to access an account in a private bank in the Caymans, containing the sum total of his father's undeclared income. She gave him the first part, and said she believed the actual amount was likely in the mid eight-figure range.

At this point, the client's patience immediately came to an end and he decided to become proactive. Hence the email to Korso, whose history of recovering the unrecoverable was well known to a small but very specific clientele.

With the invaluable aid of MD Dog, a highly skilled hacker he kept on partial retainer, Korso had tracked down the exact location of the stolen items, and amassed a wealth of other intel necessary for the job. The police ID had taken the most time to arrange as it had to be the genuine article, or very close to it, and the officer in question also had to exist in real life. But with money all things are possible, and the client was more than generous when it came to expenses.

Korso's fee was another matter. Usually he insisted on a straight thirty-three per cent of the salvaged item's market value. But while the ring was made from one of the most expensive elements on the planet, it was still only worth about six thousand dollars in total, so that was out. Neither was it realistic for Korso to demand a third of the elusive bank account. So after some back and forth, Korso had finally agreed on a straight fee of two hundred thousand dollars, after expenses. Payment on delivery. Not bad for six weeks' work.

Now it was just a matter of waiting for the client to get back to him.

Mozart's Symphony no. 41 followed Bach, and just before it reached its final notes, Korso pulled into the entranceway of the Fairway Inn, and found a spot in the shaded parking lot close to his chalet. The Fairway was a pleasant, secluded hotel overlooking the St Joseph Sound. Korso's duplex apartment, with its excellent view of the marina, was the most expensive and luxurious in the place.

The apartment also contained an additional bonus in the shape of Alison Williams, a pretty accountant here on vacation, whom he'd met at the restaurant buffet four days ago. They had gotten on, one thing had led to another, and when Korso found out she was staying in one of the hotel's less desirable rooms, he suggested she move her luggage into his apartment for the remainder of her stay. Alison happily accepted the offer, along with the spare key. He left her to do her own thing during the daytime, while he busied himself preparing for the final part of his assignment. The evenings they shared.

Now the job was practically finished, he was looking forward to spending a few full days with her before she headed back to her regular existence in the Midwest. This was the kind of female companionship that suited him best. Brief, and with no strings attached. And she was always in good spirits too. A rare quality in a companion.

Korso was just unlatching his safety belt when his cell phone chirped at him. He picked it up, checked his inbox. The anonymous text consisted of one word:

Done

He went straight to the password-protected website of a very private bank in Lichtenstein. Once past that firewall, he keyed in his long account number and even longer password and was finally transferred to his account page. He saw that the two-hundred thousand had been deposited three minutes ago. That money was already gone, automatically split into seven random amounts and wired to seven other anonymous, untraceable accounts he held around the globe. But the client had done his part. Now it was Korso's turn.

Korso took five more close-ups of the ring, ensuring every part of the inner band was clearly visible. These he attached to a simple text that read:

Thanks

Good manners cost nothing. He sent the text to the same number. Less than a minute later, a return text came back:

Likewise

And that was that. If only every transaction was as painless. The client had played fair from start to finish, which meant he'd go straight to the top of the list should he ever need Korso's services in the future. Korso still had to take the ring to the local FedEx office two miles away and have it delivered to a certain address in New Jersey, but that could wait. He wanted to take a shower and grab something to eat first.

Locking the vehicle, he saw a petite woman in cargo shorts and tight t-shirt exit the room two doors down and unlock her car remotely. She looked over as she walked to the vehicle, beaming at him while she pulled open the door. Korso smiled back. No wedding ring, he noticed. There was certainly no shortage of attractive single women around these parts. She was still watching him as she backed out of the space. He watched her go, thinking of the possibilities, then turned back and noticed Alison's rented Chevy Impala parked a few spots away. He hadn't expected her back so soon. Unlocking the front door to his chalet, he stepped inside and spotted her suitcase standing upright on the floor next to the settee.

He heard footsteps on the stairs and looked up as Alison came down. She'd combed out her afro, and made up her face. Not that she needed it. She was wearing baggy jeans and a yellow tank top, and carried a canvas bag over her shoulder.

'I thought you still had a few days left,' he said.

'I do,' she said, 'but I want to check out Miami before I head back home. Never been there before, and I hear the night life's pretty wild. I was about to leave you a note.' She came over and put her hands on his shoulders, giving him a chaste kiss on the lips. She smelled of rose water and orange blossom. Her large, dark eyes held his. 'Don't be sad, sugar pie. We had fun, didn't we?'

'We did. Want some lunch before you go?'

'Already had a late breakfast.' She picked up her suitcase, flashing him a wide smile. 'Let's not draw this out, huh?'

'Last thing on my mind.' He opened the door for her. 'You take care of yourself, Alison.'

'Always do.' She patted his cheek as she passed. 'So long, sugar pie.'

Korso watched her drive off and gave a mental shrug as he shut the door. There were worse ways to end a fling. Climbing the stairs to the bathroom, he unbuttoned his shirt and thought about the woman two chalets down, wondering how long she might be staying at the hotel.

He'd have to ask her.

THREE

On another gloriously sunny afternoon, four weeks later, in a completely different part of the world, Korso pressed the trackpad and stared at the next page of the PDF that filled the laptop screen. Unconsciously, he took a sip of his chilled grapefruit juice. He barely tasted it. All his attention was focused on the text in front of him.

He was reading pages from a slim, forty-page letterpress booklet entitled *Tamerlane and Other Poems* by an author identified only as 'a Bostonian', and printed by Calvin F. S. Thomas in 1827. Even though it was almost two hundred years old, the reproduction was still very poor for its time. And, to be honest, the poems weren't particularly memorable either. But that was all irrelevant.

What Korso was looking at was undeniably the rarest book in American literature: the very first published work of Edgar Allan Poe.

The poems were written just before Poe turned fourteen, and subsequently published by his friend, Calvin Thomas, a few years later when they were both eighteen. Fifty copies were printed, and until recently it was believed that only twelve copies were still in existence. The last one Korso knew about sold at a Christie's auction in 2009 for six hundred and sixty-two thousand dollars. He also knew this particular copy, though badly scuffed with age, would probably go for three times that if put on the market today. Maybe more.

Because what he was looking at was the recently discovered thirteenth copy of the exceedingly rare pamphlet. It was currently owned by a retired antiques dealer in Hartford, Connecticut, who had found it amongst a horde of vintage farming pamphlets in a chest of old books left to him by his deceased uncle. A real find. Even better, the retiree was seriously considering selling it privately, rather than at auction. Apparently, he'd been burned by Sotheby's more than a few times over the years and was loathe to give any auction house the standard ten per cent premium they demanded of sellers. Which was all to the good, as far as Korso was concerned. It made life that much more interesting.

When he wasn't on an active assignment, Korso spent his spare time attempting to track down some of the rarest first-editions on the planet. Since he was a lover of literature, he not only enjoyed the detailed investigative work involved, but made a substantial secondary income from it as well. He had a select roster of extremely rich clients who also shared the same passion, and who were willing to pay whatever outrageous price a seller might demand for a book they had been chasing for years, sometimes for decades.

He knew two clients in particular who would be more than happy to make an offer on this volume. Each was an avid collector of Poe's work, and both were richer than Croesus. Opening his browser, Korso went to his highly secure email account and keyed in his elaborate user name and his twenty-one-digit password.

For security reasons, Korso rarely used a cell more than once before destroying the sim card and dumping the phone, which left email as his foremost means of communication. His numerous forwarding services that guided incoming and outgoing messages ensured none of his emails could be traced to his IP address. And besides, he used a very exclusive proxy VPN. On top of which the name on the passport he was currently using wasn't even his real one – he hadn't used that in years. He owned two more passports of various nationalities, each with a completely different name inside.

In Korso's line of work, the kind of clients he dealt with, one could never be too careful. A lesson he'd learnt long ago, and never forgotten.

He composed a fairly lengthy email, detailing everything he knew about this Poe edition, coupled with a few facts about the seller himself. After attaching the PDF of the book, he added a few thoughts on the kind of offer that might be accepted and sent off personalised versions to each man. The rest was up to them. If either man was interested in taking things to the next level, Korso would get in touch with his contact in the US, who would then approach the seller directly and see what kind of response the offer brought.

Korso took another sip of juice and got up and stretched. Strolling over to the study window, he breathed in the warm, dry air as he took in the ocean view again. The sight of Caldera's volcanic islets, set amid the deep blue of the Mediterranean, never got old. It was one of the main reasons he'd rented the two-storey villa in the first place. Situated on the northern tip of the Greek island of Santorini, the house itself was in an ideal location. Since there was no beach to speak of, only smoothly sloping cliffs leading down to the sea, it was well off the tourist trail. And the few neighbours he had in the area were rarely seen in person, happy to mind their own business, and leave Korso to his.

His last residence had been a nice townhouse in Bermuda, and he'd been there for almost two years before that address became seriously compromised by some unwanted visitors. After that, he'd had no choice but to take his few belongings and find somewhere else to live. But that was all right. He made it a rule to never stay too long in one place, and the cramped island had started to feel a little too confining anyway. A year down the line and he might feel the same way about Santorini. But for now, he liked the place just fine. The future could take care of itself.

An electronic ping jolted him out his reverie. The alert meant he'd just received an email, which was something of a surprise. He hadn't expected a reply from either man quite so soon. He sat down in front of his laptop. The new message was from an unknown address, and instead of a header there was just a blank space. Frowning, Korso clicked on it.

The message was brief:

Korso, call me ASAP. You know the number. Dog.

Korso gave a small grunt as he sat back in his seat. He looked at the nine words in the message again. He'd read them correctly. Dog was actually contacting *him*. In the seven years they'd known each other professionally, that had never happened before. Not that he really knew Dog, of course, since they'd never met in person. Anytime they spoke, Dog's voice was disguised by a sophisticated modulator. It could be male, female, robotic, or even a prepubescent child's. The device apparently had a wide choice.

Nevertheless, his curiosity had been well and truly aroused.

He opened a drawer and took out one of his pre-paid burner phones. He removed the plastic packaging and switched it on. Once it was up and running, he dialled a number from memory, left the number of the new phone on the voicemail, and hung up. This was the system they always used when Korso needed something. He saw no reason to change it now the shoe was on the other foot.

Less than a minute later, the phone rang. He answered it.

'This is a first,' he said.

'Don't I know it,' Dog said. This time the voice was a man's, pitched an octave or two lower than Korso's. 'But it's not like I've got a whole lot of other options available.'

'So let's get to it. Why are we talking?'

'I'm in some very serious shit, K, and I need you to pull me out of it.'

FOUR

'Just how serious is serious?' Korso said.

'That kind of depends on your stance on personal liberty,' Dog said. 'As far as I'm concerned, this is end-of-the-world stuff.'

'So you're facing a prison term, then?'

'You got it. And we're talking well into double figures too.'

'Before we go any further, how secure is this conversation?'

'Nobody's listening in, K. You can count on it. The encryption software I use I designed myself, which means it's at least three years ahead of anything on the market. But that's the least of my problems right now. I need—'

'First things first,' Korso interrupted. 'I know you're not phoning from a jail cell. You wouldn't be that stupid. So where are you calling from?'

'I'm at my... uh, usual quarters, but that's only because of the damn ankle shackle they put on me. I'm under strict house confinement. I try walking out my front door for longer than ten seconds and this little red light starts flashing, and it's game over for me. First thing I did was try to take a look at its innards, but I never even got to first base. And I don't dare try again.' Dog sighed. 'As much as I hate to admit it, this device they stuck on me is a pretty sophisticated piece of kit.'

'Who's *they*?'

'Interpol. Cybercrimes division. And they've got enough to put me away for two lifetimes.'

'So why don't they?'

'Because they're holding out for something better, something worth at least ten of me. Maybe a hundred.'

Korso took another sip of his juice. 'Start from the beginning. What did you do? How did they catch you? And what do they really want?'

'To answer your first question, what I did was trust a kid. Which leads directly into the second question.'

'Explain.'

'Okay, a fortnight ago I had to babysit my fourteen-year-old nephew for a short time. It's not something I usually do, but I owed a favour and couldn't really say no. Family, you understand? So like every other kid on the planet he's crazy about computers, and after a few days it became obvious that he had a real gift for getting into secure places. And we're talking fairly hard to access places here. To tell the truth he kind of reminded me of myself when I was his age, a real code-monkey, so I started teaching him a few tricks of the trade to cover his tracks, and he went on from there.'

'That's not too smart, Dog.'

'Easy to say now. I kept a pretty close watch on him all through this period so he couldn't compromise my security at any point, but I wasn't able to keep an eye out every second of the day. All I know is he must have somehow slipped through my net for a few minutes, and that's all the time he needed to completely screw up my life. I found out far too late that he somehow managed to hitch a ride onto one of my special VPNs when he was trying to illegally access some e-commerce sites, which was bad enough. But then the idiot forgot everything I taught him when he yanked himself out of their systems, and he left footprints large enough to lead right back to me. And the worst sin of all, he forgot to lock one of my back doors when he came hurtling back, which meant if anyone spotted his presence in there and decided to follow the electronic trail, they could do so with relative ease.'

'And someone did just that.'

'Exactly right. So all of a sudden my firewalls might as well be made of tissue paper, because the next thing I know two Interpol agents show up at my front door and demand an interview. This is two days ago. Straight away they handed me a printout pulled directly from my own database, containing the names and contact information of thirty of my biggest clients. And let me tell you most of those clients are *very* bad people. I practically had a coronary there and then.'

In a very calm voice, Korso said, 'You know my next question, Dog.'

'Yeah, I know it. And you don't need to worry. Your name's not on any file of mine, mainly because I haven't got a clue what your real name *is*. When I did refer to you at all, it was by initial only. And K can stand for a lot of things.'

Korso breathed a little easier. This was exactly why he'd stopped using his real name two decades ago. Although, even if Dog had keyed in his current Korso moniker, it wouldn't have made too much difference. It was just a brand name he used, mainly for business purposes. If it became compromised for whatever reason, he could easily adopt another one. It would cause him more than a few problems, but he'd do it. He got up and strolled over to the window and looked out at the Mediterranean again.

'How much information of yours did they gain access to?' he asked, watching a speedboat in the distance. 'I assume it wasn't everything.'

Dog gave a throaty chuckle. 'Not even close. Basic Survival 101: never keep all your data in one place. But they still managed to grab a small section of my client list, along with clues to the kind of work I'd done for them, and a few other bits and pieces. It was enough. These agents aren't idiots, K. They know how to join the dots. I'm not about to go into details here, but what they've got on me is enough to keep me out of the sunlight forever.'

'But you're saying they don't want you.'

'What's another hacker to Interpol? The world's full of people like me. I know that and so do my two guardians. I'm just small potatoes. I haven't even been officially arrested yet, which just goes to show these two aren't amateurs at this. You know my MO, K. My whole trade depends on my total anonymity. I lose that and I lose everything. So right from the start, as soon as they found out about me, they made sure not to put my name down on any paperwork. As far as Interpol are concerned, I'm simply Suspect No. 3489.'

'How do you know?'

'I checked for myself. I may be confined to the house, but I've still got my gear and I can always find a way to access places that don't want me. Interpol's database is no tougher than some that I've had to crack. Well, okay, it's a *little* more secure than most, I'll give them that. Anyway, I figured it was worth the risk. But after finding no mentions of my name, it at least proved to me that these guys are playing the long game. And that they want to deal.'

'Are the two agents with you now? Because I find it hard to believe they'd just leave you alone in your domicile, with all your equipment right at your fingertips.'

'They're not living with me, if that's what you mean. But one's always close by, keeping watch at all times. And as for my gear, they know I need it in order to help them get what they really want.'

'Which is?'

There was a pause on the line. 'You remember the Guatemalan vice-president who got assassinated almost a year ago? It was all over the news for a couple of days. He's the one who got disembowelled while taking a leak in their congress building.'

'I remember.'

Korso subscribed to all the reputable online news sites, and he had read everything he could about the murder at the time. It seemed an unhinged political fanatic named Juan Arriola, using a fake ID that passed all security checks, had gotten himself a job with the cleaning company that had the contract to service all the government buildings in Guatemala City. Over a period of some weeks, Arriola managed to wangle himself a permanent place in the cleaning crew that handled the congress building. Once he'd established himself as a trustworthy and diligent employee, he was more or less left to his own devices during his many night shifts. And it was during those shifts that he would continue his real work of constructing a false wall at one end of a little-used, narrow supply room on the second floor. Two doors down from this supply room was the men's room closest to the office occupied by the vice-president, Cesar Dias, whenever he had to speak at committee hearings.

At some point, after filling the space behind the wall with enough dry rations and supplies to keep him going for weeks if necessary, Arriola simply went to work one night and stayed there. He lived, ate and slept in the small alcove, patiently waiting for his moment. He finally got it on the day the vice-president was due to chair a congressional hearing on constitutional changes relating to governmental transparency and accountability.

Early one Monday morning, the vice-president arrived at his office to prepare for the hearing held later that day. At some point he visited the bathroom, and when he left his cubicle he was attacked by the knife-wielding assassin. There wasn't even time for him to scream. There were no witnesses. Arriola stabbed him a total of fourteen times, then calmly left the building by one of the rear entrances, avoiding all the security cameras. At some point along the way, he got rid of the murder weapon. The police arrested him only hours later, but they never did find the knife. It didn't matter. Arriola was more than happy to confess his guilt. He didn't even ask for a lawyer. As for motive, he said he wanted to finally bring the numerous human rights offences committed by the current Guatemalan government to the attention of the world's media, and decided this would be the most dramatic way to do it.

Since the country's death penalty had been abolished several years earlier, Arriola was quickly sentenced to life in solitary at El Infiernito – or 'Little Hell' – one of the very worst prisons in South America. As far as Korso knew, he was still there.

'And that murder is somehow relevant to your current situation?'

'I'm getting to that,' Dog said. 'Now one of the names on that client list of mine is Miguel Quezada, who's one of the big-shot mafia bosses in that part of the world. He lives in a private compound just outside of Guatemala City.'

'Quezada. I've heard the name, I think.'

'I wouldn't be surprised. He's a bad one, all right. I've done a few special jobs for him over the past couple of years. The most recent was to supply him with some highly classified blueprints for a number of government buildings in the capital.'

Korso nodded to himself. 'Including the congress building.'

'Got it in one.'

'So you're saying this Quezada was the one really pulling the strings behind the assassination?'

'That's what my two new friends, Agents Verhoeven and Steinman, believe. Verhoeven also told me that she helped interrogate the killer in prison shortly after he was sentenced to life, and through the interpreter he admitted that Quezada not only financed the whole thing, but helped arrange it too. He said that Quezada also promised to give a million dollars to the radical left-wing political group the assassin belonged to if he followed two simple but very important rules.'

Now we're getting to it, Korso thought. 'And did Quezada keep his word?'

'He paid up.'

'So what were the two rules?'

'First, the killer had to use a knife on the poor guy, meaning it had to be up close and personal. No other weapon could be used. It was a knife or nothing. And not just any knife, but a very particular dagger that Quezada would personally provide for him.'

'What kind of dagger?'

'He said it was an ancient-looking thing with a polished bone handle and a jagged blade sculpted from thick jade.'

'Mayan, most likely,' Korso said, picturing it in his mind. He'd seen several ceremonial daggers just like that in museums. Usually found in Aztec tombs from the sixth or seventh century. There was also the added bonus of Arriola being able to take the knife through metal detectors without setting off any alarms. Very clever. 'And the second rule?'

'The killer had to get away with it. At least, for a short while. Now ask me why.'

Korso thought for a few moments, but nothing came. 'Okay, I'm asking.'

'Because Quezada wanted the guy to have enough time to place the still-bloody murder weapon in a jiffy bag, and mail it back to him.'

Korso snorted. 'He wanted a trophy.'

'Bingo.'

'And?'

'Isn't that enough?'

'Not nearly. What else?'

'What else. Okay, Verhoeven told me Interpol have video testimony from a drug courier who was actually invited up to Quezada's house one afternoon, about seven months ago. After he was caught in a police sting recently, he quickly turned informer to reduce his sentence. And this courier says he witnessed Quezada showing off to his house guests as he waved around this ancient-looking jade dagger with a polished bone handle, making noises about how he was master of his own destiny and this knife proved it, or something like that. This courier also said the blade itself was dark with what looked like dried blood.'

'Waving it around,' Korso said. 'You mean Quezada was actually handling the knife himself?'

'That's what Verhoeven said. I saw no reason not to believe her.'

Korso finished his juice as he sat back down at the table. He'd been processing all the disparate elements while Dog talked, and as much as he tried he could only think of one possible conclusion to all this. He set the glass down.

'The answer's no.'

FIVE

'What are you talking about?' Dog said. 'I haven't even asked you anything yet.'

'You don't need to. I can see it coming a mile away.'

It was all as transparent as glass. Interpol clearly wanted Quezada in a major way, and now they had a witness who'd seen him personally handle an antique jade knife that might be the actual weapon used to killed Guatemala's vice-president a year ago. So they figure all they need is that knife, with Quezada's prints all over the bone handle and the vice-president's blood on the blade, and Quezada's down for the count. Conspiracy to murder.

Since there was no way Quezada could have gotten that knife without knowing the assassin, it would be as close to an open and shut case as you could possibly get. It wouldn't matter how many expensive lawyers he had at his disposal. Interpol were probably already licking their lips at the thought of it.

There was just one catch.

'You must think I'm certifiable,' Korso said. 'That's the only explanation.'

'Look, if I thought there was any other way K. Or if I knew anyone better suited to—'

'Commit suicide?' Korso shook his head. It was almost comical. 'Dog, you're suggesting I break into what's almost certainly the heavily guarded fortress of a psychotic South American crime lord, who *may* be in possession of the actual murder weapon used to kill his country's vice-president. And steal it. On my own. That *is* the essence of what you're asking, isn't it?'

'Well… in a way, yeah.'

'Then let me ask you this: why would I even consider doing something that hare-brained? I'm genuinely interested.'

'To help pull me out of a bottomless hole, for starters. You and I have known each other a long time, K. That must be worth something.'

'I'm not sure "know" is the right verb to use for our relationship. Especially as we've never even met. I value your services, Dog, but let's not pretend this is something more than what it is. I employ the use of your skills whenever I come up against a particular complication that I can't handle myself. You and I are simply associates, nothing more.'

'And have I ever let you down, K? Or told you, sorry I can't help, but I'm busy with this something else over here? I'm always there when you need me.'

'And I pay you very well for it. That's how business relationships work.'

Dog paused. 'Look, I need your help, K. I've got nowhere else to turn. I'm here asking for your help.'

'I don't do good deeds, Dog. Especially when they involve insane levels of risk.'

'Hey, we're both pros so I wouldn't expect you to do it for nothing. I've managed to put away a fair amount over the years. Name a figure, and I'll pay whatever you ask.'

'This may surprise you, but money isn't my sole incentive when it comes to accepting assignments, and besides, I'm fairly flush after my last one. But that's all immaterial. My main concern right now is how much you might have told Interpol about me.'

'What do you mean?'

'It's obvious, isn't it? Not only have your guardians not placed you under arrest, but they've allowed you to stay in your residence surrounded by all your hardware. They must have done that for a reason. And the only reason that occurs to me is that you've already sold them on the possibility of someone you know going in there and grabbing this knife for you. You would need access to your equipment in order to give that person necessary back-up as and when. Am I close to the mark?'

Another pause. 'Pretty close, actually.'

'In which case, they must have some confidence in this person's abilities, or why even bother? So what do they actually know about me? Give me details.'

'You understand I had to give them something, or it was game over for me before we even started.'

'I can appreciate that.'

'Okay, so they already knew Quezada was one of my clients, and the very first thing they wanted from me was any kind of information I might have that could help them get a lead on that knife. Like blueprints for his estate in Guatemala City, or intel on his closest associates, or anything like that. Anything at all, in fact. And I had nothing. Zero. Ours wasn't that kind of relationship. I knew he was the client because I always do my research and never go into a deal blind, but I never dealt with Quezada himself. It was always two or three steps removed, and the contact I spoke with was different every time. I told Verhoeven and Steinman all that up front.'

'And?'

'And they weren't too happy about it, as you'd expect. *But*, I told them, I do happen to know a covert salvage specialist with plenty of experience at recovering lost or stolen assets, and that he's got a very high success rate at this kind of thing. I mentioned that I've worked closely alongside him on numerous jobs over the years, and that I might be able to persuade him to recover that knife. But only as a favour to *me*.'

'Stretching the truth a little there, weren't you?'

'When you're desperate, you'll say anything. And it wasn't that far from reality when you think about it.' Dog sighed. 'It seemed to satisfy them, though. And that's why I'm still here at my own place, instead of a prison cell somewhere. Look, I know I'm rowing upstream here, K, and I can't blame you if you tell me to get screwed, but if there's any way I can persuade you to help me out, just say the word and it's done. But at least think it over before you turn me down. That's all I'm asking.'

This wasn't an unreasonable request. Dog deserved that much. So Korso leaned back in his seat and proceeded to give the matter some serious consideration.

Korso didn't have friends, only associates, and not too many of those. Thinking back, he calculated he'd met only a handful of professionals who, when it came down to the final wire, could really be depended on. And Dog was a member of that very exclusive circle. Now that he thought about it, he could barely recall an assignment where he hadn't utilised Dog's special skills at some point. There was that job in Morocco three years ago, when he was tasked with recovering a portfolio containing eight genuine Monet sketches, stolen from a Lithuanian oligarch. He'd completed that assignment without any outside help, but only because of a unique and fortunate set of circumstances. That was far from the norm.

All of which meant that if Dog was permanently taken out of play, Korso would have to find a suitable replacement almost immediately. That wasn't quite as straightforward as it sounded. While it was true that there were plenty of skilled hackers around, how many of those could actually be trusted? No, Dog was a true rarity in the trade, and always came through. And Dog didn't get too curious about extraneous matters either, like digging into Korso's past, for example. That was another major plus.

Then there was the job itself. Korso didn't know nearly enough yet to make an informed decision on what was possible and what wasn't, but he'd started with less in the past. This one at least sounded unlike anything he'd done before. He'd have to find out a lot more about this Quezada, though, before he could even consider it. But on the plus side, Korso was a fluent Spanish speaker, so at least there wouldn't be a language barrier.

He smiled thinly to himself, seeing where his thoughts were leading. You could never hide from yourself. As much as he hated to admit it, part of him was already warming to the challenge.

He looked out the window at the clear azure sky, tapping a finger against his lower lip. After another minute of this, he picked up the phone again.

'I'm back.'

'I'm almost afraid to ask,' Dog said.

'Well, I won't keep you in suspense. I've decided I'm not completely opposed to the idea, although that doesn't necessarily mean I'll do it yet.'

'Oh, thank Christ for that.' Dog blew out a breath. 'Just when I thought there was no light at the end of the tunnel. Tell me what I can do to turn that maybe into a yes, K. Because whatever it is, it's yours.'

'Well, if I do this, and that's a big "if" until I know a lot more than I do now, then I'd want three things in return.'

'Name them.'

'First, anytime I require your services from now on, you provide them, gratis. And without any unnecessary delay. That means whenever I call you, my needs automatically take precedence over anyone else's.'

'When you say "from now on", you mean forever?'

'No, a lifetime of servitude isn't what I had in mind. You and I have worked together for seven years now, Dog. And we'd continue that relationship, but for the next seven years you'd be working for free. At least for me. It's not like I use you that often anyway, so it wouldn't be any great hardship. You could still charge your other clients whatever you want, as always.'

'Okay, deal. What else?'

'You'd pay all expenses. Travel, supplies, whatever I might need on this job, I get. Immediately. No questions asked.'

'That's a given. So what's the third thing? Wait, don't tell me. One million wired to one of your offshore accounts on completion? Or two million?'

'You mean you've got that much stashed away?'

'And then some. So how much?'

'I told you, money's not always my prime motivator for accepting a job. In this particular case, assuming I go ahead with it, I'd want something else instead.'

'What?'

'A face-to-face meeting with you. In person.'

There was a pause at the other end. 'I don't get it. Why?'

'Because I don't enjoy being at a disadvantage when dealing with you.'

'Okay, you've completely lost me now. What are you talking about?'

'I'm talking about all the times I've asked you to upload my details onto somebody's database. Like a month ago, when you hacked into the secure server of the Atlanta Police Department and altered Detective John Nosalle's details so that for a few hours the headshot that accompanied his record showed my face. That's just one example. You've always known what I look like, Dog, but after all this time I still know nothing about you, and that eats at me. So if I go through with this, that's one of the conditions. After that, I figure you and I will finally be on level terms.'

Korso listened to silence on the line. Finally, he said, 'Are we agreed or not?'

'You sure you don't want a cool million instead? My anonymity's worth that much to me.'

'I figured it would be, but my offer still stands. Your answer.'

'Okay,' Dog said with a sigh. 'You and me, face to face.'

'Good. Now tell me, in your opinion, who's the more level-headed of the two, Verhoeven or Steinman?'

'Well... I'd say Verhoeven's the better bet, and I think she's slightly senior as well. During my initial interrogation Steinman was the one playing bad cop, and it seemed to me he was performing more for her benefit than mine, you know what I mean? As though he was looking for approval from her in some way. But that's just my impression. I could be wrong.'

'I'll trust your instincts, Dog. Verhoeven it is. Can you dig me out an official dossier on her? I don't need everything, just a general overview of her career, character profile, and so on.'

'I could do that, sure. I'll email something over to you later today. Anything else?'

Korso thought for a moment. He already had the perfect meeting place in mind, although it would still take a lot of preparation on his part. Everything would need to be planned down to the second, but that was standard operating procedure for him. *Prepare for all contingencies* was just one of the fundamentals he swore by. It helped explain why he was still breathing when so many past associates, enemies included, had gone belly up.

'Okay, what I want you to do is to set up a meet between me and this Verhoeven,' he said. 'Just the two of us. Two days from now. You can build me up any way you like, but make sure you emphasise she's to follow these instructions to the letter...'

SIX

Grabbing the polystyrene cup from the counter, Korso took his change in coins from the girl behind the cash till, and said, '*Danke*.'

'*Bitte*,' she said, already turning her attention to the small line of customers waiting behind him.

The kiosk was fairly small compared to the other vendors on either side, yet there always seemed to be another customer waiting to be served. He'd read online reviews that said this place supplied the best coffee in the whole terminus, and he was curious to know if it was true or not. After emptying a small sachet of sugar into his cup, he grabbed a long-handled plastic spoon and stirred his drink, taking in his surroundings.

Frankfurt am Main Hauptbahnhof was not only the busiest train station in Germany but also one of its most important traffic hubs, mostly thanks to its central location. And it rarely got busier than Monday mornings from seven to nine. Korso checked his watch again. 07.54. Still another minute to go.

Thousands of commuters and tourists swarmed noisily around him in all directions. The air was thick with conversation and the sounds of humans in constant motion, while arrival and departure announcements were broadcast over the tannoy system almost constantly. Many travellers made their way along the main concourse towards their respective platforms, while others shopped or grabbed themselves a last-minute breakfast from the numerous food and drink vendors all around. He spotted a pair of uniformed *polizei*, each wearing the standard flak jackets, about a hundred feet away. They were strolling along the concourse, closely watching everyone they passed. He'd already seen another pair in similar attire chatting with a female station steward outside the Burger King near the main entrance. There would be more. In Germany, armed police were constantly patrolling the airports and larger railway terminals, forever on the alert for trouble. Especially the drug-related kind.

Korso calmly took a sip of his coffee, making sure the hot liquid made minimal contact with the moustache and beard. He gave a nod of appreciation as it went down. Strong, with good body and just a slight hint of acidity. Nice balance all round. Now he understood why people flocked here. He might even leave a starred review himself, if he remembered.

Taking another sip, he turned to his left and saw that the balding man in the three-piece suit was still texting on his phone. Or pretending to. The man was standing next to the escalators that led to the S-Bahn – or underground – platforms, and had been there for the past fifteen minutes. He had no briefcase or luggage. Every now and then he'd look up for a few seconds before looking back down at his phone. Sometimes Korso saw his lips move, even though there was nobody near him. There was a slight bulge under his left arm.

Adjusting the visor of his baseball cap, Korso turned to his right. Twenty feet away, in front of another vendor, he saw a woman in a smart, grey business suit hand over a ten-euro note. Her shoulder-length blonde hair was pulled back into a ponytail, and she wore little make-up. A black leather laptop bag hung from her left shoulder. The seller gave her some change and she picked up the paper bag containing her order and turned back to the concourse. As her gaze moved in Korso's direction, he lowered his head and took another sip while busying himself adjusting the straps of his bright red backpack. When he finally turned back, she was already looking the other way.

Directly ahead were the mainline platforms, twenty-five in total. Eleven were currently occupied by trains waiting to depart. There was open access between all the platforms and the main concourse, with no barriers or ticket gates to hinder travellers' progress when changing trains. Korso had always liked Germany for that reason; they seemed to excel at making things as efficient and hassle-free as possible.

Korso checked his watch again. 07.55. It was time.

He strolled towards the blonde woman while sipping his coffee. He was wearing dark blue chinos, a grey t-shirt, and a New York Knicks baseball cap. Just another backpacker, in other words. He'd already seen fifty single guys who looked just like him. In a busy terminus like this, it was as close to total anonymity as you could get.

When he reached the woman, he stopped two feet from her and looked at the prices on the board. The woman turned to look at him. Strudel seemed to be the main dish. The pleasant aroma of hot pastry and fruit filled his nostrils. Pulling his phone from his pants pocket, he swiped his finger across the screen and turned to the woman. He showed her the display.

She frowned at him, then looked down at the phone. In large-type English, the message read:

> We have a mutual canine friend. Do not speak, Agent Verhoeven. If I see your lips move, I leave. You will never find me again. Nod once if you understand.

Verhoeven raised her gaze to him, and nodded her head once. She would already know all this from Dog's relayed instructions, but a reminder in these situations never hurt.

Korso reversed the phone, and without taking his eyes off her, swiped his finger across the display again. He showed her the new screen.

> You and I will walk together. You will follow my lead. Same rules apply. Do not ask any questions. If I spot you contacting any of your law-enforcement colleagues I walk away forever. The jade dagger is lost. Nod again if you agree.

He watched her face as she read the text. It was an attractive face, with hazel eyes, a strong jawline, and a small mole above her upper lip. She looked up at him and nodded again. Her thin lips were clamped shut, as though with effort. As he swiped to the next screen, he saw her studying him. She was concentrating mostly on his eyes, which was fine with him. He was wearing light blue contacts over his real irises.

She furrowed her brow as she read the new screen. Then she carefully pulled her phone from her inner jacket pocket and switched it off, as instructed. She showed it to him before pocketing it again.

Korso knew she might conceivably have another GPS tracker on her person, but he couldn't check everything. Right now, speed was more important.

He motioned his head towards the S-Bahn escalators at their right. She moved away from the counter and began walking towards them. Korso left his coffee at the kiosk and walked beside her, watching her closely out the corner of his eye. But she just looked straight ahead, her lips pursed. They walked close to the balding businessman, who was still doing something on his phone. He paid them no attention.

They joined the throng of commuters taking the descending escalator. It was cramped. Verhoeven turned to him briefly, but said nothing. He didn't return the glance. When they reached the bottom, Korso took her hand in his, steered them to the right and immediately stepped onto the up escalator. She had no choice but to join him. He released her hand as they rose towards the main concourse again, buffeted by commuters in front and behind.

Halfway up, Korso saw the bald businessman coming down the other way. He was looking straight ahead, trying to appear bored and not really succeeding. As they passed within a few feet of each other, Korso turned to him and slowly shook his head from side to side in a friendly warning. The cop's expression didn't change at all. Which, of course, was the exact opposite of how a normal person would react in that situation.

Once they reached the top, Korso took Verhoeven's hand again and marched down the concourse, looking in all directions. Despite the throng of people surrounding them, he spotted the second plainclothes cop straight away. He was standing next to a bureau de change, wearing a grey suit and no tie, his dark hair cut close to the scalp. Korso didn't see a bulge this time, but he could tell the man was armed just from his posture. The cop was already manoeuvring his way through the human traffic towards them, trying his best to be casual.

Korso kept them both moving in the direction of the main entrance, his eyes searching the crowds intently. Verhoeven was keeping pace with him, not saying a word. Not even trying. Which proved he'd made the right choice in picking her. Plus, a man and a woman holding hands generally went unnoticed.

His eyes finally landed on the two *polizei* he'd spotted minutes earlier. They were still at the Burger King, still talking with the female railway employee as she sipped her coffee. He aimed directly for them, Verhoeven still mute at his side.

The two *polizei* turned in their direction when they were still about ten feet away, clearly sensing something in the air. Korso closed the distance and said, in English, 'Excuse me, officers, but I've just passed a man coming this way with a handgun under his jacket.'

The female cop narrowed her eyes, looking silently past Korso's shoulder. The male cop appraised Verhoeven for a second, before switching his attention to Korso.

'You are sure this man has a gun, sir?' The policeman's English was almost perfect.

'Fairly sure,' Korso said. 'I was a military cop. I can always tell. He's wearing a grey suit, no tie, white shirt. Light brown eyes. Dark hair shaved close to the skull. A day's worth of beard stubble. The gun looked like a forty-five automatic, but I couldn't be sure.'

The female cop was still looking past his shoulder. Her eyes flashed for a second and Korso turned to look behind him. He saw the plainclothes man about thirty feet away, walking against the tide in their direction.

'That's him,' Korso said.

The female cop pulled a mic from her jacket and began speaking into it, while the male cop said, 'Please leave this to us.'

'Gladly.'

Both cops brushed by him, hands on belts, as they moved towards the oncoming plainclothes man. Korso turned to Verhoeven, who simply met his gaze without expression. He gave a casual shrug, then led her towards a Tie Rack store further on. He already knew the layout of the terminal like the back of his hand. He'd spent four hours yesterday going over every inch of the place. So he knew that just past the store was a wide thoroughfare containing restrooms, more escalators, and the first-class waiting lounge, among other points of interest. As they walked, he heard the unmistakeable sounds of an altercation behind him. He didn't look back. Checking his watch again, he saw the time was 07.58.

Passing the Tie Rack store, Korso led Verhoeven into the wide aisleway on their left. He moved them along with the other commuters until he reached a large glass display next to the wall, with an impressive scale model of the Frankfurt HBF terminal inside. People were moving past it as though it didn't exist. Korso dragged Verhoeven to the other side of the display and came to a stop. It didn't provide much cover, but the constant horde of passing travellers would help.

Moving quickly, Korso removed his red backpack and reached in and pulled out a thin, beige, mid-length, summer windbreaker. He passed it to Verhoeven. She took it, frowned at him for a brief moment, then quickly put it on without being asked. Despite himself, he found he was starting to like her. Handing her a stylish black beret to go with it, he pulled out a dark blue blazer for himself and slipped it on while she carefully affixed the beret over her hair. The commuters passing by barely paid them any attention.

Korso checked his watch again. 08.00. Two minutes to go.

Verhoeven was watching him calmly, clearly intrigued to know what he planned to do next. Korso turned the red canvas backpack inside out, converting it into a black flight bag complete with shoulder strap. He offered his hand to Verhoeven, jutting his chin at the laptop bag she carried. She passed it to him, and he placed it inside his converted bag and slipped it over his shoulder. He removed his baseball cap and put it inside too. From his jacket pocket, he pulled out two pairs of spectacles. He handed her the black Ray-Bans, while he put on the plain reading glasses. As she donned her sunglasses, he removed his beard and moustache with a single movement of his left hand and stuck the thing in his jacket pocket.

Grabbing Verhoeven's hand again, he marched them back the way they'd come. As they were about to exit the thoroughfare, Korso spotted a woman coming their way, wearing a light jacket and blue jeans. She had a tense expression on her face as she rapidly searched the crowd in front of her. Her gaze quickly passed over Korso and Verhoeven without stopping, and then she was walking past them. Another of Verhoeven's law-enforcement colleagues, he was sure. Looking for a man with a bright red backpack.

Korso kept moving. He heard a voice over the loudspeaker announcing that the Intercity Express to Vienna would be departing from platform sixteen at two minutes past eight exactly. Korso checked his watch as the time changed from 08.00 to 08.01.

They marched across the concourse to platform sixteen, which was situated directly ahead of them. Korso could see the doors of the trains still wide open. A conductor stood on the almost empty platform, looking both ways for last-minute stragglers while checking his watch. He frowned when he saw them coming and motioned for them to hurry up.

Korso waved back and they both jogged the final few yards towards the end carriage. Verhoeven jumped on. Korso followed right after. Seconds later there was a whistle, and the automated doors made a piercing beeping sound before closing shut behind them.

SEVEN

Verhoeven showed no sign of being out of breath. As the train pulled out of the platform and steadily picked up speed, she stood in the empty vestibule and looked back at Korso without expression.

Pulling a ticket folder from his inner jacket pocket, he motioned towards the front of the train. She turned and opened the connecting door. With Verhoeven leading, they silently made their way single-file through four mostly packed carriages before reaching the first-class section of the train.

This section was much quieter, with far fewer passengers. Mostly businessmen and businesswomen. The seats were faux leather instead of cloth, and arranged in a one-two configuration, unlike the two-two configuration in second-class. The few passengers scattered around were either working on laptops, reading their Kindles, or playing with their phones. Korso judged the train was already travelling at well over two hundred kilometres an hour. The view out the windows consisted mostly of greenery, and small towns whizzing by at great speed. The ride was very smooth, as though they were travelling on an escalator.

At the end of the car, Verhoeven opened the connecting doors and they entered the next carriage, which consisted of a narrow corridor on the left, with restrooms and six-seat compartments on the right.

Korso checked the numbers above each compartment they passed and tapped Verhoeven's shoulder when they reached the one containing seats eighty-one to eighty-six. It was empty. As it should be. He'd paid for all six seats two days ago. She opened the door and stepped inside. He followed her, sliding the door shut behind him.

She took a seat by the window. Korso placed the flight bag on the floor at her feet, while he sat opposite. There was a wooden fold-out table between them. She took off the sunglasses, long windbreaker and beret, and placed them on the seat next to her.

'Am I permitted to speak now?' she said. Her voice was deeper than he'd expected, huskier, containing only faint evidence of a Dutch accent.

'It's a free country.'

'So what should I call you?'

'I don't care. Johan, if you like. A good Germanic name.'

'Well, this has all been very dramatic, Johan. Do you always take such elaborate precautions before a rendezvous?'

'Depends on the situation, Agent Verhoeven. In your case I felt the extra effort was warranted, especially as you had so many friends back there looking out for your welfare. It seems we both like to come prepared, wouldn't you say?'

She shrugged. 'Were you really military police?'

He shook his head. 'It just seemed the right thing to say at the time. Enough about me. When did Dog contact you with my instructions?'

'Saturday afternoon.'

'You talked to him in person?'

She tilted her head at him. 'Nice try, Johan, but I'm not biting. Dog will remain genderless for the time being.'

'Glad to hear it. If you'd told me, our meeting would have been over before it began.'

'Really? The hacker means that much to you?'

'You know better than that. It's simply a matter of trust. If you can't keep your word to Dog, you won't keep it with me either. Thus, any further discussion would be pointless.'

'And now you trust me?'

'As much as you trust me.'

'So do you wish to test me further, or can we move on to the task at hand?'

'The ball's in your court, Agent Verhoeven. Proceed.'

She turned to his flight bag, reached in and pulled out her laptop bag. As Korso unfolded the end flaps of the table, he saw the conductor out in the corridor. The man slid open the door and nodded at them both. '*Karte, bitte.*'

Korso removed the train tickets from the card wallet and passed them to him. The conductor frowned when he saw there were six in total.

'The others are boarding at Nuremberg,' Korso said.

'Ah, you are English?'

Korso gave him a bland smile that could mean anything.

The conductor scanned the barcodes of each ticket, and handed them back. 'Enjoy your trip,' he said, and left the compartment.

Verhoeven had already pulled out a folder and placed it on the table, along with a wafer-thin HP laptop. She opened the folder. 'How much do you know about Miguel Quezada?' she asked, leafing through the loose documents within.

'Only what I've gleaned from the archived news websites. He's one of the three top crime bosses in Guatemala. *Allegedly*, since he's never actually been convicted of any crime. He's never even been arrested, as far as I know. There aren't many photos of him. He resides in a vast private compound on the capital's outskirts, which he doesn't leave very often. They say he's involved in everything from drugs and human trafficking to murder-for-hire, all of which is probably true. And according to you, he also masterminded the assassination of the country's vice-president last year.'

She looked up from her papers. 'We have no tangible proof of that, of course. But we know he arranged it.'

'Dog mentioned a drug courier turned informer who witnessed him parading before his guests with a jade dagger, with what looked like dried blood on the blade.'

'That's right. Apparently he'd had a few drinks at the time, which partly explains the momentary lapse in judgement. And as Dog probably told you, Juan Arriola also admitted after his sentencing that Quezada was the man behind it all, and that he was instructed to send the murder weapon to a specific mailing address in the city. Although he never signed a statement to that effect, or mentioned either of those points in court. During the trial he insisted he'd planned it all himself, and that he threw the knife in a dumpster somewhere. Ever since that interview, he's steadfastly refused to make any further comment about the case. Which is regrettable, but understandable. He has a mother and father, after all.'

Korso turned to the window and watched as various shades of green sped past in a blur. 'So assuming Quezada was behind it, what was his motive? He must have had one.'

'He had one. You see, Vice-President Dias was one of those politicians who enjoyed speaking with the press more than almost anything else, especially on the campaign trail. And one of his favourite subjects was how ridding the country of crime bosses like Quezada and his ilk could only raise Guatemala's reputation in the eyes of the world as something more than a central hub for drug trafficking, money laundering and just about every violent crime known to man. Dias built his whole political career on the subject of criminal justice reform, and he remained consistent after he became Basurto's running mate in the last election, even more so after they won it. Whenever he talked about his pet cause, which was often, he'd make a point of name-checking Miguel Quezada as the perfect example of the type of crime figure he wanted brought to justice. Since Dias came from a legal background, he'd always stop short of outright libel, but over time the constant parade of innuendos and insinuations had the desired effect. The populace loved Dias's plain speaking, and wanted more. He was more than happy to give it to them.'

'Makes sense,' Korso said. 'The public always responds better to a specific enemy than some vague, shadowy threat. Just ask Germany.'

'But in this case, he picked the wrong man to use as an example. What he didn't realise was that Quezada actually considers himself a genuine patriot. He's almost fanatical about being seen as the sole protector of Guatemala's historical heritage, specifically it's ancient Mayan culture. He's constantly promoting himself as a major philanthropist and businessman, and regularly donates vast sums to museums and needy causes. But it's all dirty money, and everyone knows it. Or if they didn't before, they knew it after Dias made him a public scapegoat. I imagine any dreams he had of becoming a respectable member of the so-called legitimate business community evaporated every time he switched on the news.'

'So he decided not to take it lying down.'

'Would you, in his place?' Verhoeven leafed through some papers and pulled out a colour six-by-four. 'This is the most recent photo we have of him. It was taken three months ago, at a museum fundraising dinner set in the Intercontinental Hotel. Some of the country's top VIPs, business tycoons and entrepreneurs were invited. Quezada was one of them.'

Korso looked down at the shot. It had been taken with a telephoto lens, but the image remained sharp. The photo showed four men in conservative suits, standing next to an elegant-looking bar with drinks in hand. The man on the left was waving a finger, and his mouth was partly open. The other three were listening. Korso recognised Quezada as the man second from the right. He was a good-looking fellow in his early-forties, with a stocky, powerful build. His short dark hair was brushed forward, and he wore his sideburns long. His eyes were dark. He was the only one of the three listeners not smiling. He wore an expression of intense concentration. An observer rather than a talker. Probably looking for any hint of weakness in his three companions, and mentally filing it all away for future use.

Which showed he had brains. But then, he couldn't have lasted so long in his business without them.

'Well, it looks like Quezada's plan worked,' Korso said. 'If this photo's any indication, he's back in everybody's good books again.'

'Oh, most definitely. With Dias gone, the public soon lost interest in Quezada and where he got his money. They haven't forgotten, but as long as Quezada's not being mentioned in the news he's happy. And museum administration boards have very short memories where money's concerned.'

Korso looked up at Verhoeven. 'So how did he find his assassin?'

'It need not have been difficult. Quezada could have used any one of his numerous resources to locate the specific kind of political fanatic he needed. Someone who'd do absolutely anything, even commit murder, to promote his cause, whatever it might be. And if he had a history of mental instability, so much the better. But it seems he found the man he was looking for in Arriola, who ticked all the relevant boxes. Not only did he have a long history of mental problems, but he'd previously belonged to a non-violent human rights activist group before deciding peaceable demonstration wasn't the answer, after which he and some other like-minded members decided to jump ship and form their own splinter group. Not surprisingly, this new group contained quite a few people with criminal backgrounds, and they weren't afraid to promote mob violence to get their points across. We believe they also committed a number of robberies to fund their cause.'

Korso made a whirring motion. 'Quezada, Agent Verhoeven. Miguel Quezada.'

'I'm getting to it. Now Arriola told us that Quezada approached him personally one night and convinced him that they both shared the same cause with regards to human rights. He also convinced Arriola that everything Dias said about him in the media was a complete fabrication. That he was nothing more than a legitimate businessman who'd simply become the vice-president's enemy number one because he'd slept with the man's daughter a few times, and unceremoniously dumped her when his wife came close to finding out.'

Korso raised an eyebrow. 'Is that true?'

Verhoeven shrugged. 'I'm dubious. Dias's daughter completely denies it, which is hardly surprising. But I also think Quezada's too smart for something like that. It wouldn't fit with his character. Besides, he has a very beautiful wife already, who by all accounts adores him. No, I think he just told Arriola what he wanted to hear.'

'This couldn't have been arranged over a single meeting,' Korso said, looking down at the photo again. 'It had to be over a prolonged period of time.'

'Over the course of a month, according to Arriola. They would always meet alone, often in dark, seedy bars in the early hours of the morning, talking extensively about the better world to come. He said Quezada also gave him numerous examples of his many donations to humanitarian causes over the past decade, no doubt putting himself in the best light possible. Over the course of a few weeks, it wouldn't have been too difficult to gradually guide the pliable Arriola towards the idea of political assassination as the most effective way of getting their message across to the world. I'm theorising, you understand, but it would fit in with what we know of Quezada's behaviour. Unlike most crime bosses in that region of the world, he can be subtle when he wants to be.'

'That's probably why Dias picked on him instead of the others,' Korso said. 'I hear Quezada's only really got two rivals that come close to him in terms of strength, power and influence. Is that still the case?'

'Yes. His main competitors are Tobias Macqin and Romario Galiçia. Naturally, they all hate each other with a passion, with each man willing to go to any lengths to take over the others' organisations and intelligence networks. Violence always ensues whenever that happens. And as usual, it's often the innocent who get caught in the crossfire.'

She opened up her laptop, moved her fingers around the touchpad for a few seconds, then turned it round so Korso could see the screen. 'Galicia on the left. Macqin on the right.'

Korso studied the two colour shots. The one on the left showed an unshaven man in a yellow tracksuit, his lips around a thin cigar as he stepped out of a limo. He had an athletic physique and a receding hairline, and Korso put him somewhere in his late twenties. The other shot showed a slightly older man with a shaved head, wearing a red tank top and baggy shorts. He had a phone to his ear, and was gesticulating with his hand as he spoke.

'I'm curious,' Korso said. 'Which one would you say Quezada hates most?'

'Probably Galicia.'

'Why him?'

'Well, accounts differ depending on who you speak to, but it seems he got a job as a lowly drug runner in Quezada's organisation when he was barely out of his teens. Over the course of a few years, he built up his own crew and eventually hijacked part of a heroin shipment and then set out on his own. Naturally, Quezada went after him, but he somehow managed to survive all attempts on his life and over the years steadily built himself an organisation that now almost rivals Quezada's in terms of size. He's as cold-blooded and ruthless as they come, but Quezada still considers him an arrogant upstart who dared to rebel against his master. Quezada hates Macqin too, but that's simply business. With Galicia there's a personal element.'

Interesting, Korso thought, tapping a finger against his lower lip. 'Weaknesses?'

'You mean Galicia? Well, there are rumours that he has a fondness for underage girls, but nobody's ever been able verify it.'

'Or lived long enough to.'

'Possibly,' she said, shrugging. 'It's a sad fact that kids go missing all the time in that part of the world. Often forever. Why, what are you thinking?'

'All manner of things. What can you tell me about this compound of Quezada's?'

Verhoeven crossed her legs. 'His personal estate is set on a five-acre parcel of land, situated about one mile north-east of Guatemala City. He also owns the land immediately surrounding it. The only access is via a private road, whose entrance is constantly guarded by his men. A twelve-foot-high brick wall runs the entire perimeter of the property, protected by barbed wire and motion sensors. As for the actual layout, Quezada's lawyers pay Google Earth a large annual sum to ensure the whole site is shielded from public view.'

'However...' he prompted.

She sat forward and leafed through her folder. '*However*, I have an official source within the CIA who was able to furnish me with some recent shots taken from one of their reconnaissance satellites.' She pulled out a glossy print and passed it over to him.

The colour aerial shot wasn't that different from those seen on Google Earth, except the quality was marginally better. Quezada's estate was a ragged oblong shape surrounded on all sides by thick woodland and forest. The forested areas were probably patrolled by more guards, day and night. Within the compound he counted eight houses of varying sizes, with probably more hidden by the numerous trees and foliage scattered around. Four of the houses also had swimming pools. He saw a huge network of pathways running from property to property.

'Looks like a nice little community,' he said.

'With Quezada as sole patriarch. Like many of his kind he has a fondness for gangster movies, and it's believed he got the idea for the compound from *The Godfather*.'

Korso nodded. 'The Don's estate on Long Island. I remember. Who else lives in there? Family and close associates, I suppose?'

'Family, almost certainly. Beyond that, I'd only be guessing.'

'Let's stick with the facts,' Korso said. 'Start with his family.'

EIGHT

'His wife is a former model named Luana, whom he married eleven years ago when she was twenty-two. She's still very beautiful, and known to be tough and hard to please, though never with him. She's also mother to their three daughters. The oldest is ten, the youngest three. Quezada dotes on them like any father would, although the word is he's frustrated that his wife has failed to provide him with a male heir. At least, so far.'

'It's always the woman's fault,' Korso said.

Verhoeven's eyes crinkled as she smiled for the first time. 'Some things never change. Quezada's parents separated when he was a child, and his father moved up country and was killed in an industrial accident not long after, but we know his mother lives in one of the houses on the compound. He also has three brothers, each with a family of their own, so it's likely they also have houses there. According to my sources, none of the brothers possesses much in the brains department. It's believed that Quezada simply takes care of them out of family obligation.'

'No sisters?' Korso asked.

She paused.

He shook his head slowly. 'Don't do it.'

'Excuse me?'

'I can tell you're about to withhold some vital piece of information from me, Agent Verhoeven. It always happens, often for no reason other than to make the client feel superior. Break the mould this time, and just tell me.'

'Very well. There *is* another person in that compound, one that very few people know about. Her name is Alejandra

Davalos, and she's Quezada's personal assistant and sometime advisor.'

'You mean like a *consigliere*?'

She gave another thin smile at the *Godfather* reference. 'Not in the way you mean. She has nothing to do with his criminal doings, but focuses instead on his legitimate enterprises, of which he has many.'

'But she knows the kind of man Quezada is. She has to.'

'Undoubtedly. But *he* also knows she'll never spill any secrets about him.'

'Let me guess. She's actually his illegitimate sister.'

'Close,' Verhoeven said. 'She's his half-sister on their father's side. Her mother's identity is unknown, but she apparently died from excessive bleeding during childbirth. All records related to Alejandra's birth are missing, probably thanks to Quezada. But we know her father raised her initially, and when he died when she was four, she then lived with a foster family until adulthood. It's a secret she and Quezada have shared for who knows how long. She's kept the name of her foster family, and there are no physical similarities between the two, so nobody else suspects she and Quezada are in fact closely related.'

'How did you find out?'

'Basic detective work. I became curious about this Alejandra two months ago and after some extensive research, discovered some large gaps related to her infant years. Over a period of weeks, I finally managed to track down a lady who sometimes cleaned her father's house in Teculután, a small town in the Zacapa region, and she confirmed to me that the father's real name was Julio Quezada, and that he had a little daughter called Alejandra. Apparently, he was living under an alias there as his estranged wife's family were gunning for him over some unpaid debts.'

'Who else knows about this? From your end, I mean.'

'Just myself and Steinman at present. I haven't entered the discovery into any of my official reports yet, as it could put her life in jeopardy if the information became public knowledge. Quezada has a lot of enemies, and kidnappings are fairly common over there.'

He studied the aerial shot again. 'Which house is his?'

She leaned forward and pointed to one of the larger houses, located close to the centre of the compound. 'The drug courier said this was the one he visited that evening.'

'Describe what happened when he was there.'

'He told us he and his boss were body searched at the entrance gate here,' she said, running her finger along the image as she spoke, 'and then they were driven along the curving driveway here until they reached this house. They were greeted by one of Quezada's servants and some more guards, searched again, then led inside to the main living area where Quezada was in the middle of entertaining some other business associates. Apparently, everybody was drinking rum and had been for some time.'

She sat back in her seat again. 'He said Quezada wasn't close to being drunk, but it was clear he'd had a few already. At some point he began bragging about how nobody could hold him back from whatever he wanted to do, and that those in high places who tried would learn this lesson the hard way. At this, he left the room, and when he came back he was brandishing the dagger in question. It had a blade carved from jade, and a polished bone handle. The courier said it looked ancient, and that the blade was splattered with dark stains that could have been dried blood.'

'Dimensions?'

She pulled her hands apart. 'Around twelve inches in length, with the blade a little longer than the handle. The courier said Quezada was clutching the dagger by the handle, and making stabbing motions as he told his audience how this proved he was true to his word, and that anyone who tried to cross him would have their guts removed just like the last person who'd tried. Nobody was brave enough to ask him who he was referring to.'

'Or dumb enough. How long was Quezada out of the room?'

She frowned in thought. 'Not long, I think. Let me check.' She leafed through the file again until she found what she wanted. Pulling out several pages that had been stapled together, she scanned the first page quickly before flipping to the next page. When she was halfway down, she said, 'He was gone for almost ten minutes. That's all it says.'

'Meaning the knife could be stashed almost anywhere on the estate. Probably in a hidden vault that nobody else knows about.' He paused for a moment. 'You say he's obsessed with Mayan culture and antiquities. Does that mean he's a collector himself?'

'It seems likely, especially as he must have owned this particular dagger to begin with. But as for how serious he is, I couldn't tell you. If he's purchased antiquities at past auctions, he almost certainly did it anonymously or through an agent, so there's no way of confirming one way or the other.' She tilted her head. 'What makes you ask?'

'Quezada wasn't content with just killing Dias, he also wanted a trophy that he could gloat over and touch with his bare hands. Why else would he insist Arriola place the still-bloody weapon in a jiffy bag, and send it to a pre-arranged address? No, Quezada's a collector, all right. I know the type. And the collector mentality doesn't allow for occasional forays into his or her obsession. There's always another priceless antique, or piece of art, or rare book around the corner that the collector simply must own, regardless of cost. It's a constant hunger.'

'Yes, I agree with you.'

'In which case, there's a very good chance that Quezada's actually got himself a trophy room somewhere on these grounds, hidden from all eyes except his. An air-conditioned inner sanctum he can visit whenever he gets the urge to feast his eyes over his most prized possessions, or when he wants to add new ones. For all we know, it might even double as a safe room. Are there no building blueprints for the houses in that compound?'

'None. In Guatemala, money regularly changes hands and official records are routinely misplaced, often never to be seen again. And nobody knows which construction company Quezada used, or even if they're still operating.'

Korso studied the aerial photo again, making sure to memorise everything. 'One thing's for sure. If we assume there *is* a large vault on the premises, Quezada would have made sure nobody else besides him knows its location. I'd say the original architect is most likely buried somewhere in those woods out there, along with the builders who did the physical labour.'

'Unfortunately, you're probably right.'

He passed the photo back to her. 'So tell me, Agent Verhoeven, why all this interest in Miguel Quezada?'

She blinked at him. 'Are you serious?'

'I'm just to figure out why an agent from Interpol's Cybercrimes division is so concerned with the actions of a mob boss in Guatemala. Unless Quezada's started personally hacking into government servers himself, I'd say this is all a little outside your purview.'

'Oh, I see what you mean. No, I mainly operate out of the Organised Crimes Division. My ex-partner, Agent Steinman, transferred to Cybercrimes some years back. So when he called me with this sudden lead on Dog and told me of Dog's connection to Quezada, I put in a formal request that we work together on this, at least temporarily, and see what we could turn up on Quezada. We trust each other implicitly. He's the only other agent who knows Dog's identity, and he's already agreed to turn Dog loose without charge if we can land Quezada instead. So with that as an incentive, Dog pointed us towards you, and here we are.'

Korso turned to the window and gazed idly at the scenery rushing past. 'You're convinced you'll get a conviction if you get the dagger?'

'As much as I can be without seeing it with my own eyes. I do know that if that dried blood is Dias's, then Quezada's prints on the handle would be enough for the Guatemalans to convict him on a conspiracy charge.'

'That's a big "if" right there. Two, actually.'

'Two?'

'Quezada could easily have wiped his own prints off the dagger before replacing it back in his safe room. Don't tell me that possibility hasn't already occurred to you.'

Verhoeven looked at him without expression. 'It's occurred to us. There are no certainties. Do you think that's what he did?'

Korso shook his head. 'Unlikely. Based on what you've told me, Quezada doesn't strike me as a man lacking in self-confidence. If he truly thinks nobody can touch him, why would he suddenly doubt himself when it came to the dagger? He knows that simply owning that knife with the vice-president's blood all over it is enough to put him away, so he's unlikely to lose any sleep over his prints being on it too. He probably still fondles the thing every time he visits his trophy room. That's what collectors generally do. And you still haven't answered my question.'

'Which one?'

'The one regarding your interest in Miguel Quezada. I get that he'd be a great catch for you, but I kind of doubt that Interpol policy allows their agents to approach questionable characters like myself and solicit their help in procuring physical evidence through illegal means. Or have the rules changed?'

'They haven't changed.'

'I didn't think so. You know, if I were a betting man I'd wager your reasons for wanting to put Quezada behind bars are something other than purely professional. Exactly how long have you been after this guy, Agent Verhoeven?'

She stared right back at him. 'That's not your concern, *Johan*. Let's get back to the problem at hand. Dog seems to have a lot of trust in your abilities to procure those items beyond most people's reach, but I've nothing to back that up. In fact, we've been talking for twenty minutes now, and aside from the fact that you call yourself a covert salvage operative, I still know almost nothing about you. Not even your real name.'

'To tell you the truth, I've almost forgotten it myself.'

'In that case, I don't suppose you'd care to supply me with a few examples of previous jobs you've undertaken? Off the record, of course. Just to put my mind at ease.'

'Nothing's ever off the record. And I'm not here to soothe your brow, Agent Verhoeven. Just in case there's any doubt, I'm not doing this for you.'

'But you *are* going ahead with it?'

'I'm here, aren't I?'

'So how long have you been doing this specialist recovery work? You can tell me that, at least.'

'Less than ten years. More than five.'

She snorted. 'With what kind of success rate?'

'I've never actually worked it out, but around ninety per cent, I guess.' Korso shrugged. 'Possibly eighty-five. It's hard to say. I still turn away clients, put it that way.'

'Who approach you via word-of-mouth recommendations, I assume?'

'It's still the most effective form of advertising.'

'And might I have heard of some of these clients of yours?'

'You might.'

She gave a deep sigh. 'How is it that each time you answer a question, I seem to know less than I did before?'

'It's an art.'

'I have to say I'm not used to dealing with people about whom I know nothing. It goes against all my instincts.'

'Look at it this way, Agent Verhoeven. I'm simply a wild card with no connection to you or anyone else, so regardless of what happens, you've got plausible deniability all the way down the line. That means everything to gain, and nothing to lose.

Besides, the ball's no longer in your court, so don't waste time worrying about it.'

She exhaled loudly. 'I'll try. So what might you need from me? You understand any help from my quarter will be very limited, since it has to remain completely unofficial.'

'I kind of guessed that. All I really want from you is a phone number in case of emergencies. As an Interpol agent you have access to a vast range of contacts around the globe, mostly within the police community, whom I could never approach myself. I may not need them, but things don't always go to plan, and it'd be good to know the option's there.'

'That much I can do. So you have a plan?'

'The beginnings of one. But let's get one thing clear, Agent Verhoeven. If I get you the murder weapon used on Dias, then Dog not only goes free but also completely vanishes from your radar. Whether Quezada is convicted or not is immaterial. Are we agreed?'

'You get me that knife and Dog is let off the leash. Permanently. You have my word.'

'Good.' Checking his watch, Korso judged he had about another twenty minutes before they reached Nuremburg, where he planned to disembark. Alone. 'Now let's run through everything again, and see what we've missed.'

NINE

Korso pulled in to the kerb behind an ancient Honda pickup, and switched off the engine. He lowered the window to let in some air. Slouching down in his seat, he angled the rear-view mirror so he could still see behind him without moving his head.

Nothing back there yet. It wouldn't be long, though.

It was a Thursday afternoon. Three minutes after four. The day was warm for July, with the temperature somewhere in the late seventies. No downpour yet, but it would come. This was Guatemala's wet season.

The last time Korso had visited this particular location had been three days ago, at around the same time. He'd been driving a different car then. The vehicle he was now driving was a heavily dented grey Subaru with a hundred and fifty thousand miles on the clock. He was parked on a side street in Colonia Prados de Villahermosa, a heavily populated, working-class neighbourhood located a few kilometres south of Guatemala City.

Lining both sides of the street were sun-baked two-storey townhouses and makeshift stores, all clustered together. No one building looked the same. The biggest was a six-storey apartment house halfway down the street, with eight steps leading up to the main doors. Korso was parked about fifty feet away, on the other side of the road, but with a good view of the entrance. There wasn't much traffic this far off the main road. He watched locals of all ages strolling up and down the sidewalks, some carrying bags heavy with shopping. Some local kids were playing football in the middle of the road up ahead, pausing the game any time a vehicle had to come past.

Korso spotted movement in the rear-view and raised his eyes. The two black SUVs had just turned in and were slowly making their way towards him. He'd been following them all day, and when he'd seen they were headed in this direction again, he'd taken a chance and overtaken them so he could arrive first. It seemed he'd made the right call. He pulled a cigarette from the pack on the dash and stuck it between his lips without lighting it. He wasn't a smoker, but many locals around here were.

Without moving his head, he watched the two vehicles crawl past. The windows of each were tinted so he couldn't make out any details. Twenty feet up ahead, the lead vehicle slowed and turned in, parking directly in front of the apartment house. The second vehicle parked just in front of it. The doors of the first vehicle opened and three beefy men exited. All three wore light jackets to conceal the guns they were carrying. After looking up and down the street, the three men jogged up the steps and disappeared into the building.

Korso counted the seconds. He'd reached eighty-three when one of the men came out the front door and stood at the top of the steps. He nodded his head once. The doors of the rear vehicle opened. Four men got out. Three were dressed similarly to the first trio, and looked just as serious. They inspected the street in all directions, searching for anything amiss, while the fourth man busied himself with his phone, completely disinterested in his surroundings. This man had slicked back hair and wore grey sweat pants and a blue polo shirt. Once he was ready, he pocketed the phone and scratched his crotch as he began walking up the steps, two of his men following close behind. The man waiting at the top opened the door for them, and closed it again once they were inside. The other remaining bodyguard leaned against his vehicle, and pulled a pack of cigarettes from his pocket. He lit one and smoked, watching the street.

Korso knew the routine well enough. He'd been following Galicia for almost a week, using a different car every other day, mostly old wrecks nobody would look at twice. Which was the whole point.

He'd landed in Guatemala the previous Thursday, using the Portuguese passport that identified him as Ricardo Graves. That identity had been compromised ever since Bermuda, making it the more expendable of the three passports he owned.

Verhoeven had supplied him with the home addresses of Tobias Macqin and Romario Galicia. The latter lived in a secluded estate, situated about five kilometres east of Guatemala City, way up in the hills. So last Friday evening Korso found himself an unobtrusive spot with a good view of the entrance gates, parked the old Chevy Aveo he'd bought that day along with three other similar vehicles, and waited. He knew how to wait. He'd done it often enough. When he saw a pair of Toyota SUVs with tinted windows exit through the main gates early on Saturday morning, he started the engine and followed them into the city.

The first thing Korso learned was that the Toyotas went everywhere together. He assumed they were also bullet-proofed to the max. Their first stop was at a business hotel in the financial district. Korso parked nearby and watched as Galicia and three of his men emerged from the rear vehicle and entered the building, while those in the other SUV waited outside. It was like that for much of the day. Galicia moving from one business meeting right on to the next, from the wealthiest parts of town right down to the most depressed, and always in the presence of armed bodyguards. He was always on the go, Korso had to give him that.

Sunday had been more of the same. Korso had followed them again, this time in an old Ford station wagon, learning more about their daily routine with each passing moment. No meeting exceeded an hour, and most lasted for just fifteen or twenty minutes. Korso watched it all from a distance. It was drudge work, but necessary. The gathering of intel was always the most essential part of any assignment.

But it wasn't until around four on Monday afternoon that things became a little more interesting. That's when the two SUVs had come to this very apartment house, and Galicia had gone inside with his men.

Just like today.

Korso judged thirteen minutes had passed when he spotted the girl on the sidewalk ahead, carrying a beige backpack, coming this way. She was wearing her school uniform of navy-blue skirt, white polo shirt under a navy-blue sweater, and grey socks and black shoes. Her dark hair was pulled back in a ponytail, and Korso judged her age at around thirteen or fourteen. Certainly no older.

He'd seen her on Monday, too. Which suggested the rumours were true about Galicia. The guy at the vehicle had also spotted her coming, and gave her a small wave. The schoolgirl gave a nervous smile back as she climbed the steps of the apartment house. The bodyguard at the top exchanged a few words with her before opening the door wide. She slipped inside, and he shut it again. He grinned at the driver below before folding his arms and resuming his watch.

Korso sat back in his seat, already knowing what would happen to the girl six months or so down the line, once she was too old for Galicia, or once he'd simply lost interest and moved on to a younger conquest. For someone in Galicia's position, there was really only one way to absolutely guarantee her silence. If Verhoeven was right, she wouldn't be the first to suffer that fate.

He sat back and sucked on the unlit Marlboro as he watched the building. Over the next ten minutes he saw three women and a man exit separately, while two men entered, also separately. These two were questioned briefly by the bodyguard at the top before they were allowed inside. When the front door opened again and an old man exited, Korso removed the ignition keys and got out of the car. He locked the door, crossed the street and strolled up the steps. He was wearing jeans and a button-down short-sleeved shirt, just like a million other guys. He also hadn't shaved in three days. That, combined with his dark hair and naturally olive complexion, was pretty much the extent of his protective colouration for this job. It seemed to have worked well enough so far. Nobody was confusing him for a tourist.

As he approached the front entrance, the bodyguard stepped forward and said, '*¿A dónde vas?*'

Korso stared at him as though he were crazy. '*A mi apartamento. ¿Por qué?*'

'*¿Qué número es?*'

'*El treinta y tres,*' Korso said, sarcastically rattling his car keys, hoping Galicia wasn't on the third floor. '*¿Algo mas?*'

The bodyguard glared at him for another second, then stepped back. With a final shake of his head, Korso pushed open the door and entered the building.

It wasn't an upmarket place. There was no inner door, or even a proper reception area. Just an open lobby area, with the elevator to his right. There was a wide hallway directly ahead, with four rows of ancient mailboxes set against the left wall, and a staircase further down on the right. He heard a loud TV blaring out from one of the apartments ahead. A mother yelled at her screaming kids from another.

Ignoring the elevator, Korso climbed the stairs to the second floor and looked down the corridor. He heard loud music coming from somewhere, but saw nobody. He walked down the long hallway and turned left at the end. There were five more apartments located back there, two on the left, three on the right. At the end of the short hallway was a door to the fire stairs. He took these stairs to the third floor, where he passed an old woman carrying a full bag of washing in the corridor, but saw nobody else.

He climbed the main stairs to the fourth floor, and when he entered the hallway he saw two of the men he'd seen earlier.

They were standing outside the corner apartment at the far end. The taller one had his arms crossed, while the other played on his phone. Korso lit his cigarette while he strolled down the corridor and blew out smoke. It tasted disgusting, but he'd put up with far worse on other jobs. He saw the taller bodyguard say something to his colleague, who immediately pocketed his phone. They both watched Korso approach.

He barely paid them any attention as he reached the end of the hallway and turned left. But he now knew they were stationed outside room 412. The apartment next door was 413, with 414 at the end, right next to the fire stairs. Taking another drag of the cigarette, Korso pushed through the door and descended the stairs. He hadn't seen the other two bodyguards around, but figured they were most likely covering the rear exit. Once he was outside the building again, he threw away the cigarette and walked to his car and got back in.

He waited.

Seventy-one minutes later, the girl exited by the front entrance, head lowered to her phone as she walked back the way she'd come. On the surface, she was unchanged from the girl who arrived over an hour before, except she seemed a little more passive in her posture. Minutes later, Galicia and his four men exited. Galicia seemed in a particularly good mood. Along with the guy at the entrance, they all got back in their respective vehicles. Korso watched as they drove off down the street in unison.

Once they were gone from sight, Korso got out of the car and walked back to the apartment building.

-

The lock took him less than fifteen seconds. Pocketing his tools, Korso pushed open the door and entered room 412.

It was a medium-sized studio apartment, with the single window overlooking a vacant lot below. Directly under the window was a king-sized bed. The two large pillows each had indentations. He saw no point in taking a closer look at the ruffled sheets. He already knew far more than he wanted to. There was a tiny kitchenette in an alcove on the right, along with an open door showing a small bathroom with a shower. He peered inside. Two damp towels hung off the rail, and he could smell a combination of men's deodorant and citrus shower gel.

Korso took in the rest of the room. Other than the bed, the only other furnishing was a large wooden wardrobe set against the left wall. It almost reached the ceiling. He opened the doors. Inside, hanging from wire hangers, were four freshly laundered towels. He pushed them aside and studied the interior closely, tapping the sides, the rear plate and the floor. The main body was pine, but the rear plate was only thin board. Shutting the doors again, he slid the wardrobe a few inches away from the wall. It didn't take much effort. He lightly tapped the wall behind the wardrobe and nodded his head at the sound. He calculated the concrete was about an inch thick at most. Noise insulation wasn't exactly a high priority for landlords in this neighbourhood.

Exiting the room, he walked next door to apartment 413. He could hear the muffled sounds of stadium noise coming from inside, either from a TV or radio. He rapped a knuckle against the door three times, and waited.

After a few seconds, the door opened and a bare-footed, unshaven man in his mid-forties appeared, wearing tracksuit bottoms and a vest that showed off his paunch. A thin cheroot poked out the side of his mouth. Looking Korso up and down, he narrowed his eyes.

'*¿Quién eres?*' he said.

'*Me llamo Ricardo,*' Korso said, pulling from his pocket a thick roll of quetzal notes, tied with a rubber band. He held it up for the guy to see. '*Tengo una proposicion de negocios que podria beneficiar for both of us, but especially for you. Can I come in?*'

The man blew smoke out the side of his mouth as he thought it over, his eyes focused on the money. Finally, he shrugged, and opened the door wider. 'Sure, why not.'

Korso peeled off a two-hundred quetzal note and handed it to the guy as he entered the apartment. 'That's just for listening.'

The man checked the watermark, then shut the door and followed Korso inside.

The room layout was a mirror image of next door, but with a few more furnishings. In the middle of the room was a twin convertible sofa bed with an adjustable back. Facing it was a wooden coffee table and a large LCD TV on a stand, the station currently tuned to a local football match. There were four empty bottles of beer on the table and a half-full ashtray. Thankfully the window was open, so the smell was bearable. The only other furniture was a small work desk in one corner, with a pair of vinyl conference chairs on either side.

'You want a beer?' the man asked.

'Sure.'

As the man went over to the kitchenette, Korso saw another clothes cupboard standing against the wall to his right. But this one was smaller, and positioned a few feet closer to the window.

The man came back with two opened bottles of Gallo Beer and handed one to Korso.

'What's your name?' Korso asked, taking a sip of the cool lager.

'Mateo.'

'How's the game, Mateo?'

'I've seen better on the street outside.' He picked up a remote from the coffee table and muted the sound. Perching on the sofa, he said, 'Ricardo, right? Tell me about this business proposal. Is it legal?'

'Perfectly. It might also be the easiest thing you've ever done.' Korso took one of the conference chairs, set it down next to the sofa, and sat. 'A few questions first. Who lives next door, in 414?'

'Some guy and his old lady. I don't know their names, or what they do – they're out most of the time. I haven't heard them for the last few days.'

'And 412?'

'No idea. Every now and then I hear the bed squeaking in there, or the toilet flushing, but that's about it.'

'What about the tenants directly above and below you? Are they noisy?'

Mateo shook his head. 'Haven't heard a squeak from upstairs for over a month, so it could be vacant for all I know. As for downstairs, they sometimes play their TV loud at night, but during the day it's pretty quiet. They're probably at work, like everybody else.'

Korso nodded. 'And what about you, Mateo? What do you do for a living?'

'Auto mechanic.' He took a long slug of beer and puffed on his cheroot. 'This is my day off, in case you were wondering.'

'I wasn't. Tell me, how much do you earn in a year? On average.'

Mateo's brow became furrowed. 'Is that any of your business?'

'Not unless you want it to be.'

After a brief pause, the man shrugged. 'Last year I made maybe thirty-five thousand.'

Korso placed the roll of notes on the coffee table. 'There's ten thousand quetzales, Mateo. I've got another roll just like it in the car, making twenty thousand in total. That adds up to over half a year's salary. It's yours, if you want it.'

Mateo gently put down the bottle, looked at the roll of money, then back up at Korso. 'Who am I supposed to kill?'

'I already told you it couldn't be easier. All you have to do to earn that money is move out of this apartment by midnight tonight. Permanently.'

'Are you serious?'

'Do I look like I'm joking? Rent or borrow a van, pack your stuff and grab a motel room for the night, or stay at a friend's. Or drive down to Montericco and lie on the beach for the next six months. I don't care what you do, Mateo, but I want you out of here within the next few hours. Do that and the twenty thousand is yours. What do you say?'

'I don't get it. What the hell's so special about this room?'

'One of the conditions for taking that money is that you don't ask me any questions. Now do we have a deal, or should I try one of the other tenants?'

Mateo continued looking at him as he picked up the bottle and drank the rest of his beer. He set the bottle down on the table, belched, and said, 'Never did like this place much anyway. Brother, you got yourself a deal.'

TEN

Korso was just about to capture Queen's Knight when the sound of a door being unlocked echoed throughout the apartment, immediately pulling him out of the game.

That was the problem with playing chess against yourself. Matches often became so all-consuming that you could lose track of time and forget the outside world even existed. And this one had just reached a particularly interesting point. With a faint pang of regret, Korso placed the peg of his white pawn back in its hole, and closed and latched the lid of the travel chess set. He had every intention of continuing it at some point. He got up from his chair and walked over to the kitchenette counter, where the small speaker was currently recharging, along with a Samsung Galaxy. Korso lowered the speaker volume a few notches so it wasn't quite so deafening, unplugged the smartphone and opened up the web browser.

It was 16.02 on the following Monday, a little less than four days since Mateo had exchanged his apartment keys for the twenty thousand. Once the deal had been made, it had taken the mechanic less than two hours to vacate the room. He'd borrowed a friend's van to remove his possessions, Korso helping with the bulkier items. All he'd left behind was the small work desk and the two chairs, which were sufficient. Then Korso went out to the car and grabbed the cheap Japanese-style futon he'd picked up that afternoon, and brought it back and unrolled it on the floor. That was it for his living arrangements.

After a decent night's sleep, Korso went out early the following morning and drove into the city. He spent a few hours picking up the very specific tools and items he required, such as the old folded wheelchair leaning against the far wall, and the black bin bag on the floor next to it, which contained a few more essentials. After Korso returned from his shopping trip, he got down to the serious work. He'd completed the noisiest parts of the operation by the middle of Friday afternoon, before the other tenants started coming home from work. Saturday was spent fine-tuning the details. Sunday and most of Monday, he either played chess or read. Marking time.

Now it seemed the waiting was finally over.

As soon as his bookmarked page loaded up, a video stream filled the display screen. He'd placed the miniature IP spy camera in the north-east corner of 412 on Saturday morning, close to the ceiling. It was painted the same tan colour as the wall, and almost impossible to see unless you were actually looking for it. The RTSP stream was fed through to a password-protected web page in real time. Considering the size of the camera lens, the footage was of excellent quality. Not high-definition exactly, but not far off. And no choppiness either. The audio came from a state-of-the-art microphone he'd placed under the window. It was even smaller than the camera.

He saw the two bodyguards had already entered the room and were busy checking it over in preparation for their boss's arrival. Korso couldn't tell if they were the same ones as before, but he thought it likely. Galicia wouldn't want too many of his own people knowing about his abnormal sexual proclivities. One guy was patting down the pillows and straightening the bed sheets. The other was doing the same with the towels in the bathroom. From the speaker, he heard one say, '*…need to get some new bed sheets before Thursday. These could do with a wash.*'

'*I'll bring some over tomorrow*,' the other one said.

The first guy turned and approached the clothes cupboard. Korso's breathing slowed as he watched the man pull the doors open and check the interior. After a few more seconds, he closed them again, apparently satisfied. Korso breathed out again.

Still watching the screen, Korso stepped over to the apartment's connecting wall. There was a large hole in the concrete at knee level, measuring two feet square. The wall was just over an inch in thickness. All that could be seen on the other side was a square section of board, denoting the back of the clothes cupboard the bodyguard had just checked. After carefully measuring everything out in each apartment on Friday morning, Korso had used an industrial circular saw to cut through the wall that same afternoon. It had taken him less than thirty minutes to complete, since the hole didn't have to be particularly neat or precise. But the whole process had been very noisy. Fortunately, he had no immediate neighbours to complain about the racket. The cleaning up afterwards had taken much longer. Later that night, he left the saw in a very obtrusive spot on a nearby street. As expected, it was gone when he checked the next morning.

Korso removed his shoes and sat cross-legged on the floor and continued watching the real time footage on the display. The two men in 412 each gave the room one final look, and then they turned towards the door. Korso heard one say, '*Go tell the boss everything's ready*,' as they were leaving the apartment.

The moment the door clicked shut behind them, Korso got up and knelt before the hole. He tapped the backing board along the sides until the adhesive gave, and a square section the same size as the opening in the wall fell into the wardrobe. He reached in, pulled the piece of board out and set it on the floor.

It had been a dicey moment when the bodyguard checked the interior. Korso had spent a lot of time cutting the rear section away, and then carefully replacing it using a temporary mounting adhesive. He'd also used a little papier-mâché to fill in the cut, and painted over it with a water-based paint the exact same colour as the thin wood. The whole effect had looked good to Korso's eyes, but it was hard to be completely objective about your own work. But the bodyguard hadn't even bothered to move the towels out of the way for a better look. If he had, he might have spotted the join, but he hadn't noticed a thing.

One of life's truisms was that people often only saw what they expected to see.

Korso grabbed his phone and patted his shirt pocket to make sure he still had the two most essential items. They were still there. Aware that one of the guards was stationed right outside, he gently dragged the four hangers to the left and poked one leg through the hole, then the other. Just as silently, he crouched down in the wardrobe and pushed open the left door all the way, before closing it again. He did the same with the right door. Neither one made a sound. He'd oiled the hinges yesterday, so he'd have been surprised if they creaked.

Korso continued to wait.

Less than two minutes later, he heard the apartment door opening. He looked down at his phone and saw Galicia strut into the room, wearing a short-sleeved patterned shirt and chinos, head bobbing to whatever beat was playing in his head. He looked wired. Probably coked to the eyeballs. The door clicked shut behind him. As before, he was doing something on his phone. Probably texting the poor girl to see where she was. He laid down on top of the bed and crossed his legs, one hand absently massaging his crotch as he continued doing things on his phone with the other.

Breathing through his mouth to minimise noise, Korso leaned his head back against the side of the cupboard and waited some more.

Less than ten minutes later, Korso heard the apartment door open again. He looked down at his phone and saw the same girl enter the room. She was wearing a school uniform, as before, and carrying the same backpack. A grinning Galicia jumped off the bed and went over to her. They hugged, then kissed. Korso put the phone down and simply listened. He didn't need to see. Reaching into his shirt pocket, he pulled out the two disposable syringes, each once containing a clear solution. He put the one with the lesser amount back in his pocket. This one contained fifty milligrams of Propofol, while the other contained a much smaller dosage of the same sedative. He removed the cap, flicked the barrel three times to remove any remaining air bubbles, and depressed the plunger. A few drops squirted out of the needle.

He was ready.

'Celina, baby,' Galicia said, finally. 'You don't know how much I missed you the last few days. You miss me too?'

'You're all I think about, Romy,' she said. 'I love you more than anything, but I've been really worried too. I'm sure Mom thinks I'm seeing someone after school. I tell her I'm only hanging out with friends, but I know she doesn't believe me. I'm afraid—'

'You told her nothing about us?' he cut in. 'Nothing at all? Don't lie to me now.'

'*Nothing*. I promise. But, Romy, I don't know what—'

'Hey, she's just worrying like mothers everywhere, that's all. Don't worry about it. Anyway, I know just how to make you feel better. Now go get ready, and make sure you put on that little nightdress I like. But don't take too long this time, okay? We don't want what happened last time, do we?'

'No. I'm sorry, Romy.'

'Don't be sorry, baby. Just go and get yourself ready like a good girl.'

Korso picked up the phone again and saw the girl shuffle off towards the bathroom, shutting the door behind her. Good. One less problem to worry about.

He saw Galicia already unbuttoning his shirt as he walked over to the apartment door, a huge grin spread across his face. He drew the latch across and turned the key in the lock, then made his way across the room towards the window. While he was moving away from the wardrobe, Korso put down the phone and with one hand still gripping the hypodermic, silently pushed both doors open.

Without making the slightest sound, Korso crawled out of the confined space onto the floor of the apartment, and quickly got to his feet in one fluid motion. Galicia was standing at the window now, maybe fifteen feet away. If he turned round at any point, the game was over. He'd yell out, the bodyguards would burst in, and bullets would fly.

Padding along the hardwood floor in his stockinged feet, Korso silently crept up behind Galicia while he was busy pulling the drapes across. Even better, he could hear the man humming a tune to himself as he no doubt imagined the pleasures soon to come. The rustle of the drapes being drawn covered Korso's final few steps, as he closed the distance to just a few inches.

Standing directly behind the man, Korso reached round and clamped his left hand hard across Galicia's mouth, hugging him tight to his chest at the same time. The man struggled in sudden alarm and tried to shout as he reached up with both hands. Korso kept the pressure on, keeping him off-balance by dragging him back along the floor. With his other hand, he plunged the hypodermic needle into the carotid artery in the guy's neck. He depressed the plunger quickly, and in less than a second the solution was in the man's bloodstream, the strong sedative already speeding towards the brain.

The effects were almost instantaneous. Galicia's struggles quickly became weaker, his breathing shallower. His grip on Korso's arm diminished until his hands fell away completely, and within seconds his head slumped to the side. Korso kept his hand clamped over the man's mouth for another few seconds, just to be sure.

Korso dragged the now unconscious man back and laid him down in front of the wardrobe. The gangster's breathing was perfectly regular, as though he'd just fallen asleep. The fifty milligrams of Propofol meant he'd stay that way for another couple of hours at most, depending on how much coke was in his system. Korso got up and crossed the room, placing his ear against the bathroom door. He heard the sounds of the girl brushing her teeth. He pulled the second syringe from his shirt pocket, and spent a few moments getting it ready.

He knocked on the door, and in a reasonable imitation of Galicia's voice, said, 'Okay if I come in for a second?'

'Come on in,' the girl said.

Korso turned the knob and gently pushed open the door, then quickly bulldozed into the tiny space before the girl could get a handle on the situation. She was still fully dressed, and had a toothbrush half raised to her mouth. Her eyes widened when she saw it wasn't Galicia. Korso clamped his free hand over her mouth before she could scream. With his other hand, he injected the needle into her carotid artery, depressed the plunger, and held on to her for the few seconds it took for her eyes to close as she slipped into unconsciousness.

He checked her breathing, and gave a nod of satisfaction when he saw it was just as regular as Galicia's. *Minimal collateral damage* was another good rule to live by. Even more so when it involved innocents. He laid the girl down gently on the tiled floor. He'd only given her twenty-five milligrams, so she'd be out for no longer than ninety minutes. He closed the bathroom door and let her sleep. With any luck, she wouldn't even have a headache when she awakened.

More to the point, she wouldn't have Galicia in her life anymore.

ELEVEN

Once Korso retrieved his spy cam and microphone from their hiding places, he dragged the unconscious Galicia through the man-sized gap into apartment 413. Leaving him on the floor, Korso reached through and gently pulled the cupboard doors shut again. He also dragged the four wire hangers across until the towels were in exactly the same positions as before.

Grabbing the mounting adhesive he'd used previously, Korso squeezed a small amount of the fixative all around the edges of the square section of backing board. He carefully positioned the piece into the rear plate of the wardrobe once more, making sure the fit was absolutely perfect. Once he was satisfied, he held it in place for a full minute before taking his hands away. He tapped the section lightly with his index finger. The board remained in place. It wouldn't have to hold forever, just for a short while.

He checked his phone display. 16.18. Based on the amount of time Galicia and the girl had spent together on the two previous visits, Korso figured he had about an hour to play with. Not that he'd need it.

Korso crossed the room and brought over the black bin bag and opened it up. He pulled out the neatly folded clothes from within and set them on the floor next to Galicia. He'd picked up the garments at a thrift store on Friday. Next, he brought the wheelchair over, which he'd found in a nearby pawn shop. Like the clothes, it looked well used, but it was still fully operational. After making sure the wheel brakes were locked, Korso gently pushed the padded seat down in the middle, and the sides of the wheelchair slowly slid away from each other until it all clicked into place. Korso then reached back into the bag and pulled out the last few items he needed.

Fifteen minutes later, the crime boss who'd entered apartment 412 was gone. In his place, sitting slumped in the wheelchair, was a much older man with grey hair hidden under a black baseball cap, and grey beard and moustache. Korso had purchased the hairpiece, facial whiskers and spirit gum from a well-known theatrical supplier in Frankfurt and brought them with him. They hadn't been cheap, but the effect was worth it. Galicia was dressed in an old black suit jacket, white shirt buttoned to the neck, and navy-blue trousers. Korso had also fitted him with a soft, flesh-coloured neck brace, the temporary kind used by a patient after an operation or by the victim of a car accident. It would ensure Galicia's head remained mostly upright and wouldn't drop forward suddenly with the movement of the wheelchair, or flop around like a rag doll. Korso leaned down and placed a pair of tinted reading spectacles over his closed eyes, then stepped back for a better look.

To a casual observer, Galicia definitely looked like a fifty- or sixty-something man who'd suffered some bad luck. Except for the hands. They were a dead giveaway. Korso stepped forward and carefully crossed Galicia's arms, tucking each hand into an armpit. That was much better. It was also a more natural position for a dozing man.

Placing his travel chess set on Galicia's lap, Korso went to the kitchenette and pocketed his micro speaker. No sense in leaving that behind. He also took the folding tactical knife he'd picked up at a hardware store, for emergencies. Hopefully he'd never need it. Fitting a faded red baseball cap over his own head, he took a last look around the apartment to see if he'd missed anything. All that was left were a few surplus clothes he hadn't needed, and a well-thumbed Cormac McCarthy paperback he'd finished earlier. In Spanish, of course.

He had everything he needed.

After unlatching the door, he pulled it open and went back to the wheelchair. He pushed the sleeping man gently out of the room into the hallway, partly facing the fire stairs so the bodyguards couldn't get a good look. Out the corner of his eye, Korso saw the two men outside 412 watching them both closely. He didn't pay them any attention.

'Be right with you, Pop,' Korso said as he shut and carefully locked the door.

Pocketing the key, he gripped the handles again and turned the wheelchair so it was now facing the two men outside the next room.

'And away we go,' he said.

As Korso pushed the unconscious Galicia down the short hallway, he gave the two men outside 412 a friendly nod. Both men ignored the gesture. They looked like the same ones as before. The taller man had his hand inside his jacket, his dark eyes darting between Korso and the man in the wheelchair. The other one was leaning against the wall and seemed a little less intense, but looked just as unfriendly.

Korso pushed Galicia past his very own watchdogs, turned the corner and continued down the long corridor towards the front of the building. He knew they were still watching him closely, but just ambled along like any normal son taking his old man out for some fresh air. He could have utilised the mirror app on his phone to check what they were doing behind him, but he decided against it. If either man decided to follow him, he'd hear it. But all he heard were his own footsteps and the faintly squeaking wheels. He finally reached the end of the corridor without incident, and parked the wheelchair in front of the elevator.

He pressed the call button. Machinery whirred from down below. He bent down to his charge, moving his mouth as though he were speaking to his father. Galicia remained unconscious. In his peripheral vision, Korso could see the two bodyguards were still at their posts. The elevator arrived and the door opened. He gave Galicia a gentle pat on the shoulder and pushed him into the tiny space, pressing the button for the ground floor.

When the door opened again, Korso pulled the wheelchair out of the elevator and stopped it a few feet from the front entrance. He went over to the main door, pulled it open and saw the other bodyguard at the top of the steps outside. The man turned to him. Although he was wearing sunglasses today, Korso could tell it was the same guy who'd interrogated him four days previously.

'You mind holding this open for a second?' Korso asked.

'What for?' the man growled.

'So I can bring my dad out.'

Korso waited. The man's curiosity soon got the better of him, and he peered into the lobby and saw the grey-haired man with the neck brace sitting in the wheelchair. With a shrug, he came inside and held the door against the wall, while he studied the man in the wheelchair with vague interest.

'Thanks,' Korso said, and proceeded to push his charge through the doorway and out into the sunlight.

Straight ahead were the two SUVs, once again parked right out front. As before, one of the drivers was leaning against his vehicle watching the street. His attention was now squarely on Korso at the top of the steps.

Ignoring him, Korso flipped the anti-tip bars up at the back of the chair, and locked the push-pins into place. Then, tilting the chair back slightly so Galicia wouldn't topple forward, he took the full weight and carefully bumped the wheelchair down the eight large steps. It took him almost a minute before he reached the bottom, the driver silently watching him all the way down. Korso was in no rush, and he knew the slightest error could cost him everything. Once on the sidewalk, he slowly lowered all four wheels to the ground, flipped the anti-tip bars up again, and relocked the push-pins.

After making sure Galicia was still in position, Korso steered the wheelchair away from the driver, who was still watching them both with a faint frown, and headed off in the same direction from which the girl had come. Just like before, over a dozen kids of varying ages were laughing and shouting as they played football in the middle of the road. Probably the very same ones. They all ignored him as he passed.

Korso kept going, his attention focused on avoiding the many potholes in the uneven sidewalk as he approached the little side street up ahead on the left.

He finally made the turn twenty seconds later, and once he was partially in the shadows, stopped the wheelchair for a moment. He let out a long breath he hadn't realised he'd been holding. Patting Galicia's shoulder affectionately, he studied the cul-de-sac ahead of him. It was essentially a short, narrow alley with a single dwelling at the end, and a few entrances for the buildings on either side. Like most residences in this neighbourhood, steel bars protected each door. Four vehicles were parked on the left-hand side of the alley. He was the only pedestrian. There was nobody else in sight.

Korso kept going, stopping when he reached the third vehicle down, a boxy, thirty-year-old Nissan Sentra saloon with a bad paint job and a huge dent in the passenger side door, along with a host of smaller ones at the rear and front. The car had cost him less than five thousand quetzales, but the engine was solid and that was all that counted. He'd parked so there was three yards of space between it and the vehicle behind.

After locking the wheels on the chair, Korso opened the front passenger door and placed his travel chess set in the glove compartment. He went to the rear and opened the trunk. Even after removing the spare wheel, there wasn't a whole lot of room in there. Not that Galicia was in any position to care.

Korso was just about to remove Galicia's neck brace when he turned to check his surroundings one last time. And that's when he saw Galicia's driver, watching them from the mouth of the alley fifty feet away, his right hand already reaching inside his jacket.

He began walking towards Korso.

TWELVE

As casually as possible, Korso turned his attention back to the man in the wheelchair. Staying in character, he leaned down to say something to his supposed father as they prepared for their drive. Meanwhile, he was rapidly sifting through the few options available to him, searching for the most effective way to deal with this new obstacle. On the plus side, at least there were no witnesses around. Not yet anyway.

In his peripheral vision, he saw the driver was now only thirty feet away and closing fast. Turning a little so his left side was out of view, Korso reached into his pocket and grabbed the folding tactical knife. It had a three-inch, serrated, stainless-steel blade. Not much use against a gun, but it was all he had. He pulled his hand out, keeping it close to his side, one finger on the flipper tab at the base of the blade. All it would take was one press, and the knife would instantly flip open and lock.

Rising up, Korso saw the driver a few feet away and widened his eyes in fake surprise. He was maybe an inch shorter than Korso, but thickset, with arms like tree trunks. The man stepped over to the gap between the cars and looked inside the open trunk, right hand still inside his jacket. Korso judged there was now about three feet between them.

'What's the problem?' Korso asked, adding a slight tremble to his voice. 'Look, we don't have much money, but—'

'Just stay there, don't move. Something's not right here.' The driver wore a deep frown as he studied the man in the wheelchair. He pulled the gun, a .45 semi-automatic, from his shoulder holster and pointed it at the open trunk. 'Why's this open?'

'Once my dad's in his seat, I stick the wheelchair in there. It folds up.'

The man turned to the invalid in the chair. 'Take off his cap.'

'Sure, whatever you want. Just don't hurt him, okay? He's dozing now, and he's only been out of hospital for a few days. He was hit by a car and—'

'I said take it off,' the driver said, raising the gun.

'Okay, okay.' With his knife hand still at his side, Korso reached down with the other and removed the baseball cap from Galicia's head, taking care not to dislodge the hairpiece. He was glad he'd paid for a good one, it still looked convincing. He dropped the cap on the ground. 'There, it's off.'

The driver was studying Galicia with narrowed eyes. His instincts were good, Korso had to give him that. He hadn't come to any conclusions yet, but he would very soon. 'Now the glasses and neck brace. Get rid of them.'

'Whatever you say.'

Keeping one eye on the gun, Korso moved around to the back of the chair, marginally closing the distance between them in the process. There was only two feet between them now. His left hand was still out of the man's view. Using just his right, Korso reached down and unclipped the foam brace, and gently unravelled it from Galicia's neck.

With the driver's attention focused on Galicia, Korso raised the brace, preparing to drop it on the ground. Instead, he threw it towards the driver. At the same, he rushed forward while pressing his left index finger against the flipper tab. The tactical knife instantly sprung open, and the blade locked in place.

'What the—' the driver cried out, and then Korso lunged the knife towards his face.

The driver instinctively raised his gun arm, blocking the move, and the blade connected with the bony part of his forearm instead. Half an inch of it sunk into flesh. The man screamed in pain and staggered back, blood gushing from the wound. The gun fell from his grip and clattered to the ground. Korso followed its progress and was about to dive for it when he saw the man's left foot accidentally make contact with it as he backed away. The gun skittered under the Nissan, out of reach.

Korso swore and lunged forward, slashing at the man again. But the driver quickly backed away further into the middle of the street. He had his right hand pressed against the wound, still in pain, but his eyes were now completely focused on Korso. He'd had a shock, but he'd recovered quickly. The adrenaline was probably helping too. As Korso stepped into the street to follow, the man released his bleeding forearm and reached for something behind him, under his jacket. The hand reappeared almost instantly, this time gripping a knife.

And not just any knife, but a carbon-steel Ka-Bar, with a seven-inch serrated blade.

The driver looked at Korso's puny folding knife and grinned. 'Man, you just made the worst mistake of your life. I'll cut you into little strips and feed the pieces to my uncle's pigs.' Completely ignoring his bleeding arm now, the driver began moving towards Korso again, knife hand extended out in front of him.

Korso moved to the left, and the driver moved to his own left in response, at the same time jabbing playfully with the knife. He had the longer reach. Those four extra inches of steel made all the difference. But Korso knew a few little tricks of his own. There were other ways to level the playing field. Each man continued to circle the other warily, leaving just three feet of space between them. Valuable seconds passed. Korso knew this had to end quickly, before any passers-by in the street spotted them. But neither could he rush things. That road led to destruction.

As they warily mirrored each other's movements, Korso waited patiently for the driver to attack first. He was the one bleeding, after all. Korso just kept his focus on the driver's left shoulder, waiting for the tell. It would come. It always did. The moment he saw the man's left deltoid tense, Korso jerked his body back an instant before the driver's arm shot out towards his chest. The blade swished past with space to spare.

Korso smirked. 'Loser.'

The driver lost his grin, his eyes flashing in anger at the insult. Korso watched the man's right shoulder, readying himself for the inevitable follow-up to come. Adjusting his position so only his right side was facing his attacker, Korso kept his left leg straight, while raising his right foot a millimetre off the ground in readiness. Waiting to strike.

The moment the driver's deltoid muscle tensed again, Korso dropped his left shoulder and pivoted on his left foot so it was pointing away from the target, and then thrust his right foot straight out and up in the classic taekwondo side kick. As the man jabbed the now empty air with the knife, the edge of Korso's foot immediately connected hard with the man's abdomen.

Bone met hard muscle, his pivoted left foot adding extra power to the kick. The driver's body bent inward, and he grunted loudly as the air left his lungs. Instead of lowering his leg, Korso remained in the same stance and chambered his knee, immediately kicking his foot out again towards the man's face. The outside edge of his shoe struck the driver's left jaw solidly, and the man completely lost his balance and fell back to the ground.

Korso didn't waste a moment. He darted forward and stamped his foot down on the man's left wrist, hard. The driver groaned in pain, the hand opened and the Ka-Bar rolled out of his grip. Bending down, Korso dropped his own knife and grabbed the Ka-Bar by the handle. He clamped his free hand against the man's forehead, and with the other plunged the blade deep into the man's throat, just below the Adam's apple. He kept the knife in place to reduce the amount of arterial bleeding. It didn't help much. The man's struggling eased off immediately, and he stared up at Korso with an expression of disbelief on his face. Nobody believes it when their time finally comes.

Adjusting his footing to avoid the heavy stream of blood spurting onto the ground, Korso kept his grip on the knife steady and watched the man's eyes gradually lose focus. After a few more seconds, the lids finally closed and the bleeding came to a stop as all life left the body. Once he was sure the man was dead, Korso removed his hand from the knife.

He looked up towards the mouth of the alley, expecting to see concerned bystanders. But nobody was there. A silver sedan passed by in the street. A yellow pickup went past the other way. He could hear the joyful sounds of those kids playing football out there. Life was still going on. Nothing had changed. Wanting to make sure it stayed that way, Korso dragged the corpse back by its collar until it was lying in the space between the two vehicles.

After checking his clothes for blood stains, and finding none, Korso went over to the man in the wheelchair. He reached under Galicia's armpits and hefted the unconscious man out of the chair and folded him into the trunk, laying him on his side with both knees tight up against the chest. He leaned in and checked the man's breathing again. Still steady and regular. He closed and locked the trunk.

He folded up the chair and slid it onto the back seats. Looking around, he saw the neck brace, baseball cap and spectacles he'd dropped, and threw them in too. He took one last look at the dead man on the ground, the knife still lodged in his throat. Korso's fingerprints weren't on any database, and any he'd left on the knife would be badly smudged anyway. And since he'd never touched the handgun the driver kicked under the car, he simply left it there.

After retrieving the tactical knife he'd dropped, he got into the driver's seat and shut the door. Pulling out his phone, he blocked the caller ID and dialled 120.

Moments later, a female voice said, 'Police. What's your emergency?'

Korso told her he was calling from Colonia Prados de Villahermosa and gave her the street name and the number of the apartment house. 'There's this mafia big shot over here right now, in apartment 412, and he's in there having sex with this school kid. I swear she can't be any older than twelve years old. And he's got armed bodyguards outside the room, outside the front entrance, all over the place, making sure nobody interrupts them. This goes on every other day, and I've had enough. I'm in the apartment next door and I can hear everything that's going on in there. It's disgusting. I've got a daughter the same age.'

'Please calm down, sir,' the dispatcher said. 'You say this is happening right now?'

'As we speak. You need to get the police over here as soon as possible. Apartment 412. Oh, and I overheard one of the other tenants say this guy's name is Romario Galicia. I don't know if that means anything to you?'

'Romario Galicia? Are you sure of that name, sir?'

'That's what I said. Look, just get some police over here, fast.'

Korso ended the call, and turned the key in the ignition. The engine coughed into life. He carefully eased the car out of the space and drove towards the end of the alley. After checking both ways for traffic, he turned right. The kids in the street paused their game briefly to let him through and he carried on for a few yards past the apartment house. Parking by the side of the road, he kept the engine running and turned in his seat. The doorman was still at his post on the top step. The man took a few steps forward and craned his neck to see if the driver was on his way back, and then returned to his post again. He didn't seem too concerned yet. Korso faced front and checked the time on his phone: 16.44.

Less than five minutes later, straight ahead in the distance, Korso saw two black pickups with police lightbars turn into the street. No sirens. No flashing lights. They made their way towards him. Seconds later, a third police vehicle followed them. This one was a black saloon car, but one with a lightbar. Again, no siren. The mere mention of Galicia's name had seemingly worked wonders. And while they wouldn't get their hands on the man himself, their presence ensured the kid would immediately come under police protection.

Korso waited for the police vehicles to pass. Then he pulled out and steered his prize away from there.

THIRTEEN

Less than an hour later, Korso turned into a very private and exclusive road, located about one mile north-east of Guatemala City. Almost immediately, he pressed the brakes at the sight of the steel swing-arm barrier in front of him. It ran the whole width of the narrow, tree-lined road. There was no sidewalk past the barrier, only empty road. Korso could make out a set of arched gates in the distance, with part of a driveway beyond. That was all. To the left of the barrier was a small concrete guard box, against which a casually dressed man leaned, smoking a cigarette. He had a submachine gun slung over his shoulder.

At the sight of the car, the guard straightened up and stamped on his smoke. He gripped the SMG as he approached the driver's side. Korso wound down the window.

'What do you want?' the guard said.

'I've got information your employer will want,' Korso said. 'I'm here to deliver it personally.'

The man smirked as he looked at the state of the vehicle. 'Are you expected?'

'I doubt it.'

'Name.'

'Graves.'

'Okay, Graves, you give me this information, and I'll make sure it gets passed along to my boss.'

'Sure you will. Would you prefer I turn around and leave? Because I guarantee you'll be the one who gets his legs chopped off when your employer discovers you refused me entry. I'd check first if I were you.'

The guard sighed and shook his head as he slowly unclipped a small walkie-talkie from his belt. He raised it to his mouth just as casually and spoke under his breath to someone at the other end. There was an immediate response that Korso couldn't make out. But the guard reclipped his radio to his belt, strolled back to the guard box and went inside. A second later, the steel arm began to swing inwards. The guard emerged again, and said, 'Stop at the entrance gates at the end. Somebody will meet you there.'

Korso nodded, and slowly steered the Nissan through the widening gap.

It was a pleasant drive, if brief. The peaceful tranquillity of the trees and woods on either side of him were a breath of fresh air after the clamour and smog of Guatemala City during rush hour. He had to applaud Quezada's choice of surroundings.

When he reached the gated entrance at the end, he pulled the handbrake and got out of the car. The steel gates were set between two brick posts and ran the entire width of the road. Set within the gates, on the far right, was a smaller, door-sized gate with a gravel path leading to a windowless concrete structure beyond. Past the entrance gates, he saw a section of the driveway as it began to curve to the right. The rest was hidden by more trees and foliage on either side. He listened to the tweeting of birds all around.

There was a sharp metallic *clack*, and Korso turned to see two men step through the door-sized gate. The first man was stocky, with a goatee and shoulder-length dark hair pulled back in a tight ponytail. He wore a shoulder holster over his short-sleeved shirt. It held a large calibre revolver. The second man was younger and taller than his partner, and clean-shaven. He wore jogging pants and a long-sleeved shirt and carried a semi-automatic in his right hand.

The taller one stayed back, while the stocky one took a good look at the Nissan. Nothing showed in his face. Finally, he turned his attention to Korso.

'Your name's Graves?' he said.

'Yes,' Korso said.

'You've got information for me.'

'So you're Mr Quezada?' Korso frowned. 'That's odd. You don't look much like your photos, and I notice you've also lost some height too. Also, the guard back there must have misunderstood. It's not information I've brought, but something more tangible. Something that the real Mr Quezada wants very badly.'

The man glanced at the back seats. 'That wheelchair sure doesn't look like it's made of gold. So what else you got?'

Korso motioned with his finger and walked to the rear of the car. He inserted his key and opened the trunk. After removing the hairpiece and whiskers, he took two steps back. Both men peered at the man contained within, the taller one leaning in for a closer look. Galicia was still unconscious, still breathing regularly.

After a few seconds, the stocky man turned to Korso, his face just as blank. 'So?'

This told Korso he wasn't talking to the brains of the team. His taller colleague, however, was another matter. He slowly raised himself up to his full height. There was a light in his eyes that hadn't been present before. He led his partner out of hearing range and whispered in his ear. Korso closed the trunk, and waited.

They soon finished their private discussion and strolled back. The stocky one was smiling again as he pulled the gun from his holster. It looked like a .357. 'Good of you to drop him off,' he said. 'We'll take it from here. You can hitch a lift back on the main road.'

'And if I choose not to?'

The man aimed his gun at Korso's chest. 'Take one guess.'

Korso shook his head sadly. 'I'd always heard Mr Quezada was a smarter man than most. But it seems I was wrong if he's got a moron like you working for him.'

The stocky man lost the smile. 'Take a look around. We're surrounded by forest on all sides. All private land. Where we bury you, nobody will ever find you. Now who's the moron?'

'Pull the trigger then. But I guarantee you'll be joining me shortly after.'

'And why's that?' the taller one said.

'Because if Mr Quezada's as smart as his reputation suggests, he'll expect a detailed account of how his most hated enemy arrived at his front door, unconscious, in the trunk of a car. And once he finds out your friend here's killed the only person who can give him those details, he's going to be very unhappy. I'd hate to see a man like that in a bad mood. He's liable to do anything. Don't you agree?'

'I could make you tell us.' The first man aimed his gun at Korso's left foot. 'I don't have to kill you.'

'But we both know that's how it would end, so I'll give you nothing, no matter how many holes you put in me.' He turned back to the taller man. 'Of course, there's a much simpler solution. Just introduce me to Mr Quezada and I'll explain everything to him in person.'

'I don't like it,' the stocky man said. 'And I don't like you.'

Korso ignored him. To his partner, he said, 'Why delay things? You know he'll want to see me.'

The taller one said, 'Search him, Ramirez. From head to toe.'

'Look—'

'Just do it. He's right. The boss will want to talk to him.' He pulled out a walkie-talkie, pressed the transmit button. 'It's Dante. Open the gates.'

Ramirez's face became sullen, but he put the gun back in its holster. Korso made sure not to smile as he raised his arms high into the air.

–

Korso steered them through the gates, keeping the speed at a steady fifteen kilometres per hour. Ramirez sat in the passenger seat, his Smith & Wesson pointing at Korso. The one called Dante sat in the rear. After Ramirez body-searched him, Dante had repeated the process until he was fully satisfied. They were thorough, he had to give them that.

The large compound was a little oasis of tranquillity compared with the hustle and bustle of the city just beyond the walls. Trees everywhere you looked, set amidst beautifully manicured gardens. Korso followed the gently curving driveway around, passing a stucco bungalow with a small swimming pool on the left, and a two-storey house on the right, this one mostly hidden by trees. Other than two elderly male gardeners, one of whom was sprinkling a flowerbed with a hose, he saw nobody else.

The gravel driveway soon opened up into a large open courtyard, with four park benches spaced out around it, and a lushly designed, single-storey villa as its backdrop. Rotating sprinklers silently watered different parts of the huge front garden. A set of wide steps led up to a regal front entrance, which suggested this was Quezada's house. To the right of the building, the driveway spurred off towards a huge annex building that had to be a garage. Korso counted seven up-and-over doors in view, but the structure looked deep enough to hold over three dozen vehicles inside.

Korso pressed the brakes and the vehicle came to a gentle stop directly in front of the main house.

'Out,' Ramirez said, motioning with the gun. 'Keys first.'

Korso killed the engine, passed him the ignition keys, and got out of the car. Ramirez and Dante joined him, one standing on either side.

They all looked up at the house and waited in silence. After a minute, the front door opened and an athletic-looking man with dyed-blond shoulder-length hair emerged. He wore a short-sleeved shirt and tan chinos. Standing on the top step, he looked down at them with an air of superiority. Then he slowly descended, his eyes never leaving Korso's face for a second. Once he'd reached the bottom, Korso saw that he was somewhere in his mid-forties, with a narrow face that made his sunken eyes seem larger than they were. His cheeks were lightly pockmarked.

'This better be good, Dante,' he said, still studying Korso as though he were a laboratory rat. 'You know the rules. Mr Quezada doesn't like strangers on his property unless he's personally invited them.'

'I know, Mr Ozan. But this guy's delivered something the boss will want to take a look at himself.'

'Show me.'

Dante made a hand signal to his less intelligent partner, and Ramirez stepped over to the rear of the vehicle and opened the trunk. Ozan rubbed a hand against his cheek stubble and sauntered over. He gazed down at the man contained within. A second was all it took for the recognition to show on his face. He leaned in closer for a better look, while placing two fingers against the captive's neck.

'Propofol,' Korso said. 'He should regain consciousness any time now. If he hasn't already.'

Ozan looked at Korso with more interest. 'It's really him.'

'Of course.'

Turning back to the trunk, Ozan pulled out his phone and took four quick shots of his captive. Then he leaned down and slapped Galicia's face hard. When he got no response, he did it again, even harder. After the third slap, Galicia groaned and slowly raised a hand to his face. He opened his eyes and squinted at the four men staring down at him, as though still in a dream. When he saw Ozan, his eyes widened.

'You remember me?' Ozan said.

Galicia nodded dumbly, his previous arrogance all gone.

'Good.' Ozan smiled. 'It's always better when they know what's coming.' He pulled his arm back and struck Galicia in the face, his knuckles connecting with the man's jaw below the ear. Galicia's head snapped back from the impact, and he went out like a light.

Ozan closed the trunk and turned to Korso. 'How?'

'That I'll tell to Mr Quezada, and nobody else.'

'And what exactly are you hoping for in return?'

'Same answer.'

'What's your name?'

'Ricardo Graves.'

'Well, Graves, Mr Quezada is very particular about who he sees and who he talks to, which is why I have to check you out first. I want some answers from you, and the quicker you give them to me, the quicker you get to see the man himself. Are we clear?'

Korso blinked slowly. 'I understand your words, Ozan. And I'm willing to tell you everything you want to know, but I'll only do it with Mr Quezada present. I hate explaining myself twice.'

'Watch your tone, friend. You're in a different world from the one you just left, with a whole new set of rules. Mr Quezada's got no patience for arrogance, and that goes double for me.'

'I'll make sure to remember that,' Korso said.

'Let me put one in his leg, Mr Ozan,' Ramirez said. 'I'll make him sing for you.'

Ozan sighed. 'Ramirez, shut your stupid mouth. Open it again only when I ask you a question, not before. Dante, you've searched him thoroughly?'

'Twice. He's completely unarmed. Nothing in the vehicle, either.'

Ozan nodded vaguely as he pursed his lips. After a few moments, he said, 'Watch him,' then put a little distance between them as he pulled out his phone again. He pressed a button and raised it to his ear, then spoke in hushed tones for about a minute. Finally, he ended the call and returned to Korso, his face showing nothing.

'Dante, you and Ramirez stay with the car,' he said. 'Graves, you come with me.'

FOURTEEN

As Ozan led him through the main entrance, Korso knew he was entering completely unchartered territory. Up to this point, everything had been planned down to the smallest detail, but now that he'd made it inside there were no longer any certainties. Everything now depended on how Quezada would react to this unexpected intrusion into his private life.

The small lobby area was very tastefully designed, with white marble floors, white stucco walls, and plenty of space. The ceiling was much lower than he'd expected, which automatically made the place feel more welcoming and homely. Not what he'd imagined at all. There were two paintings on display, one on either side of him. Korso recognised the styles straight away. The one on the left wall was a minor Picasso piece, possibly from his later years, showing a bullfight. The painting on the right was much larger: a brightly coloured carnival mural by the great surrealistic Guatemalan artist Carlos Mérida. The room also contained four doorways leading off to other parts of the house. Taking pride of place at the very head of the room was a large Mayan Chacmool stone sculpture, portraying a genderless reclining figure with its head facing ninety degrees from the front, and supporting some kind of bowl on its stomach. The stone was chipped in places, and generally smoothed over with time. It looked over a thousand years old.

Ozan led him towards the furthest door on the right, past the mural. He opened it and Korso followed him into an arched hallway, with another door at the end, maybe thirty feet away. There were three doors running down the right, all shut. Light was provided by floor-to-ceiling windows all down the left side. They overlooked a medium-sized swimming pool and patio area, with another beautifully designed garden area set further back. The sun was fading, the horizon already streaked with orange. A beautiful long-haired woman wearing a thin robe lay on one of the four sun loungers by the pool, doing something on her phone. He had no doubt he was looking at Luana, Quezada's wife. On Google, he'd seen plenty of shots of her from her modelling days.

Ozan reached the door at the end and knocked gently three times. A voice came from within and he opened the door, motioning for Korso to enter.

Korso nodded at him and stepped into a large office area. The room's design was contemporary minimalist, with the opposite wall completely taken up by modern bookcases, each filled with hardcover editions. A small bar area took up one corner of the room. To Korso's left, floor-to-ceiling windows looked out onto the same garden area he'd just seen from the hallway, and there was also a sliding glass door at the far end. To his right was a large executive work desk containing some legal pads and three large widescreen monitors, each with its own silicone keypad. A woman with long black hair parted down the middle, wearing a pale-yellow sleeveless summer dress that accentuated her dusky complexion, sat in front of one of the monitors. Her back was to Korso, and she was humming to herself as she keyed in figures onto an Excel spreadsheet.

Next to her, a familiar-looking man was leaning against the desk, silently sipping from a glass of iced water as he watched Korso. Miguel Quezada looked younger than the man in the photo, but the eyes were still just as dark, just as intense. His black hair was now cut very short, but he still wore his sideburns long. He had on loose linen beach trousers and a baggy white shirt, open to the chest. His only jewellery was an antique gold ring on the third finger of his right hand.

Korso looked back at Quezada and remained silent. He was a guest in the man's house and thought it prudent not to speak unless he was asked to.

Quezada held out his hand to Ozan, who had followed Korso into the office. Ozan went over and handed his phone to Quezada. The crime boss set his glass on the table and looked down at the display with a slight frown. Soon, the frown disappeared and the hint of a smile appeared at the sides of his thin lips.

'How sure are you, Javier?' he asked.

'One hundred per cent, Miguel. It's him. You'll see.'

Quezada swiped an index finger across the display a few times, nodding to himself. Finally, he gave the phone back to Ozan. He picked up his glass again, looked at Korso.

'An impressive calling card, Graves,' he said.

'That was my intent, Mr Quezada.'

'Alex,' he said, still watching Korso, 'that's enough for today, I think. We'll continue where we left off in the morning.'

The woman stopped typing and turned. He could now see she wore wire-rimmed spectacles with round frames. She also had a very pleasing profile.

'If you're sure, Miguel.' She saved the document, turned off the screen, and stood up.

'Graves, allow me to introduce you to my associate, Alejandra. She's been an essential part of my business for some years now. In many ways, I consider her my right hand. Alex, be nice to the man.'

'I'm always nice.' She turned to Korso, her brown, almond-shaped eyes studying his with mild interest, along with a hint of amusement. She brushed her hair away from her face with a palm. 'Pleased to meet you, Mr Graves.'

'The honour's all mine, Miss Alejandra,' Korso said, conscious that he wasn't exactly dressed to impress. Nor had he shaved in three days. 'It seems everywhere I turn in this place, I see more beauty. It's very disorientating.'

She raised an eyebrow. 'Well. Your guests aren't usually this polite, Miguel.' She gave a fleeting glance to Ozan, and added, 'Or as charming. Where did you find him?'

'I'm about to find out. Run along now, little Alex.'

'Yes, *sir.*' With a smile, she picked up a linen bag from the floor, slung it over her shoulder, and walked over to the sliding glass door. Waving to Quezada, she gave Korso a quick final glance, and then she was gone.

Korso turned back to his host.

'You know how to make a first impression, I'll grant you that,' Quezada said, motioning towards the chair Alejandra had just vacated. 'Now to business. Sit.'

Korso sat. He also knew without looking that Ozan was standing right behind him. Probably with a gun in his hand.

'Okay,' Quezada said, 'Ricardo Graves, if that *is* your real name, you said you'd only speak with me, and so here I am. Now tell me everything.'

FIFTEEN

Korso talked. In great detail, he told Quezada how he'd shadowed Galicia and his men every day for over a week, and how he'd finally found out about the gangster's predilection for underage girls through sheer doggedness. Which was a lie, but it served to make his accomplishment seem even more impressive. As Korso told of the schoolgirl, and recounted her secret liaisons with Galicia at the apartment house, he could see the muscles in Quezada's jaw tense up. His face became darker, and he clenched and unclenched his right hand.

'This girl,' he said, his voice calm, controlled. 'How old is she?'

'I'm not sure,' Korso said. 'I'd say no older than thirteen. Possibly less.'

'I see. Go on.'

Korso continued. He told of his appropriation of the neighbouring apartment, his many preparations to get everything ready in time, and finally his abduction of Galicia that very afternoon, right in front of his own men.

'Once I had Galicia tucked up safely in the trunk,' he went on, 'I parked outside the apartment house and called the police. I told them I was a tenant, and that some gangster named Romario Galicia was having sex with an underage girl in 412. As soon as they showed up in force, I left and drove here.'

'Why bother calling the cops at all?' Ozan said. He was now sitting a few feet away from Korso, his left hand hidden from view.

'Once Galicia's bodyguards discovered their boss was gone,' Korso said, 'they'd want answers, and the girl would be their first obvious port of call. There's no telling what they'd do to her once she woke up, but I doubt it would be beneficial to her.' He shrugged. 'I felt she'd be safer in police custody than theirs.'

'And this all took place less than two hours ago?' Quezada asked.

Korso nodded. 'It can be checked easily enough. A man of your influence must have plenty of contacts in the police department.'

Quezada gave Ozan a look. The other man pulled his phone from his pocket and stood up. He walked over to the windows, pressing buttons as he went. Quezada was still leaning against the desk with his arms crossed, watching Korso, his expression giving nothing away. Korso heard Ozan talking in hushed tones to whoever was at the other end of the phone. He couldn't make out any words.

'I know you're not Guatemalan,' Quezada said, 'but I can't place your accent. Where are you from?'

'Portugal, originally.' Korso thought it best to stick with the nationality on his current passport. 'But I move from country to country, wherever the work is.' He lowered his gaze to Quezada's right hand. 'That's an impressive ring. Is it Mayan?'

'It is indeed.' Quezada made a star of his hand, smiling down at the ring. 'It once belonged to King Pakal. You know of him?'

Korso nodded. 'Pakal the Great. Ruler of the ancient Mexican city of Palenque, which borders Guatemala, for much of the seventh century. He eventually died at the grand old age of eighty. His tomb and sarcophagus were discovered in the 1950s, weren't they?'

'1952, to be exact. In the Temple of Inscriptions. You know your history, Graves.'

'It's always been my favourite subject. That's a very impressive Chacmool sculpture in your lobby, by the way. I'm no expert, but it looks to be over a thousand years old.'

'Eleven hundred and seventeen years, actually.' Quezada noticed Ozan had finished his call. 'Well?'

'My man just confirmed most of what he told us, but with a few additions. He said they received an anonymous call at around four forty-five this afternoon. Three units raced down to an apartment house in Zone 21 and found armed bodyguards inside and out. Three of them got themselves arrested for pulling guns. The cops found the girl, still dressed but unconscious, in the bathroom of 412.' He gave a thin smile. 'No sign of Galicia, of course, but one of the uniforms discovered the hole in the wall, so they know it was a professional snatch. None of the bodyguards admitted to seeing any guy pushing an old man in a wheelchair, but some kids on the street outside said they saw the two of them go past while they were playing football. Some uniforms checked one of the side streets around there and found a guy's corpse behind a parked car, with a very large knife lodged where his Adam's apple used to be. Nobody claims to know who he is.'

Quezada turned to Korso, his face darkening. 'Well?'

'Just one of Galicia's men,' Korso said. 'He sensed something was wrong and followed me. I had to deal with him, so I did.'

'And you didn't think that worth mentioning?'

In fact, Korso had purposely held that part back in order to see how extensive Quezada's intelligence network was. Now he knew. But he said, 'It was just a minor complication, that's all. I didn't think it was relevant.'

Quezada stepped forward until his face was just inches away from Korso's. His anger was almost palpable. 'Listen to me very carefully, Graves, because I'll only say this once. When I ask you to tell me everything, that means *every*thing. You leave nothing out. *Nothing at all.* Do you understand?'

'Yes.'

'*Do you understand?*'

'I do now.'

Quezada nodded once and stepped back, his anger suddenly vanishing as though it had never existed. 'Continue, Javier.'

'So anyway,' Ozan said, 'my man over there says they're not exactly breaking their backs looking for Galicia, especially with so little to go on. They figure it's just business as usual, and are happy to leave it at that. If he turns up at the bottom of a lake a week or a month from now, no big deal. Just one less problem to worry about.'

'Good. And the child?'

'She woke up soon after they broke in, but couldn't tell them anything useful. All she knows is some guy she'd never seen before slammed into the bathroom and stuck a needle in her neck, and the next thing she knows she's surrounded by police asking her questions.' He paused. 'And Miguel? She's twelve years old.'

'Twelve,' Quezada said, his voice as cold as ice. 'Practically Nilsa's age.' He took a deep breath, let it out just as slowly. 'Javier, have Dante take Galicia to the usual place, but quietly. I want nobody else on the estate to see him, understand? *Nobody*. I'll want to talk to him personally after supper, and I'll want you and Dante there too, so make sure you bring your instruments.'

'They're all polished and ready to go.' Ozan smiled as he pulled out his phone again.

Quezada returned his gaze to Korso. 'I still have a few more questions.'

'I thought you might.'

'Now you've delivered Galicia to me, and I'm grateful. That degenerate scum's been a thorn in my side for a long time. But while you've told me how you did it, you still haven't given me the why. What is it you expect in return?'

'I expect nothing, Mr Quezada. You were right the first time. Galicia's little more than a calling card to help get me through the door. After all, you're not an easy person to meet. As far as I'm concerned, he's a gift. Yours to do with as you will.'

'Very generous of you. And that's all?'

'Not quite. He also serves as a résumé of sorts. You see, I'd very much like to work for you, Mr Quezada. In a specialist capacity, that is.'

'You want to work for me,' Quezada repeated, fondling his ring.

'Mr Quezada's already got thousands of people on his payroll, Graves,' Ozan said. 'What makes you so unique?'

'I think I've just proved myself in that regard, don't you? I imagine Mr Quezada's instructed his people to bring him Galicia's head more than once over the past few years, with clearly limited success. I've achieved what they couldn't, and in a fraction of the time. I'd say that makes me unique.'

Ozan's eyes turned to slits. He opened his mouth to speak, but Quezada raised a hand, and he closed it immediately.

'And just what is your specialty, exactly?' Quezada asked.

'At its most basic level, I suppose you could call me a solver of problems. Specifically, those problems to which nobody else can find solutions, as evidenced by the man in the trunk of my car. But most of the time I'm tasked with recovering assets, often stolen, that might otherwise remain lost.'

'For whom?'

'For people like you.'

'Such as? Give me examples.'

'I'm afraid I can't supply you with names or references, Mr Quezada. The main reason I'm still alive is that I never betray the confidence of a client. It's an ironclad rule.'

'Very convenient,' Ozan said with a sneer.

'I can see how it would seem that way, which is why I sidestepped that little problem by providing Mr Quezada with a practical demonstration instead.'

'Yeah? For all we know, you could be a cop.'

Korso stared at Ozan. 'Seriously? Nobody's ever said that to me before. Anyway, Mr Quezada already knows I'm not Guatemalan, so even if I were law enforcement I'd have no jurisdiction in this country.' He turned back to his host. 'But what do your instincts tell you, Mr Quezada? After all, they've kept you alive this long.'

'Definitely not law.' Quezada smiled for the first time. 'I can always tell. So can you, Javier.'

Ozan shrugged, acceding the point. Quezada tapped his fingers on the table top as he studied Korso's face. Seconds passed. Nobody spoke. Korso could hear the faint sounds of children's laughter coming from another part of the house.

'So why seek my patronage?' Quezada said, finally. 'Why not approach Galicia instead, say, and present him with the drugged body of one of his enemies? Maybe even me?'

Korso snorted. 'You're joking. I had to pass through three levels of security just to get this far, including two full body searches, and that's only because I brought along something of worth. No, I always do my research, Mr Quezada, and what quickly became obvious to me was that you're a survivor. Being one myself, I know the type intimately. You've lasted this long in a business that doesn't encourage long lifespans, and you can only have done that by making as few mistakes as possible. And the few you have made, I expect you only made once. Galicia, on the other hand, is young and arrogant and a slave to his passions, and men like that might as well have targets tattooed onto their foreheads. Especially in your business. I'm fairly sure you would have gotten him eventually, but I just figured, why wait?'

'Why, indeed?' Quezada took another sip of his water. 'I seem to have forgotten my manners. You want something to drink?'

'Thank you. Mineral water will be fine.' Korso breathed a little easier. Having a drink offered to you was always a good sign in negotiations of this kind.

'Javier, refresh mine as well.' Quezada said. 'Plenty of ice. And whatever you want for yourself.'

Ozan mutely took Quezada's glass tumbler and walked over to the small bar in the corner. Korso could tell from the sullen expression that he and Ozan weren't going to be friends anytime soon. Not that he'd really expected otherwise. He knew his very presence here was disrupting the status quo, and that always produced resentment amongst the faithful. And he had a feeling Ozan had known Quezada for a long time, perhaps since childhood, so to be mixing drinks for the new guy wasn't exactly helping his mood.

Not that Korso cared. He wasn't here to keep Ozan happy.

They waited in silence while Ozan pulled two fresh glasses from the shelf behind the bar, and then took two small bottles of mineral water from a refrigerator hidden under the counter. When Ozan returned with the drinks, Korso took his with a curt nod of thanks.

'Javier,' Quezada said, taking his own glass. 'I've been thinking about that other problem of mine. No names. You know the one I mean. We were discussing it again yesterday morning.'

Knotting his brows together, Ozan jutted his chin at Korso. 'For him, you mean? I don't know, Miguel. I think maybe we need to discuss it some more before you think of handing it over to a complete stranger. After all, we still don't know anything about this guy.'

'Yes.' Quezada nodded slowly. 'There is that. Still…'

Completely in the dark as to what they were talking about, Korso said, 'I think the less you know about me, Mr Quezada, the better for you in the long run. We've got no shared history, so there's no real way to connect me to you, meaning complete deniability all the way down the line. As I'm sure you know, in certain sensitive situations, often the best way to guarantee no comebacks is to assign the problem to an outsider.'

'Maybe… maybe not.' Quezada waved a hand, immediately brushing the subject aside. 'Never mind that now. Where are you staying?'

'I don't know yet. A lot depends on the outcome of this meeting.'

Quezada set his tumbler down and walked round to the other side of the table. He opened a drawer and pulled out a thick envelope. After a brief check of the contents, he slid it across to Korso.

'Take it,' he said. 'Get yourself a room at a hotel in town while I think on this some more. Try the Hilton. And upgrade your wardrobe too. Give Ozan your cell phone number on the way out, and he'll get back to you. It might be tomorrow, it might be the day after. And it might not be the answer you want.'

'I can't ask for anything more.' Korso stood up, putting down the glass and pocketing the bulky envelope without even looking. 'I appreciate your time, Mr Quezada.'

But Quezada just ignored him. He sat down at his desk and clicked the mouse, his mind already on other things.

SIXTEEN

Once they were outside the villa, Korso paused on the top step and gave Ozan his cell phone number. Ozan keyed it into his own phone. 'Piece of advice, Graves.'

Here it comes, Korso thought. 'And what's that?'

'Get yourself a better vehicle before you come back. *If* you come back. That piece of shit down there belongs in a scrapyard.'

Korso just smiled and descended the steps, hearing the front door shut quietly behind him. He saw his car was parked in the same spot, now facing the other way. Ramirez was glaring at him from the driver's seat, waiting to escort him off the property. But Ozan had a point. In these surroundings, the Nissan was nothing less than an embarrassment. He reached the bottom step and walked around the car. He was about to open the front passenger door when he saw someone sitting on one of the garden benches overlooking the courtyard.

It was Alejandra. Sitting with one leg folded under her as she carefully painted her fingernails. She was also pretending not to notice him. Behind her, the steadily darkening sky was a stunning mix of purples, pinks and oranges. Magic hour.

'Let's go,' Ramirez said.

Ignoring him, Korso ambled over to Alejandra, glad to have a chance to talk with her again. For a number of reasons. 'Hello again, Miss Alejandra.'

She paused and looked up at him. A brief smile crossed her lips. 'Hello, Mr Graves.'

'Ricardo, please. Or Ric, if you prefer.'

She didn't say which she preferred, just continued brushing purple varnish across the nail of her index finger. It belonged to a nice hand, with almost perfect bone structure. Finally, she said, 'So your meeting with Miguel went satisfactorily?'

'I'm not entirely sure yet. He said he'd call me tomorrow, or the next day. We'll see. You're very colour co-ordinated this evening, Alejandra. At least, temporarily.'

She looked down at her yellow dress and green sandals, then stared back at him with a puzzled expression.

'That shade of nail varnish matches the sunset almost perfectly,' he said.

She smiled again, for longer this time. 'I wish I could say I'd planned it that way.' Looking past his shoulder, she said, 'You're being summoned.'

Korso turned to see Ramirez standing by the side of the car, making angry beckoning gestures at him.

'Just ignore him.' Korso gave him a friendly wave, and turned back to Alejandra. 'As long as I'm with you, he won't do anything.'

She studied him for a moment before returning to her nails. 'You're not much like the others.'

'Others?'

'The other men who come here, summoned by Miguel for one reason or another. Or watchdogs like Ramirez over there. They're mostly frightened little thugs, often with mean eyes, and usually with manners similar to the gorillas they resemble.'

'I can be mean too.'

'So can we all, but not all the time. That's the difference.'

Korso watched her work for a while, then said, 'May I offer you a lift, Alejandra?'

She glanced at the Nissan and snorted. 'I'm fine, thank you. Besides, I'm not sure that thing will even make it to the front gate.'

'It'll make it. It's what's under the hood that counts. So you live on the grounds, then?'

Alejandra moved on to her middle finger. 'What business is it of yours?'

'I don't know. Only you can answer that.'

After a short pause, she said, 'I'm staying here for now. I use one of the spare bungalows when Miguel needs me close to hand. The rest of the time, I have my own place in the city.'

'The best of both worlds. Very wise.' He looked around, completely ignoring Ramirez still standing by the car. 'It's a big estate, isn't it? I spotted two more smaller houses on the drive in. Are there many others on the grounds?'

'Hmm, ten in all, I think. No, eleven.' She paused, frowning up at him. 'You know, I'm not sure? As you say, it's a large compound, and I'm sure there are plenty of areas I've never even visited.'

'Perhaps if I'm invited back, and you're free, you could give me a short, guided tour. We can discover the rest together.'

'Getting ahead of yourself a little, aren't you, Mr Graves?'

'I find it saves time in the long run.' He smiled. 'Well I better be off before my friend over there sets the dogs on me. Very nice meeting you again, Alejandra.'

She just smiled back in response, and he turned and strolled to his car. Ramirez glared silently at him as he got back behind the wheel and turned the key in the ignition. The engine roared loudly into life. Korso got in the passenger side.

'You're really pushing your luck,' Ramirez growled.

Korso turned to him and said nothing. He saw Alejandra watching them both, and gave her a wave that she didn't return. Then Ramirez crunched the gears, stepped on the gas and slowly steered them back towards the front gates.

SEVENTEEN

Korso found an empty parking space on a side street close to the city centre, not far from Plaza Mayor. It was still Monday evening rush hour, so the area was heaving with traffic. Leaving the keys in the ignition, he grabbed his overnight bag and shut the door without locking it. Regardless of the car's poor condition, he had no doubt it would be gone within the hour. He walked five blocks east, stopping only to purchase some off-the-shelf shirts and a pair of trousers along the way, before finally signalling for a taxi.

Thirty minutes later, he was towelling himself off after a well-deserved shower and shave. He'd followed Quezada's advice. Using some of the cash he'd been given, he took a premium suite at the Hilton. Set amidst the sprawling gardens of an exclusive residential estate on the outskirts of the city, the hotel provided a pleasant counterbalance to his last few days in Colonia Prados de Villahermosa. Feeling fresh and clean at last, he put on one of the shirts he'd bought, along with the new pair of tan chinos, and took his glass of iced mineral water out onto the third-floor balcony. There was a small table and two chairs out there. On the table was his travel chess set. He sipped at his drink as he gazed down at the floodlit gardens below. The cool, gentle breeze coming in from the west felt good against his skin.

Tomorrow he'd find himself some more presentable wheels, but for now Korso simply reflected on his current progress and tried to figure out what might come next. So far, things had gone about as well as he could have hoped. He'd grabbed Galicia without anyone knowing a thing. As a result, he'd not only been introduced to the target himself, but it seemed possible that Quezada might give him another assignment almost immediately. He clearly had something in mind, but without further information Korso couldn't begin to guess at the problem to which he hinted.

Could be another competitor he wanted taken out of the game. Maybe even Tobias Macqin, his other main rival. Anything was possible. He also couldn't help wondering what might be happening with Galicia at this very moment. Or *to* him. Quezada's remark about a personal visit, accompanied by both Ozan and Dante, certainly didn't bode well for the man.

Without any kind of prompting, his thoughts naturally turned to Alejandra. Although Verhoeven had briefed him on the woman, Korso hadn't actually expected to run into her so quickly. Fortunately he'd turned on the charm a little at their initial meeting, which seemed to have paid dividends if her presence later at the front of the house was any indication.

If she was staying in one of the bungalows on the property, then he felt sure it would have its own garden. So why did she decide to sit on one of the benches in front of Quezada's? There could only really be one reason. She wanted to see Korso one more time, learn a little more about him. Which was fine with him. Any edge he could get was worth exploiting to the full, and if she was actually interested in him, so much the better. That she was also very attractive was merely the icing on the cake. It also seemed obvious, based on that quick dismissive glance she gave Ozan when she was introduced to Korso, that there was some kind of history between the two of them. Which would help explain Ozan's general hostility towards Korso after she'd left. That added another interesting element to the mix. Whether or not it developed into anything further was another matter.

Everything depended on Quezada now. If he wanted another meet, fine. Another step forward. If he didn't, then

Korso would have to make a decision. Either start again from scratch and come at the problem from a different angle, or abandon the job altogether. And giving up on an assignment went completely against his nature. He knew there was always more than one solution to any problem, you just needed to look for it. That was a lesson he'd learned at a very early age.

Hopefully, it wouldn't come to that. Only time would tell.

Korso felt a brief vibration against his hip, and took his phone from his pocket. That was another factor that marked this job out from the others. He rarely used a cell phone more than once, and here he was using the same one over and over again. It was a weird feeling. For the foreseeable future, he was no longer living off the grid. But of course for the role he was playing it was essential that he be contactable day or night. Whatever the job demanded.

He'd received a text message. The sender was anonymous, from a number he didn't recognise. Korso opened it up.

How's things? Good, I hope? Your canine pal.

Korso had to smile at the casual phrasing. He hadn't actually thought about Dog since he'd landed in Guatemala, but he could see how the hacker might be getting fidgety right about now. He quickly keyed in an equally vague message and sent it off.

Things are fine. Don't expect regular posts from me.

A few seconds later, a return text came back:

Understood. Just worried – that's all.

He understood Dog's anxiety, but absolute security could be guaranteed only if nobody else knew what he was up to. And that included Dog.

Korso put down the phone. He studied the remaining positions on his chessboard again and considered his next move.

–

Nobody called on Tuesday.

Korso spent the morning purchasing a silver Honda Civic from the same dealer from whom he'd bought the four previous wrecks. The vehicle was only ten years old, and after a lot of haggling, he'd finally handed over forty thousand quetzales for the vehicle. But at least he now had a car that looked a little more presentable. Personally, Korso couldn't care less about appearance, but for the role he was playing he had to look the part.

For the remainder of the day, when it wasn't pouring down with rain, Korso either ate or swam in the main pool, or reclined on one of the loungers as he caught the sun and played chess against himself. He hated being non-productive, this way he could at least keep his mind active while darkening his natural olive colouring a little more, so as to better blend in with the rest of the populace.

Wednesday brought more of the same. And even more rain. Whenever it stopped, Korso sat out by the pool again, keeping to himself and talking to nobody. In between chess matches, he made his way through a book about Mayan rulers of the ancient world, which he thoroughly enjoyed. Nobody called. He knew they would, that they were making him wait on purpose. But you had to allow people their little power games. Korso knew the art of patience better than anyone.

On Thursday morning at 11.13, he was drinking juice on the balcony when his phone trilled. After the sixth ring, he took the call.

'Hello?'

'Graves?' The voice was Ozan's.

'Yes.'

'Come out to the house. He wants to see you right away.'

EIGHTEEN

Korso arrived at the arched gates thirty-five minutes later. After another comprehensive body search from two men he'd never seen before, followed by a very thorough search of his vehicle, he was finally allowed into the compound. Ozan met him once again at the front of the house, before escorting him back to the same office in the south-east wing. The office was empty. As Ozan went over to the sliding doors, Korso glanced at some of the titles in the leftmost bookshelf. Quezada had some tantalising books in his collection.

'Over here,' Ozan said, breaking him out of his reverie. He was motioning for Korso to pass through the open doors into the garden.

Wearing a baggy short-sleeved shirt and casual linen trousers, Quezada sat at a circular marble table under the shade of some morro trees, doing something on his laptop. 'Graves,' he said, stopping what he was doing, 'glad you could come.'

'Thanks for inviting me.'

'Sit down. I like an early lunch. If you want something that's not here, I can have it brought out for you.'

Neatly arranged on the table were bowls of diced mango, pineapple, fresh avocados and other fruits, along with plates containing cold cuts, bread, freshly made enchiladas and more besides. There was also a jug of iced water, and two jugs containing orange and grapefruit juice. Quezada was eating mango chunks with the aid of a long fork.

'This looks just fine,' Korso said, taking a seat directly opposite.

Quezada made a brief hand gesture, and Korso turned to see the back of Ozan as he quietly disappeared into the house. So it was just the two of them for now, although he had no doubt they were still under observation. Quezada probably had a gun secreted somewhere on his body as well, just in case. Korso knew he was still under probation, and Quezada was too sharp and too paranoid to let down his guard for a second. Especially with a stranger.

'I believe a healthy diet cures all ills.' Quezada poured some grapefruit juice into a glass, pushed it across the table to his guest. 'The enchiladas are vegetarian, but you can add whatever meats you want.'

'Vegetarian works for me.' Korso wasn't all that hungry, but he placed two enchiladas onto an empty plate and took a bite out of one. As he chewed, he slowly nodded his head in appreciation. 'Delicious.'

'I expect nothing less in my own house.'

Korso looked around as he ate. The vast garden was surrounded on three sides by fifteen-foot-high fruit trees set amongst thick foliage. Fifty feet away, close to the house, was the swimming pool and the lounge chairs he'd spotted before. Nobody was there now. He could make out garish-coloured birds in the branches of the nearest trees, singing songs to each other. He could also hear the faint barking of dogs somewhere in the distance, and figured they were probably on the grounds somewhere. The place was big enough. The whole scene was all very calm and relaxing, but Korso didn't let himself be fooled for a second. He was in the very heart of the lion's den, where the slightest wrong move could prove fatal.

Quezada finished the last few chunks of his mango and pushed his plate aside. Wiping his fingers with a napkin, he said, 'Have you heard of the name Manuel Pineda?'

Korso frowned as he sipped his drink. Nothing came to mind. 'Can't say I have.'

'Let me introduce you.' Quezada swivelled the MacBook Air around. 'This Pineda's another thorn in my side. A large one.'

Korso groaned inwardly when he saw what was on the screen. It was an official photo showing a moustached man with piercing grey eyes and short black hair, wearing a dark uniform with five gold chevrons on each shoulder epaulette. The shot looked like it had been taken in his office. There was plenty of oak or teak in the background, along with part of a Guatemalan flag. The man seemed to be in his mid-forties, and despite the deep ridges running down from his nose to the sides of his mouth, his face had a well-fed look about it.

'A policeman?' Korso asked.

'Not just any policeman. Pineda's the deputy chief of DOC, the Division of Joint Operations, and has close ties with DIFEP, the Division of Special Police Forces, DIPAFRONT, the Division of Ports, Airports and Border Posts, and most of the other divisions as well. He's also got influential friends all the way up to the highest levels of the Ministry of the Interior, which explains how he's risen so high in the National Civil Police in such a short time. Like any good politician, he knows how to network to get ahead, and he also knows how to cover his tracks. We looked, and there's nothing in his past to use against him. Not a thing. Pure as a virgin from head to toe. A year from now he'll be chief of the whole department, and after that, who knows? With his connections, the sky's the limit.'

Korso understood what Quezada meant. He could see steel behind those grey eyes. 'I assume he doesn't like you very much.'

'You could say that,' Quezada said. 'For the past eleven months he's targeted me personally, while mocking me in public at every available opportunity. In that time, he's conducted police raids on every single one of my legitimate businesses in the city, based on nothing more than unfounded rumours from "secret sources", his men often destroying huge amounts of my inventory in the process. I own any number of restaurants and nightclubs around the city, and thanks to him every single one of them also gets raided by the police on a monthly basis, usually during their busiest periods. And every raid somehow gets full media coverage too, with my name always at the forefront as the "alleged owner" of the premises in question, which doesn't exactly do my business reputation any favours. But in purely financial terms, you can imagine what that kind of continuous official harassment does to a venue's popularity. Over the past year, all of my walk-in businesses have lost money, and some I've had to shut down entirely.'

Korso frowned. 'Surely these businesses only account for a fraction of your gross income. Besides, a man in your position must have an army of lawyers at their beck and call. Aren't they doing anything about it?'

'I don't care about the money, Graves. All I care about is putting an end to this bastard's vendetta against me once and for all. As for the legalities, every motion my lawyers file against the city gets dismissed in a heartbeat, and there's no court of appeal for people like me. We both know how the world works, and I've been declared Public Enemy Number One by those at the top. Additionally, three of my best lawyers have each told me they've had visits by armed masked men in the middle of the night, and each had threats made against his family if he continued to file motions on my behalf. I could hire more, but what's the point?'

Quezada poured some orange juice into a glass and took a sip. 'And Pineda hasn't stopped with just my legitimate businesses. He also targets my heroin and coke distribution outlets on the street, practically on a weekly basis. His secret police execute my soldiers and runners whenever they feel like a little target practice. I've had three manufacturing plants burned to the ground, with the workers still inside. The media don't hear about that part, of course. I've also had two shipments seized before they even reached their respective ports, with all the legitimate cargo confiscated, all without any kind of due process. Lieutenants of mine have been taken from their homes in the middle of the night, never to be seen again, and my own sources tell me he's the one responsible. I've lost count of how many men I've had to replace, and you can bet each and every one spent their last moments in a dark concrete room with blood-splattered walls, spilling everything they might know about me or my business, no matter how small or insignificant.'

Korso knew Quezada was right. Even after a long history of human rights violations, from kidnapping and torture to outright murder, police forces in many Latin American countries still operated with little oversight. And Guatemala's reputation was one of the worst in that regard. So he thought it more than likely that this Pineda was utilising the NCP as a private army to advance his own agenda. But that was all perfectly fine with Korso, if it meant Quezada had special need for his services once more.

'These lieutenants who were grabbed,' Korso said, 'they don't know anything about you, right? Or more specifically, your actual involvement in the drug trade?'

'Of course not. There are at least seven layers of separation between me and my street-level workers, but that's not the point. The *point* is, these kidnapped employees are able to give Pineda just enough so that he can plan his next attack on my enterprises. None of my people work in a vacuum; if they did they wouldn't be able to operate at all. But all Pineda needs is a name or an address, just one small lead and he can…'

Quezada looked towards his office, a smile slowly spreading across his features. Korso turned round to see the man's wife walking towards them, holding the hand of an equally beautiful girl. She looked no older than ten, with huge eyes and curly dark hair down to her waist. They were both wearing short-sleeved, ruffled, knee-length summer dresses. The mother's was pale blue, the child's was white.

Korso gently closed the laptop screen as they grew closer.

'Nilsa,' Quezada said happily, both arms outstretched. 'Why aren't you in class? I thought you had English this afternoon.'

The girl ran to her father, returning his hug and giving him a kiss on the cheek. 'Silly,' she said, 'that's later. I wanted to come and have lunch with you. Mama too.' She glanced at the dishes on the table. 'Where are the strawberries? They're my favourite. And I want some lemon ice-cream too.'

'I told you Papa was busy, sweetheart,' Luana Quezada said in a weary tone, giving Korso a brief glance. 'You can see he's with someone.'

'I can always spare a minute for my best girl.' Quezada released his daughter, and said, 'Mr Graves, allow me to introduce my eldest, Nilsa. And my wife, Luana.'

'Hello,' Nilsa said. Her mother said nothing, barely paying any notice to him.

'Very pleased to meet you both,' Korso said, noting that all of Quezada's warmth seemed to be directed towards his daughter. 'Young lady, you're going to be even more beautiful than your mother, and that's saying something.'

Nilsa blushed, gifting him a huge smile before returning her attention to her father. 'Why can't I have lunch with you, Papa?'

'Mama's right, baby. I'm a little busy at the moment. You both have your lunch together, and I'll come see you as soon as I'm done. Deal?'

She pouted, then sighed heavily as she gave him another kiss. 'Okay.'

Smiling at her husband, Luana took her daughter's hand and led her back to the house. Quezada watched them go, the smile slowly fading from his features.

'You're a very fortunate man, Mr Quezada.'

'In some ways.' He noticed the closed laptop then, and gave Korso a brief nod of acknowledgement at his foresight.

'I don't think your wife was very happy to see me,' Korso said, taking another bite of his enchilada.

'Don't let it worry you, Graves. Luana's just naturally suspicious around strangers.'

'Understandable. I hope you don't think me out of line, but is she aware of how you conduct your business?'

'She never asks, and I don't tell her. But she's no child in the woods, if that's what you mean. There's very little about the world that surprises her, and she's aware of the lengths to which some men must go in order to provide for their family.'

'*Everybody behaves badly*,' Korso said, patting his lips with a napkin, '*given the proper chance*.'

'Hemingway,' Quezada said, smiling. '*The Sun Also Rises*. His first and finest novel.'

'I agree.' Korso frowned at him, feigning surprise. He'd already seen the book's title when he'd passed through the office. 'Do you prefer the Spanish translation or the original English version?'

'English, of course. A writer like Hemingway used words so sparingly that too much can get lost in translation. I've got a first edition in my office, personally inscribed by the author, among other treasures. I may show it to you sometime.'

'I'd appreciate that very much. Rare books happen to be a passion of mine.'

'Are they now?' Quezada studied him thoughtfully for a few moments, and then said, 'So, to business. We were discussing the problem of Manuel Pineda.'

'It does seem as though he's got a particular grudge against you.'

'Obviously. Yet I still have no idea why.'

Korso looked up from his food, and saw Quezada was genuine. He hadn't seen it. Which was interesting. But then, when you were too close to a problem it was sometimes hard to spot the obvious. Vice-President Dias, a man who made a point of baiting Quezada in the media every chance he got, gets assassinated almost a year ago to the day, and less than a month afterwards Pineda takes his place by declaring his own war on Quezada. Perhaps Dias had been a mentor of Pineda's at some point in their past. If so, it would have been a little-known relationship, as Quezada clearly hadn't unearthed it in his research of the man. But Pineda had to have knowledge of the assassin's interview in prison, where he'd admitted off the record that Quezada had been behind the murder. To Korso, the connection was too obvious to ignore, yet not only had Quezada not seen it, but also nobody close to him had even brought up the possibility, or investigated it further. Which meant nobody else knew of Quezada's involvement in Dias's assassination. Not even his second-in-command, Ozan. Very interesting indeed.

One thing was for sure: Korso wasn't planning on enlightening him on the subject. Not unless it profited him to do so.

'Knowing how you make your living,' Korso said, 'I can think of one or two possibilities why Pineda might have it in for you.'

Quezada's smile didn't quite reach his eyes. 'Granted, there are a host of reasons why we might not be the best of friends, but there are hundreds more like me operating within these borders, and most are far worse than I am.'

'But nowhere near as successful. You're right at the top of the tree, Mr Quezada. That's why I approached you in the first place. As for the why, it could be anything. Your people might have killed a friend or colleague of Pineda's during a police raid, and he holds you responsible. Or it might even be something very minor in comparison. He could have any number of motives for coming after you personally.'

'Well, I've had enough, Graves. This has been going on for a year now, and I want him removed. Permanently.'

'So why haven't you?'

Quezada glared at him. 'Say that again.'

'I mean you must have an army of assassins on your payroll, Mr Quezada. Why haven't you ordered one of them to simply take him out? With the right amount of preparation, anybody can be got to. Vice-President Dias's murder a year ago proves that.'

Quezada's eyes grew vague at the mention of Dias. 'I'm glad you brought him up, because he's the main reason I can't be overt about it.'

'I don't get you.'

'It's very simple. Dias was another one who believed I was the devil in human form, and any time a news camera came within ten feet of him, he made no secret of that fact. So naturally, after he was murdered, I was thought to be the one behind the assassination, despite there being no evidence against me. But the rumours still continued, and it's taken a lot of time and effort on my part to dispel them. So if Manuel Pineda *were* to be murdered now, even by a stray bullet, those in charge would immediately consider me the prime suspect, and all my work would be undone. I can't allow that to happen. That's why I've given express orders to all my people, all the way down the line, that Pineda is not to be touched. Not under any circumstances.'

'I'm beginning to see where this is going.' Korso reached for an apple. 'And why you called me in today.'

'I was hoping you might. You know, I was impressed by your handling of Galicia, removing him from that apartment building right under the noses of his own men. And I especially appreciated the sleight of hand, how you made the police look one way while you went in the opposite direction, leaving behind almost no trace of your existence. Except for that one corpse, of course.'

'So you want me to grab Pineda for you without anyone knowing? To be honest, I'm not sure employing misdirection would help in this case.'

'I'm well aware of that, Graves. Kidnapping Pineda, no matter how it was done, would be no better than putting a bullet in his brain. The powers that be would simply assume I was responsible for his going missing, and come after me even harder. I want to avoid that scenario altogether.'

'Which leaves just one possibility. You want Pineda to suffer an accident. A fatal one.'

'Exactly. I'm glad you understand. And, of course, there has to be no doubt that his death *is* completely accidental. And I mean no doubt whatsoever. Otherwise I'm in an even worse position than before, which I refuse to allow.'

Korso took a large bite of the apple, thinking quickly.

'I'm not trying to put myself out of a job,' he said, 'but don't you have people of your own who could do this?'

'Graves, I've got men who can hit a target the size of a coin from over a mile away, and I've got even more who can happily remove a man's intestines and feed them to him, all without batting an eyelid. But if I want a specialist who prefers to use a scalpel rather than a meat cleaver, then I'm forced to look outside my comfort zone. And since you've proved with Galicia that you can be subtle when the situation demands it…' He displayed both palms to Korso. 'So tell me, can you handle this problem of mine, or can't you?'

Korso nodded. 'It's what I do.'

NINETEEN

Quezada didn't smile, but he was clearly pleased. For his own part, Korso wasn't entirely sure what he felt. He'd had to accept, or the job would have been over before it even started. And turning down the offer would merely be signing his own death warrant, as Quezada couldn't possibly let him live after divulging his plans. Quezada would likely have iced him on the spot and had his men bury the body in the woods outside. Nobody would ever know, or even care. Except Dog, of course.

Nevertheless, the idea of eliminating a high-ranking police official complicated things greatly. Killing a crime boss was one thing, but a cop took the situation to a whole new level. To make matters worse, if Pineda's campaign against Quezada was any indication, he was most likely an honest cop too. At least comparatively. So if Korso actually *did* what Quezada was asking him to do, and Agent Verhoeven ever found out the truth – and she'd struck him as a very competent detective – he'd find himself on Interpol's list of most wanted fugitives until the end of his days. The whole point of his existence was to stay in the shadows. That's where he thrived. Added to which, he wasn't an assassin. Killing wasn't his area of expertise and never had been.

It wasn't a matter of morals, which generally came very low on Korso's list of priorities, but of survival. Everything else was secondary. But he also knew there had to be a way of satisfying both ends of the spectrum. He just didn't know how yet.

'You realise this might take a little time to arrange, Mr Quezada,' he said. 'Whenever I take on an assignment I always insist on researching the situation thoroughly, conducting my own reconnaissance on the target, taking note of every single problematic area to minimise the risk of things going wrong on the day. In this case, I'll need to—'

'This time you'll do things a little differently. Remember, you're being brought into this project at a late stage, Graves, so you won't be surprised to learn I've already ticked some of those boxes on your list.'

And there went the first warning bell. Korso just hadn't expected it so soon. Keeping his expression neutral, he said, 'What do you mean?'

'I mean I've had Pineda under surveillance for quite a while now. For the past two months I've been accumulating data on him on a daily basis, waiting for the right time to use it. Open that laptop again.'

Opening the MacBook Air, Korso quit out of the photo app and watched Pineda shrink to nothing. He saw a single untitled folder on the desktop, already open. Inside the folder was an Excel file, also untitled. Korso opened it up.

It was a spreadsheet showing an itinerary. Precise timings on the left-hand side, with comments keyed in on the right. Each page made up a single day. Korso noticed straight away there were no names, not even initials. Nothing to indicate Pineda was the target under surveillance. That was encouraging. The first page was dated Monday, May 16. There was no year. He read through the first few entries:

> 06:36 – Suspect opens bedroom drapes.
>
> 06:43 – Movement downstairs.
>
> 07:13 – S leaves house by front door. Opens garage. Pulls out onto 10A Avenida. Drives east.
>
> 07:15 – S turns right at end of block, then left onto 17 Calle. Continues driving east.

07:18 – S stops at red lights. Now smoking e-cigarette.

07:20 – Green light. S continues east.

Korso looked up at Quezada. 'Okay, I have to admit this isn't bad. I wasn't expecting your men to be this thorough.'

'I believe in details,' Quezada said as he peeled a fresh avocado. 'My people know if I ask them a simple question and they can't answer, they're of no further use to me. And I rarely give second chances.'

'Are the timings and notes this comprehensive all the way through?'

'All the way up to the present day. Or yesterday, to be more precise.'

'How many people have you got on surveillance?'

'Four men in total, one man per car. Different cars every day. Two assume active duty on Monday for a full twenty-four hours, the other two take their place at midnight Tuesday, and so on and so on. I've used them all before for similar tasks, so they know the level of detail I expect from them.'

'And you've read through everything so far?'

'On a daily basis. This is one project very close to my heart, Graves.'

'I appreciate that. Can you give me a brief overview of Pineda's routine? Assuming there's such a thing as an average day for him.'

'Weekdays, he mostly spends at the district headquarters in the city.' As he talked, Quezada carefully cut the avocado down the middle, pulled the fruit apart and removed the pit. He began slowly cutting the fruit into thin slices. 'He works six days a week, Monday to Saturday. He makes at least three visits to the nearby police gym each week, always at lunchtime. Those days vary, as does his lunch hour. Every now and then, he's called to speak at a constitutional hearing in the congress building, but mostly he sticks to his own office. As far as I can see, Pineda leads the typical life of a government bureaucrat.'

'What about his personal life? Is he married, with kids? If not, does he have a fiancé, or a regular girlfriend?'

'He was married before. She died.' Quezada put down the knife and nibbled on one of the slices of fruit. 'There's a woman he's been seeing for eighteen months now, a forensics analyst who works in the same building. Like him, she's a widow. They spend the night together two or three times a week. Sometimes at his place, sometimes at hers. My sources tell me it's a casual relationship, that neither of them plans to get married again.'

Korso quickly scanned through the next page, saw more of the same. 'What's his home like?'

'Pineda lives in a two-storey townhouse on the southern outskirts of the city, in Zone 14. A very unassuming residence for a man in his position. He bought it twelve years ago, just after he got married, and he and his wife lived there together. No children. Apparently, she either couldn't have them, or didn't want them. Since her death three years ago, he's decided to remain there alone. For the time being, at least.'

'How did the wife die?'

'Natural causes. I played no part, if that's what you're thinking. She developed bone cancer four years ago, and died from an abdominal haemorrhage in hospital a year later.'

'You're very well informed.'

Quezada shrugged. 'It pays to know your enemies.'

'You said Pineda lives there for the time being. Does that suggest he's planning to move anytime soon?'

'Eighteen months ago, he put a down payment on a spacious two-bedroom condominium in a thirty-storey tower block that's still undergoing construction. His condo's on the south-east corner of the twenty-first floor. The building site takes up an entire block. It's located close to the police academy, about four kilometres from his office. They estimate it'll be completed in about six months' time, which in this country means twelve.

But for him, it would theoretically mean a ten-minute drive instead of an hour. Not that it'll ever reach that stage.'

Korso thought for a moment. Armed with this additional piece of data, a number of options had immediately occurred to him. One in particular.

'This tower block, how far along are they with it?'

Quezada furrowed his brow. 'The main core and superstructure was completed a few months ago, and they're currently affixing stone panels to the exterior. Once that's finished, I expect they'll move straight on to the interior.' He studied Korso with interest. 'You like the building site?'

'Don't you? All kinds of accidents can happen on such sites, most of them due to either negligence, mechanical error, or both.' He paused for a few moments. 'I don't know about you, Mr Quezada, but if I'd put a large amount of money down on a brand-new condo, I'd want to make occasional visits to the site in order to check on its progress. Wouldn't you?'

'I would.' Quezada smiled. 'And it seems Pineda's no different. He checks on his own condo on an almost weekly basis.'

'Really? You mean he actually goes up to the twenty-first floor and physically checks on his own apartment?'

Quezada nodded. 'Like I said, usually once a week after he finishes work. But never the same day twice, and not always every week.'

'I know safety regulations are fairly lax here, but I'm surprised somebody can just walk onto a working construction site whenever they feel like it.'

'They can't, as a rule, but Pineda's not just some guy off the street. He generally shows up after hours, when most of the workers have finished for the day, and usually while still in uniform. And no site supervisor is going to refuse a high-ranking cop entry, not if he wants to keep his job. He's sometimes accompanied by one of his subordinates, a sergeant, I believe. I can't recall the name now, but it's in the log. But he also arrives in uniform. Which means they can go wherever they want.'

'Okay, that makes sense. So when was his most recent visit?'

'Six days ago. Friday evening, in fact.'

'And did Pineda come alone?'

'He did that day.'

'Six days. So it's likely he'll go again either tonight or tomorrow?'

'Possibly. If not this week, then likely early next week, based on his past behaviour. Possibly even on Saturday or Sunday. He's done it before.'

'There's no construction going on at the weekends?'

'Saturday mornings occasionally, but I don't keep a close eye on the place. That's something you'd have to find out for yourself.'

'Okay. Well, tonight or tomorrow's far too soon to do anything. Sunday or early next week would be better, but that's out of our control. I assume you can supply me with complete architectural blueprints for the building, as well as a plan for the construction site itself? Along with official IDs and uniforms, if necessary?'

'We can supply whatever intel and materials you might need, don't worry about that.' Quezada popped the last slice of avocado into his mouth. 'So now you've found yourself a starting point let's move on to the next item. For this job I've decided I want Javier to accompany you until you reach the finish line. I assume that's agreeable to you.'

As if on cue, there came the second alarm bell. And an even bigger one than the first. 'Hold on, Mr Quezada, I prefer to work solo on these kinds of—'

'I don't care what you prefer.' Quezada's eyes hardened in an instant. They could have been glass marbles for all the emotion they showed. 'Remember you approached me, Graves, not the other way around. I don't really know anything about you other than what you've told me, and that makes me very wary. So for something this important I want someone I trust implicitly to be my eyes and ears.'

Korso remained silent. He had no bargaining power here. Having Ozan alongside him threw a major spanner into the works, but he was powerless to do anything about it. Quezada was the one who set the rules. He certainly didn't want to aggravate the man further by getting into an argument he couldn't possibly win. Also, the man hadn't blinked in almost a minute. That wasn't a good sign.

'Now do we fully understand each other?' Quezada said. 'Or do you have any further objections you want to share with me?'

'No objections at all, Mr Quezada. Like you said, you're the boss.'

'Good.' Quezada's features relaxed, and he blinked again. 'Very good. Now I don't want us to get off to a bad start, so I should tell you that if this project reaches a satisfactory conclusion – which I'm sure it will – then I can guarantee that you'll have a very important, and very well-paid, role in my business affairs for the foreseeable future. I value loyalty and reliability above all else, and I'm more than willing to pay handsomely for it. After all, that's why you approached me, correct?'

'That's exactly right.' He paused. 'I don't want to appear tactless, Mr Quezada, but since we're on the subject of pay...'

'Yes, I thought we might get around to that,' Quezada said. 'Following the successful completion of this particular job, I'll immediately transfer a sum of one hundred thousand US dollars straight into your account. I hope that's acceptable to you.'

It wasn't phrased as a question. And the fee seemed pretty miserly for someone of Quezada's financial standing, but Korso wasn't doing any of this for the money. 'That's perfectly acceptable,' he said.

'Fine, fine.' Quezada sat back and stared up at the azure sky, the subject now closed. There were few clouds in view, although the weather forecast predicted a downpour later. Still facing away from Korso, he said, 'Alex mentioned that you and she talked on Monday, after your meeting with me.'

'We did. After Ozan saw me out, I spotted her out by the front of the house. I went over and we chatted for a minute.'

'What about?'

Korso had the distinct feeling Quezada knew exactly what they had talked about, so he stuck to the truth. 'She said I wasn't like the other men who came to see you, which I took as a compliment. I offered her a lift, but she said she always stays on the grounds whenever you need her close by. We discussed the compound a little and I suggested she might give me a guided tour should the chance ever present itself again. She didn't say whether she would or she wouldn't. Was I out of line?'

Quezada turned to him. 'No, but I'm naturally protective of Alex, and like to know what's happening around her. I'm the same with all those I care for. You like her, don't you?'

'I'm only human.'

'Yes, she has that effect on men. Sometimes, the wrong kind of men. Just be aware that her continued well-being is something I take a great deal of interest in. And that if anyone were to affect that well-being in a negative way, even in the smallest way, I wouldn't be best pleased. Do we understand each other, Graves?'

'Perfectly. It's always good to know where you stand.'

'Glad you see things my way.'

Quezada stood up, indicating their conference was over. Korso did the same. 'I'll tell Javier to meet you at the front gates, and you can both take things from there.' He came round and walked Korso back towards the house. Sliding the doors open, he motioned for Korso to enter the office first. Korso saw Alejandra already there, sitting before one of the PCs as she copied something down onto a legal pad. Today, she was wearing a long-sleeved, orange-and-white baseball shirt, and dark green pants.

'Alex,' Quezada said, 'I wasn't expecting you till later. You've had lunch?'

She turned to him with a smile, and didn't seem surprised at Korso's presence. 'Not today. I had a big breakfast.' To Korso, she said, 'Hello again, Mr Graves.'

'Afternoon, Miss Alejandra.'

Quezada said, 'He was just telling me that the last time you two spoke, he asked if you could show him the grounds when you next had the chance. Perhaps now might be a good time. Unless you're too busy, that is.'

'Sure.' She put her pen down on the pad and got up. 'I don't mind.'

'Good. Take him out the front way, will you? When you get back, we'll go over the thing we discussed yesterday.'

'No problem.' She glanced at Korso. 'Would you like to follow me, Mr Graves?'

TWENTY

As Alejandra led him back through the front lobby, Korso said, 'I hope I didn't put you on the spot back there.'

She gave a shrug as she approached the front door. 'Not much fazes me, Mr Graves.'

'Ricardo.' Korso sometimes had difficulty remembering his actual first name, especially as he hadn't used it in over twenty years. But the one on his current passport served the purpose well enough.

'Ricardo, then.' She opened the main door and waited for him on the top step. 'By the way, I generally prefer people to call me Alex. Alejandra's far too formal.'

'I don't know. I quite like it.'

'You don't have to live with it.' They made their way down the steps. She noticed Korso's new Honda Civic, which he'd parked outside the garage, and nodded her approval. 'Much better. At least that one's not such an eyesore.'

'Or as embarrassing to drive. You kind of forced my hand in the matter, Alex.'

'Somehow I doubt anyone's ever forced you to do anything you didn't want to do.'

'You might be surprised.'

Once they reached the gravel courtyard, she guided them left towards the extended communal garage. There was a stone pathway ahead that ran parallel to the garage, which almost immediately split off into two smaller paths. The left fork continued under more tree cover and veered inwards, towards the main part of the estate, while the right-hand path gently curved back towards the front gates.

Alex took the left fork. They strolled in silence for a while, surrounded by trees and flowerbeds on each side, sometimes interspersed by small open spaces containing stone benches or the occasional wooden gazebo. He knew there had to be gardeners around, but he didn't see anyone. Maybe they were on their lunch break. Korso listened to the *caw-caw*s of unseen birds warning others off their territory. It was all very tranquil, with little clue that the outside world even existed.

'You should feel honoured,' she said, finally. 'Miguel doesn't usually allow people to walk around the estate this freely.'

'Well, I've got you here as my guardian.'

She gave him a sideways glance. 'Is that what I am?'

'You tell me.'

'I'm just giving you a guided tour, like you asked. Sometimes what you see is exactly what you get. Nothing more.'

Very rarely, in Korso's experience. And definitely not behind these four walls. 'My mistake. I have a tendency to overthink things, Alex. It's a hard habit to break.'

She smiled. 'That's why they call it a habit, I guess.'

Korso returned the smile. He knew that Quezada was using Alex as a means to dig up more information on him. Since Korso hadn't supplied a wealth of personal details, he couldn't exactly blame him. Nor did he blame her. He was sure she'd recounted their previous conversation word-for-word, and suspected she'd do the same again this time. After all, she and Quezada were related by blood, even if they were the only ones who knew. But Korso wondered how deep their connection really went. There was something about this half-sister of Quezada's that he couldn't quite put his finger on. Something a little off behind the eyes, as well as in her general demeanour. Just a feeling, but he'd learnt long ago to trust those kinds of feelings. They'd kept him alive on more than a few occasions.

As they cleared the cover of the trees, Korso saw a two-storey white stucco building coming up on their right, partially hidden by foliage. Lots of glass. Very modern. He said, 'These are for relatives, I suppose?'

'Mostly. Though some are reserved for close friends, along with important business associates. This one belongs to Miguel's older brother, Raul, and his family.'

'And which bracket do you fall under, Alex?'

'I already told you my role here. If you're asking if there's anything else between me and Miguel, the answer's no. If you've seen his wife, then you wouldn't even ask.'

'Actually, I was introduced to Luana earlier, though I'm not sure I registered on her radar.'

'Yes, she can be aloof with anyone outside the immediate family, including me. But then she was a successful model before; they all learn how to do that from an early age.'

She pointed at another two-storey house coming up on the left. In the front garden, sitting on a chaise lounge under a large parasol, was a woman in shorts and a shirt. She was playing with her phone, while nearby a very small boy played with a dog. 'That house belongs to another of his brothers, Gabriel. That's his wife and son.' Alex waved, and the woman saw her and waved back, then returned to her phone.

They continued walking, passing the occasional lamp post with LED lights at the top. They passed by more residences, each house seemingly placed at random. Sometimes Alex told him who lived inside, sometimes she didn't. He had to be very careful not to show undue interest in anything he saw, as that could only cause him problems if it got back to Quezada. One thing did give him pause, though. Ever since they'd left the main house, he'd been keeping his eyes peeled for any sign of security cameras on the property. So far, he hadn't seen a single one. Which was more than a little puzzling, particularly for someone as naturally paranoid as Quezada.

But what he was really looking for was a building that wasn't a residence. Somewhere away from the main house, some external building that could conceivably be used to house a hidden trophy room. Assuming he even had one, that is. That was the whole reason he'd asked to be shown around in the first place, but Alex hadn't yet shown him anything that could qualify. And he couldn't think of a way to bring up the subject that wouldn't immediately create suspicion.

Looking at the ground, she said, 'So, what is it you're actually doing for Miguel? Or am I better off not knowing?'

'I can't really go into it, Alex, but it mainly involves research at this stage. I've even been assigned Ozan to help, if you can call it that. Between you and me, I have a sneaking suspicion he and I aren't ever going to be close friends. You must know him better than I do. Can you give me any tips?'

'Don't show weakness, never share personal information, and always keep him right in front of you.'

Korso stopped and looked at her. 'Now that sounded like it came from the heart.'

'You asked.' She shrugged. 'Take my advice or ignore it, it's up to you.'

He'd suspected she and Ozan shared some kind of history, and that response had pretty much confirmed it. 'I always take good advice,' he said. 'Thanks.'

'Don't mention it.'

'I won't.'

From the direction of the sun, Korso could see they were gradually making their way towards the front part of the estate again. He was starting to wonder if Alex's residence was one of those he'd passed on the drive in, when she pointed and said, 'That's mine over there.'

He looked in the direction of her finger, and noticed a small bungalow with a gabled roof, mostly hidden by tree cover like almost every other house they'd passed. There was a large patio area out front, but not much else. The house almost seemed like an afterthought.

'Looks cosy,' he said.

'It's nice enough on a temporary basis, but it's all a little too quiet for me. I'm looking forward to returning to my own apartment in a week or two.'

'Independence counts for a lot.' Turning his head to the right, he spotted part of the boundary wall through a gap in the trees, maybe a hundred feet away. 'I've lost my bearings a little. All I see are trees and more green. How far away are we from the main house now?'

'Not far. We're practically right in the middle of the estate now. I'd say another few hundred yards straight ahead, and we'll be back where we started.'

And still no sign of the one thing he'd hoped to see. He decided it was time to stoke the fire a little, see what sparked. 'Eleven,' he said.

Alex turned to him, adjusted her glasses. 'Excuse me?'

'Before, you said you weren't sure how many buildings there were on the compound. So far, I've counted eleven, and that includes those two houses I passed on the drive in and out. Or twelve, if you include the communal garage. So now you know.'

'I don't count the garage,' she said, 'but the total still comes to twelve. There's still one more to go before we reach Miguel's house. Through the gap in these trees here.'

She led him down a narrow dirt track, almost hidden between a group of juniper conifers. Once they were out in the open again, Korso saw a large, single-storey brick building directly ahead. This one had a completely flat roof, and there were few windows in evidence. It looked more like a utility building than an actual residence. Trees closely surrounded the building on all sides, many of them overlooking it from above, which made it very easy to miss. He couldn't remember seeing it on Verhoeven's aerial shot. But it clearly wasn't a secret either. At the front, under a portico with two support columns on either side, was a set of double glass doors. Next to the entrance, two middle-aged employees in dark green overalls stood with their backs to the wall, taking a smoke break. Two long rakes were lying on the floor at their feet. The man noticed Alex and they each gave a hesitant wave. Alex returned the gesture.

'Interesting,' Korso said. He wasn't about to get his hopes up just yet, but the building certainly looked promising. 'What's its purpose?'

'I'll show you,' she said.

As Korso followed Alex towards the front entrance, the two gardeners decided this was their cue to get back to work. Stamping on their smokes, they each picked up their tools and, without a word, shuffled off towards the gardens at the rear of the building.

Korso saw no identifying signs on the glass doors. Each door had a steel pull handle set at waist level. The glass was heavily tinted, so Korso couldn't see much beyond his own reflection. There was a large keyhole under the left pull handle. He expected Alex to pull a key from her pocket, but she just pulled the right-hand door open, motioning for him to go in.

Stepping inside, he found himself at the head of a wide aisle that ran down the centre of the building, which he estimated was about two hundred feet in length, and about the same in width. On the left side were two open doorways, one close by, the other near the end. Three more doorways ran down the right. LED spotlights in the ceiling and hidden fixtures in the walls provided illumination that approximated natural daylight. It was all very minimalist, with the white tiled floor contrasting well with the polished natural stone walls. Korso saw no security cameras anywhere, or none visible to the naked eye. The sound insulation was excellent. Other than the faint hum of the air-conditioning, the place was as quiet as a tomb.

'You know what this place reminds me of?' His voice echoed faintly. 'A museum.'

'Funny you should say that.' Alex led him towards the first doorway on their left and motioned for him to go in first.

He stepped through and entered what was clearly a display room, one filled with all kinds of historical treasures. Skylights in the ceiling let the natural daylight in, which explained the scarcity of windows around the building. All around him were examples of life-sized Mayan sculptures, sacred masks and head-dresses, stone reliefs and huge partial monoliths covered in carved text and hieroglyphics. Everything was encased in large, museum-quality, glass display cases. The Chacmool in the lobby of the main house was majestic, but it had only been a taster. This was the real thing.

He turned in a slow circle, trying to take it all in at once. 'Impressive. Very impressive.'

'Isn't it?' Alex said. 'Helping to protect and preserve ancient Mayan cultural artefacts is one of Miguel's ruling passions. There are over fifty museums here in Guatemala, most of them privately owned, and there always seems to be one in desperate need of financial aid to avoid going under. Since Miguel's well known for his interest in Mayan art and culture, as well as his philanthropy, he's usually the first person on their list when they're searching for donors. As I'm also in charge of his charitable works, it's usually me who gets the call. But nine times out of ten Miguel gives me permission to send them however much they need, no questions asked. And in return they often supply him with a gift or memento as a token of their appreciation. This room houses most of those gifts, which gives you a clue as to how much they appreciated his aid. Everything in here's at least one thousand years old.'

Korso didn't doubt it. Verhoeven sure hadn't been kidding when she'd talked about Quezada's ongoing quest for respectability, and his role as self-proclaimed protector of his country's historical heritage. This room was a testament to that fact. He'd found Quezada's trophy room without even trying, but only because it was right out in the open for all to see. Korso walked between the display cases, carefully checking each and every artefact inside. Looking for the jade dagger, already knowing it wouldn't be here.

'The pieces in this room alone must be worth millions,' he said, once he'd finished his inspection. Naturally, there was no dagger. 'And I don't mean quetzales.'

'At least fifteen million dollars, US,' Alex said. 'And that's a conservative estimate.'

'So where's the security? There are no guards in sight, and no cameras either, unless they're very well hidden. The front doors aren't even locked. I don't get it.'

'It's very simple. Anyone who works or lives inside these four walls can come here whenever they want, as long as it's in their own time and they treat the property with respect. Miguel trusts his staff, and they in turn know that he'd go ballistic if they ever betrayed that trust, even slightly. But not many take up that offer. For most of them, once they've seen everything in this display room, why would they want to visit it again?'

'What about the other rooms? Are they much the same?'

'Not at all. The room next door is actually a cinema. Miguel has a few favourites that he likes to watch on a regular basis. Opposite, there's also a gym, an indoor spa, and a game room. We can take a look if you like.'

'If you don't mind. It's always enlightening to see how the rich spend their free time.'

Alex took him to the room directly opposite, the game room. One side contained over a dozen retro arcade machines, some with their own seats, others with their own dance platforms. None were switched on at the moment. There were also six pool tables scattered around the room, along with four full-size snooker tables. At the far end was what looked like a bar area, with a large counter running across the room. He didn't see any liquor bottles on display, but there was a large commercial refrigerator set against the wall.

'All the sodas anyone could ever want, but no alcohol,' Alex said, in answer to his unspoken question. 'His people can do what they want outside, but in here he wants everybody dry.'

The next room on that side was the indoor spa. The area was partitioned off into individual sections. A decent-sized swimming pool took up the central part of the room, along with a pair of steam rooms, six individual shower rooms, and three hot tubs. The place looked spotless, and was obviously cleaned on a regular basis.

The room at the end on that side contained the gymnasium – fully stacked, of course – and basketball court. In addition to the usual weights and treadmills, Korso saw enough state-of-the-art machinery and equipment to make most commercial gyms envious.

'Does Mr Quezada workout here?'

'No, these three rooms along here are primarily for the house and personal staff. He has his own personal gym at the house, along with his own swimming pool and private spa.'

Finally, she led him to the home theatre, directly opposite the gym. There wasn't much to see. Oak panelling on all four walls. A large projector screen at the front. Facing the screen were three rows of five luxurious leather seats, each one with its own side table.

'Very nice,' he said. 'I can think of a few films I'd enjoy watching in here. Mostly older ones, featuring men in hats. What about you, Alex? Any favourites?'

She shook her head. 'Not much of a movie-goer, I'm afraid. I'm more a music lover. Live music, that is.'

'You don't say.'

Korso was mentally juggling a lot of balls in the air, but when the time was right he planned on asking Alex out on a date. And after that, who knew? Anything to ingratiate himself further with Quezada. That he also liked her made things a little easier. With that end in mind, it was useful to know what interested her and what didn't.

But he was currently wondering whether he was any better off now than he had been thirty minutes ago. Alex had not only given him a cursory tour of the property, but she'd also shown him around the very thing he'd been hoping to see: Quezada's personal display room. Except it wasn't, really. It couldn't be. Regardless of the treasures the room undoubtedly contained, there had to be another one, an inner sanctum, that housed all the stuff Quezada kept for himself. The real gold that he didn't dare show anyone.

In every room he'd visited so far, Korso had been paying very careful attention to the walls and the floor, looking for any sign of a hidden panel that might grant entry to a hideaway known only to Quezada. But he'd seen nothing. It was entirely possible that there was another chamber hidden somewhere in this very building, but he'd need to physically measure each room's dimensions and match them against the dimensions of the building's exterior. If they didn't match, then that meant an extra space nobody else knew about. But that would take time, and a certain amount of free licence, neither of which he had right now.

'Seen enough?' Alex asked.

'I think so. I'm sure you've got other work you should be getting on with, as have I. But I'm grateful for your time. It's been educational.'

'You're welcome, Ricardo.' She led him back to the main entrance, and they stepped outside. 'It's always a pleasure to meet someone who truly appreciates art when they see it.'

He turned to her, looked into her eyes. 'I can appreciate art in all of its forms. That also includes the living, breathing kind.'

'Are you flirting with me?'

'I'd say that's entirely possible, Alejan… sorry, Alex.'

As they began walking in the direction of the main house, Korso said, 'So I was thinking that after I've completed this research job for Mr Quezada, I might take you out to dinner somewhere, and then you might take me to a live gig afterwards, since you must know all the best venues. If that sounds agreeable to you, of course.'

The smile was back on her face. 'Well, I'm not opposed to the idea, let's put it that way. But no promises. It's still early days. Let's see how things pan out first.'

Korso nodded at the diplomatic response. 'I know how to be patient.'

TWENTY-ONE

Once they reached their original starting point, Korso told Alex he looked forward to seeing her again and then watched her go back into the main house. He returned to his car and began the slow drive to the front gates.

He felt today's visit had gone better than expected. Not only had he been given a further assignment, but the target's sister was considering the possibility of a date in the near future. And a closer relationship with her, combined with a successful outcome to the Manuel Pineda situation, could only augment his status within Quezada's personal orbit, allowing him a little more freedom to move around in the process. On the down side, he hadn't found the safe room, but he hadn't expected it to be that simple. Nothing in life ever was.

When he reached the guard house by the front gates, Korso tapped the brakes and brought the car to a complete stop. He looked up at the cameras covering the entrance. He knew they were watching him, making him wait, but he didn't mind. He counted four CCTV cameras within his sight. There were probably more that he couldn't see. And that was the strangest part of all. There seemed to be no shortage of security at the perimeter of the property, but almost none once you were inside. As anomalies went, that was a big one, since it didn't fit with what he knew of Quezada. But there had to be a reason for it.

Korso turned his head and gazed absently at the thick foliage to his right, not really seeing it. He had no idea how much time had passed when the answer suddenly came to him.

A tapping on the window yanked Korso out of his thoughts. He turned to his left and saw Ozan glaring in at him, dyed-blond hair tied back in a short ponytail. He was wearing a light summer jacket, no doubt to hide the gun holster. 'I've been waiting for you.'

'And now I'm here,' Korso said.

Ozan walked round to the passenger side. He threw an overnight bag into the back and took his place in the front seat. 'You're not understanding me, Graves. Miguel wants me to watch over you for the next few days, and that's exactly what I'm here to do. And keeping me waiting is not a good start. I expected you here fifteen minutes ago. Where have you been?'

'You know where I've been.'

'Yeah, I know. With Alejandra, getting a nice little tour of the grounds. Just what makes you think you'll be around long enough for it to matter one way or the other? And that's another thing. I don't like you sniffing around her. She's not for you. You want to stay on my good side, consider her off-limits from now on.'

'You have a good side?'

'Are you listening? I said keep away from her.'

'I heard what you said. Take it up with Mr Quezada. He was the one who suggested she show me around.'

'Forget Mr Quezada. I'm the one telling you right now.'

'I'm not answerable to you,' Korso said. 'Just so we're clear on the subject.'

Ozan gave a sigh. 'You're still not getting the bigger picture here, so let me lay it out for you. Miguel – Mr Quezada to you – assigned you the job of dealing with this Pineda asshole, and that's fine. I gave him my objections, but he wants to see how you handle this specific problem, and he's the boss. Now since I'm your only link to Miguel, that means everything has to go through me, understand? You need essential information on somebody? I arrange it. You need supplies, hardware, IDs? Me, again. So if you start pissing me off like you're doing now, then maybe one of those requests gets delayed at the worst possible moment, and the whole operation goes south. Who do you think will get the blame if that happens, you or me?'

'I take it this is a rhetorical question.'

'Miguel and me,' he went on, as though Korso hadn't spoken, 'we've known each other since we were kids. You could say we're practically brothers. We both grew up on the streets together, and I've had his back ever since. And I don't trust you, Graves, or whatever the hell your name is. There's something about you that doesn't smell right, what with you showing up out of the blue with Galicia in the trunk of your car, all wrapped like a Christmas present. It seemed too good to be true to me then, and I still feel that way now.'

Korso shrugged. 'You're wrong. But if that's what you believe, I can live with it.'

'Don't be too sure about that.'

'I hope that's not a threat, Ozan. But while we seem to be clearing the air, maybe now's a good time to mention that you're not my only link to Mr Quezada.'

Ozan's eyes narrowed as he thought this over. 'You mean Alejandra?'

'We've already exchanged phone numbers. In fact, we just provisionally arranged a dinner date a few days from now.' The lie came easy, especially as there was no way Ozan could check for himself. He felt sure Alex would tell him nothing. 'I understand you two have a history, but you've got to let her go sometime. But more importantly, if I ask you for something specific on this job and I don't get it, then don't be too sure Mr Quezada won't get to hear about it. And who do you think will get the blame then, you or me?'

Ozan's sunken eyes stared hard at Korso. 'Are you threatening me?'

'I wouldn't be that dumb. I'm just here to do a job, and whenever I commit myself to something I do it to the best of my abilities. If you've lasted this long as Mr Quezada's right-hand man, then I can only assume you share that same level of commitment.'

'So?'

'So, since we're going to be working together on this, I suggest we forget whatever personal issues we might have with each other, and just get on with being the professionals we clearly are. Mr Quezada wants a successful conclusion to his immediate problem. I've got a pretty good idea of how to do it. Are you going to help me or hinder me? It's up to you.'

Ozan stared at him without blinking for a few more seconds. Then he sank back into his seat, extended his arm out the window and waved to the camera. The gates immediately began to open inwards. 'A job's a job,' he said.

'That's exactly how I see it.' Korso glanced at the rear seat. 'So what's with the overnight bag?'

'Where you go, I go.'

'Just as long as you're not thinking of sharing a room with me,' Korso said, steering them through the gates. 'That's where I draw the line.'

TWENTY-TWO

Forty-eight minutes later, Korso parked the car across the street from the site where Manuel Pineda's new home would be. For the most part the journey had been a muted one. Neither man had had much to say to the other. They'd made one stop along the way, to a photographic supply store, where Korso suggested that Ozan get them some telephoto zoom monoculars. He expected Ozan to protest, but the man just went into the store and came out a few minutes later with a plastic bag containing his purchases.

The Casa Nueva Condominium was situated just off CA-9, the four-lane highway that ran through the city like a central artery. A huge billboard above the site entrance showed an artist's impression of the finished apartment block and promised its grand opening the following January. Korso thought it optimistic. A chain-link perimeter fence surrounded the whole site, with hoarding wooden fence panels behind it. A private hospital was its immediate neighbour on the left, while a huge car dealership took up most of the block to its right. The thirty-storey building was the tallest structure for a mile in all directions.

Quezada had been correct in his summary. The superstructure was all there, with stone panels having been affixed to about seventy per cent of the exterior. The top seven levels were still in their skeletal form, and completely open to the elements. At ground level the worksite was a hive of activity, with supply trucks arriving or exiting through the open main gates, and over a hundred construction workers in neon orange hi-vis overalls and yellow hardhats continually on the move inside. There was a lone man stationed at the entrance, who checked the identification and work orders of everyone who entered. Through the main entrance, Korso saw all kinds of construction vehicles moving around in there, including excavators, bulldozers, concrete mixers, forklifts, conveyers and more besides. Next to the building, and standing almost as tall, was a huge tower crane. Korso watched as the operator expertly swivelled the long working arm towards the twenty-fifth storey, where a clutch of workers were waiting to haul in the canvas-wrapped supplies hanging from its hook.

Korso said, 'Let me have one of those scopes, will you?'

Ozan pulled two boxes out of the black shopping bag at his feet, and handed one over. The brand wasn't one Korso recognised. Probably a knock-off anyway. Opening the box, he pulled out the monocular and extended it to its full length. He aimed it at the crane, put his eye to the lens, and gently rotated the dial for the zoom, increasing the magnification until it was at its maximum setting.

The tower crane looked close enough to touch, with enough detail that he could almost make out individual rivets in the lattice mast. He panned the scope up the mast and along the jib until it was aimed on the tower block itself. Korso could make out the individual faces of the construction workers on the fifteenth floor as they all waited for the package to reach them. He could also see part of a girder poking out of the canvas. He moved the scope along to the south-facing side, and gave a thin smile when he saw the small cage about halfway up the building.

'So what are we looking at?' Ozan asked.

'That buckhoist running up the south face,' Korso said. 'See it?'

'You mean the temporary elevator? What about it?'

'There's usually at least two construction elevators on a building of this size, one for carrying materials and heavy equipment, and the other for personnel. That cage looks as though it could just about hold four people, maximum, if they all breathed in at the same time. Which means there's probably another hoist on the west face, out of our view, with a much bigger cage that they use to transport the heavy stuff. Maybe two, depending on how much they have to transport on a regular basis. We can check the other side later, to be sure.'

'Okay. Let's say you're right.'

'Well, Mr Quezada told me that Pineda visits this site on an almost weekly basis to check on the progress of his condo.' He pointed to the south-east corner apartment on the twenty-first floor. 'Which would make it that one there. And unless he uses the fire stairs to climb those twenty-one floors, the only other way up is by elevator. So if we assume the other buckhoist is used for supplies and materials, then this one on the south face is probably the one he uses.' He turned to Ozan, who was peering at the building through his own scope. There was now an unlit cigarette between his lips. 'You planning on smoking that?'

'I might.' Ozan slowly lowered his monocular and pulled a disposable lighter from his pocket. 'What's it to you?'

'Just make sure you open the window first.'

'And if I don't?'

'Then one of us leaves this car.'

Ozan smiled at him. He flicked the button of the lighter and a small flame appeared. He released it, the flame died. He flicked it again, the flame appeared again. Korso kept his expression neutral as the other man went through this pantomime a few more times. Sensing he was getting nowhere, Ozan finally pressed the button to lower the window. Traffic noise filled the interior. He lit the cigarette and took a drag. 'So you're thinking Pineda might have a sudden fall in one of those elevators the next time he pays a visit?'

'Accidents still happen,' Korso said, 'even in these safety-conscious times. Three workers died in Tehran a couple of years back when a construction elevator plummeted twenty floors. There were two more accidents just last year, one in Karachi, and another in China, both on building sites. Over a dozen workers died in those two alone.'

'I don't know,' Ozan said, tapping ash out the window. 'A few nobodies getting it in an elevator crash is one thing, but you make one of the victims a high-ranking cop and that instantly ramps everything up by the power of ten. With someone like Pineda, who's everybody's favourite golden boy, making it *look* like an accident isn't good enough. There has to be no doubt at all that it *was* an accident, or Miguel's worse off than he was before. Because you can bet your ass there'll be a whole load of investigators and analysts on the scene, not just from the insurance companies representing the property and the construction company, but from the police end, and probably from the Ministry of the Interior too. And every one of them will be swarming over the crash site with a magnifying glass, looking for the slightest clue that switches it from an accidental death into a homicide.'

'I'm aware of the parameters of the job,' Korso said. 'Mr Quezada was very clear on the subject.'

'Just as long as you don't forget. So what now?'

'Have you got an up-to-date version of the surveillance log?'

Ozan pulled a phone from his pocket. He swiped the screen a few times, and said, 'What do you want to know?'

'Pineda's most recent visit was last Friday evening. Skip to that day and read out to me exactly what happened.'

Ozan began scrolling quickly through the log, then gradually slowed until he said, 'Okay, Friday afternoon, Friday afternoon… right, Friday evening. Here we go: "*18:16, Suspect exits underground car park and turns east on 1A Calle. Nobody else visible in the car.*" There's a few more notes on his route, and then it says, "*18:25, Suspect arrives at same construction site as before. Parks outside main entrance. 18:26, Suspect approaches open gate and enters property. Speaks with security guard. 18:27, Suspect leaves guard and walks towards apartment building. 18:29, Suspect takes outside elevator up to twenty-first floor, alone. 18:30, Suspect exits elevator and—*"'

'Which one?' Korso said. Ozan looked up at him. 'Which elevator? It's kind of important.'

Ozan lowered his gaze again. 'Okay. "*18:35, Suspect enters elevator and descends. 18:36, Elevator reaches ground level. Suspect leaves elevator and walks towards entrance.*" He looked up at Korso, eyes glaring. 'The stupid asshole doesn't say which one. Goddammit, I'll tear out his—'

'No need to make a production out of it. Just call up and ask.'

Still muttering to himself, Ozan pressed some buttons and raised the phone to his ear. Seconds later, he said, 'No names. You know who this is, right? Good. Now, about the person you're keeping an eye on. Which elevator does he use to visit his apartment at the building site? … Is that right? Well, next time make sure you put it in the log, or I'll take a baseball bat to your knees. And while we're at it, how many other elevators are there? … So does our boy ever use that one instead? … Okay. Now listen, we never had this conversation, you understand? Wipe it completely from your mind and never mention it to anyone.' He ended the call, turned to Korso. 'Pineda always uses the south elevator. My guy says there's also a second hoist running up the west side of the building that they use for heavy loads, but he's never seen Pineda use that one.'

'Good. We're narrowing down the possibilities by the second.'

'Except you still haven't told me how you plan to make this look like an accident. If you can't do that, then none of this is worth shit.'

'That part's easy.' Korso raised the monocular and focused it on the underside of the hoist cage, but all he could see were shadows. 'There's a particular fluorosulfuric acid variation that should do the job well enough. In its normal form, sulphuric acid will corrode most metals, including stainless steel, which is what the rack and pinion systems that work these elevators are made from. The only problem is the whole process can take quite a while. But the specific compound I'm thinking of is not only a hundred times stronger, which means results in seconds instead of weeks, but it also has the added bonus of making the resulting corrosion look as though it was caused by rapid oxidation.'

Ozan blinked at him.

'Rust,' Korso said. 'Severe rust. The acid also dissipates quickly once exposed to the air, so there won't be any trace of it after the accident.'

A slow grin began to spread across Ozan's features. It wasn't a pleasant smile. 'I'm starting to like the sound of this. Tell me more.'

'Not much to tell. The rack and pinion system's pretty simple. There's a drive assembly built into the top of the elevator, and two pinions attached to the lift's motor. They move along a permanently mounted gear track, allowing the cage to move up and down as and when required. Each of those rollers in the pinion is supported by two needle bearings, which remove the sliding friction you get in normal elevators with cables and drive shafts. Now if I were to place a ten millilitre glass ampule of this acid compound above those bearings, along with a radio-controlled micro-detonator to break the neck of the ampule at a specific moment...' He showed a palm. 'The acid splashes down, corrodes the steel bearings in seconds, along with the detonator, at which point the elevator drops all the way to the ground at a rate of two hundred kilometres per hour. It'll take just under four seconds to drop the full two hundred and fifty feet. Nobody's going to survive a fall like that. And with no evidence of foul play, the accident investigators will have no choice but to log it as accidental death caused by mechanical failure.'

'And you can guarantee that. Absolutely, without question.'

'I can guarantee the first part, that there'll be no evidence of foul play. As for the rest, trying to predict human behaviour in people you've never even met is a complete waste of time. I can offer up scenarios, but I can't control how the investigation will play out. All I know is Mr Quezada won't end up as the scapegoat.'

'You think Miguel will buy that?'

'That's his decision. Once I give him the layout, he'll either give me the go-ahead or he won't. But I think he'll see this as an opportunity too good to pass up.'

'You want to go see him now?'

Korso shook his head. 'Not yet. I want to get a few other details sorted out first, which is where you come in.'

'I'm listening.'

'I need to get on-site before the end of the working day, while there are still plenty of other people around. Just to get a feel of the place. So you need to get us some hi-vis overalls and hardhats, preferably in the same colours as those worn by the construction workers. Also, some clipboards.'

'Next?'

'I want blueprints for the whole worksite, as well as complete architectural blueprints of the building itself. I assume you've got contacts who can supply those without too many problems?'

Ozan gave a contemptuous snort. 'Anything else?'

'Official IDs, identifying us as safety inspectors come to make a routine evaluation of the building site.' Korso pulled out his phone, went to Google and typed in a few key words. He clicked on the third result that came up from a website belonging to a Guatemalan legal firm. He speedread through the text until he found the relevant paragraph. 'Here we are. Multiple reforms were made to Guatemala's labour laws in 2016, particularly those relating to occupational health and safety. It says here that Decree 1441 is the bill that regulates any and all inspection procedures carried out by representatives of the Ministry of Labour, whenever and wherever they see fit.'

He put the phone on the dash. 'So that's what we'll be. Safety inspectors representing the Ministry of Labour. The IDs don't need to be genuine, but they have to closely resemble the real thing, with government seals and everything. If photos are required, pick two guys that look vaguely similar to us and use photos of them. I'm not about to use my own face, and nobody will be looking all that closely anyway. How fast can this be done?'

Taking a last drag of his cigarette, Ozan gave a shrug as he flicked the stub out the window. 'Couple of hours at most. So what will you be doing through all this?'

'Taking care of the finer details. Speaking of which, give me the number of a reliable chemist within your organisation. You must have hundreds on your payroll. I'll want him to pass me on to another chemist with no connection whatsoever to Mr Quezada, and then I'll use that guy to manufacture the very specific acid compound I need.'

'I got just the man.' Ozan scrolled through his contacts list until he came to the one he wanted. He read out the chemist's name and number, which Korso keyed into his own phone. 'Tell him I sent you, and he'll give you as many names as you want.'

'Just one will suffice.' Korso turned to Ozan. 'Look, we've only got the one vehicle, and I need this one. What are you planning to do for transport?'

'Don't worry about it. I'll have a car delivered within minutes of you leaving.' Ozan grabbed his overnight bag from the back seat, opened the door and got out. 'You just do your job, bright boy, and I'll do mine.'

TWENTY-THREE

Korso started the engine, waited for a gap in the traffic, and drove away. He didn't have a particular destination in mind, he just wanted to be away from Ozan for a while. The man was tolerable in small doses, but no more than that. Korso drove in a westerly direction until he spotted a makeshift shack up ahead, with CANTINA painted in a large scrawl above the open entrance. He parked on the street and turned off the engine.

He took a seat at one of the empty tables on the sidewalk. He was the only customer. Latin rock blared out from an unseen radio in the back. When the middle-aged owner finally appeared, Korso ordered a plate of shrimp ceviche and a glass of light beer. She nodded once, and then headed back to the kitchen.

Korso pulled out his phone and dialled a number from memory. He left a brief message at the prompt, and hung up. Soon, the owner returned with a cold bottle of Gallo Light and a clean glass. Korso was pouring the beer when his phone trilled at him. He took the call. Temporarily switching back to English, he said, 'Hello, Dog.'

'Hey, K. How's things?' Dog's voice was male again, but set at a much higher pitch than before. 'Please tell me things are going well.'

'They're progressing. More than that, I can't say.'

Dog sighed. 'I bet you're a whiz at the poker table. So what do you need from me?'

'Additional information. That dossier you sent me on Verhoeven is fine for what it is, but there's still something missing.'

'Like what?'

'I don't know, that's why I'm calling. But there has to be a reason behind Verhoeven's obsession with nailing this guy, and I want to know what it is. I've a strong hunch that there's something personal between them, but that could cover almost anything.' He thought for a moment. 'Tell you what, check the current status of her previous partners at Interpol, as well as those when she was with the Dutch National Police. See what turns up. And also check for any overseas assignments she had that brought her over to this part of the world prior to the vice-president's assassination. You never know, their paths may have crossed at some point.'

'I can do that. When do you want this by?'

'What else is more important?'

'Good point. Don't go away, I'll call you back in a few ticks.'

'I'll be here,' Korso said, and hung up.

He sat back and sipped his beer, watching the pedestrians and traffic passing before him while he thought about Verhoeven. Back on the train, he'd warned the agent not to keep anything back. But in refusing to reveal her reasons for wanting Quezada so badly, she'd done it anyway. This kind of omission happened on every job, without fail. He'd never really understood why. But there was more than one way to crack an egg, and at least with Dog on the case, Korso had a better-than-evens chance of finding the answer. It was more than simple curiosity. If for any reason Verhoeven decided not to keep her end of the deal, then Korso wanted some kind of effective ammunition that he could use to persuade her otherwise. And he'd always considered information to be the best kind of ammunition of all.

The waitress came back with Korso's spicy shrimp salad and set it down on the table along with some small flatbreads and a clean fork. Korso took a few bites of the tasty ceviche, then scrolled down his phone's contact list until he got to the number he wanted.

After seven rings, a guarded male voice said in Spanish, 'Hello?'

'Ozan gave me this number,' Korso said, switching back again. 'He told me you'd be able to give me a recommendation. I want the name of a good chemist like yourself, but someone legit with absolutely no connection to your current employers.'

There was a pause on the line. 'Uh, Ozan, you say? I'm not sure I know that name.'

'Really? You sure you don't know who I'm talking about? Maybe you'd like me to interrupt him from whatever he's doing so he can call you himself and confirm my bonafides. Because we can go down that route if you want.'

'No need for that. Uh, can I ask what the job might entail, and what your basic requirements are?'

'Sure. I need someone who can do a simple mixing job for me, strictly off the grid, but using legit ingredients. There's money in it, obviously. But this someone has to be licensed, reliable and able to keep his or her mouth shut and not ask too many questions. They also need to reside here in the city.'

The chemist thought for a few seconds, then gave Korso a name and a cell phone number and said this guy should be able to handle whatever Korso threw at him without complaint. Korso thanked him and ended the call. He tried the new number. It rang for a full minute without any response. He was just about to hang up when a man's voice suddenly came on the line, 'Yes? Who is this?'

'A prospective client,' Korso said. 'I was given your name by a colleague of yours. I need a mixing job done fast, and he said you could handle it without asking too many questions. Was he correct?'

'That depends on what kind of mixing we're talking about. There are certain chemicals I won't touch, if you know what I mean.'

'I think I do. No, what I'm after is a specific fluorosulfuric acid variation, and I need someone who knows what they're doing to prepare a very small quantity for me.'

'Fluorosulfuric acid? How small a quantity?'

'Forty millilitres should be more than enough, to be divided into sealed ten-millilitre glass ampules. I'll want to test one out before I hand over your fee, of course.'

There was a pause. 'I need to ask another question. Will you be planning to use this acid on anything organic?'

'No, nothing living, if that's what worries you. I actually need it to corrode a device made from stainless steel.'

There was a small chuckle. 'Oh, it'll definitely do that, and faster than you might think. Have you used it before?'

'Once or twice. I'm familiar with its effectiveness.'

'In that case, I think we can do business. How quickly do you want it?'

'Any time this afternoon would be good. Is that achievable?'

'Anything's achievable with money.'

'Give me a realistic figure, an address, and a time to come pick it up.' The chemist gave him all three. 'I'll bring cash,' Korso said, and hung up.

He returned to his snack, mentally planning out the rest of the day as he ate. Fifteen minutes later, he was settling the bill with the waitress when his phone rang again.

'K, it's me,' Dog said, using the same modulated voice as before. 'You good to talk?'

Korso watched as the owner retreated to the kitchen. 'I am now,' he said, switching back to English again.

'Okay, so I've been delving a little more into Verhoeven's professional background, and I found one or two titbits that should be of interest to you. One in particular.'

'Go on.'

'So she's had a total of five partners during the course of her successful and colourful law-enforcement career, including my friend Steinman, who was with her when they both worked out of Interpol's Terrorism division. But I checked and cross-referenced the other four, and they're all still alive and breathing. One retired from the Dutch force four years ago, and currently operates a small private detective business in The Hague. As for the other three, they're all still in law enforcement in one form or another. So if you were thinking she might be out for revenge for the murder of a partner, that's a dead end. Her boyfriend's a partner in a highly successful legal firm in Paris, and he's fine too. Same story with her immediate relatives.'

'But you found something else instead.'

'Well, I found out you're on the right track, K. As you know, she was headhunted by Interpol eight years ago and transferred to their headquarters in Lyon, France. And it turns out one of her very first cases with them involved a junior customs attaché working out of the Dutch consulate in, guess where – that's right – Guatemala City. He was thought to be supplying diplomatic credentials to certain individuals suspected of being involved in human trafficking, allowing them to enter and exit countries without any record being made of their presence. So Interpol and the Dutch government came to an under-the-table agreement, and Verhoeven was sequestered to this consulate under the guise of a police attaché to keep a close watch on this other guy, and see how deep it went and make sure there were no other embassy staff involved.'

'Interesting. And I take it our boy was one of those involved in human trafficking?'

'His name does get a mention, although nothing was ever proved against him.'

'Naturally. How long was Verhoeven sequestered to this consulate?'

'Eleven weeks.'

'Almost three months?' Korso raised an eyebrow. That was a long time for a single assignment. Of course, the case might have had additional complications of which they were unaware, but that still meant plenty of spare time in an exotic country. And a lot can happen in three months. 'Did she make any friends while she was there?'

Dog gave a sour chuckle. 'You're way ahead of me, K. Seems over the course of her stay, our super-agent had a romantic fling with a local detective who'd been supplying her with background material. Nothing specific about that in the file, of course, but it's pretty obvious if you read between the lines. And it seems one of *his* ongoing cases concerned some priceless Mayan antiquities that had recently been stolen from a private collector in Antigua. From what I read, Interpol figure this cop must have gotten a little too close to the real culprits, because a week before Verhoeven wrapped up her own case and returned to France, the cop's beaten and bloody corpse was found in a ditch by the side of the main highway, minus its head. Which was never found, by the way. Nor were the perpetrators.'

'Priceless Mayan antiquities,' Korso repeated to himself.

'That's right. So if this cop lit some kind of fire under Verhoeven, and she suspected our boy was behind his murder, that could explain why she's been so hot for him ever since.'

'It could.'

'And there's something else. Once she'd successfully completed her assignment, she immediately put in a request to be transferred to Interpol's Organised Crime Division. The request was accepted, and that's where she's been ever since. What do you think of that?'

Korso thought it was better than expected. None of it could be considered conclusive in any way, but that wasn't the point. It seemed reasonable to think that Verhoeven and her lover would have compared notes with each other about their respective workloads. That's what fellow professionals did. So if she was aware the chief suspect in his theft case was a certain Miguel Quezada, then it was only natural that she'd place him as the prime suspect in the cop's brutal murder. It also suggested their relationship was more than just a simple holiday fling. Only love could account for Verhoeven holding on to a grudge this long, which would also explain why she'd declined to share this information with Korso.

'It's definitely food for thought,' he said. 'I'm not sure how much good it'll do me, but at least you've filled in a few gaps. I don't like working blind.'

'You and me both. So is there anything else I can do?'

'Not right now. I've got a full day ahead of me, and I need to get back to it.'

'Well, the last thing I want is to hold you up, so I'll sign off. Be careful, K.'

The line went dead. Korso frowned at the phone in his hand for a few moments, deep in thought. He took a sip of his now lukewarm beer, and carefully keyed in another number from memory. He raised the phone to his ear and listened to the ringing tone.

It was picked up, and a familiar feminine voice said, 'I don't know this number.'

'But you remember the voice, don't you?'

There was a brief pause. 'Johan,' Verhoeven said.

'As good a name as any. How's the weather with you?'

'Right now? Grey, windy. How about you?'

'Warm. The sun's out at the moment, but I've noticed a few clouds already forming. I predict heavy rain ahead.'

'Hmm, it's hard to tell whether you're being literal or not. I suppose it's pointless asking where you are.'

'Take a guess. You'll probably be right.'

She sighed. 'Tell me, do you enjoy being purposely vague, or is it something that just comes naturally?'

'A little of both, probably.'

'Thus proving my point. So can I assume you want something else from me other than a weather report?'

'You can. In fact, I've got a few questions I'm hoping you can answer…'

TWENTY-FOUR

Striding along the sidewalk towards the site entrance, Korso glanced at Ozan at his side. He looked the part at least. They both did. They were dressed almost identically in orange hi-vis overalls and bright yellow hard hats. The hard hat also had the added benefit of concealing Ozan's dyed-blond hair, which wasn't really a look one expected of a Ministry of Labour representative.

Each man carried a clipboard filled with official paperwork. In reality, they were photocopied pages from an old computer repair manual Korso had bought from a street seller that afternoon, shortly after collecting his fluorosulfuric acid samples from the chemist. The chemist had done everything exactly as Korso requested, and also supplied him with a misshapen bar of scrap metal for testing purposes. Wearing a pair of heavy-duty rubber gloves, Korso had chosen one of the four ampules at random, broken the neck and dripped the contents onto the piece of scrap metal. He was pleased to see the stuff eat through it in a matter of seconds. He'd paid the man in full, and added a bonus too.

Ozan was also carrying a thin attaché case. Inside were two ring binders, each one containing more random photocopies from the same manual. Korso had learnt that you could never have too much paperwork for this kind of thing. He checked his watch: 4.15 p.m. Still an hour and a quarter away from quitting time. He saw the site watchman standing in front of a small prefab sentry booth, idly watching them as they approached.

They were still a few feet from the front gates when a huge loader suddenly braked at the entrance, preparing to leave. Both men stopped. The noise from the idling diesel engine was deafening, almost drowning out the continuous ear-splitting din of jackhammers, cement cutters, electric saws, drills and welding machines battling for supremacy behind it. Through his open window, the driver shouted something to the watchman down below as he waved his arm, and both men laughed. The truck driver said something else to the man, then he crunched the gears loudly and pulled out onto the street and drove away.

Korso began walking again. 'Remember, just leave all the talking to me. Don't say anything. Silence is always more intimidating in these situations.'

'Silence?' Ozan said with a snort. 'In this place?'

'You know what I mean.'

As they closed the distance, Korso saw the young watchman studying each of them. 'See your IDs?' he said finally. He almost had to shout to be heard.

Korso reached into his pocket, pulled out his thin wallet and flipped it open to the photo ID card, while Ozan silently did the same with his. The IDs certainly looked real enough to him. He didn't know how Ozan had done it so quickly, but even the photos looked like them. If you didn't look too closely.

The man scanned the cards briefly, and his frown intensified. 'Safety inspectors?' He took a single step back and grabbed a clipboard from a shelf in the cabin. He glanced at the top sheet. 'No mention of an inspection on my schedule.'

'That's the whole point, son,' Korso said. 'Better get your site foreman over here. We'll need to talk to him.'

The younger man pulled a fat walkie-talkie from his belt and pressed the transmit button. There was a brief garbled conversation that Korso couldn't even begin to decipher, and a few moments later the young man clipped the walkie-talkie back onto his belt. 'Won't be a minute.'

Korso just nodded his head. He saw plenty of workers moving around with purpose, carrying tools or supplies from one place to another, but didn't see anyone carrying a walkie-talkie. He looked over to the main building and saw the ground floor was still pretty much exposed to the elements. Unlike the floor above, the windows hadn't yet been fitted with glass, and the doorways were still nothing more than gaping holes to allow for easy access for the workers constantly coming and going.

After a couple more minutes, he noticed a stocky, bearded man coming their way from the direction of the tower block, talking on his phone as he walked. Unlike the other site workers, he wore a yellow hi-vis jacket over a white shirt and tie, and a white hard hat. Once he'd closed the distance, he pocketed the phone and nodded briefly at the watchman, before turning his attention to Korso and Ozan. He glanced from one to the other, and said, 'I'm Bolanos, site foreman. I'm also a busy man, so who are you and what do you want?'

'Everybody's busy,' Korso said. He briefly showed the man his ID, before pocketing it again. He didn't want to push his luck with this guy. 'We're inspectors employed by the Ministry of Labour, here to make sure all necessary safety regulations are being followed under Decree 1441 of the Labour Law, 2016. Now this is more a formality than anything, so nothing to worry about. I've already been looking around and I can see all your people are wearing steel-tipped safety boots, hard hats and hi-vis overalls, so that's a good start.'

The foreman glanced briefly at Ozan, who gave him his best silent glower back. Bolanos turned back to Korso with a puzzled expression. 'Why all the interest? We had three guys from your department out here a month ago. And then another safety inspector a couple of months before that.'

'Standard procedure nowadays,' Korso said. 'You'll probably get another visit a month or so down the line as well. Hey, it's not my decision. I'm just a cog in the machine, and I go where they tell me.'

'Yeah, I know all about that. Well, I guess it's okay. You got any authorisation at all, Mr…?'

'I assumed our IDs would be sufficient,' Korso said. 'But you're welcome to go through our work orders if you want.' He turned to Ozan. 'Let me have the first folder.'

Ozan opened his attaché case and pulled out one of the ring binders. He passed it to Korso, who opened it and started flipping through the two hundred pages of meaningless rubbish contained within. 'I have to warn you these are fairly extensive in scope. Maybe we should go find an office somewhere where you can go through it all?'

'No way.' Bolanos was shaking his head at the sight of all the paperwork. 'I got no time for all that. You want to inspect the site, that's fine with me. Bruno, give each of these men a visitor's badge.' The watchman turned and stepped into his booth, while Bolanos said, 'How long will you be? We finish at 5.30 sharp.'

'We'll be long gone before then.' Korso offered his hand. The site foreman shook it. 'I appreciate your time.'

'No problem,' Bolanos said, all smiles now. 'Glad to help.'

The stocky man left them and walked off while Bruno emerged from his booth and passed over two PVC badges, each one with VISITA in large black capitals on a blue background. 'Make sure you wear these at all times,' he said.

'Right.' Korso clipped his badge to his chest while Ozan did the same with his. They left the younger man and entered the main site.

Once they were far enough away, Korso said, 'Walk slowly, and make sure to scribble notes in your clipboard occasionally, so it looks like we're actually working.'

'You don't have to spell it out,' Ozan said. 'You do realise if we were genuine inspectors we'd split up at this point and get the work done in half the time? You ever think of that, bright boy?'

'I did. But as it turns out, you're the rookie and I'm the senior inspector guiding you through your first field assignment. But we can split up if you want. It's not like I need you for anything.'

'Yeah, you'd just love that, wouldn't you? Forget it, I'm sticking to you like glue.'

With a shrug, Korso continued strolling through the work site, making mental notes as he went. Korso had already memorised the site layout from the blueprints Ozan provided, but there was no substitute for seeing the location in person. Workers moved busily all around them, too wrapped up in their own tasks to pay either man any attention.

Since he already knew there'd be a night security guard posted at the main entrance, Korso began with a careful tour of the whole perimeter, taking note of the best access points. The ten-feet-high chain-link fencing surrounding the site was the standard type, with three lines of barbed wire set at a 45-degree angle at the top, supported by angled brackets spaced out every few feet. But he couldn't see any security cameras, which was good news. He was particularly interested in a spot on the north side, where two rows of portable toilets had been placed close to the fence. They'd make excellent cover for a surreptitious entry at night, especially if the security guard was occupied elsewhere.

When he reached the west side of the building, he finally saw the second buckhoist he'd hitherto only heard about. The hoist car itself was a large steel box without windows, measuring about twelve feet by eight. That one had to be used primarily for heavy equipment and supplies. It was currently stopped on the fifteenth floor.

He turned to see Ozan at his left, staring up at the elevator and looking as though he'd rather be anywhere else than here. Korso could empathise. He wished the same thing.

Making his way around a group of four ear-muffed workers drilling into the outer foundation, Korso steered them towards the south section of the work site, where he saw the other buckhoist was currently at ground level. Unlike its partner this car was a small yellow box about five feet square, with steel grated walls. It was also empty.

Korso walked over to it. At the top of the car was a steel railing to protect the motor pack on the roof that powered the elevator. Opening his clipboard to consult his 'notes', Korso turned to Ozan. 'Cover me for a moment. If anybody else comes this way, let me know.' Ozan gave a single nod in return.

Stepping over to the rear of the car, Korso took a penlight from his trouser pocket and switched it on. It was dark back there, even in daylight. Looking closely at the steel slidings and the casing that connected the car to the central mast, he soon found the section housing the pinions that carried the car's weight. Beside that was a protective steel fascia, about twelve inches by four. It was affixed to the outer casing with eight Phillips screws. Korso knew this section housed the bearings that enabled the car to move up and down the slidings. Since technicians and engineers had to have ready access to these inner workings, the protective covering had to be detachable. After satisfying himself that everything was where it should be, Korso pocketed his penlight and stepped out into the open again.

Ozan turned to him. 'Are we good?'

'So far. We'll check the twenty-first floor now.'

They entered the building through a nearby open doorway that looked like it might eventually be a fire exit. The continuous whine of numerous electric saws at work was much louder inside than out. Korso walked down a short passageway and stopped at a T-junction at the end, which opened onto another access corridor running from left to right. There was nobody to the left, but to his right he could see the backs of two men as they transported a wheeled piece of heavy machinery somewhere.

Korso followed them and had only walked a few feet when he came to another short passageway, at the end of which was the temporary access gates for the elevator outside. The lift door was the kind that you raised up manually. He leaned down, slid it up, and stepped into the small steel cage. Ozan followed him in and pulled the door down again. There was barely room for both of them. A simple control panel was affixed to the wall by the door, containing a single column of buttons numbered one to thirty, along with a large red stop button at the bottom. The buttons were all big enough to accommodate men wearing bulky safety gloves. Korso pressed the one marked 21.

The car began to ascend. It was noisy, but the ride was a smooth one. As they slowly rose into the air, Korso glanced up at the steel ceiling inches above his head. But the steel plate was completely featureless, even in the corners, and therefore of no use to him.

The elevator stopped at the twenty-first floor as gently as it had started. Korso pulled the access door up and entered the tower block again. There was no passageway on this floor, just a large open space that would probably end up as someone's living room. Ozan walked towards an open doorway straight ahead while Korso stopped and studied the area immediately surrounding the elevator entrance. The ground was thick with debris and dust. But stacked against the wall to the left of the elevator were six huge industrial sacks of concrete mix, all unopened. They looked as though they'd been there for some time. He knelt down next to the sacks, inspecting the floor, then looked towards the elevator entrance, making sure the line of sight ticked all the criteria. He finally nodded to himself, knowing he'd found the perfect location for a spy-cam.

He joined Ozan, who stood in an empty corridor outside with his clipboard open. A number of unfinished doorways lined this corridor. Ozan pointed towards the south-east corner up ahead. 'See that open doorway at the end there? That's Pineda's condo.'

Mentally picturing the floor layout from the blueprints, Korso saw he was right. Mostly to himself, he said, 'So he gets off the elevator, walks down this corridor and enters his apartment. Spends four or five minutes looking around the place, probably imagining how the place will look once it's finished. Then he walks back down this corridor, gets back on the elevator and descends. Okay, that's fine.' He turned to go.

'Hey, don't you want to check out the man's condo?'

Korso stopped and looked at him. 'What for? I've seen everything I need to. It's time to go.'

'Where?'

'To check in with your boss, and discover if this has all been a waste of time or not.'

TWENTY-FIVE

When Korso finally finished going through his proposal, Quezada leaned back in his chair and gazed up at the ceiling.

They were back in his private office in the south-east wing, having arrived fifteen minutes ago. Once they were seated, Korso recounted every aspect of his strategy, wasting as few words as possible. Now he waited patiently for Quezada to decide while Ozan got up and went to the bar and began fixing himself a drink. It was 5.33 p.m.

Quezada finally leaned forward and placed both palms on his desk. 'Javier, I want your objective opinion. What do you think?'

'You already know my thoughts on this whole Pineda problem, Miguel,' Ozan said, pouring Evian into a glass. 'As for the plan, I can't see anything technically wrong with it.'

'But...?'

'But even if everything goes off like clockwork, there's still no guarantee that whoever's in charge of the investigation won't decide to pin it all on you anyway. Even Graves admits that much. I still feel we're stirring up a hornets' nest here, Miguel. Especially when there are plenty of other methods to—'

Quezada waved a hand. 'We've already been over all that, Javier. Many times. So let's stick to the relevant points, shall we? Graves, I have to say I expected something a little more intricate from you, especially after how you dealt with Galicia. This all seems a little more rudimentary in comparison.'

'The more complex a plan becomes, the more that can go wrong,' Korso said. 'As for Galicia, the method I used to kidnap him was actually the simplest I could think up for that situation. But for your particular problem, where you want the subject to die in a manner that couldn't have been anything but accidental, this – in my opinion – is the best and easiest way to do it. The construction site's sitting right there, waiting for us to utilise it.'

'And if I disagree, and veto this idea altogether?'

'Then I'll find another way. But whichever method I were to end up using, it would always be my second choice.'

Quezada considered that for a moment. 'When would you want to set it all up?'

'Tonight, if possible. So we'll be ready if Pineda decides to visit this weekend. I just hope he's already got other plans for tonight, otherwise we'd be in for a long wait.'

'We'll know for sure within the next few minutes. Javier, call your observer and tell him to notify you as soon as Pineda leaves his office.'

Ozan pulled his phone from his pocket. 'So you're going through with it, Miguel?'

'I'm still considering, but it doesn't hurt to know the man's plans for tonight.' He turned back to Korso. 'So once you've prepared everything to your satisfaction, what then?'

'Then it's simply a waiting game. Since Pineda could pay a visit anytime over the weekend, I'd need to stay fairly close to the target area for the next two days, just in case.'

'You *and* Javier, you mean.'

'I didn't, but if that's the way you want it…'

'That's how I want it. *If* I decide to approve it. What about this site foreman? After the accident, he might suddenly remember the two unnamed safety inspectors who turned up unannounced days before, and decide it was more than coincidence.'

'Unlikely. He told me they've had two similar inspections within the last three months, so there's nothing unique about this one. To him, it's just business as usual.'

'Good. And this fluorosulfuric acid mixture you mentioned? You already have this?'

'I picked up three ampules this afternoon. The fourth I tested myself, and it works just fine. The chemist who mixed it for me has got no connection to you, by the way.'

'You're acting as though there's no doubt I'll give you the go-ahead. I'm not sure I like that.'

'I just like to be prepared for all eventualities, that's all.'

Quezada silently studied him for a while longer. The seconds soon turned into a minute. Finally, he said, 'Very well, Graves. You have my permission to proceed. Assuming Pineda goes straight home from work now, and then Javier will help you set everything up tonight. He'll also wait with you over the weekend in case Pineda decides to visit then. Are we in agreement?'

'We are.'

'Pineda's still at police headquarters,' Ozan said, returning to his seat with his drink. 'My guy will call me back the moment he leaves.'

'Good.' Quezada absently rotated the antique ring on his finger. 'We'll wait.'

Korso glanced at the two bookcases lining the opposite wall. 'You mind if I take a look at your collection to pass the time?'

'Be my guest, but treat them gently. Some of the books on those shelves are worth more than your life.'

'I treat all books with respect, Mr Quezada.'

Korso got to his feet and approached the leftmost bookcase. Quezada's collection was made up mostly of hardcovers, arranged in alphabetical order by author. He could have browsed for hours, days even, but this was work. He went straight to the H section again and there was Hemingway, represented by seven thick hardcovers of varying sizes. All looked old, and all were in excellent condition.

He reached down and carefully pulled out the volume of *The Sun Also Rises* that he'd spotted before. He stared at the dust jacket. The front cover was a beautifully stark Hellenistic illustration of a scantily clad woman sitting by a tree, while the back bore a sketch of Hemingway rather than the usual photo. Korso knew right away that he was holding a near mint first-edition of the famous novel, published by Scribner's with an initial print run of 5090 copies. He opened the book to the first page and wasn't surprised to see the author's familiar signature on the front endpaper. He carefully turned to page 181 and smiled when he saw the infamous misspelling of *stopped* with the third *p* in the centre.

Korso felt a nearby presence, and turned to see Quezada standing at his right, watching him closely.

'You went straight to the page with the typographical error. I'm impressed.'

'So am I,' Korso said. 'I've never seen a copy in such fantastic condition. It looks as though it could have been printed last year rather than a century ago. I'm guessing the original owner must have stored it somewhere safe the moment he got it signed, and kept it there, unread, for years.'

'You're not far from the truth. One of Hemingway's favourite nephews received the copy as an eleventh birthday present. The boy's mother wrapped it in plastic and stored it in the attic and told him he could read it when he was old enough. When the nephew died just five years later in a boating accident, everyone forgot about the book, including the mother. Seventy-three years later, one of my scouts discovered its existence and, after verifying its history, purchased it from the estate.'

'Incredible find.' Korso carefully placed the rare volume back on the shelf. 'Something like this, in such pristine condition, would easily fetch a seven-figure sum in today's market. And it's probably not even the most valuable book in this room.'

'Not even close.' Quezada was still studying Korso carefully. 'You really do have a genuine appreciation for rare artefacts, Graves.'

'They're a passion of mine, Mr Quezada. And since I also make my living locating and recovering them, I consider myself a more fortunate man than most.'

Quezada smiled. '"Find a job you enjoy doing, and you will never have to work a day in your life." Do you know who wrote that?'

'Mark Twain, if memory serves. Whom I imagine is well represented in this collection of yours.'

Quezada waved nonchalantly towards the right bookcase. 'Seven first editions, four of them signed. You know, I believe I may have something else for you once this little problem has been put to bed. I'm still working out the exact details, but I think you'll find it very interesting.'

'I'm already intrigued.'

'I thought you might be. But let's stay focused on the task at—' Quezada stopped short as the piercing sound of a howling wolf filled the office.

The ringtone was cut off mid-howl as Ozan took the call. He grunted a few times, then hung up. 'Pineda's left the office. He's heading home as we speak.'

'Good,' Quezada said. 'So you both know what to do next.'

TWENTY-SIX

At 11.44 that same evening, Korso and Ozan were parked in the same spot as before, watching the Casa Nueva construction site entrance from the other side of the mostly empty street. They'd been there for almost an hour. After leaving Quezada's compound, Korso had driven them back to the Hilton, where they'd each disappeared into their respective rooms and made preparations for the night ahead. Somehow, Ozan had managed to wrangle himself the suite right next door to Korso.

With the car windows rolled down, Korso heard the oncoming vehicle before he saw it, the engine sounding as though it had been tuned to its loudest possible setting. Two seconds later, Korso saw it: a red Toyota pickup with huge wheels and a raised chassis, speeding eastwards at about sixty kilometres an hour. It looked about to pass by them when the driver hit the brakes and the vehicle screeched to a sudden stop, almost directly in front of the main entrance. The driver revved the engine loudly a few times. A thumping bass beat could be heard from within the vehicle.

A few seconds later, another pickup arrived from the opposite direction, going just as fast. This one was a silver Honda. The driver was heading straight for the Toyota and looked about to crash right into it. But when it was just twenty feet away, there was another ear-splitting squeal of brakes, the wheels locked, and the vehicle skidded to an equally dramatic halt until there was a gap of just three inches separating the two vehicles.

Doors opened and kids of both sexes emerged from the cars and bounced onto the street, all whooping and hollering over the loud beat. None looked older than twenty. Most were either holding beer bottles or drinking from pocket-sized bottles of Quetzalteca whiskey. Two girls in tiny tank tops and even tinier shorts started writhing and dancing on the sidewalk. Within seconds, two of the guys joined them. Pretty soon everyone joined in.

It was Friday night in the big city, and that meant party time. Or at least, that's how it would appear.

'Dumb kids,' Ozan said in a sullen tone. 'I pay them to be here at 11.30, and the little assholes show up fifteen minutes late.' He steered out onto the street and turned right at the next intersection, slowly making his way along the northern perimeter. Theirs was the only vehicle moving. And no other pedestrians either. Not this late.

Korso kept his eyes on the security fencing. When he finally spotted the tops of the portable toilets he'd noticed before, he said, 'Right here will do.'

Ozan pulled into the kerb, killed the engine and switched off the headlights. Korso pulled the navy backpack containing his equipment from the rear seat and slipped his arms through the straps. He was wearing a black turtleneck, black trousers and a black cotton beanie that could be converted into a ski mask if necessary. Reaching back, he grabbed the section of rolled carpet he'd brought along as well.

As he was opening the door, Ozan said, 'How long?'

Korso checked his watch. It was 11.50. 'An hour should do it, all being well. Just be here when I get back.'

'I'll be here. You just do your part of the job.'

Korso said nothing, just exited the car and gently shut the door. Even from this far away, he could hear the impromptu party going on at the main entrance. It wouldn't last much longer. Another ten minutes or so and the two pickups and their passengers would be gone. A temporary distraction was all that was required. The last thing they needed was the security guard calling the cops. He checked his surroundings and saw nothing but a few business premises and the private hospital on the other side of the street. Every window was dark. The sky was overcast, so no moonlight. Streetlamps provided the only illumination. There were still no other vehicles in sight.

He approached the fence and when he came to one of the angle brackets supporting the barbed wire at the top, he unrolled the thick carpet. He folded it once to double the protection, and flung it over the bracket, pulling the rug downwards so it caught on the sharp barbs. He slowly climbed up the fence and carefully hauled himself over the top, ensuring his body made contact with the thick material and nothing else, before landing on his feet on the other site. After removing the rug from the fence, he rolled it up again and hid it between two of the mobile toilets, ready for use later.

Korso spent a minute peering at a spot in the darkness of the site behind him, waiting for his night vision to kick in. A minute later, he got to his feet and headed towards the elevator on the south side.

–

It was 1.08 a.m. when Korso retrieved the carpet from its hiding place and flung it over the fence. He'd seen nobody since he arrived, and nobody had seen him. All the pieces were in place and everything was where it should be, just waiting to be activated on his signal. The two micro cameras on the twenty-first floor were easy, although he could have done without the long hike up the fire stairs. Battery life wouldn't be a problem since they could each be activated remotely, as and when required. But he'd spent the most time on the placement of the two ampules beneath the motor assembly, where one millimetre either way could make the difference between success and total catastrophe. It would have been hard enough working in daylight, but with only a small LED penlight to work with, the whole operation became a test of nerve and patience.

His Honda Civic was still parked in the same spot. He could see Ozan in the driver's seat, his face partially illuminated as he did something on his phone. After making sure they were still the only two humans in sight, Korso hauled himself back over the fence again. Retrieving the carpet, he opened the front passenger door and got in.

Ozan was looking at him, a .45 semi-automatic now gripped in his left hand.

'Put that away.' Korso threw the carpet onto the rear seat. 'I don't like having guns pointed at me, especially in my own car.'

'You shouldn't surprise a guy like that. I almost gave you a third eye.' With a smirk, Ozan slowly put the piece back in its holster. 'Well? Is it done?'

'It's done. And it smells like death in here. I told you to open a window if you planned on smoking.'

'Oh, yeah, you did. I guess it just slipped my mind.'

Korso knew it was pointless to argue. Ozan clearly felt the need to play these little power games, so Korso just let him. He'd suffered far worse hardships in his time.

After placing his backpack on the rear seat, he said, 'Okay, let's go.'

'Where to?'

'The hotel, of course. We've got a day ahead of us tomorrow.'

Ozan snorted as he started the engine. 'Yeah, waiting around for something to happen, which it won't.'

'Possibly. But I'd still prefer to be awake if something *does* happen. You see where I'm going with this?'

Ozan drove them away without answering.

TWENTY-SEVEN

Saturday was a no-show. Korso knew it would be, but had to be ready anyway. Ozan informed him that Pineda spent the morning at home, and most of the afternoon out shopping in town with his girlfriend. The couple had gone back to her apartment in the early evening, and he'd stayed with her overnight.

Fortunately, the nature of the job meant Korso and Ozan didn't need to spend too much time in each other's company. Because he had a two-man team constantly watching Pineda, Ozan knew he'd get plenty of warning if he were to start driving in the Casa Nueva's general direction. That meant neither man needed to be in close proximity to the other, just as long as they stayed in the same general area. Korso handled this by spending the first half of the day reading or playing chess alone at the cantina he'd visited before, and the latter half at another sidewalk diner two blocks away. As long as he kept ordering snacks or beverages every now and then, the owners didn't mind how long he stayed. Neither establishment was doing a roaring trade anyway, especially as it rained all day. He didn't ask where Ozan spent his time, all he knew was that he'd get another call when Pineda started coming their way.

Sunday started out much the same as Saturday. Korso spent the morning and early afternoon at another sidewalk diner he'd found in the area. He got a call from Ozan at around 10 a.m. to inform him that Pineda had arrived back home after leaving his girlfriend's place. After a light lunch of pepian stew and flatbread, Korso settled the check and changed venue again, moving onto the original cantina he'd visited twice previously. There were three other customers, making it the busiest he'd ever seen the place. After ordering some table snacks and a bottle of light beer, the owner left him and went back to chat with her other customers.

At 4.06 p.m., Korso was taking a break from a particularly involving chess game, and was just watching the traffic pass by, when his phone started chirping at him. He picked it up.

'Just got word he's on the move,' Ozan said. 'Heading north.'

'How long?'

'A few seconds ago. Why, you thought maybe I had myself a little siesta before calling you?'

Korso held back a sigh. Ozan had to turn every simple conversation into another confrontation. 'Just tell me where he is now.'

'Wait one… Okay, four blocks from his house now, still heading north.'

'Meaning he's more than thirty minutes away from us, and could still be going anywhere. I can pick you up now, or wait until it's more definite. I suggest the latter.'

'Fine,' Ozan said, and terminated the call.

Korso considered returning to his game for another few minutes, but decided there was no point and closed the lid of his travel chess set. He signalled the owner for the check.

The phone chirped again at 4.15. 'Still headed our way. This could be the day.' Ozan gave an address three blocks east of Korso's current location. 'Come pick me up.'

'On my way,' Korso said, and left the cantina and walked the thirty feet to his parked Honda. He got in and less than two minutes later arrived at the address he'd been given, which was a two-storey dive where guests could book rooms by the hour. Ozan was waiting out front, listening to whatever was being said through his Bluetooth earpiece. When he saw the Honda, he came over and got in on the passenger side.

'Heading into the downtown area now,' he said to Korso. 'Might be going to the office, or he may be coming here. Could go either way.'

'No, it couldn't,' Korso said, and pulled out and drove them back to the construction site. 'He's on his way. You know it as well as I do.'

After a short pause, Ozan smiled. 'Yeah, I guess I do at that.'

'The guy who's supplying you with this information, can he hear you talking to me?'

Ozan looked offended. 'What do you take me for?'

'You don't want to know.'

Korso parked on the side street bordering the southern perimeter of the construction site. There were plenty of spaces. He picked one with a decent view of the elevator mast running up the side of the building. The eight-foot-high wooden fence panels behind the chain-link fence prevented him from seeing much, but since he couldn't spot the buckhoist, he assumed it was currently at ground level. There was almost no other moving vehicle on this side street. It had rained buckets that morning, but this afternoon the sun was out with barely a cloud in the sky. He turned off the engine and looked up at the twenty-first floor. There was no movement up there, or anywhere else on the site. Hadn't been since early Saturday afternoon when the last of the overtime workers had left.

Meanwhile, Ozan was providing him with a running street-by-street commentary of Pineda's movements. Korso tuned most of it out and focused instead on the precise sequence of events that he'd gone over a hundred times already, once more visualising every single detail in his mind. At 4.39, Ozan said, 'He's just driven past the police building, still heading our way.' He smiled. 'Looks like we're on.'

Korso reached over, opened the glove compartment, and pulled out the small drawstring nylon bag in there. He opened it up and pulled out two small electronic transmitters. One was black, the other granite. After switching both devices on, he put them back in the glove compartment. 'Is your man reliable?' he asked.

Ozan frowned at him. 'Which one?'

'The one currently speaking into your right ear. Because if he's got a brain in his head, he'll know straight away that whatever happens next is no accident.'

While Ozan leaned back and pondered on that, Korso pulled his phone from his pocket and opened the Firefox browser. He went to the first bookmarked site and gave a mental sigh of relief when he saw a fish-eye image of an empty, unfinished hallway, featuring two door-sized openings on each side, and a large open area at the end.

'That looks familiar,' Ozan said, frowning at the screen.

'It should. It's Pineda's apartment.' Korso had drilled a small hole just above the entrance to Pineda's condo, fairly close to the ceiling, and placed one of his micro spy-cams in the opening. The tiny internal lithium battery was only good for transmitting two hours' worth of footage, so there was no point in activating it before he actually needed it. He was just grateful the thing was still working. You never knew for sure until you tried.

He went to his second bookmarked site. After a brief delay, he saw a wide angled, ground-level shot of the elevator entrance on the twenty-first floor, the camera set at a 90-degree angle to the lift entrance. He'd secreted the second spy-cam partly underneath one of the sacks of concrete mix by the exterior wall. But since he'd positioned it, some more cement sacks had been placed against the wall further along, partially obscuring the view of the elevator entrance. The line of sight was still good, just not as clear as it could have been.

'Christ, couldn't you have found a better vantage point?'

'It was fine on Friday night,' Korso said, propping the phone up on the dash. 'Somebody must have added some more sacks of cement after I placed it, probably yesterday morning. Other than a couple of blind spots, it's still good enough for our needs.'

'We'll find out soon enough. So what about after?'

Korso turned to him. 'After?'

'After things go boom, those two spy-cams will still be up there, right? What's to stop either one of them being discovered over the coming days?'

'Me. I plan to go in again later tonight and remove them both. Nobody will know they were ever there.'

'Think of everything, don't you? So when were you planning on letting me—?' Ozan stopped mid-sentence, raising a finger to his ear. After a short pause, he smiled. 'Our boy's just three blocks away now. Almost game time. Give me the URL for one of those feeds so I can access it on my phone.'

'I can do better. Reach down under your seat.'

Ozan did as instructed, reaching under the passenger seat and pulling out an 11-inch iPad Pro. It was a counterfeit model, but good enough for their purposes. Korso told him to open Safari and access the page he'd bookmarked. Soon, the same fish-eye shot of the apartment hallway appeared on the display, in far better quality than on Korso's phone. Ozan grinned as he rotated the iPad onto landscape mode. 'Just a shame we couldn't get a camera inside the elevator too. I'd pay good money to see the look on that bastard's face when this shit goes down.' He chuckled. 'See what I did there?'

Korso just looked at him as though he were a lower form of life. 'Updates would be helpful,' he said.

'He's just arriving now.' Ozan swivelled in his seat, peering out the rear window. 'Can't see him, but my guy says he's just parking up now, outside the main entrance.' He faced front again, listening. 'Now he's getting out of the car... Okay, he's locking the doors, and talking on the phone to somebody... And now he's walking over to the front gates, still on the phone...'

'And it's definitely Pineda?' Korso said, watching a couple walk down the other side of the street. 'We need to be sure.'

'Take a pill or something.' Ozan faced front again, wearing a smile that was even more smug than usual. 'Your nerves are showing. If it were anybody else, my guys would know it within seconds. They've practically been living with the man the past few months… Okay, the security guard's come over to the gate, and they're talking… Pineda's showing his ID now, and the guard's unlocking the gate. Now Pineda's stepped inside.' He gave a loud sigh. 'Shit, I hate not being able to see any of this.'

Korso reached into his shirt pocket and pulled out a small black key fob. It had a single button on the front and a tiny LED light at the top, which was currently inactive. There was also an on–off slide switch on the side.

Ozan looked at it with a strange gleam in his eye. 'Hand me that remote,' he said. 'I'll activate the detonator.'

Korso blinked at him.

'You heard me. You may be the ideas man, but Miguel put me in charge of the operational end, so I'll do the honours.'

Korso turned the fob in his hand, thinking. Finally, he said, 'You press the button exactly when I tell you. Not one second before. Not one second after. Are we clear?'

'You giving me orders now?'

'Listen to me, Ozan, If any part of this operation goes wrong Mr Quezada will lay the blame solely at my door, not yours, and we both know it. So if that hoist doesn't happen to drop at the exact moment it should, and Pineda somehow survives, then I'll need to find a way to leave the country before your boss sends a hit squad after me. But not before I break your neck, you understand? I'll have nothing else to lose at that point, and killing you means one less hunter on my tail. So I repeat: you press that button exactly when I tell you. Not before, and definitely not after. Are we clear on that?'

Ozan took a deep breath. 'We both want the same result here. Hand me the remote, and you got my word I'll press it on your say-so.'

Korso handed him the device.

'Not that I couldn't handle you,' Ozan added.

'Naturally.'

Korso abruptly turned his head at the familiar sound of the elevator doors being opened, somewhere off to his left. Neither man said a word. They just listened. The sound of a metallic door sliding shut. After a short pause, machinery whirred. Almost immediately, Korso saw the buckhoist come into view as it began its slow journey up the mast. He leaned out his window and watched it all the way, mentally counting the seconds.

He'd reached a count of forty-nine when the hoist came to a stop at the twenty-first floor. Korso stared down at his phone display, while Ozan leaned in for a better look. They watched the static, wide-angled shot of an empty room, and waited.

Finally, movement. From the left, Pineda appeared from behind one of the sacks of cement as he walked away from the elevator towards his apartment, out of the shot to the right. He looked exactly like his photos. He was wearing a loose-fitting long-sleeved shirt, casual chinos, and white sneakers. There was no sound. He was only visible for a couple of seconds, and then he disappeared off-screen.

'Definitely him,' Ozan said, sitting back and switching his attention to the iPad. They watched the empty apartment hallway in silence. After a few nervy seconds, the back of Pineda's head came into view as he strolled down the passageway, before disappearing through the first doorway on the left.

That would be the guest bedroom, assuming the building blueprints were correct. There was no telling what the guy was doing in there. Both men watched the screen in silence. Korso's eyes gradually switched to Ozan's left hand, as his fingers carelessly played with the remote control. 'Don't do that,' he said.

Ozan suddenly became aware of what he was doing and stopped. 'Relax, it's not even switched on.'

'Doesn't matter. It's not a plaything. If you drop it you could damage the circuits inside, and then we're back to square one.'

Still staring at the screen, Ozan sighed. 'Okay, okay, I get the message.'

A minute passed. Two. Then Pineda emerged from the guest bedroom and strolled over to the doorway diagonally opposite and entered what would be the main bedroom. Another three minutes passed in silence before he came out again. He was on his phone once more, gesturing vaguely with his hand as he talked. He turned right and ambled off towards the top of the screen, into the main living area. Seconds later, all that could be seen were his sneakers as he turned to his right and vanished out of shot.

Time passed slowly as Korso stared at the static view of the unembellished hallway. Neither man spoke. Without taking his eyes off the screen, Ozan absently reached into his jacket pocket with his free hand and pulled out a pack of Marlboros. Korso was about to say something, when Ozan thought better of it and slowly put them back again.

Korso judged around five minutes had passed when Pineda's sneakers reappeared at the top of the screen. Both men tensed as the rest of him followed. No longer on the phone, Pineda strolled casually down the hallway towards the entrance, giving the left wall a possessive pat as he passed. Although he didn't look up at the camera, his facial features couldn't be clearer. There was no doubt at all. It was Pineda.

'Looks like he's seen enough,' Korso said. 'Turn on the remote.'

Ozan immediately thumbed the on–off switch on the side of the key fob. The tiny LED at the top flashed green, and stayed that way.

They kept watching as Pineda continued walking towards the camera. When he disappeared from the bottom of the frame, Korso immediately turned his attention to the smartphone on the dash, waiting for him to appear on the right side of the display.

Ozan also leaned forward for a better look. 'You feel it yet, bitch?' he said under his breath. 'Because it's coming.'

'When I give the word,' Korso said. 'Not before.'

'Yeah, yeah, yeah.'

They waited. The passing seconds felt like an eternity.

Finally, Pineda appeared on the right of the screen, heading directly towards the elevator. He was still walking at the same leisurely pace when he suddenly stopped in the centre of the screen, just before the sacks of cement that obstructed the view of the elevator itself, and looked down at something on the floor. Crouching down on his haunches, he picked up a small object and carefully inspected it, turning it this way and that.

'What the hell is it?' Ozan whispered, moving in closer.

'Could be anything. Maybe a coin.'

'A lucky coin. Yeah, I like that.'

Whatever it was, Pineda dropped the object into his shirt pocket as he got to his feet again. He carried on walking towards the elevator, and less than a second later he was out of shot entirely.

'He's inside now.' Ozan's thumb hovered over the button. 'He's got to be.'

'Wait. Keep watching in case he comes out again.' Korso leaned out the window and craned his head up towards the twenty-first floor. The hoist was still up there. Two hundred and fifty feet away. Motionless.

A second passed. Two. Three. Four.

Then movement, as the hoist began its slow descent.

'*Now*,' Korso said.

He didn't see Ozan press the button, and the detonator was too small to make any noise. To the naked eye, nothing untoward had occurred. The hoist passed the twentieth floor and continued descending at the same speed. Korso knew it would take a few more seconds for something to happen, *if* it was going to.

'Well?' Ozan called out from behind him. 'Why isn't it falling?'

'Shut up.'

Korso just watched the elevator continue its slow descent. The hoist had just passed the nineteenth floor when it made a sudden jerk, and briefly halted in its tracks. Korso heard the harsh sound of grinding metal up there, along with the unmistakeable sound of someone screaming in fear. He'd heard sounds just like it before. Then there was an almighty tearing sound as the hoist began to hurtle towards the ground, as though somebody had cut the strings. Korso watched it frantically pick up speed as it sped past the floors. After the initial tearing noise, there were no more sounds. Which made it worse.

The four seconds it took to hit the ground felt like twenty, and Korso watched it all the way. When it hit the earth, the noise from the impact was tremendous, especially after the silence of the drop. The fencing blocked his view, so all he could see was an eruption of machine parts as the one-tonne metal cage smashed into the ground. The mast scaffolding rocked slightly from the impact, but remained upright.

Then silence.

It took a few seconds before the usual city sounds came into focus again. Traffic sounds. Beeping horns. Barking dogs. Sirens somewhere off in the distance.

Korso pulled his head back in and turned to see Ozan standing out in plain view beside the car, staring open-mouthed at the spot where the hoist fell.

'Get in,' Korso said. 'We need to move. Now.'

Ozan got back in the passenger seat and slammed the door shut, still grinning like it was Christmas Day. 'Man, did you see that? It was beautiful. Just beautiful. Everything I imagined it would be.'

'I'm happy for you.' Korso started the engine. The street they were on was still quiet. It wouldn't stay that way for long.

'Hey, what the hell are you doing?' Ozan said. 'We need to stick around and wait for the ambulance, get confirmation he's really dead.'

'You've got observers who can do that. But if you want to stay behind, I'm not stopping you. Just make it quick because I'm leaving right now. What's it to be?'

'Okay, okay. Let's go then.'

So Korso drove.

TWENTY-EIGHT

Korso spent the next two days at his hotel, continually checking the news sites for updates on Sunday's incident. He had no idea if Ozan was still in the next-door suite, although he thought it unlikely. Now the assignment was completed there'd be no further reason for him to stick around.

As for Manuel Pineda, the deputy chief of DOC had been officially declared dead at the scene by the chief coroner, who'd arrived shortly after the first ambulance had shown up. By the time the media turned up in force, Pineda's corpse had already been removed from the scene. However, a number of forward-thinking bystanders did manage to film two of the paramedics as they manhandled a heavily covered stretcher into the back of an ambulance, and it wasn't long before every single news site carried the same shaky cell phone footage.

According to an unnamed source in the department, almost every bone in Pineda's body had been smashed upon impact, and his face and upper body almost obliterated from the steel cage crumpling in on him. As a result, positive identification had to be confirmed mostly through his fingerprints and existing medical records. Further construction of the condominium building had also been put temporarily on hold until the police analysts, insurance investigators and all other interested parties had completely finished inspecting the scene of the accident.

And that was how the media referred to it – the scene of the *accident*. That or the *crash site*. Nobody was calling it the scene of a possible homicide, although several bloggers strongly hinted at the possibility when the news first hit. Those assumptions had all but disappeared by mid-Monday, however, as it quickly became evident that this was nothing more than a terrible calamity, and one that would have happened to the next person – or persons – who used that elevator, regardless of their identity or position.

On Tuesday morning, an official police statement was finally released to the media. In essence, it said that after an extensive examination of the crash site, investigators had discovered no evidence of foul play, and that unless something new came to light, Manuel Pineda died as a result of mechanical failure in the elevator buckhoist, caused by extreme rusting of the needle bearings in the motor assembly, along with part of the pinion system.

This was exactly what Korso had been hoping to hear. As a matter of course, he continued searching the web for all mentions of Quezada's name in connection with the crash, but found nothing that might cause him concern.

At 4.32 p.m. on Tuesday, Korso was speedreading through a news blog site when the landline in his suite began to ring. It was the first time he'd heard it since he'd arrived. He got up, walked over to the work desk and picked up the receiver.

'Graves?' a male voice asked. Not Ozan's.

'Yes. Who's this?'

'Come now, don't you recognise my voice?'

'Now I do.' Korso was just surprised Quezada would actually call him in person.

'Come on over,' Quezada said. 'We've things to discuss.' There was a click, and the line went dead.

Korso took the same route as before and, despite the rush-hour traffic, reached the front gates of the compound less than thirty minutes later. After the expected formalities were done with, he was finally allowed through. Ozan was waiting at the front door again, smoking a cigarette and talking to one of his men. Korso recognised him. It was Dante, whom he'd met that first day. They both turned to watch Korso as he got out of the car. Ozan said something to Dante, who nodded and descended the steps. At the bottom, he purposefully ignored Korso and carried on towards the garage.

Korso climbed the steps. 'How's Mr Quezada today?' he asked.

'You'll find out soon enough,' Ozan said, and crumpled what was left of the cigarette between his fingers.

Dropping the remains on Korso's shoe, Ozan turned and entered the house. Korso shook his head and followed. This time, Ozan led him through the entrance lobby and turned into the second doorway on the left, into a wide hallway with dark tiled floors. On the left was a luxurious private spa, complete with aquarium and Turkish bath. On the right, there was a tinted, sliding glass door leading to a closed-off gym area. Ozan slid the door open and waited without expression. Korso stepped through, heard the door shut behind him, and saw Ozan walk back the way he'd come.

The private gym was essentially a smaller version of the one in the annex building that Alex had shown him. This one was pleasantly air-conditioned and windowless, with illumination provided by soft down-lights embedded in the ceiling. Quezada was jogging on one of the two treadmills, listening to whatever was coming through his earbuds as he sipped from a water bottle. Wearing just shorts and sneakers, he looked a fine specimen of a man in his late forties, with a flat, well-toned stomach, and lean biceps and defined deltoids. He was barely sweating. This workout was clearly a daily regime for him.

Finally, Quezada turned off the machine and slowed his pace to a complete stop. Removing his earbuds, he said, 'I didn't expect you so soon.'

'Traffic was a little lighter than usual. I like this gym of yours, Mr Quezada.'

'One of my favourite rooms in the house, maybe the whole compound. I believe a man who doesn't take care of his body on a regular basis deserves everything he gets. That's something I feel more strongly about with each passing day.' He wiped a towel over his face and took another sip of water. 'You did well, Graves. Very well indeed.'

'So you're satisfied with how it all turned out?'

'You could say that.' He reached down, picked up a t-shirt from the floor and slipped it on over his head. 'Ozan had his doubts about your plan, as did I, but I'm glad to say you proved us both wrong. Through my sources, I've been keeping up to date with the investigation, and it seems clear from all the available evidence, or lack of it, that Manuel Pineda's tragic death was the result of an industrial accident caused by mechanical error.' He gave a sad shake of his head. 'And he had so much still to give. By the way, I deposited your fee to your overseas account less than an hour ago. Along with a fifty per cent bonus for accomplishing it all so quickly.'

'That's… unexpected. I'm grateful.'

Quezada waved it away as though it were nothing. Which it probably was to him. Leaving his empty water bottle, he said, 'Come with me,' and made for the door.

Korso followed him through the house, passing more rooms until they reached a huge kitchen area at the end. The floor-to-ceiling windows looked out onto a colourful garden he hadn't seen before. The kitchen island in the centre of the room was full of freshly sliced vegetables and meats, while a sixty-something woman in a starched white uniform and blue apron stood at a cooker, stirring the ingredients of a large pot. She greeted Quezada with a smile and ignored Korso entirely.

'Smells good, Maria,' Quezada said, opening the nearest refrigerator.

'Black bean soup, sir. It's a new recipe I'm trying. I hope you'll like it.'

'I always do.' He pulled out a large water bottle filled with a prepared protein shake. He popped the top and drank half the contents in one go. 'Maria's been with me for over ten years now. I consider her the best cook in the city, maybe even the whole country.'

'Quite the recommendation.'

Bringing his shake along, Quezada led Korso through another doorway into another hallway, with more rooms on the left. From one, a little girl squealed, '*Daddy, Daddy.*'

Quezada's features crinkled into a genuine smile as he led Korso into a brightly decorated playroom filled with toys of all kinds. All four walls were painted in bright primary colours, and piles of colouring books and games were stacked up against one. A little girl with pigtails, who looked like a younger version of Nilsa, was sitting at a low circular table in the centre of the room, busily colouring a drawing she'd made. Sitting next to the little girl was Alejandra, with boxes of coloured crayons in front of her.

'Daddy,' the girl said, 'look, I drew a picture of you.'

'Did you now? Let's see.'

While Quezada went over to inspect his daughter's portrait of him, Alejandra smiled at Korso. 'Hello. I was wondering when we might see you again.'

'I've been wondering the same thing. How are you, Alex?'

'Well, I'm currently trying to teach little Anna here the rudiments of art, and not having a whole lot of success. She's at that age where everything has to be purple. Even trees and lakes. So how's your research project going?'

'Just completed it today. Which now puts me in mind of that final conversation we had, about the possibility of a dinner date.'

'Yes, I remember that as well. Well, it just so happens I'm not doing anything this evening—'

'Alex,' Quezada said, looking up from his daughter's drawing, 'if you could put your own interests on hold for the moment, Graves and I have a few things to discuss first.'

She gave a shrug. 'Sorry, Miguel.' To Korso, she added, 'You remember where my bungalow is, don't you?'

'I remember.'

'Maybe I'll see you later then. If you have time.'

'I'll find time.'

Quezada kissed his daughter and motioned for Korso to follow him. They exited the playroom and entered another room further down the hallway. This room was smaller and sparsely furnished. Three luxuriously quilted chaise longues were arranged geometrically in the middle of the room, each with their own slide-out table. The walls were all white, with one wall containing a number of built-in sliding wardrobes, and what looked like a refrigerator as well. Floor-to-ceiling windows looked out onto the same garden Korso had seen from the kitchen, along with a sliding door. Outside, the sky was already darkening as the sun began to set.

'This room I use for my more reflective moments,' Quezada said. He approached one of the cupboards and slid the door across. Inside, Korso saw three single-stemmed glass hookahs arranged along one shelf. On another, a pair of sleek games consoles, along with various devices that he didn't recognise. From the top shelf, Quezada grabbed hold of a pair of wrap-around ski-style welding goggles. He silently handed them to Korso, who looked them over with a faintly puzzled expression. The goggles had been modified so the panoramic lens was now completely blacked out by a black rubber overlay. There was also a sticky rubber seal on the inside, to further restrict the wearer's view. Meaning anybody wearing these would be essentially blind.

Now Korso knew why he'd been invited here. Especially in light of the cryptic comments Quezada had made on Friday night. He thought quickly as he looked around the room. The moment his glance fell on the refrigerator, a possibility came to him.

'I imagine you have questions,' Quezada said.

'One or two.'

'Well, put them on hold for now. I plan to show you something, but for reasons of security I'll require you to put these on first. Do you trust me?'

'I don't trust anyone.'

Quezada smiled. 'An honest answer. I like that. But you needn't worry, you're not in any danger here.'

'I'll take your word for it. Uh, Mr Quezada, before I put these on, is there any chance of getting a drink? A soft drink, I mean. My throat feels like a desert.'

'You should have said.' Quezada walked over and pulled the refrigerator door open, displaying the contents. 'Take your pick.'

The fridge was packed with bottles and cans of soft drinks of all kinds. Ignoring the Coca-Colas and Sprites, Korso suppressed a smile when he spotted two bright yellow cans of Schweppes Indian Tonic Water at the back. Perfect. He reached in and pulled one out. 'I don't suppose you have a straw, so I can sip as we walk?'

Frowning a little, Quezada opened a small cabinet set just above the fridge, which contained rows of clean glasses amongst other paraphernalia. He rummaged around and pulled out a fresh pack of white plastic straws. 'Thought so. My girls won't drink anything that doesn't come out of one of these. Maria's got fresh packs stashed everywhere.'

'Kids always know best.' Korso popped the can open and inserted the straw, took a quick sip of the bitter citric drink. 'Much obliged.'

'And now the goggles.'

Korso took the headgear and stretched the elasticated silicone strap over his skull, placing the goggles carefully over his eyes. With the rubber seal tight against his skin, he saw nothing but complete and utter blackness. No matter how much he manipulated his cheek muscles to try and let in a little light at the sides, the soft rubber seal around the mask matched their every move as though it were glued to his face.

'This must be what a sensory deprivation tank feels like,' he said. 'All I see is blackness.'

'That's the whole point. Now you'll be walking in front of me, but I'll be keeping my hand on your right shoulder at all times. When I steer you one way, you go that way. When I stop, you stop. And be sure never to touch those goggles until I tell you otherwise, not even to scratch. Do you understand?'

'Perfectly.'

'Good. Let's go for a walk.'

TWENTY-NINE

Korso heard a door slide open, and Quezada placed his left hand on Korso's right shoulder. A small nudge was all Korso needed to start moving. Since he'd already been warned about asking questions, he decided to keep his mouth shut.

His feet touched grass, and he filled his lungs with fresh air. He heard the sounds of birds singing nearby. He continued walking in a straight line, changing course only when Quezada steered him in a certain direction, which was often. Probably to disorientate him. Every now and then Quezada stopped him dead, then turned him in a semi-circle one way, then full-circle the other way, then again a few more times. Within a few minutes, Korso had completely lost his bearings. He couldn't even feel the sun on his face. He stopped counting the seconds in his head as well. There was no point. Quezada could have doubled back at any time and retraced his steps, and Korso would never know. Although he had a fairly good idea of their ultimate destination, he wouldn't know for sure until they finally got there. And maybe not even then.

He took an occasional sip of his tonic water as he walked, even though he wasn't particularly thirsty. Mainly so Quezada would get used to his doing it, and not pay it any further attention. Korso had actually chosen the tonic less for its taste, which was pleasant enough, and more for its unique ingredients. Specifically the minute amount of quinine that gave the drink its harsh bitter quality.

Korso figured about six minutes had passed before his feet touched solid concrete again. In that time, he'd heard not one human voice. Not even a distant one.

A few seconds later he was brought to a halt. There was the sound of a door opening in front of him. Quezada's hand urged him to move. Korso took another sip of his drink and stepped forward. The air was cooler inside, and his footsteps echoed slightly. There was also a faint hum coming from the air conditioning, which he recognised from when Alex had shown him around the previous week.

He was in the annex building. Had to be. Korso mentally pictured the layout again. Wide hallway straight ahead. Display room on the left-hand side, with a private cinema at the end. On the right was the game room, followed by the spa, and then the gym.

Quezada pushed Korso forward down the main hallway, until he figured they'd covered half the length of the building. At which point Quezada brought him to a halt, and said, 'This next part will make you dizzy, so prepare yourself.'

'I'm ready.'

Quezada took the drink from his hand and quickly rotated him one way, then the other, over and over and over. By the time Quezada stopped Korso barely knew which way was up anymore. His dizziness was total. The fact that he couldn't see only amplified the effects tenfold. Already feeling himself veering to the right, he held out his free hand and found Quezada's shoulder, using it to stay upright from the intense vertigo. After a few moments, Quezada handed back his drink, then guided him forward with both hands.

'Keep your arms close to your sides,' he said. 'Don't try reaching for anything.'

'Understood.'

Still feeling the effects, Korso made sure to sip more tonic water as he was urged onwards. He thought they might have entered one of the rooms, but he wasn't sure. The vertigo had skewed his hearing too.

Finally, Quezada indicated he wanted Korso to stop. Korso halted. He sucked some more of the tonic through the straw and listened hard. Hoping for something, anything. Then came a very faint rumbling sound, as though something heavy was being wheeled carefully along the floor. The noise stopped. Not long after he heard an electronic *blip*, followed by the sound of something emerging from somewhere else. Like a CD drawer popping out of a hi-fi system.

Korso raised his right hand to his mouth, squirted some of the drink onto his palm and simultaneously stumbled to the floor, as though he'd lost his balance. He felt his back connect with something solid as he landed. Like a wall or a partition. But he made sure to keep the half-empty can upright. He couldn't afford to make a mess on the tiles. That would ruin everything.

'Sorry,' he said, 'still dizzy, I guess.'

He raised his free right hand into the air, hoping Quezada would help him up. With an impatient sigh, the man grabbed Korso's now damp hand and hauled him to his feet. Quezada made an exclamation of disgust. 'If you even think about puking up, it'll be the last action you ever make.'

'I'm fine now,' Korso said. 'It won't happen again.'

'Make sure it doesn't.'

Korso stood still and listened carefully. He heard eight barely distinguishable beep tones, like somebody pressing a keypad. A few seconds of silence was followed by what sounded like a metallic object making very light contact with another object. Not a key. Something else. He couldn't begin to guess what that something might be. After a short period of silence, there was a solid metallic *click*, immediately followed by the unmistakeable sound of a heavy door opening electronically.

'Open sesame,' Quezada said, and carefully pushed Korso forward ten paces before stopping. Another beep tone, and Korso heard the door begin to close behind him. Quezada then did the rotation thing again, one way, then the other, and so on. Not enough to cause vertigo this time, but by the end of it Korso had no idea from which direction he'd come.

'Okay,' Quezada said, 'you can remove the goggles now.'

Keeping his eyes closed, Korso reached for the strap with his free hand and carefully removed the goggles from his face. The sudden influx of light stung his eyelids. Slowly, he began to open them.

He was standing in the middle of some kind of safe room, or panic room. Most billionaires had one hidden away on their properties, although Korso doubted any of them were quite like this.

The room was about twenty-five feet square, with irregular-shaped stone feature walls and ceiling, making it seem as though the whole thing had been carved out of rock. Illumination came from down-lights expertly hidden in the cracks of the stone ceiling above. In the centre of the room, right next to Korso, were a sleek modern work desk and a director's chair, along with a plush ottoman beside it. He set the goggles down on the desk as he looked around. A pair of comfortable-looking settees faced each other from either end of the room. Next to one settee was an open door, showing part of a corridor and more doorways beyond. In front of one of the remaining walls were eight oblong marble plinths, probably steel-reinforced like the walls, with all but one bearing a museum-quality glass display unit. Contained within each of these was a unique treasure of some kind.

One contained an old untitled book resting on a wooden stand. Another contained an intricately designed gold crown. Another contained a centuries-old Chinese vase. He had no idea what dynasty, but assumed it was one of the rarest ones.

Korso's heart jumped a beat when his eyes fell on the fourth display case. Under the glass was a knife. It was positioned at a slight angle over a black mount fixed to the base, with a double-T steel wire armature holding it in place. It looked ancient, with a handle made from polished white bone. Unfortunately, that was as much as he was able to verify. The blade itself was concealed within a plain black wooden scabbard. None of it was visible, so there was no way of telling if it was jade or not, and he wasn't about to ask. The less interest he showed in the dagger, the better for his continued health. But he did notice that none of the display cases had locks on them. At least, none that were visible.

He turned to the opposite wall and saw numerous framed pieces of art, along with various other collectibles. In one frame, the smallest on the wall, he recognised a page from one of Leonardo da Vinci's codices, featuring the familiar reversed handwriting and five small engineering diagrams. He saw two much larger pieces that looked like Picassos from his early Cubist period, and probably were. Another frame contained a Manet still life, of a vase of flowers standing alongside five oranges. In stark contrast to these paintings was a copy of the iconic *Action Comics #1* from 1938, already sealed within its own airtight CGC-graded case. Korso noticed the grade was 9.4, which would make it the most pristine copy in existence. There was more on the wall. Much more. He spent a few minutes looking at everything.

'This is a lot to take in in one go,' Korso said. He turned to see Quezada watching him with a faint smile on his face. 'I thought I'd seen all Leonardo's codex pages, but I've never seen that piece before.'

'Few people have. But it's a beauty, isn't it? And I've always loved his mirror writing, at least on an aesthetic level. It just looks right, for some reason. They say he mastered the skill to prevent competitors from stealing his ideas, but I doubt someone of his genius would have used such a simple code. It doesn't fit in with his character.'

'I agree,' Korso said. 'He probably wrote that way just because he could. Those two Picassos are magnificent, by the way. How early are they?'

'The one on the left was painted in early 1910, shortly after he and Braque pioneered the Cubist movement. The other dates from early 1912.'

'And over there on the right, that's a Cézanne?'

'You have a good eye. What about this vase here? Can you identify the dynasty?'

Korso came over and studied the ornament, taking careful note of the intricate fish carvings and the yellow and cyan colouring. Chinese history wasn't really his area of expertise, but he knew just enough to get by. 'Late eighteenth century would be my guess. And that's only a guess.' When Quezada gave an affirmative nod, Korso said, 'Qing Dynasty?'

'Well done.'

Korso stepped over to the display case containing the unidentified hardcover book. 'But I'm really fascinated by this volume here. There's no title on the spine or the front, but in my estimation it looks over five hundred years old.'

'You're very close. This book was actually published in 1543, part of an initial print run of between four- to five-hundred copies.'

As soon as Korso heard the date, he knew. 'Copernicus' *On the Revolutions of the Heavenly Spheres*, the first time anybody publicly dared to theorise that the earth wasn't the centre of all things. I've never seen a first edition in such good condition...' He paused.

'Something bothers you?' Quezada asked.

'Well, as rare as this book is, I also know there are two hundred and seventy-six other first editions just like it still in existence. Yet almost everything else in this room is unique in some way or another. So I'm naturally curious as to what makes this volume so special. Unless...'

Quezada just looked at him. 'Unless?'

'Well, I know that the editor added a short preface to the original manuscript, against the wishes of Copernicus' disciples. And I know that one of them, Rheticus, used red ink to cross through the offending text in as many copies as he could get his hands on. It was probably only a handful, though, since only one recorded copy is known to have survived.'

'You're looking at the one surviving copy.'

'Amazing,' Korso said, shaking his head. 'I'm fast running out of superlatives.' He turned to the other wall again. 'I also see your copy of *Action Comics #1* is graded 9.4, yet I know for a fact that the highest recorded grade for that issue is 9.0. How's that even possible?'

'Anything's possible with money, Graves. Surely you realise that by now. Any time I have a piece graded or certified, I pay additional large sums to the relevant people, and they in turn make sure that all records concerning my particular piece are sealed or deleted from the record entirely. My privacy is worth any amount of money.'

'I can believe that.' Korso pointed at a space on the display wall that was marked only by two support hooks. 'Looks like something's missing there.'

'You're right. But hopefully for not much longer, and I've partly you to thank for that. That's one of the reasons I brought you here.'

'To help you fill it, you mean?'

Quezada gave him an enigmatic smile. 'Possibly, but we can discuss that all later.'

'Curiouser and curiouser. Not that I'm complaining, but what's the other reason for my being here?'

'The simple answer is I don't meet very many people who can truly appreciate my passion for the rare and obscure. Yet you struck me as one of the exceptions from our very first meeting.' He looked down at his Mayan ring. 'Few have even heard of King Pakal, yet when I mentioned his name you were able to give me a concise two-sentence summary of his life almost without thinking, and you're not even Guatemalan.'

Korso shrugged. 'As far as I'm concerned, history has no borders. I've always been fascinated by exceptional figures from the past, which is probably why I'm so good at what I do. And in my opinion, anybody who managed to live to the age of eighty, in an era where the average life expectancy was half that, automatically qualifies.'

'I completely agree,' Quezada said, glancing at his ring again. 'Although he was a great ruler too, let's not forget.'

'I'm just surprised that ring isn't on display in here, taking pride of place.'

'Well, this particular item has a special meaning to me. I've always felt a deep connection with Pakal, since he was a true survivor like myself, and wearing this always makes me feel closer to him in some way. As though he's giving me guidance almost. I never seem to tire of looking at it, either, which is rare for me.'

'Can I ask where you got it?'

'Via public auction, like most of the items in here. This once was at Sotheby's of London, almost seven years ago. A descendant of Alberto Ruz Lhuillier, the archaeologist who discovered Pakal's burial chamber, had come into possession of some of her great uncle's discoveries, including a number of smaller pieces from the tomb that never reached museums. This ring was the most important of those finds, since she also had written corroboration from Lhuillier that it had been found on the third finger of Pakal's right hand. Naturally, as soon as I learned of this I wanted the ring, and no price was too high.' He motioned towards the rest of the room. 'As you can see, I generally get what I want.'

Korso surveyed the room once more. 'There is somebody else who'd appreciate this room as much as me, you know.'

'You mean Alejandra?' Quezada smiled. 'Maybe she already has.'

Korso let that one go. His gaze fell on the partially open doorway that hinted at more rooms beyond. 'You seem to have all the comforts of home in here. Assuming we aren't already back *in* your home, that is. We could be anywhere on your compound.'

'Which is the whole idea. A great man once said, "Your secret is your prisoner; to reveal it you become its slave", a sentiment I wholeheartedly agree with. I'm the only living person who knows the location of this room, and that's how it'll stay.'

As Korso let his eyes sweep the room again, a frown began to appear on his brow. 'Wait a second. Something's not right here.'

Quezada gave a small semblance of a smile. 'I was wondering when you'd notice.'

Korso approached the nearest wall and peered closely at the stonework, sometimes moving his fingers along the cool surface. He did the same with the others. But, except for the doorway, the surfaces of all four walls were completely smooth, with not a crack in sight. 'I don't see any joins at all. Where's the entrance?'

'If I didn't tell you how we arrived, why would I reveal how we leave? Speaking of which, it's time you put those goggles back on. It's already late, and I've still got a lot to do.'

Grabbing the welding mask from the desktop, Korso took a final look around Quezada's inner sanctum, allowing his gaze to briefly slide over the dagger again. The length of the knife was right, matching the dimensions Verhoeven had given him. The handle also fitted the description, thus ticking two boxes out of a possible three. But the blade itself still remained a mystery. The only way he was going to know for sure whether it was jade or not was by doing what he'd set out to do: come back and check for himself.

Which presented a whole new set of problems.

But at least now he knew the vault actually existed. And its existence also confirmed Korso's theory as to why Quezada had no CCTV cameras within the compound. Security cameras inevitably meant the use of security guards to keep watch, and Quezada was too paranoid to allow anyone to see him travelling to and from his private hideaway whenever he felt the urge. But that lack of electronic surveillance would also work in Korso's favour.

Assuming he was right, of course. Nothing could be taken for granted. Not with someone like Quezada. Who was already checking his watch. It was clear from the man's expression that his patience was running out. So Korso quickly placed the goggles over his face and, for the second time that day, entered a world of complete and utter darkness.

THIRTY

The walk back was just as protracted and confusing as before. Once again, Korso heard no human voices at any point along the journey. But he did hear the familiar nocturnal cawing of chachalacas and toucans all around him, which suggested he'd been inside longer than he realised. The air felt a lot cooler too.

After about fifteen minutes of walking in various directions, Quezada finally brought them to halt, and said, 'You can take them off now.'

Removing the goggles, Korso saw they were right back where they'd started: in the garden outside Quezada's relaxation room. Night had already fallen. He checked his watch, saw it was quarter to seven. The numerous street lamps scattered around the property had already been turned on, giving the whole compound a serene residential feel. The sound of distant sirens was the only clue that they were still within city limits.

'I advise you not to mention this little excursion to anyone,' Quezada said, taking the goggles back. 'You don't strike me as the garrulous type, but I'm giving you fair warning regardless.'

'No warning necessary, Mr Quezada. I don't think anyone would believe me anyway. So when do you want to talk about filling that blank space on the wall?'

'Tomorrow at noon, in my office. I'll give you all the relevant details then.'

'I'll be here.'

'Just make sure you're on time. You know your way to Alex's house?'

'Well, it all looks a little different at night, but I should be able to find it okay.' He pointed south-west. 'It's in that direction, right?'

Quezada gave an affirmative nod. 'Just keep moving in a straight line, and make sure not to veer off the track at any point. Do you understand me?'

'Couldn't be any clearer, Mr Quezada.'

'And remember what I said about Alex. Treat her as you would that Qing vase I showed you.'

'I won't forget.'

With a curt nod, Quezada turned away and opened the sliding doors to the room they'd left while Korso turned in the direction of Alex's bungalow and began walking. Contrary to what he'd said, Korso knew exactly where he was going. His internal compass rarely let him down, and over the years he'd learned to trust it implicitly. Since he knew the annex building was between the main house and Alex's, he made sure to make a wide detour around it, just in case Quezada was keeping an eye on him. You could never be too careful.

A few minutes later he saw the little bungalow he'd seen before, almost completely enveloped by the surrounding trees. The lamp post just beyond the front patio provided more than enough light to see by. Korso saw the lights were on in the house as well. He approached the front door and when he didn't see a bell, knocked twice.

Seconds later, the door was opened and Alex appeared, wearing a tight-fitting one-shoulder black dress that ended just above her knees. She'd also straightened her hair and made up her face, but still wore her spectacles. Korso thought she looked ravishing.

'Hi, I wasn't expecting you so soon,' she said, fiddling with a hoop earring. 'I'm still getting ready. Come on in.'

'You already look ready,' he said, following her into the house. 'Why try and improve on perfection?'

'Oh, just keep talking that way and you and I'll get along just fine.'

Closing the door behind him, Korso entered a modest-sized living room area as Alex dashed off through another doorway. 'I won't be a minute,' she called out. 'If you want a drink or anything, the kitchen's on your right. There's some iced tea in the fridge.'

'I'm good, thanks.'

The living room was furnished simply with a modern settee, two matching easy chairs and a glass coffee table. A huge LCD screen practically took up one wall. There were no other decorations, no ornaments or houseplants, no framed pictures. No personality. It looked like a room in an upscale hotel. He perched on one of the chairs and listened to the tinny samba music coming from the bedroom, probably from her phone.

Looking down at his navy polo shirt and grey working chinos, he felt distinctly underdressed after seeing Alex in her evening wear. But that would give him a genuine reason to stop off at his hotel before they went out. There were a few other things he needed in addition to a change of clothes. His LED penlight for one, as well as a few other essential items he'd have to find quickly. The hotel might have what he wanted. If not, a few notes in the right hands would do it. The rest he'd play by ear.

A little later, Alex emerged from the bedroom looking just as pretty as before, and proclaimed herself ready. They left the bungalow. She didn't bother locking the front door. As they began walking in the direction of the garage, she asked, 'So is your business with Miguel finished?'

'For today. But he wants to see me again tomorrow at noon, so it seems I'll be around for a while yet.' They walked a while. 'He also left me with a warning. About you.'

'Really? What did he say?'

'That I should treat you with kid gloves, or words to that effect. He seems very protective of you.'

She gave a derisive snort. 'The last time I looked, I was a grown adult. I don't need anyone looking out for my welfare, but you try telling Miguel that. He thinks none of us can possibly survive when we're outside these four walls away from his oversight.' She shook her head, and murmured under her breath, 'If he only knew.'

'Knew what?'

She smiled at him. 'Doesn't matter. Are you hungry? I know a place in Zone 10 that does the best *plato tipico* in the city. And afterwards, there's a newly opened club that I've been wanting to try out. More lounge than club, really. Their house band's supposed to be pretty great, and I'd like to see for myself.'

'Sound good to me. Can we stop off at my hotel first? I'd like to change out of my work clothes before we eat.'

'You waited for me. It's only fair I do the same for you. Equality, right?'

'Very progressive of you.'

'I try my best. Let's pick it up a bit, shall we? I'm ravenous.'

THIRTY-ONE

At the hotel, Alex nursed a sangria mocktail in the downstairs bar while Korso went up to his room and quickly changed into a black long-sleeved shirt, black trousers, and dark jacket. He also stocked up on a few items he might, or might not, need. It was always best to be prepared. A brief visit to the hotel gift shop supplied him with the final two items on his list, both of which fitted easily in his jacket pocket.

Once they were back in the car, Alex gave him accurate directions to Zone 10, and they arrived at their destination fifteen minutes later. The whole street was lined with restaurants of the upscale variety, but the one they wanted was the only place with a tuxedoed doorman outside the front entrance. As Korso found them a parking space nearby, he said, 'You sure we'll get a table? It looks packed in there.'

'Don't worry,' Alex said. 'They know me. Anyway, I booked ahead.'

They approached the restaurant on foot. The doorman saw Alex coming and greeted her like an old friend, opening the door for them both. Once inside, a grinning maître d' also recognised Alex and immediately led them to an empty table for two. It seemed to be the only empty table left. The whole place had a modern middle-eastern vibe, with plenty of gold everywhere and walls covered in Arabic street art. A colourful marimba band was playing upbeat jazz on a slightly elevated stage in the middle of the room, while around them couples and groups noisily enjoyed their meals.

Alex ordered some white wine for them both. The maître d' went away.

'Good choice of venue,' Korso said. 'I just hope the food lives up to the décor.'

'Trust in me, Ricardo. I know all the best places. I've been meaning to ask, do you prefer Ricardo or Ric?'

'Whatever works for you, Alex. I'm easy.'

'Ric, then. In my book, one syllable's always preferable to three.' They watched the band for a while in comfortable silence. A waiter came with a menu and a bottle of wine. He opened it at the table and poured them each a glass. Alex waved the menu away and ordered the speciality of the house for each of them.

'Hope you don't mind,' she said.

'Not at all. I trust in you.' Korso clinked glasses with Alex and toasted their continued good health. He sipped his wine, then said, 'I've been wanting to ask you a question since we first met, but I honestly don't know how you'll take it.'

'Is the question personal?'

'Aren't they all?'

She chuckled. 'Good point. Well, you won't know until you try.'

'Okay, it's about your boss, Mr Quezada. Or Miguel, as you refer to him. You do know what he does, right?'

'Of course, I've been handling his paperwork for almost a decade, remember?'

'I meant the side of his business that doesn't require paperwork.'

She blinked at him over her glass. 'I'd have to be pretty dumb not to be aware of how he really makes his living, wouldn't I? I only need to key two words into a search box and there it all is, right in front of my face, often from hugely reliable sources.'

'So my question is, how do you feel about that?'

'How do I feel?' She thought for a moment. 'Not sure how to answer that one. Maybe I'll tell you when I get to know you better. *If* I get to know you better.' She smiled. 'In any case, I could ask you the very same question, couldn't I?'

'You wouldn't believe me if I told you.'

'Wouldn't I? Interesting. Okay, perhaps we'll leave that for another time. But there is something else I want to ask you.'

'Go ahead.'

'Are you married?'

'Straight for the jugular. I like that. No, I'm not. And I don't foresee it ever happening in my lifetime.'

She tilted her head. 'And why's that?'

'I move around a lot, sometimes at a moment's notice. That kind of lifestyle's not really conducive to a long-term relationship.'

'That's a little more honesty than I expected, Ric. So what does that make me? A prospective one-night stand or something?'

'Hopefully more than that. I can still like you without wanting to marry you, can't I? They aren't mutually exclusive. Anyway, you're too smart to marry somebody like me.'

She gave a snort. 'Nobody's smart when it comes to affairs of the heart, don't you know that? I've made my share of mistakes over the years. None of us are infallible.'

'You're referring to Ozan?'

She sighed. 'You had to bring up his name, didn't you? And we were getting along so well. Yes, Javier was a major error of judgement on my part, I have to admit. What can I say? He caught me at a weak moment, that's all. But at least when I realised my mistake I had the good sense to end it quickly, before things had a chance to get serious. Not that that's stopped him from trying to continue where we left off, of course. He's not someone who easily takes no for an answer.'

'I've noticed that.'

'I'll bet you have. So, has he caused you any problems yet?'

'Well, he tried flexing his muscles with me initially, but backed down some when I brought your name up as a potential ally when dealing with Mr Quezada. I might also have mentioned how you'd more or less agreed to a date with me. I don't think he liked that.'

'Did he warn you to stay away from me at pain of death? He does that.'

'More or less.' Korso shrugged. 'Since then we've kept our distance whenever possible, although he still shoves the needle in at every opportunity.'

'And that doesn't bother you?'

'About as much as a little dog yapping at me at the end of the street bothers me.'

Her face grew serious. 'You shouldn't underestimate him, Ric. Javier's anything but a harmless little dog.'

'I know that.'

'So, regarding this mysterious research project of yours, was Miguel satisfied with your results?'

'It sure looks that way. He says he's got another project for me tomorrow.'

'In which case, Javier already knows about it. And that means he'll hate you even more now.'

'I'm not sure that's possible.'

'Oh, believe me, it is. He can hold grudges like nobody I've ever known, and the last thing he's doing is wishing you more success. As far as he's concerned, you're this dirty outsider who's dared to trespass on his personal domain, and the sooner you're completely removed from the equation, the better. And you can believe he'll already be thinking up ways to achieve that, probably right at this very moment.'

Korso sipped some more of his wine and sat back in his seat. Alex was correct, of course. The only surprising part was that Alex was openly suggesting it herself. He hadn't expected her to be this honest with someone she barely knew.

While he was musing on that, their waiter returned, carrying a large, loaded tray. He carefully arranged their dishes of grilled pork and beef, stewed beans, chismol, fried plantain and rice on the table, wished them a pleasant meal, and left again. It all smelled wonderful.

After a few mouthfuls, Korso said, 'You're right, the food easily surpasses the décor.'

'Told you.'

As they ate, Korso said, 'Alex, I know Mr Quezada likes to take a close interest in your life, but how much of what you and I discuss tonight will actually get back to him?'

'What you mean is, exactly how much will I tell him?'

'I'm just curious, that's all. For someone so naturally paranoid, Mr Quezada seems surprisingly open to a stranger like myself spending quality time with someone he clearly cares about, who also knows every aspect of his private and business life. That strikes me as out of character. Unless it's not. No offence.'

She snorted again. 'I love it. You're practically accusing me of being Miguel's personal informant, but I shouldn't be offended?'

'I'm not doing very well, am I?'

'Don't worry.' She waved it away. 'Honesty means a lot more to me than manners, and besides, it's a fair question. Miguel wanted to know all about our conversation at the front of the house, that very first evening we met. Did you know that?'

'I suspected. He probed me about it as well, and I got the distinct impression he already knew the answers before I told him.'

'He did. But that's Miguel for you. He demands to know everything about everybody, which is one of the reasons why he finds you so interesting. You're still very much an enigma to him, and he doesn't meet many of those anymore. As for what goes on tonight, he'll know exactly what I want him to know, and only that. I know when to give and when to hold back. We all have our little secrets, don't we?'

'We wouldn't be human if we didn't,' he said.

They resumed eating. The waiter returned and silently refilled their wine glasses, then left them again.

'That guy's getting a good tip,' Korso said.

Alex nodded. 'They always seem to appear at the exact moment you want them to, don't they? Just one of the reasons I like it here.'

'So did you know Miguel before he met Luana?'

'A year or so before. Why?'

'Speaking of enigmas, she's another one.' He told her about his one and only encounter with Luana, when Nilsa tried to persuade her father to join them for lunch. 'While Miguel was all smiles with his daughter, it seemed to me that he was almost keeping his wife at arm's length. Like he was displeased with her over something. Maybe they'd simply had a row that morning, but it seemed to go deeper than that. Or maybe I'm just overthinking things again.'

Alex had already finished her food, and sipped her wine as she looked at the couples dining at the surrounding tables, all of whom were busily engaged in their own conversations. 'You're not overthinking things. I don't think he's displeased with Luana so much as... actually, I don't know what word to use. I know he still loves his wife, but now there's an underlying sadness between the two them, and it's been like that for the last six years.'

Korso finished dabbing the last of the sauce with a piece of flatbread, and looked up at her. 'Six years is a very specific period of time.'

'Isn't it?' She continued sipping her wine as she studied him. 'Let me ask you this. Do you have any idea how disappointing it is for someone in Miguel's position to be father to three beautiful daughters, and yet still have no male heir?'

'Well, I wouldn't automatically discount any of the daughters from following in his footsteps. Hardness of character isn't defined by gender. Some of the toughest people I've ever met have been women.'

'I couldn't agree more,' she said, a slight upturn at the corner of her mouth. 'But in Guatemala the male still rules the roost to a large extent, and Miguel wants nothing more than to carry on with that tradition. His daughters are the apples of his eye, and he'll do his best to ensure they remain as pure and virginal as they can, for as long as they can.'

'Okay, but Luana's still young. What's the problem with trying again? The law of averages is with them.'

'Not anymore. There were some complications when Anna was born three years ago, and the doctors informed Luana she couldn't have any more children after that. But that's not the reason for Miguel's change of behaviour towards her.'

'So what is?'

'They had a son… and they lost him.'

THIRTY-TWO

Korso didn't try to hide his surprise. This was a brand-new wrinkle, one that had even evaded Verhoeven's net. 'Lost him?' he said. 'You mean a miscarriage?'

'Worse even than that. He died in his sleep, just a few hours after entering this world. Sudden Infant Death Syndrome they called it, but nobody ever really knew the exact cause. One second he just stopped breathing, and that was that. They tried everything to get his heart beating again, but nothing worked. Miguel's never really gotten over his death, although you'd never know it.'

'And this happened six years ago?'

She nodded.

'You were with them at the hospital?'

Alex shook her head. 'No hospitals. Once Miguel found out Luana was carrying his son, he became obsessed with her safety and not only forbade her to leave the compound, but kept her pregnancy a complete secret from everyone outside of the immediate family. He had one of the houses converted into a fully operational maternity unit just for her. He also recruited a handpicked medical team and midwife to stay on site for the full term, in case of emergencies. One week before the due date, they moved Luana into the sterile unit and she was under constant medical supervision from then on. When she finally went into labour, the conditions couldn't have been more favourable. I wasn't there, but I heard the delivery went as smoothly as anyone could have hoped for. But still the baby died. Poor little thing.'

Korso sat back in his chair. No wonder this little detail had slipped past Verhoeven's radar. Nobody outside the compound knew the first thing about it. Only the medical team knew the whole story, and pay-offs combined with fear of reprisals would ensure they wouldn't talk to anyone. Which made it all the more surprising that Alex was revealing it to him now.

'No offence,' he said, 'but if this is such a big secret, how come you're privy to it?'

'Well… I was having some personal problems a few years back – it wasn't Javier, before you ask – and I wasn't dealing with it very well, and it was affecting my work. So one day Miguel locked the office door and got out an expensive bottle of whiskey from his cabinet and said I was going to keep drinking until I'd gotten it all out of my system and we'd found a solution to whatever was ailing me. After a while he decided to join me, and it wasn't long before we were both absolutely blitzed. But before we passed out, he started telling me in great detail about the son he lost, which was probably the first time he'd ever opened up about it to anyone. But by the time we finally got our senses back the following day Miguel was already acting as though nothing had happened. To be honest, he was so drunk he probably forgot what he'd said, and I wasn't about to bring the subject up again.'

'Probably a wise move.' Korso already knew the hidden connection between the two of them, and why Quezada had confided in Alex, but decided now wasn't the time to bring it up. Maybe never. 'What about Luana? How did she take it?'

'Miguel said she dropped into a deep depression that lasted for months. Of course, Miguel, being the alpha male, just kept it all inside and went on with life and kept himself busy with work. But after that confession I finally understood why, on a certain day every year, Miguel just disappears for twenty-four hours straight. Nobody sees him until the following morning. He never tells anyone where he's been and nobody ever dares to ask.'

Korso had a fair idea where Quezada spent those missing twenty-four hours. And he had an inclination he wasn't the only one. He decided to trust his instincts and risk it.

'I know where he goes,' he said. 'And so do you.'

She looked at him without expression. 'Is that so?'

'I believe it is. Tell me, what are your thoughts on Cezanne? Or Picasso, specifically his Cubist period?'

'I've never been much of a fan of still lives, but I could stare at a Picasso all day.' Alex carefully put down her glass and looked at him. 'So Miguel actually showed you his special room?'

Korso nodded. 'Shortly before I knocked on your door. I was heavily blindfolded during both journeys, which means it could be anywhere, for all I know.'

'Wow. That's… interesting. But what's even more interesting is the fact that you're telling me. Because if I know Miguel, he'd have warned you very severely not to speak a word of that room's existence to anyone. And that includes me.'

'He warned me, which means my life's effectively in your hands now. And that's not a figure of speech.'

'So why?'

'To prove a point.'

'Which is…?'

'Trust is a two-way street, Alex.' He shrugged. 'And since I doubt that Miguel would want the details of his infant son to be shared outside of his close inner circle, maybe this is simply my way of keeping us on a level pegging.'

'Well. We each seem to be learning all kinds of new things tonight, don't we?' Alex smiled as she raised her glass. Korso raised his too, and they clinked glasses. They drank.

'That's two large goblets you've had now,' she said, putting hers down. 'And this is a pretty strong wine. It's my opinion that you're no longer fit to drive.'

'You're right. I think it's taxis from here on in.'

'Along with cocktails, and loud music, and maybe a little cha-cha-cha,' she said, moving her shoulders in time with the last three words.

'All of those things sound appealing, as long as you're in there somewhere too.'

'Just no more talk of Miguel, okay? Or Javier. Or anyone else in the compound. That's not how I want this evening to go.'

'Deal.'

'Good.'

They watched the band for a while, and the waiter arrived to clear the table in readiness for dessert. Conversation soon turned to music, movies, likes, dislikes, all those subjects that normal people discussed when getting to know each other. They drank more wine, with Korso carefully pacing himself so he wouldn't get smashed. He was still here on business. As much as he enjoyed Alex's company, his main objective of retrieving the jade dagger was always at the forefront of his mind. And since opportunities invariably presented themselves when you least expected them, he needed to be in command of his faculties at all times.

Once Korso paid for the meal, they left the restaurant and took a taxi to Zone 3. The place she'd heard about was called the Bajo Centro Lounge, located in a side street just off 12 Calle. It didn't look like much from the outside, with just the bare minimum of neon. Inside, the bar was small and dimly lit, with plenty of booths and tables scattered around. The place was only half full, but Alex said it was still early and would get likely busier as the night went on. There was a long bar running along one side, and a small stage at the end of the room. A five-piece group were playing some kind of chilled-out funk thing that had the clientele nodding their heads as they drank and smoked. Several couples, drinks in hand, were dancing in the small open area in front of the stage.

Alex took Korso's hand and led him to the bar. She ordered cocktails for each of them, smiling as she moved her shoulders in time with the groove. 'Those guys aren't bad at all,' she said. 'Nice funky backbeat, and I like that bassline too.'

'Looks like you've picked another winner,' he said.

'*Alex*,' a feminine voice screamed from behind them. 'Hey, is that really you?'

Korso turned at the voice and saw two young couples sitting in a booth against the opposite wall. One of the women, heavily made up and with bright orange hair, was already half out of her seat as she stared wild-eyed at Alex.

'*Malina?*' Alex said, a look of disbelief on her face. 'No *way*.'

'It's me, baby.' Malina rushed over and clasped Alex in a bear hug. 'In full living colour. Jesus, where the hell have you been all these years? I missed you.'

'I missed you too,' Alex said, hugging her back just as tightly.

When they finally let go of one another, they began arguing about how long it had been. At some point, Alex introduced Korso as her date, and the three of them made their way back to the booth, where more introductions were made. Alex didn't know the other three, but everyone was friendly and it wasn't long before they were all getting along as though they'd known each other from the cradle. The bartender brought the cocktails over and went away with orders for more. And more after that. There was much talking and laughter, accompanied by even more drinking.

Although Korso consciously held back from getting too tipsy, Alex had no such inhibitions and was clearly enjoying being with people who wanted nothing more from her than good company. As the evening progressed, the cocktails gradually got stronger and more plentiful. Korso and Alex took to the cramped little dance floor often, sticking especially close to each other during the slower numbers. Korso wasn't much of a dancer and was just content to let Alex lead the way and make all the moves. And she seemed to know a great many of those.

The hours passed quickly. As the place became busier, smokier and noisier, Korso and Alex became progressively more lascivious and wanton with each other.

They were doing a slow writhing shimmy to one number when Alex moved in even closer and put her arms around

Korso's shoulders. He wrapped his around her waist and their lips met, still moving in time with the beat. When they finally came up for air, she said, 'So, are we having fun?'

He shook his head. 'Worst night of my life so far.'

She laughed, kissed him again. 'Smooth talker. You're not quite as drunk as you make out, are you?'

'Most people aren't. I notice you're no longer slurring your words either.'

'I'm pleasantly inebriated, without actually being wasted. I've got a pretty high threshold for alcohol, amongst other things. But then, I had years of practice.'

'You mean with Malina back there?'

'Her, and others. Believe it or not I was a very bad girl back in the day, managed to get up to all kinds of mischief.'

'I can believe it.'

'Except I happen to be thinking of a different kind of mischief right now.' She kissed him again, for longer this time.

'You're not the only one,' he said, once he was able to speak.

'So the question is, where to next? Yours or mine? I have to admit, I've never been inside the Hilton before. Is it nice?'

'It's just a hotel room, much like any other.' He checked his watch, saw it was almost one-thirty in the morning. 'But since I've got an early conference with you-know-who nine hours from now, I'm thinking your bungalow might be a better bet. If that's okay with you.'

'That's fine with me. Come on, let's split.'

Korso waited as Alex said her goodbyes to Malina and the others. Once outside, it only took them five minutes to find a taxi, and when the cab driver finally pulled up in front of the arched gates of the compound, Korso was genuinely surprised to discover twenty minutes had passed them by. He and Alex had spent the entire journey wrapped up in each other, paying little attention to the outside world.

After paying the driver, he and Alex were buzzed through the side door. Thanks to her presence, Korso was given a very brief body search by a guard he'd never seen before, and then they were allowed in. They strolled back to her bungalow in each other's arms, talking little, encountering nobody else on the way. Other than the omnipresent buzzing sounds of cicadas, the whole compound was quiet.

As soon as Alex let them into the bungalow, they grappled messily with each other's clothing as they quickly made their way to the master bedroom.

And for the next hour or so, that's where they stayed.

THIRTY-THREE

Korso stared up at the ceiling and listened to Alex's breathing. She was snuggled up against him with her head close to his, one arm across his chest. It had been the perfect end to a very enjoyable evening. Afterwards, she'd advised him to regather his strength before their next go round, and then within seconds she'd fallen asleep herself. That had been ten minutes ago. Her breathing pattern was now slow and regular, signalling that she'd entered the non-REM stage of her sleep cycle. Korso reached over for his watch on the bedside table, saw it was 3.26 a.m. Just over two hours until sunrise.

Enough time. He hoped.

Carefully disentangling himself from Alex's arms, Korso slowly slid out of the bed and looked around the room. His clothes were still on the floor where he'd dropped them. He picked them all up, taking extra care with the jacket containing his car keys and the other items. Walking on the balls of his feet, he carried everything into the living room and quickly got dressed. He went back and peered into the bedroom. Alex was in the same position, her breathing still steady and regular. With any luck, her alcohol intake would ensure her sleep remained undisturbed for the next few hours.

He gently pulled the door closed and returned to the living room. The streetlamp outside provided more than enough light to see by. He retrieved the items from his jacket pocket and set them carefully down on the coffee table: his small LED flashlight, a basic multi-tool complete with scissor attachment, three thick elastic bands and two folded packs of cellophane gift wrap. The last five items he'd picked up at the hotel gift shop. He removed the plastic packaging from the packs of gift wrap and unfolded the cellophane sheets until they were flat on the table. One sheet was blue, the other purple.

Unfolding the scissors from his multi tool, Korso cut two small square sections from the purple sheet and one from the blue. Each section was roughly two inches square. He placed the first purple section over the lens of the flashlight, followed by the blue sample, and then the second purple piece. The order didn't actually matter, just the ratio of purple to blue. Holding the sheets tightly with one hand so they completely covered the light source, Korso used an elastic band to secure them to the flashlight, twisting the elastic a few times to ensure everything was as tight as possible.

Now he had a black light.

Korso took out his wallet and extracted a 200 quetzales bill. He switched on the flashlight and aimed the ultraviolet beam at the note. Thanks to the special UV ink embedded in the banknote, the perched quetzel bird, the coat of arms, the Mayan glyph, and the security strip shone in all their fluorescent blue-and-white glory.

Perfect. He pocketed all his items and put on his shoes.

He opened the front door and stepped outside. Everything was the same as before. But for the ever-present chirruping of the cicadas, the whole compound was silent. A quarter moon was visible in the almost cloudless sky. Not much natural light, but better than nothing. Keeping out of the range of the LED lamp post twenty feet away, Korso stepped off the patio and began walking in a north-easterly direction.

He thought back to when Alex had first shown him around. From her bungalow, she'd led him through a large gap in the trees somewhere ahead, and after they'd emerged from cover they made their way down a narrow dirt track that was almost hidden between some juniper conifers. Not that easy to find in the daylight, let alone the middle of the night. And he wasn't about to risk turning on his flashlight. It wouldn't be much help in its current configuration anyway. He'd just have to trust his internal compass.

He kept walking.

Shortly, he came to the grouping of trees he remembered. He walked along the border until he found the large gap he wanted, stepped into the deeper shadows of the trees and kept going in the same direction. A few seconds later, the sky briefly became visible again and he spotted the small grouping of juniper trees to his right. The dirt track took a little longer to locate, but after that it was a matter of simply staying on course.

When he emerged out into the open again, he saw the single-storey annex building directly ahead of him. There were no lights in this part of the compound, but there was enough moonlight for Korso to make out the familiar portico entrance with the two support columns on either side.

He was about to walk towards it when he heard a faint rustling sound to his right.

Korso crouched down immediately, placing one hand on the ground for support. He didn't move another muscle. Tuning out the white noise of the cicadas, he listened hard. He soon heard the rustling sound again. It was coming from the same direction, off to his right. Maybe twenty, thirty feet away. It was hard to be sure. But it sounded like someone, or something, moving through foliage. Possibly one of the compound residents, suffering from insomnia and out for a midnight walk. Or maybe nothing but a cat out on his nightly prowl, or a couple of birds mating. He strained to hear a voice, or specific sounds of movement, some clue as to the cause of the noise.

Nothing.

He waited.

Korso had dressed all in black for this very reason. The tree cover behind him meant anyone looking in this direction would just see nothing but a dark shape, more or less indistinguishable from the trees. Breathing only through his mouth, Korso didn't move an inch. A minute passed. Two. Then came the same rustling noise again. Leaves being disturbed. It was hard to judge distances in the dark, but the sounds definitely seems closer than before.

In his peripheral vision, he spotted movement to his right. Maybe twenty feet away from his position. He slowly turned his head a few inches, and soon saw what looked like a human male shape moving in the direction of the front gates. The shape was mostly obscured thanks to the thick foliage between them, but Korso could make out the pale clothing well enough. It was hard to miss. The shape stopped moving. Korso didn't make a sound, didn't move a millimetre. He just listened. After a few seconds, he heard a man's voice speaking, but was unable to make out the actual words.

Had to be one of Quezada's men. But was he making a regular patrol of the grounds, or was he responding to a sighting of Korso? As far as he could tell, the tone sounded offhand and casual, but he couldn't be sure. The man stopped speaking. After a few more seconds, the shape moved off until it was soon lost from view.

Still breathing through his mouth, Korso remained in the same position. He wasn't about to rush into things.

Finally, after three more minutes, Korso felt confident the danger had passed. He slowly got to his feet and continued walking towards the annex building, looking in all directions as he went. If there was one, there could be others. And the patrols could be hourly. Security cameras or no, Korso couldn't afford to let his guard down for a second.

At the glass entrance doors, he stopped and peered into the hallway beyond. It was dark in there. But was it also locked at night? He'd brought a few of his lockpick tools along with him, but they only worked on simple tumbler mechanisms, and he doubted the locks on these were standard. With a mental shrug, he grabbed the steel handle on the right-hand door, and pulled.

The door opened freely. So Alex had been right, after all.

Korso entered the building, took two steps and stopped. Now for the moment of truth.

He pulled the flashlight from his pocket and switched it on. Crouching down, he aimed the UV light at the tiled floor and moved it around a little. And there, right in front of him, glowing blue-white like a beacon in the darkness, was a small splash of dried liquid. And then another one, just a few feet further on.

When Quezada had presented him with the blacked-out goggles yesterday, Korso had had to think fast. He knew there was a decent chance that Quezada was going to show him his inner sanctum, and if so, this would be his one and only chance to get a lead as to its location. So when he'd asked for a soft drink from the fridge, he'd picked the tonic water for a very specific reason. And that reason was the quinine that gave the citrus drink its bitter taste. And quinine, like semen or urine or blood, was known to contain fluorescent molecules that show up under a UV light.

Once Quezada led him into this building, Korso had begun sipping his drink with far more regularity than before. Whenever he took liquid through the straw, he spat small amounts onto the floor in front of him. Since Quezada was walking behind him, always pushing him onward, he couldn't actually see what Korso was up to. But Korso still kept it to a minimum, not wanting to push his luck. That was the main reason why he'd hoped Alex would invite him back tonight, before Quezada's cleaning staff had a chance to come and delete all evidence of his presence here.

He walked slowly down the hallway at a crouch, flashlight aimed at the floor, following the sporadic markings he'd left for himself. About halfway down, he found the sixth marker, but that's where it stopped. So it must have been close to that spot when Quezada spun him around and completely skewed his sense of direction. He turned to his left and saw the entrance to the display room. To his right, the entrance to the game room, while a little further down was the entrance to the spa. He turned left, towards the display area, continuously moving the light around the floor as he walked. But he saw no fluorescent markings. Not even inside the room itself.

And he knew for a fact that he'd spat out a little more tonic water right after Quezada pushed him onward. Which meant that wasn't the room. He returned to his starting point and continued moving the thin UV beam around the floor as he began walking very slowly towards the game room.

He'd just passed through the doorway when the black light picked up something on the floor. Korso bent down for a closer look and saw a tiny luminescent drop of dried solution, no bigger than the head of a match. But it was enough.

So the game room it was.

Korso turned and played the black light over the rest of the room. The UV beam wasn't all that strong, but he could just about make out the arcade machines against one wall, along with the pool and snooker tables that took up most of the central floor space. He began making his way slowly down the left side of the room, past the pool tables, checking every inch of the floor with the light. He spotted no more luminescent markers down there. But he was about halfway down the room when he caught a flash of something at the corner of his vision. At waist level.

He turned his beam towards the pool table directly to his right. The light highlighted another tiny splash on the side cushion, near the middle pocket. Encouraged, Korso continued down the room and eventually saw another small splash of quinine on the floor, next to the very last pool table. Beyond that was the bar area at the rear.

He moved around the L-shaped bar top and entered a larger-than-usual back bar area, with the huge fridge unit stacked against the rear wall. Moving the UV light around the floor, he suddenly paused at the sight of a badly smudged handprint, all lit up like it was Christmas morning. It was positioned close to the bar counter. Dotted around the palm print were a few more luminescent spots of dried quinine. Korso crouched down and laid his own hand on top of the print without actually touching it. It was the same size, and clearly caused after he'd squirted his palm with tonic water and 'accidentally' stumbled to the floor during Quezada's tour of the facility. It must have been the bar counter his back collided with when he fell.

So this was where they had ended up.

Korso got to his feet and stepped over to the refrigerator. It was a commercial six-footer, as tall as he was, and made from stainless steel. It was also on wheels. He reached around and got a hold of the back of the cabinet and tried pulling it away from the rear wall. It moved easily. The fridge slowly rolled outwards at a near-perfect 90-degree angle, the wheels on the tiles making the exact same rumbling sound he'd heard the previous evening. He also noticed a steel pull handle set into the rear of the fridge.

Shining his flashlight at the wall behind, Korso saw a twin electrical socket set a few inches off the floor. The main power lead from the fridge was plugged into the left-hand socket. The right socket was unused. Other than that, the wall was featureless. Except he knew it wasn't. It couldn't be. He ran his palm all over it, the polished stone cool against his skin. It felt smooth, with no evident cracks. Kneeling down, Korso slowly moved the flashlight beam along the skirting board at the base of the wall, looking for a switch or button, something that might reveal the keypad Quezada had used to access the safe room. But there was nothing there either.

Frowning to himself, Korso stepped back to the bar. It was made from marble. Under the counter on this side were four small storage cubicles. The middle two held empty glasses and tumblers, all neatly aligned in rows. The two on either side were empty. Korso crouched down and moved his flashlight around the first empty shelf and saw nothing except a few old rags. He tried the other empty shelf, running the beam all around the interior.

He stopped. Moved the light back. Something dark right at the rear, in the upper corner. Hard to make out. Could be a piece of dirt, or a spider, or anything. Korso reached in and felt around back there. His fingers finally touched something small, hard and smooth.

A switch.

Korso flicked it to the right. From behind him came a sound he recognised: an electronic *blip*.

He got to his feet again, aimed the flashlight, and saw a square section of the wall had slid away to reveal a standard keypad with twelve black buttons, five of which were highlighted by luminescent fingerprints.

He continued to watch, fascinated, as an automated drawer underneath the keypad slowly extended itself out from the wall towards him.

There were no accompanying sounds. No flashing green lights. Once the tray was fully extended from its slot, Korso saw it measured about ten centimetres square and one centimetre deep. It was made from some kind of metal, and it looked fairly solid. Other than a partial luminescent fingerprint in the centre, it was completely featureless with no further clues as to its purpose.

Although Korso had an idea about that.

The purpose of the keypad was a little more clear cut. Quezada would have wiped his hand after helping Korso up off the floor, but he couldn't get rid of all the traces of quinine Korso had transferred to his fingers. The evidence of that was looking right at him. The 1, 2, 3, 6 and 0 keys all glowed brightly under the UV beam, while the other keys – 4, 5, 7, 8, 9, *, # – all remained dark. So he now knew what numbers Quezada had pressed, but not the order, nor how many times that number was used.

But when he moved in closer, he saw that wasn't entirely accurate. The 0 and 1 keys had been pressed more than the other three. He saw three smudged fingerprints on the 1 key, and two more on the 0 key, but only one smudge on each of the others. Which would make the inputted numbers 1-1-1-0-0-6-3-2. In addition, Korso noticed three tiny holes on the top of the keypad. He shone the UV light down into one and saw a tiny reflection bouncing off something. So maybe they held LED indicator bulbs. No way of telling yet.

Odd that there was no digital display, though.

Or maybe not so strange. After all, Quezada had built this safe room for his own solitary use. He alone knew which numbers to press, and in which order, so why make it easier for anyone else to conceivably break in? Especially as nobody was supposed to be aware of the room's existence in the first place.

The tray was another matter. Korso studied the partial print in the centre without touching the surface. Except it wasn't a print, exactly. It looked like Quezada had merely brushed the side of his little finger against the surface as he did something else, leaving behind a faint smudge that would have gone unnoticed but for the wonders of a UV light. Korso thought back to the previous evening, remembering the eight tones he'd heard as Quezada entered the combination on the keypad. A few seconds after that, he'd heard what sounded like a metallic object making very light contact with another metallic object. Shortly after that, the safe room door had opened automatically.

Clearly, entering the combination was just the first part of the entry process, while this tray somehow constituted the second part. Since he'd heard Quezada placing something metallic on the tray that suggested it was a weighing scale. And undoubtedly a precision scale, accurate to three or four decimal places. So that being the case, once Quezada had entered his code he'd placed his personal totem on the scale, and as soon as the weight was logged and approved the door would automatically open. Open sesame, indeed.

But get the weight wrong, even by a milligram, and it was game over. Just because there were no security cameras on the grounds, that didn't automatically mean there were no alarms, and if Quezada ever found out someone had tried breaking into his inner sanctum he wouldn't have to look too far to find the culprit. And then Korso really was a dead man.

So it was all or nothing. Tricky.

As for this personal totem of Quezada's, that wasn't too hard to work out. Not only would it have to be something small and metallic, with a weight that never varied, but also it had to be something Quezada could get his hands on immediately. And only one item ticked all those boxes: that ancient gold Mayan ring he always wore. But therein lay the problem – if the man never took it off his finger, how could Korso possibly find out how much the damn thing weighed?

He was walking back to the bar and musing on the problem when he heard a faint squeak. It sounded like it was coming from elsewhere in the building. He froze mid step, waiting for the sound to repeat itself, but there was only silence. Korso slipped around the bar counter and kept close to the wall as he ran out of the room.

Out in the hallway, he came to a halt and turned towards the main entrance. The double doors were still closed. He turned a complete circle. No sign of anyone in any direction. He pursed his lips. He'd definitely heard something, but there was no way to be sure the sound had come from within these walls. It could have come from anywhere.

Frowning, he made his way back to the rear bar. Reaching under the counter again, he flipped the small switch back to its original position and breathed a sigh of relief as the small scale slid back into its slot in the wall. Then the square section of wall silently slid back into its original position, concealing all signs that anybody had been there at all. He ran his palm over the polished surface of the wall, and still couldn't figure out where the joins were. It really was an amazing piece of work.

Once he'd moved the refrigerator back to its original position, he opened the door and grabbed a bottle of mineral water.

After moistening one of the rags, he used it to completely wipe away his handprint on the floor. It had served its purpose. It might only be visible under a UV light, but Korso saw no reason to take unnecessary chances. He also wiped away all other traces of tonic water, not only from this room but from the hallway too.

Once he was done, he checked his watch and saw it was 4.30 a.m. Exiting the annex building, he made his way back to Alex's bungalow, all his senses on high alert as he kept a close eye on his surroundings. But he didn't see anyone. He didn't hear anyone. He reached the bungalow without incident, and entered the same way he'd left.

Stripping down to his boxers, he carried his clothes back to the bedroom and placed them on the floor. Alex, snoring lightly, was still lying in the same position as when he'd left her. He removed his boxers and slid between the sheets.

As he laid his head back on the pillow, Alex said, 'Welcome back.'

THIRTY-FOUR

'I thought you were asleep,' he said, keeping his voice relaxed.

'I was just about to say the same thing.' Her large eyes held his. She didn't look sleepy at all. 'I wake up and see you missing from my bed, along with all your clothes. It sure makes a girl wonder.'

Korso turned to her, touched her cheek. 'I just went for a late-night walk, that's all. I tend to do my best thinking during the hours of darkness.'

'Uh huh. Thinking about what, exactly?'

'About the day ahead, and what Mr Quezada might have in store for me next. Let me ask you something. Back when he showed you his special safe room, did you by chance notice a blank space on the display wall, marked by two display hooks?'

'I don't recall anything like that. Why?'

'Well, I did. And apparently I'm going to help him fill that space later on, although I've no idea what the item itself might be, or what I might have to do to obtain it. But I also have this strange feeling Ozan will be involved somehow, and that gives me cause for concern. Hence, the insomnia.'

'I see. Well, I'm glad you're taking my warnings about him seriously.'

'*A wise man will hear, and will increase learning,*' he said, embracing her again. He pulled her in closer. 'Seriously, Alex, what made you ever say yes to that guy in the first place? You must have known what he was like.'

She reached up and lightly rapped a knuckle against his forehead. 'You sure know how to kill the mood, don't you? What is it, like a super power?'

'I'll retract the question if you want.'

'No, I don't mind talking about it, though there's really not that much to tell. You're right, though. I was at a pretty low ebb at the time and wasn't really thinking clearly. Javier simply struck while the iron was hot. Isn't that what predators generally do?'

'What caused this low ebb?'

She sighed. 'Four years ago, someone I loved very much was taken away from me. Violently. Are you sure you want to hear this?'

'I asked, didn't I?'

'Let me ask *you* something then. Do you believe in that old term, "finding your soul mate"? That there's a perfect someone waiting for you somewhere in the world, and that sooner or later the fates will bring the two of you together?'

'Lots of people do. Can't say I'm one of them, though.'

'Well, I do. And I found mine. His name was Sander. He was a senior associate at one of the private equity firms Miguel uses, and I used to deal with him whenever Miguel needed information on a particular corporate concern he planned to invest heavily in. And from the moment we met, we just clicked. No other way to explain it. We enjoyed the same things, laughed at the same things, and so on and so on. So when Sander asked me out, I naturally said yes. We started dating regularly and it wasn't long before things started getting serious between the two of us, which was a whole new experience for me. We were just crazy about each other. When he finally asked me to move in with him, I told him I'd think about it. Which I did for all of five seconds. I'd have said yes to anything he wanted at that point. I already had our future life together all planned out.' She sighed. 'God, I loved him.'

Korso waited. When she didn't say anything further, he asked. 'What happened?'

'Sander was leaving his office building one evening, when three unidentified men approached him in the street. Witnesses said one pulled a gun while the other two threw a bed sheet over him. Then they hustled him into a car and drove off. That was the last time anybody saw him alive. I was at my apartment, waiting for him to come and collect me. We were supposed to be going out to a restaurant. The police got a description of the car, but none of the witnesses thought to take a shot of the licence plate. Or maybe it all happened too fast. Who knows? Anyway, the police didn't find the car. Even Miguel, with all his street contacts, couldn't get a single lead on the kidnappers.' She absently brushed a hand through her hair. 'Four days later, thanks to an anonymous tip, the police found Sander's remains in an abandoned warehouse way out in Zone 21. They said he'd been badly tortured, and that he'd died from three bullets to the head. His father and older brother ended up identifying the body. I couldn't bear to.'

'I'm sorry, Alex.'

She gave him a sad smile. 'Everybody was sorry. Especially Miguel. But as you can probably imagine, I was pretty much a zombie for months afterward, so it's not hard to understand why I succumbed to Javier's limited charms when he moved in on me. I don't think I really cared about anything at that point.' She shrugged. 'Luckily, I regained my sanity not long after.'

'Did you ever find out why he was grabbed?'

'Not then, and not now. And if anyone does know, they aren't telling. Miguel said the men could have been working for any one of the firm's clients, and maybe this client felt he had a financial grievance of some kind and wanted to get to the truth. He's probably right. This kind of thing happens all the time in Guatemala, to the point where it's almost standard business practice. These days it's often hard to distinguish between the legitimate businessmen and the real criminals.' She took a deep breath. 'Anyway, it's all history now. Can we talk about something else?'

‘Well, there is something I’m still curious about.’

‘Mm-hmm?’ Alex began walking her fingers lightly down his stomach, and kept on going. ‘And what’s that?’

‘Before, you told me Mr Quezada has a habit of disappearing on a specific day every year.’

Alex gave him an angelic smile as she slowly caressed him. After a while, she said, ‘Mm-hmm? So?’

Korso’s breath started to get a little tighter. ‘Uh… well… I was just wondering what day that might be.’

‘Is that really what you’re thinking about right now?’

‘Not completely, no.’

After what seemed like an eternity, she said, ‘It’s the eleventh of March. Anything else you want to ask me?’

‘My mind seems to have gone blank.’ With great effort, Korso gently removed Alex’s hand, and he rolled her on to her back. He looked down at her. ‘I don’t think we should talk anymore.’

She smiled up at him. ‘I was wondering when you’d get the message.’

THIRTY-FIVE

Korso awoke to the sound of a very feminine clearing of the throat. He opened his eyes and saw Alex standing in front of the full-length mirror at the other end of the room, brushing her hair. She was wearing a loose white blouse and navy slacks. She saw him watching her. 'Good morning.'

'Hi. You look great. What time is it?'

'Thanks. And it's almost nine.'

'Where are you going?'

'To see Miguel. We've got a few matters to discuss, and then I've got to go into town for a dull business lunch at one of our investment banks, closely followed by two more conferences this afternoon. Which means I'll be out for most of the day. Your meeting with Miguel's at twelve, right?'

'Yes.'

'Well, you can stay here until then if you like. There's some cold cuts in the refrigerator, and some eggs too, I think.'

'Sounds perfect.'

She put on her glasses and put her hairbrush down on the dressing table. She came over and perched on his side of the bed, then took his hand and brushed her lips across his palm. 'Last night was good, wasn't it?'

'Better than.' He raised himself up and kissed her.

'Will I see you later?'

'That kind of depends on what Mr Quezada has in store for me. But I hope so.'

She released his hand. 'Just be careful with Javier. I mean it.'

'Don't worry about me, I've dealt with his kind before. The trick is to never let your guard down for a second, and always be prepared for the double-cross. Or even the triple-cross.' He paused. 'Alex, could you do me a small favour?'

'What?'

'You've got plenty of influence around here. Could you get someone to go pick up my car from where we left it? I doubt I'll have time today. The keys are in my jacket there.'

'Sure, that's easy enough.' She got up off the bed. After finding his keys, she grabbed a laptop bag from the dressing table and gave him a wave as she left the room.

Once Korso heard the front door close, he leaned back against the headboard and grabbed his phone from the bedside table. He keyed in a brief text and sent it off.

While he waited for a reply, he considered what Alex had told him last night about losing the man she loved. He couldn't help but think of the direct similarities to Verhoeven's own situation, based on what Dog had learnt, and wondered if that was the real reason she'd been reluctant to reveal too much about Alex's history back in Frankfurt. Unfortunately, it wasn't something Verhoeven was likely to confirm one way or the other – especially to someone she barely knew – and bringing up such a personal subject would cause far more problems than it would solve. In all likelihood, it would have to remain an unsolved mystery. But it was an intriguing one nonetheless.

Less than a minute later, the phone rang. He took the call. Switching to English, he said, 'I need information, and I need it fast.'

'Jeez, not even time for a hello,' Dog said. This time it was an old lady's voice. 'But considering the circumstances, I forgive you. What kind of information?'

Korso told Dog about Quezada's antique gold ring, including what he knew of its history and where he bought it. 'He told me the Sotheby's auction took place in London almost seven years ago. I don't know how many auctions they held in 2015, but this particular one shouldn't be hard to track down. Now what I want from you is every piece of technical data you can find on the ring, but most importantly I need to know its exact weight. And when I say exact, I mean to as many decimal places as possible. Three at the absolute minimum. Now I know for a fact that these international auction houses weigh and measure every piece of jewellery that passes through their fingers, so I'm counting on there being a record of it somewhere. If it's not in the auction catalogue itself, then it'll be in the original appraisal and valuation.'

'I'm dying to ask why,' Dog said, 'but I know better. Anything else?'

'Not right now.'

'Assuming I can do this, you want me to call you back or will a text be enough?'

'Text first. I might be busy. If I need to speak with you later, I'll call.'

'Right. Be safe.' The line went dead.

With that out of the way, Korso gazed at the opposite wall and called to mind the date Alex had given him this morning: March 11. And last night, she also mentioned Quezada's infant son had died six years before, making his birthday 1-1-0-3-2-0-1-6 when typed into a keypad. Which just happened to match those highlighted numbers in the game room exactly. He nodded to himself, confident he was making progress. Though it still left him with the second part of the puzzle to deal with, and that wasn't exactly going to be a walkover.

But there were still preparations to be made. And the sooner he got started on that, the better. He picked up his phone again.

–

'A rifle?' Korso asked.

'Ah, this is more than just a rifle.' Quezada got up from his seat and came round his desk to stand before Korso. As before, they were back in his office. Unfortunately, Ozan was also present. As soon as Korso arrived at twelve, Quezada had wasted no time in apprising him of the day's main objective. 'What you'll be retrieving for me just happens to be one of the rarest, not to mention most lethal, handheld weapons on the planet.'

'And it's all because of you, Graves,' Ozan said from behind him.

Korso didn't bother turning round. To Quezada, he said, 'What's he talking about?'

'He's talking about how you very kindly delivered Galicia to me last Monday.' Quezada's smile resembled a shark's. 'We had a very productive discussion with Mr Galicia later that evening. *Very* productive indeed. It took a lot of time and effort on Javier's part, but among other things, Galicia finally revealed to us that he'd made a deal with a specialist Russian arms dealer named Sorokin to purchase one of the few surviving examples of a genuine Norinco ZM-87. And that exchange is set to go ahead this very afternoon, not forty kilometres from where we're standing.'

Korso blinked at him. 'A ZM-87. Interesting.'

Ozan gave a contemptuous snort. 'You're saying you already know about this gun?'

'I've heard of it,' Korso said, still looking at Quezada, 'although I've never seen one in person. Not many people have.'

'Perhaps you can enlighten us on its capabilities then,' Quezada said.

Fully aware that he was being put on the spot again, Korso said, 'It's a portable laser weapon that was developed by the Chinese-owned Norinco corporation, back in the late nineties. Its primary purpose was to inflict permanent blindness in enemy personnel within a two- to three-kilometre range. It performed as advertised. But as soon as word got out that these guns were actually going into production, the UN introduced a protocol that immediately banned the worldwide use of all blinding laser weapons. By the time that ban became official, Norinco had already produced approximately twenty-two of the things, a few of which had already been sold abroad. Nobody knows where they are now, although the US have alleged that they've been used in recent years by both the Russians and the North Koreans against some of their Apache helicopters. They're probably right about that.'

Quezada nodded. 'I'd say it's more than a probability.'

'But there is one thing I know for a fact.'

'What's that?'

'The ZM-87's not actually a rifle, or even a handheld weapon, but rather a kind of laser minigun. It apparently weighs about eighty pounds, and it comes with its own tripod mount along with a thick cable that connects it to the power unit. Very few men can carry that kind of weight.'

'You're absolutely right, Graves.' That shark smile was back. 'However, what you may not know is that Norinco also produced a handful of portable variant prototypes before production was completely shut down. Or that this prototype closely resembled China's principal light assault rifle, the QBZ-95, also made by Norinco, which is still used to this day by both their army and police forces. Very sleek, very portable, and very light. It's this particular model that I'm proposing to buy today.'

'Okay, that I didn't know. And the price tag?'

'Twenty million dollars, US. Payment to be made in emeralds.'

Korso let out a soft whistle. He was about to open his mouth when there was a knock on the door. He turned and saw Ozan go over and open it. It was Dante again, who seemed to act as Ozan's second-in-command. He leaned in close and spoke softly into Ozan's ear for a few seconds, darting glances at Korso as he talked, until Ozan clapped him on the shoulder and he left. Ozan shut the door and resumed his position against the wall.

'Problem?' Quezada asked.

'Nothing to worry about, Miguel. Just a few last-minute details Dante was checking out for me. It's all good.'

Korso wondered. He slowly turned back to Quezada, and said, 'So does this Sorokin know he's dealing with you now, or is he still under the belief that Galicia's the buyer?'

'That's a very good question. As it turns out, one of Galicia's last actions on this earth was to call up Sorokin personally, informing him that because he was currently under close watch by the government he wouldn't be able to be present at the final exchange himself, but that his trusted first lieutenant would be there to act as his proxy. I know how paranoid these Russians are, so I thought it wise to retain the status quo, or at least give the appearance of it. Anything less and this Sorokin might have gotten cold feet and abandoned the deal altogether. I didn't want that.' He smiled. 'I must admit, Galicia sounded very convincing. I almost believed him myself.'

'And would this mythical first lieutenant of Galicia's resemble the man currently standing behind me?'

'He might,' Ozan said. 'He just might at that.'

'So that just leaves the question of what I'm doing here. It seems to me you've got more than enough men to oversee the handover. What can I possibly bring to the party?'

'Your expertise, of course. When we first met, you told me you specialise in these kinds of transactions, especially those that involve the trading of rare and unique assets, so I'm holding you to that. I want you there not only to inspect the weapon, but to test it as well. When you're satisfied it's the real deal, Ozan will hand over the emeralds. Once Sorokin's inspected them to his satisfaction, each party will go their separate ways.'

Korso frowned. 'I'm to test the rifle. You mean on a human subject?'

'Of course. How else will you know if it works?'

'So who's the guinea pig?'

'Somebody you haven't met before. He'll be coming along with you, ostensibly as back-up. But he's someone I've had serious doubts about for a while, and so I consider him to be dispensable.'

'Sounds simple enough on the surface.'

'It is,' Ozan said.

'Except in these kinds of situations, things have a habit of escalating.' To Quezada, he said, 'How many of us are supposed to be present at the handover?'

'Four men only. Javier, yourself and two others. The emeralds will remain in Javier's possession until the actual exchange is made.'

'Only four? How come?'

'One of Sorokin's many conditions was that we're to bring no more than that to the handover, and that includes our test subject. He sees an extra man and the deal's off. He'll simply go elsewhere. He knows there are plenty of other interested parties who'd be happy to get a hold of this particular weapon.'

'Okay. What time, and where?'

'Two o'clock this afternoon. As for the where, it's an abandoned church near Antigua. Javier can tell you the exact location once you're on your way. No reflection on you, but the fewer people who know the details, the better. Javier only learned of it twenty minutes ago.'

'You mean Sorokin chose the location himself?'

'He insisted on it,' Ozan said. 'Or no deal.'

Korso was thinking fast. He didn't like this, not any part of it. He didn't much like the idea of permanently blinding somebody without good reason. Even his worst enemies deserved better. And he certainly didn't like being thrown into an ongoing operation at the very last minute, without any kind of preparation on his part. But then, that was surely the whole point. And refusing to go wasn't a valid option either. Especially not when he was so close to the prize. 'Will this Sorokin have the same number of men with him?'

'So he says.' Quezada shrugged. 'But Russians are all natural born liars, so I wouldn't be surprised if he brought an extra man along.'

'In which case, what's to stop the guy from bringing a whole army with him and reneging on the deal entirely? He could use the four of us as target practice, and then fly back to Russia with the ZM-87 plus twenty million in untraceable gems.'

'Ordinarily I'd agree with you, but it just so happens that Sorokin's got a fairly solid reputation within the international arms trade and is known to always keep up his end of the deal. And as you know, reputation counts for a great deal in the more specialist markets. But in any case, we've safeguarded ourselves against the possibility of treachery.'

'Believe it or not, Graves,' Ozan said, 'this isn't our first time out at this kind of thing. You're not the only professional around here.'

'I know that,' Korso said. 'So let's say there are four of them. And they'll all be armed to the teeth, right?'

Quezada snorted. 'Naturally. What's your point?'

'Well, I only mention it since I'm currently lacking in that department.'

'I don't expect you to go into this empty handed. Javier here will supply you with what you need. Anything else on your mind?'

Plenty, Korso thought, *but nothing I can say out loud*. 'Well, there is the question of remuneration.'

'Yes, I thought that subject might crop up. So for your participation in today's activities you'll receive the same amount as before – but that's without the bonus. I feel that's more than sufficient for a single afternoon's work, don't you agree?'

'No argument from me.'

'Excellent. So I'll leave you in the capable hands of Javier here, and he'll help you get equipped.' Quezada turned and reached for an aluminium laptop case, complete with shoulder strap, lying in the centre of his desk. He picked it up and the contents rattled. He looked over at his right-hand man, who came over and took the case from him. 'Protect this with your life, Javier. And don't forget, I'll want a complete progress report the moment the deal is done.'

'I won't forget, Miguel.' He slipped the case over his shoulder.

'Until later then, my friend.'

'Until later.' Javier turned to Korso. 'Let's go.'

THIRTY-SIX

Once they'd descended the steps out front, Ozan began walking towards the garage building to their left. Korso walked alongside him, checking his watch. It was already 12.20. He had to admire this Sorokin. Clearly no fool, he'd left Quezada with no time to set anything up prior to the meet. Korso would have done exactly the same in his shoes.

'This church,' he said. 'How far away is it?'

'About an hour's drive,' Ozan said. 'Don't worry about it, we've got time.'

Up ahead, Korso noticed a door along the side of the building was partly ajar. He could hear voices coming from within. Ozan came to a stop next to the door. 'Okay, inside.'

Korso pulled the door open and entered the building. Inside it was vast, basically just one huge open area. Except for the low ceiling, it looked more a mini hangar than a garage. He counted thirteen vehicles lined up along one side, and fifteen more opposite. About half were SUVs of various makes, while the rest were a mix of normal day-to-day run-arounds and various supercars, the latter no doubt part of Quezada's personal fleet. He spotted a black McLaren 720S standing next to an ordinary grey Nissan Skyline, with two sleek Ferraris – one red, the other purple – bracketing a light-blue Toyota Yaris. He also noticed a bright-yellow Lamborghini in there, and what looked like an Aston Martin at the end.

Two men were standing next to one of the larger SUVs, a black BMW X7 with tinted windows. According to Quezada, one of these two was destined not to come back the same person as when he left, or possibly destined not to come back at all. Both men were laughing at something. Korso recognised the stocky shape of Ramirez as he casually loaded shells into a Fabarm STF/12 pump. He also wore a shoulder holster with the same .357 Magnum that he'd aimed at Korso when he'd first arrived. Attached to his leg and belt was a thigh holster, containing a Skorpion SMG and four spare magazines.

Korso hadn't seen the other guy before. He was taller than Ramirez, and wider in the shoulders. He had short dark hair, was unshaven, and looked to be in his late-twenties. He also wore a shoulder holster containing a semi-automatic, as well as a thigh holster containing a MAC 10 and more ammo. He was sighting down a Russian AK-103 assault rifle. He saw Ozan and Korso approaching and swivelled the barrel Korso's way.

'Budda-budda-budda, instant jam,' he said. Still grinning, he lowered the weapon and looked it over like a man in love. 'Man, this gun is sick.'

Ramirez laughed. Ozan gave a light chuckle. Korso said, 'If you point that at me again, you better pull the trigger.'

The unshaven man looked up at him. 'Or what?'

'Or I'll take it from you.'

He grinned. 'Well, now, I'd sure like to see you try. Yes, I would.'

'All right, all right,' Ozan said. 'That's enough. Flores, don't antagonise our superstar, he's the sensitive type. Ramirez, tell me you've checked this vehicle thoroughly and made sure everything's in full working order. Because if it breaks down along the way, I guarantee you'll be walking back here on a pair of stumps.'

'Just finished checking everything from head to toe, boss. I swear this vehicle's in such good shape it could have just come off the assembly line.'

'It better be.'

Ozan leaned into the passenger side of the vehicle, and Korso watched as he quickly pressed a series of buttons on the stereo.

He couldn't see which ones. But a second later, a special drawer underneath the glove compartment slid out automatically. Ozan placed the laptop case in the drawer, pressed three more buttons on the stereo, and the drawer slid smoothly back into its recess.

Ozan beckoned Korso with a finger and began walking towards the rear of the room. Korso kept pace with him. As they walked, he noticed a single door set into the rear wall on the left-hand side. It looked like a fire exit, but instead of push bars, there was just a steel handle and a keypad underneath. Once they reached the door, Ozan put his body in front of the keypad while he pressed some buttons. There was a loud *clack*, and Ozan pulled the door open and entered without a word.

As Korso followed him inside, the fluorescent lights flickered on in stages. He turned to his right and saw they were in a long, narrow room that ran the width of the building. The walls on either side of him were lined with weapons of every conceivable type: assault rifles, submachine guns, handguns, pump shotguns, combat shotguns, mortars, anti-tank rocket launchers, grenade launchers, long-range sniper rifles and more besides. Korso figured there was enough hardware in here to not only start a war, but to finish it as well.

Over a dozen workbenches were lined up against the right-hand wall. One bench contained nothing but stacks of gun holsters, while another held empty magazines of all shapes, makes and sizes. Another desk held piles of gun cases, rifle bags and cleaning kits. Two of the workbenches held nothing but grenades, all displayed in open crates. There were more crates of ammunition stacked against the wall under the benches, each one clearly labelled by calibre size.

As Korso moved slowly down the room, he let his gaze wander over the weapons on either side, taking careful note of everything he passed.

'Make your choice,' Ozan said. 'Just don't take all day about it.'

Korso kept going until he reached the workbench containing the crates of M87 frag grenades. Alongside these were three boxes of black police stun grenades, or flashbangs. Purposely ignoring these, he turned back to Ozan and suddenly pointed to the column of Israeli assault rifles on the wall behind him. 'What about those IWI X96s up there? I assume they're the fully automatic versions, right?'

As Ozan turned to look, Korso quickly grabbed two flashbangs from an open box, and stuck one in each trouser pocket. You never knew when they might come in handy.

'Wouldn't be much point if they weren't,' Ozan said, taking one of the Israeli rifles off the wall. He turned back to Korso with a smirk. 'You got good taste in weapons, I'll give you that. These babies are real state of the art. But you best lower your expectations. Miguel said I have to equip you, but it's up to me to decide with what. So take whatever handgun you want, and even a shotgun if you feel brave enough, but forget about any assault rifles you see in here. That goes for the SMGs as well. They're not for you.'

'Are you serious?'

'As a heart attack. I already told you, I don't trust you, Graves. Especially not in a confined space with an automatic weapon.'

'But I'm supposed to trust you three, is that it?'

'I really don't care,' Ozan said, removing the gun's magazine. After a brief check, he rammed the mag home again. 'You may be here as a consultant, but I'm still the one running the show. And that means I make all the decisions. You don't like that, take it up with Miguel.' He grinned. 'See where it gets you.'

Korso saw there was little point in arguing. Ozan clearly held all the winning cards. But he did wonder whether it had been his idea to bring Korso along, or Quezada's. Because the answer could put a whole new slant on the afternoon's proceedings. But it wasn't a question he could ask now. He doubted he'd get an honest answer anyway.

Instead, he moved down the room until he came to the Glocks. They'd rarely let him down in the past. There were three columns of the semi-automatics in a variety of models. About thirty in all. He pulled a Glock 17 from the wall, ejected the full magazine and checked the chamber to make sure it was empty. He peered down the sight, checked the muzzle. Aiming at the floor, he dry-fired a few times and nodded at the fluid action. He also spotted a trap door set into the floor, about twenty feet to his left. He hadn't noticed it before, and wondered if that was where Galicia had been taken for his fatal interrogation.

'Finally found something you like?' Ozan asked.

Korso didn't answer but walked back and grabbed a suitable shoulder holster from one of the workbenches he'd passed earlier. He also took three empty magazines from the next bench along. On the floor underneath were two crates of 9mm ammunition. He opened one up, grabbed two handfuls of rounds and placed them on the surface. He began loading one of the empty magazines.

To his right, out the corner of his eye, he saw Ozan loading some extra magazines for his own IWI. Korso turned back to his work. He'd picked this workbench specifically. On the wall to his left was a collection of combat shotguns. All looked pristine. But they weren't what interested him. Directly underneath the shotguns were two rows of ultra compact 9mm pistols, each piece designed to fit easily into a pocket or a handbag. The smallest was the Smith & Wesson M&P Bodyguard, and Korso spotted five versions of that particular model on the wall. It was only five inches in length, and three-quarters of an inch thick, with a six-round magazine. So small you could almost fit one inside your palm.

Korso wanted one. But he didn't want anyone else to know about it. Especially not Ozan. He continued loading his magazine and waited for the right moment. It would come. If it didn't, he'd have to create it himself.

He didn't have to. He was halfway through loading his second magazine when he saw Ramirez enter the room to his right.

'What's the problem now?' Ozan said, turning to him.

Ramirez glanced quickly at Korso, then leaned in to Ozan and began speaking in a low undertone about something or other. While both men were turned away from him, Korso stepped to his left, grabbed one of the micro compact S&Ws from the wall and dropped it into his jacket pocket in one fluid motion. By the time the two men had finished talking, he was already loading the final few rounds into the third and last magazine.

'You done yet?' Ozan said testily. Ramirez had already left. 'It's time to go.'

Korso inserted the now full mag into the Glock 17, and fitted the gun into the holster, while the spare magazines went into separate Velcro pouches underneath. Removing his jacket, he slipped his arms through the holster, carefully tightening the rig straps so that the gun was riding high up, near his armpit. He put his jacket back on. 'I'm ready.'

'Finally.'

Ozan waited for Korso to leave the room first. He followed him out and shut the door behind him, making sure it was locked. Korso saw Ramirez getting behind the wheel of the BMW. Through the tinted windows, he spotted a figure already sitting in the back.

As Korso reached for the other rear door on the passenger side, Ozan opened the front door instead. 'Uh, uh. You're up front, next to Ramirez.'

'With you and Flores sitting right behind me? I don't think so.'

'You do just what I tell you. I'm running today's assignment, and I'm telling you to get in the front.'

'And I'm telling you that isn't going to happen. Leave me behind if you want. I'll forego my fee and hope Mr Quezada understands. But whatever happens, there is no way on earth that I'm getting in that front seat with you two behind me.'

Ozan's eyes narrowed. 'Meaning what exactly?'

'You know what I mean.'

'Spell it out for me.'

'I'm saying I like to see what's around me at all times, and I can't do that by sitting up front. Tell you what, the three of us can toss a coin. Odd one out rides shotgun.'

Ozan shook his head. 'Not happening.'

'Well, it looks like we're at an impasse. How do you suggest we solve it?' Korso just looked at him, and waited.

Ozan glowered silently, aware that the other two were watching him closely from within the vehicle, curious to see how he'd deal with this potential threat to his command. He had to know Korso wouldn't budge, and he couldn't risk giving another order that was going to be ignored.

'Flores,' he said, finally.

Flores opened the door on his side and got out. 'Boss?'

'You're riding up front with Ramirez. I'll sit in the back with our sensitive friend here.'

'Sure, boss,' Flores said, and reached into the vehicle for his weapon.

'See?' Korso said, getting into the rear seat. 'There's usually a simple answer to every problem.'

Ozan got in on the other side, weapon at his flank, and slammed the door shut. 'Okay, Ramirez. Let's move.'

THIRTY-SEVEN

Ramirez steered them steadily through town, avoiding the worst of the traffic, and eventually took the westbound slip road that joined them up with the CA-1 highway. Korso had studied the maps. He knew that if they carried on this route they'd shortly have to take the south-west RN-10 turnoff, which in turn would take them directly into Antigua.

Nobody had spoken for the last ten minutes. The radio was tuned to some hip-hop station. Over a syncopated backbeat and deep bassline, a male rapper was busy waxing poetic about various social injustices that affected his people. It wasn't really Korso's genre, but the guy's lyrics were pretty good. The volume was loud, but bearable.

As he drove, Ramirez kept sneaking glances at Korso in his rear-view. He was clearly trying to be subtle about it, and failing dismally. Korso also noticed a few silent exchanges going on between him and Flores, consisting mostly of nods and vague hand gestures. Something was definitely up, and Korso knew it was centred around him. It didn't take a genius to figure out what. There was only one fall guy in this vehicle, and all arrows seemed to be pointing towards Korso.

But was it Ozan's idea, or Quezada's? That was the real question.

Ozan was still looking out the window on his side. Up front, Flores was playing with his phone, while Ramirez kept his eyes on the road ahead. While they were all occupied, Korso reached into his pocket and removed one of the flashbangs. Bringing his hand around to his back, he carefully secreted the grenade in the tight space between the two seat cushions. Not all the way in, but deep enough so it wouldn't be immediately visible.

As he was bringing his hand back out, Ozan turned from the window. Korso continued the movement, and tapped a knuckle against the window. 'This bullet-proofed?'

'What do you think?'

'I think Mr Quezada learned long ago never to take unnecessary chances. So do you plan on telling me where we're going, or is it supposed to be a last-minute surprise?'

Ozan turned to the window again. 'Our destination's an abandoned church beyond the northern end of Antigua, up in the hills, about five clicks from Vuelta Grande. Happy now?'

'When you say abandoned, you mean some kind of ancient ruins? Because those places generally attract tourists.'

'Uh, uh, not this one, bright boy. All this place attracts are flies and the occasional junkie. The church was built some time back in the 1920s, and got itself burned down about thirty years later. The villagers who lived around it gradually shifted two miles east and just left the building up there to rot, and that's how it's been ever since.'

'Sounds like you've been there before.'

Ozan shrugged. 'It's all new to me. It's not even on Google Maps. I just asked around until I found someone who came from that area. He told me it's a perfect site for an exchange like this. Plenty of open space, not many hiding places.' He leaned forward and nudged Flores' shoulder. 'Find another station. That shit's getting on my nerves. And turn it down.'

'Sure.' Flores pressed a button on the stereo, and the rap was replaced with some generic pop music with a bouncy salsa beat. He also lowered the volume a little.

'You know Sorokin and his people are at the site right now, don't you?' Korso said. 'Just waiting for us. They probably arrived hours ago.'

Ozan snorted. 'Like we haven't realised that already. Christ, who do you think you're dealing with here?'

Korso had nothing to say to that. He looked down at the thin metal case between Ozan's feet. On either side of the steel handle was a combination lock featuring six small dials. 'Those locks there won't keep out anyone for very long, which means you've got another deterrent in there. What is it?'

Still looking out the window, Ozan said, 'Why should I tell you?'

'Why shouldn't you?'

Ozan turned to him, and then shrugged. 'You ever hear of polonium before?'

'Sure. A rare and highly volatile radioactive heavy metal, arguably the most lethal known material in existence. Especially to humans. The Kremlin's been known to employ the 210 isotope as a method of assassination against so-called political dissidents and defectors. Nasty way to go.'

Ozan smiled. 'It's also got a half-life of up to six months. So now you know the kind of safeguards Miguel was talking about. Someone tries opening this case without inputting the right code and a small vial cracks open inside. It only contains a few milligrams of the stuff, but anybody who touches those stones in the next six months won't live long enough to regret it.'

'Except if Sorokin knows about the polonium, then all he has to do is open the case in a controlled environment and then simply wait out the six months.'

Ozan shook his head. 'Sorokin knows there's some kind of lethal radiation in there, but we haven't told him what. For all he knows, he'd have to wait another twenty years before he could touch the stones.'

Korso had to admit it was a pretty effective deterrent. He'd employed similar measures himself in the past, although never with something as lethal as polonium-210. He might even consider using it in the future. Assuming he survived today, of course. Leaning back in his seat, he thought about what might lie in store once they arrived at the meeting site. There were a few ways this could go, and he tried his best to anticipate all of them. An impossible task, but he had to at least try. But his thoughts were suddenly interrupted when the phone in his back pocket vibrated twice.

He pulled the phone out and saw a new text message in his inbox. The sender was anonymous. He opened it up.

> Found 2 sources for Pakal ring: Sotheby's & Christie's. Not in catalogue, but appraisal in Soth. dbase lists wt. as 4.2349g. Christie's appraisal 28 yrs old & lists wt. as 4.2350g. Call if questions.

Thanks again, Dog, Korso thought. He studied the two figures. There wasn't much he could do about the slight disparity between them, except split the difference and hope for the best. Once he'd memorised the two weights, he keyed in *4.23495g* and sent it to another number. A local number this time. Then he deleted both messages, just like he'd already deleted everything else on this phone.

Never leave anything behind. That was the rule.

'Don't tell me,' Ozan said, watching him. 'A message from your mother.'

Ramirez laughed.

'From Alejandra, as it happens. Just letting me know she'll be free for dinner again this evening. She really is a lovely girl.'

'Yeah,' Ozan said, turning back to the window, 'she is.'

He said nothing else. No insults. No threats. No dire warnings to stay away from his woman. That alone convinced Korso he wasn't supposed to last out the day. As far as Ozan was concerned, he was already a dead man walking.

THIRTY-EIGHT

Korso knew they were close to their destination when he saw the huge, long-dormant Pacaya volcano in the distance. Even from miles away, the famous landmark was difficult to miss. But once they came within reach of Antigua's city boundaries, Ramirez quickly steered them northwards, bypassing the city centre altogether. As they twisted their way up and into the hills, away from the tourists and the volcanoes, the road gradually became rougher, narrower, more treacherous. They were entering the rural countryside now, and it wasn't too long before theirs was the only vehicle in sight.

The few residential dwellings Korso saw looked as though they'd been cobbled together overnight, using whatever materials were at hand. Corrugated steel shacks were abundant. Most were brown with rust. One or two seemed to double as makeshift corner stores, stocking basic foods and supplies for the locals. There were no road signs in sight. Most of the side roads they passed were basic dirt tracks. Ramirez kept checking his GPS to make sure they were still headed in the right direction.

Ozan's cell phone rang at one point, the howling wolf ringtone immediately drowning out the sound of the radio. Although Korso couldn't hear the other part of the conversation, it was clear from the respect in Ozan's voice that it was Quezada, probably making sure everything was on schedule.

They finally arrived at their destination at 1.52 p.m.

The old church was situated on four or five acres of otherwise flat land on a gently sloping incline, close to the top of the hill. Bordered on three sides by pine trees, the field was mostly featureless, while the ground surrounding the building's remains was thick with overgrown grass and weeds. As for the church, it was essentially a ruin, though not the kind you'd want a snapshot of. If you didn't know it had once been a place of worship, you'd have a hard time guessing. There was no roof, and no crosses or cherubs in sight. The adobe wall at the front was mostly still complete, but huge sections of the side walls were missing. Large blocks of mortar and stone were piled up next to one of the missing sections, which looked like a fat V. Long-term exposure to the elements had gradually smoothed over all the rough edges.

Another SUV was parked twenty feet away from this missing section of wall. It was a dark grey Toyota with tinted windows. As Ramirez brought the BMW to a gradual halt near the front entrance, a man wearing an army camouflage jacket, black cargo pants, and black cap emerged from the open archway and held up a hand. He was carrying a large assault rifle in his other hand, while a semi-automatic poked out of his side holster. As he watched the BMW come to a stop, he spoke into his earpiece.

'He doesn't look Russian, boss,' Flores said.

'So what?' Ozan said. 'Turn off the engine.'

Ramirez killed the engine and set the handbrake. He turned to the rear. So did Flores. He was smiling. He had a revolver in his left hand. It was aimed at Korso.

'I warned you about pointing guns at me,' Korso said.

'So you did.'

Ozan turned in his seat. He was also holding a .45, aimed at Korso's midriff.

'Now I want you to place both hands against the headrest in front of you,' he said. 'Do it now. Flores, if he makes a single wrong move, put one in his shoulder.'

'Be glad to, boss.'

Korso did exactly as he was told, placing both hands against the headrest. 'You're running true to form, Ozan. Let me guess, *I'm* to be the test subject, right?'

'I always said you were a bright boy,' Ozan said. 'Just not bright enough. Or fast enough.' He reached under Korso's jacket, pulled the Glock 17 from his shoulder holster, and stuck it in his waistband. He patted Korso's jacket pockets, and raised an eyebrow when his fingers made contact with the little S&W in there. He pulled the gun out. 'When?'

'Does it matter?'

'Let's see what other goodies you palmed.' Passing the S&W to Flores, he patted Korso's legs and stopped when he felt the stun grenade in the right trouser pocket. 'Sneaky. Okay, I want you to take your right hand off the headrest and very carefully remove that from your pocket and give it to me. And that pin better still be in there or you'll experience first-hand what it feels like to be gut-shot.'

'I'm moving now.' Korso took his right hand away, reached into his pocket and slowly pulled out the stun grenade, still intact. After handing it over to Ozan, he placed his hand back on the headrest. Ozan checked the rest of his body, all the way down to his feet. Finding nothing else, he sat up again, gun still aimed at Korso's stomach.

'Ramirez,' Ozan said, 'stop looking at us and keep watch on that guy over there.'

Ramirez turned to the front again.

'I've got a question,' Korso said. 'If that's allowed.'

Ozan shrugged. 'We've still got time to spare.'

'Whose idea was it to put me on the spot today, yours or Quezada's?'

'You mean *Mr* Quezada.'

'Whatever. So who made the call?'

'You're the smart one. You figure it out.'

'To be honest, I'm seeing your fingerprints all over this one, Ozan. Quezada's too shrewd a businessman not to know a good thing when he sees it. He knows I can deliver what I promise, and so he's bound to have further uses for my services. But to you I'm just another competitor vying for the big man's attention, and that's more than you can bear. Then there's the matter of Alex, of course.'

Ozan sighed. 'You're no competition at all, Graves. The world's full of nobodies like you, all of them desperate to be a big-league player. I've handled assholes like you before, and I'll handle plenty more. Take my word for it, by this time tomorrow you'll be nothing more than a footnote. Not even that.'

'And I'm sure you've already figured out how to explain my absence to Quezada?'

'Nothing to figure out. You got greedy and tried to sabotage the deal, so we had to blow you away. I'll say we used a local as the test subject. Miguel will understand. As for Alejandra, sometimes she needs a friendly nudge to help her decide what's good for her and what isn't. She doesn't realise it, but I'm actually doing her a favour.'

That 'sometimes' had immediately snagged Korso's attention. He tried a hunch. 'You mean like the favour you did for her four years ago, with that financier?'

'You two,' Ozan said, still watching Korso, 'take up positions outside. I'll be out shortly. Ramirez, pass me the car keys before you leave.'

'Boss?'

'You want me to repeat myself?'

Ramirez removed the keys from the ignition and passed them back to Ozan. Flores grabbed the assault rifle at his side and got out. Ramirez reached over to the passenger side footwell, grabbed hold of his shotgun and got out his side. Both men stayed close to the SUV. Sorokin's man was still standing in the same spot, watching them.

'Sander,' Korso said. 'That was his name, wasn't it?'

'What do you know about it?'

'Only what Alex told me last night in bed.' He was glad to see Ozan's jaw muscles tense at that. Anything to keep him off balance. 'She mentioned how she finally found her soul mate four years ago, and described how he was snatched outside his office one night by three armed men, and how his mutilated remains were discovered in an abandoned warehouse a few days later. And she also mentioned how, when she was at her very lowest point, you decided to move in and stake your claim on her. That's some incredible timing.'

Ozan gave a careless shrug. 'That's all ancient news. Besides, the cops figured it was probably just one of his firm's clients who was behind it.'

'Sure. Except we both know better, don't we? I haven't seen a photo of this Sander, but I'm guessing he was a fairly attractive specimen. And probably an alpha type as well. It's no wonder you saw green. You must have known you'd never get a shot at Alex with him on the scene, so far easier just take to him out of the equation altogether. But then that's your solution to everything, isn't it?'

From the way Ozan was tightly clenching his gun, Korso knew he'd gotten pretty close to the mark with his guesses.

'I think you better watch your mouth,' Ozan said.

'Or what? You'll have me blinded? Maybe killed outright? Please don't.'

Ozan slowly relaxed his grip on the gun and smiled. 'I'll enjoy watching your last moments, Graves. You can always tell the measure of a man by the way he faces death. My guess is it won't take long before you start blubbering like a baby.'

'So if I'm dead anyway, where's the harm in admitting you were behind it all?'

'So what if I *was*? Anyone could see the man was a born loser. Alejandra was better off without him.'

'Really? I wonder how your boss would take it if he ever found out it was you who ruined Alex's life. He takes a very close interest in her well-being, you know.'

'I know more than you can imagine, Graves. And I know for an absolute fact that Miguel doesn't have the slightest problem with that guy's sudden disappearance. Just the opposite. But I get the feeling you're stalling now, and time's getting short.'

Ozan opened his own door and grabbed the IWI, then backed out of the car while motioning with the handgun. 'Get out your side. No tricks.'

'I'm all out of those,' Korso said. Except that wasn't quite true. Opening his door with his left hand, he shifted his body round and tucked his right hand – currently out of Ozan's view – into the space between the seats and plucked out the second flashbang he'd hidden there. As he stepped out into the fresh air, he tucked the thin tubular grenade under his shirt sleeve with the pull ring facing outwards. His jacket sleeve covered the bulge well enough. He closed the door. Ramirez stepped back a few paces, out of Korso's range. He held his shotgun over the crook of his arm and was watching Korso closely.

There was no traffic noise at all. Other than a few bird calls, and the faint buzz of an unseen prop plane somewhere in the distance, all was quiet.

Sorokin's man spoke into his earpiece. Seconds later, a second man appeared as he climbed over the discarded blocks of mortar by the missing section of wall. He was dressed the same as the first and looked similarly armed. A third armed man stepped out of the Toyota, dressed in identical fatigues to the other two. They'd clearly bought their clothes at the same army surplus store.

'Graves,' Ozan said, 'stand over there, in front of the vehicle. Ramirez, make sure you keep your gun on him at all times. If he makes a wrong move, put one in his ankle.'

Korso did as he was told, and stepped over to the front of the BMW. He leaned back against the hood and gazed up at the sky. To the north-west, maybe two clicks away, he could make out a small, single-engine aircraft. That had to be the prop plane he could hear. It was flying low and moving in a large circular arc, as though it were in a holding pattern.

Ozan was checking his watch. To the first man, he said, 'Two o'clock exactly. Where's Sorokin?'

Try looking upwards, Korso thought.

'Give me a name,' the other man said.

'Ozan. I'm representing Romario Galicia. I was told Sorokin would be here. I don't see him.'

'He's around. Where are the gemstones?'

'Close by. Let's get on with it.'

The first man pulled a small military-grade walkie-talkie from his belt. He spoke a few words into it and placed it back on his belt. 'He's on his way.'

Korso still had his eye on the prop plane in the distance. He watched as the pilot suddenly pulled the plane out of its holding pattern and started heading in their direction.

THIRTY-NINE

It wasn't long before all eyes were looking upwards, the plane's engine growing louder with each second. Korso understood now why Sorokin had picked this remote spot for the exchange. It was the only flat piece of land for miles around, just the right size for a small prop plane to land safely.

'That's him now?' Ozan asked, shielding his eyes from the sun. 'Who's the pilot?'

'He is,' the first man said.

'A man of many talents, huh? Hope he speaks Spanish too.'

'He does, along with five other languages.'

'That's just showing off. Flores, go and check the ruins. Make sure there's nobody else hidden away back there. We don't want any last-minute surprises.'

'Right, boss.' Flores walked over to the first man. After a brief exchange of words, Flores passed through the archway entrance and disappeared from view. The first man didn't move from his position, and kept his attention on the other three.

As the plane approached, Korso watched the nose drop a little as its altitude and speed gradually decreased. Once it passed the pine trees, Sorokin throttled back and the plane's altitude dropped sharply. Korso recognised the model now. It was a Cessna 172 Skyhawk, the most common single-engine plane on the planet. When it was just fifteen feet or so from the ground, the plane levelled out suddenly and as the rear wheels touched earth, its speed dropped down even further. Korso watched the plane bump its way along the uneven ground towards them. When it was about a hundred feet away, the small Cessna came to a halt and the nose propeller wound down. It was a very good landing, on mostly unforgiving terrain with little room for error. Sorokin was clearly a skilled pilot.

Moments later, the cockpit door opened and a medium-sized man got out. He was wearing a dark windbreaker, tan chinos, black baseball cap and sunglasses. The man reached in, pulled out a large bag from the rear cabin, and latched the door shut. Lugging the bag over his shoulder, he made his way towards them on foot.

Meanwhile, Flores reappeared at the arched entranceway. He walked over to Ozan and said something out of Korso's hearing range. Ozan nodded, then waved him back to his original position. Judging by their body language, Korso assumed Sorokin had kept his word about the size of his entourage.

Sorokin reached the Toyota and passed the gun bag to his man standing there. They both walked towards the BMW. The other gunman joined them, following close behind. When they were thirty feet away from the BMW, all three came to a stop. The first man dropped the gun bag at Sorokin's feet and unzipped the top. At a hand signal from Sorokin, he then joined his colleague near the ruins.

Sorokin removed his sunglasses, tucked them in his pocket. He gave Korso a cursory glance, before turning his attention to Ozan. He pulled out a phone and swiped it a few times before finding what he wanted. He shifted his gaze from the display to the man in front of him, and then back again.

To Ozan, he said, 'You match your photo perfectly.' His Spanish was faultless.

'So do you,' Ozan said.

'And how is your employer? He sounded very agitated the last time we spoke on the phone. He tried to hide it, but I could tell something was badly wrong.'

'He's fine, considering the circumstances,' Ozan said. 'The real reason he's not here is that one of his competitors attempted to kidnap him during a business meeting last Monday. We just about managed to get him to safety, but during the escape he suffered two bullet wounds, and we also lost a lot of men in the process. As you can appreciate, since then he's become very wary about leaving the protection of his estate.'

As Ozan spoke, he kept glancing at Korso as though daring him to contradict the statement. But Korso said nothing. There was a time for everything, and this wasn't the right moment. But it would come.

Sorokin was shaking his head sadly. 'Yes, that would explain it. We live in troubled times, to be sure.' He turned to his man standing at the archway. 'Hector, check their vehicle.'

Ozan raised a hand. 'Hold on—'

'Just a formality,' Sorokin said. 'Before we get down to business, I want to be absolutely sure there's nobody else hiding in the car. I'm sure you understand.'

Ozan lowered his hand and watched as Hector approached the vehicle.

The gunman opened the front door and peered inside. He closed it and opened the rear door, and looked around the interior, checking the trunk area too. Once he was satisfied the vehicle was empty, he shut the door. 'All clear, Mr Sorokin.'

'Good.'

Hector walked back towards the church remains, coming to a halt twenty feet away from his colleague. Meanwhile, Sorokin motioned towards the bag at his feet. 'As you can see, I've brought the asset. I assume you've brought the payment.'

'Right here.' Ozan turned back to the BMW and opened the front passenger door. Korso watched as he pressed the combination on the stereo. Seconds later, he emerged from the vehicle, holding the laptop case.

'Fine,' Sorokin said. 'So this is how it will work. There'll be no deviations. One of your men will bring the case over and unlock it for me. Once I'm convinced there's no danger, he'll bring the bag containing the ZM-87 and its accessories back to you. Each of us will inspect our wares carefully, making sure everything's as it should be. Now I realise that while I'm checking the stones, you'll need to check that the prototype works as advertised. But I have to warn you that if the barrel of this ZM-87 veers in our direction at any point, then I won't be responsible for what happens next, but I can guarantee that not all of us will survive this afternoon. Maybe none of us will.' He shrugged. 'I know I'm stating the obvious, but I find it's always best to make the ground rules clear right from the very start, so that there's no confusion later.'

'We're all professionals here,' Ozan said, 'and I want this whole transaction to go as smoothly as you do. What say we just get on with it?'

'I couldn't agree more. Whenever you're ready.'

Ozan stepped over to Ramirez and held out the laptop case. 'Okay, Ram—'

'Not him,' Sorokin called out.

Ozan lowered the case and turned to Sorokin. 'What?'

'I said not him. Nor your other gunman over there. That one standing in front of the BMW. Have him bring me the emeralds.'

'Why him?'

'Because I can see he's the only one of us who's unarmed. Why, do you have a problem with that?'

Ozan thought for a moment, and then said, 'Why would I have a problem?' He walked over to Korso and placed the laptop case on the hood of the SUV. In a quiet voice, he said, 'Well, it looks like you've been nominated. The combination's 5-3-8-5-9-0. Got that? And if I think for a moment that you're telling him something you shouldn't, I'll make your death worse than you could possibly imagine.'

Korso looked at the small case. While Ozan and Sorokin had been talking, he'd been spending his time figuring out how to make the best of an already tense situation – where neither party trusted the other – and seeing what he could do to help sow the seeds of further discord. And now a golden opportunity was being presented to him, allowing him the chance to stoke the fire a little and reshape that distrust into something approaching enmity. But he still made no move to take the case.

'Remember what I said about shooting you in the gut.' Ozan raised the assault rifle. 'That's still an option. Don't think I won't do it.'

'I'm aware of that.' Korso looked up at the clear sky, stretching the seconds out as much as possible. He counted to eight, figuring that was just enough time to keep everyone's nerves nicely on edge. He turned back to the vehicle and picked up the case.

'Good,' Ozan said. 'Now walk over there, nice and easy. Open the case for him, and then when he gives you the bag, you bring it back to me. Are we clear?'

'As day.' Korso turned and began walking towards the waiting Sorokin at a steady, languid pace. He wasn't in any rush. Far from it. The gunman on Sorokin's left kept his eyes on Korso, while the other one focused all his attention on Ramirez and Ozan by the BMW.

When there was about four feet of space left between them, Sorokin said, 'Stop there.'

Korso came to an immediate halt.

'Open the case.'

'You sure you want me to?'

Sorokin blinked. 'What do you mean by that?'

Keeping his voice low, Korso said, 'I mean that this case is booby-trapped. Apparently, there's an ampule of polonium-210 that'll rupture and irradiate everything inside if anybody tries to gain access without entering the correct combination first.'

Sorokin studied the man before him closely. 'This was explained to me by Ozan, although I wasn't aware it was polonium-210. But you *have* the correct combination, yes?'

'I do. But I've also been chosen as the test subject for your prototype rifle, which means I'm the very definition of expendable. Blinded by your laser weapon first, and then if I'm lucky, a double tap to the head to put me out of my misery. That's all I've got ahead of me.'

'Which explains why you're unarmed. I can empathise, but I fail to see the point you're trying to make.'

'My point is I know Ozan and I know how he works, and the art of the double-cross is almost second nature to him. It's my belief that there *is* a booby trap inside this case, but not the one he's told you about. I'm thinking there might be something a little more impactful in there, like a mini flashbang, for instance. Something to disorient your senses for a second or two, giving Ozan and his men all the time they need to wipe you all out.'

'And why would—?'

'Sorokin,' Ozan called out, 'what's the hold up over there?'

'Be patient,' Sorokin called back. 'I'm just making sure everything's as it should be.' To Korso, he said, 'So even if this were true, you still haven't explained Ozan's motive for double-crossing me. Other than the obvious, what else does he gain?'

'Well, I imagine he'll receive the eternal gratitude of his boss, along with a handsome bonus. That's often enough for loyal lapdogs like him. But, to be honest, bringing back the ZM-87 *and* the emeralds is motive enough. Everybody likes to have their cake and eat it. And let's face it, twenty million dollars isn't exactly pocket change.'

Sorokin smiled. 'Well, it's a nice theory, but I have my doubts. It so happens I've dealt with Romario Galicia twice before, and each transaction went through without—'

'Who said anything about Galicia?'

FORTY

The smile on Sorokin's face evaporated. 'What do you mean?'

'I mean Galicia's been dead for over a week now,' Korso said. 'He *was* kidnapped. By me, last Monday. I presented his drugged body to a man named Miguel Quezada as a calling card in order to help me gain employment with him. It succeeded to a degree, although it seems I've somehow fallen out of favour since then. But before we set out, Quezada did admit that he and Ozan spent a few pleasurable hours later that Monday, torturing Galicia for every last piece of information he could give them. You've heard of this Quezada, I assume?'

'I know of the man.'

'So that's how he found out about this deal. Then he got Galicia to call you up and explain how he wouldn't be able to come himself, and that his best man, Ozan, would act as his representative. I imagine that's why Galicia didn't sound too good on the phone. He was probably seconds away from death. Anyway, Quezada wants this weapon as badly as Galicia did, maybe more so, and he probably figures that if anything goes wrong today, then Galicia will get the blame. After all, nobody else knows he's even dead yet. If Ozan's lied to you about that, what else might he have lied about?'

Sorokin absently rubbed behind his ear as he evaluated Korso's words. 'One thing occurs to me. If you *have* been elected as today's lab rat, then it's clearly to your advantage to somehow drive a wedge between Ozan and myself. Would you agree?'

'There's a very easy way to check whether I'm telling you the truth or not.'

'And what's that?'

'Tell Ozan to get his boss on the phone. Say you need to speak with him in person before handing over the weapon.'

Sorokin nodded his head slowly. After a few moments, he looked past Korso's shoulder and called out, 'Ozan, join us for a moment. We may have a slight complication.'

'What are you talking about?'

'Come over here, and I'll explain.'

Korso didn't turn around to look. After a few moments, he heard footsteps behind him. He saw Ozan stop a few feet away to his left, his gaze switching between Korso and Sorokin, assault rifle aimed at the ground in the low ready position. Korso was glad to see his Glock 17 was still tucked into Ozan's waistband. He still had plans for that gun.

'What's this guy been telling you?' Ozan said.

'Oh, nothing much,' Sorokin said. 'Just that he's going to be used as the prime test subject once you get this weapon in your hands. Is that correct?'

'What difference does it make to you?'

'It could make all the difference in the world to me. For one thing, it means neither of us really cares if this man lives or dies at any point during today's exchange. In other words, he's a totally dispensable asset.' He looked at Korso. 'No offence.'

Korso shrugged. 'Facts are facts.'

'So?' Ozan said.

'So he's dispensable, and as far as you're concerned, so am I. No, don't bother arguing, it's simply the way of things. You're on one side, I'm on the other. Now let's say your man here unlocks the case and opens it up for me to evaluate the stones. Isn't it possible that, instead of the radioactive deterrent you mentioned before, there's something else in the case that's triggered to go off the moment it's opened? Something non-lethal like a small flash grenade, say, that would incapacitate us for long enough that you and your men can gun us down? Now I'm not saying that's going to happen in this instance, but you have to admit it's possible, right?'

'Most things are,' Ozan said, 'but you're on completely the wrong track here. There's no grenade in that case. We're both here to complete a deal. You get your stones, while we get our ZM-87. This guy's just trying to set us at each other's throats, that's all.'

'I considered that, but that doesn't make his point any less valid. So what I'd like is for you to get Romario Galicia on the phone for me. I can't say I completely trust the man, but he's been scrupulously honest in both of our previous business dealings, which is a rarity in my trade. So if he assures me I've got nothing to worry about, then I'm sure we can go about our business as planned.' He showed his palms. 'Am I being at all unreasonable?'

Ozan looked at each of them, thinking furiously. He had to know he couldn't turn down the request, but neither did he have the power to bring the dead back to life. After a few moments, he pulled his phone from his pocket. 'I'll try, but it may not be possible.'

'Really?' Sorokin tilted his head. 'And why's that?'

'Well... Mr Galicia's been in a lot of pain ever since he was shot last week. His doctor's been prescribing him a pretty powerful sedative and painkiller combo, which means he might not be conscious right now.'

'Try anyway.'

Ozan pressed several buttons on the screen and brought the phone to his ear.

While everybody's attention was on this little drama, Korso cupped his right hand and shifted his arm so the real flashbang began to slide down his shirtsleeve. When he felt the pull ring make contact with his middle two fingers, he held the stun grenade in place and waited. Unfortunately, he knew the concussive effects of the flashbang would be greatly diminished out in the open air, but he felt sure it would be more than sufficient to suit his purposes. It would have to be.

Ozan was still waiting for his call to go through. Assuming he was making one at all. Finally, he said, 'This is Ozan… Yeah, I'm there now. Is the boss around?'

Korso looked at Sorokin without expression. He didn't say anything. There was no need. He'd achieved what he set out to do. Now it was all a matter of timing. Moving just his eyes, he took careful note of everyone's position around him. Sorokin was directly opposite, watching Ozan at Korso's left. To Sorokin's right was his watchdog, his own assault rifle in the standard 45-degree, low ready position. He was about six feet away from Korso. He kept most of his attention on Ozan. Every now and then his gaze switched to Korso, then back to Ozan again.

One unarmed man against seven heavily armed men. A far from perfect situation, but you could only work with what you were given. Besides, they wouldn't all be shooting at him. And now Korso had three out of the seven standing in very close proximity to each other. That was a good start. Better than he could have hoped for.

But most importantly of all, he still had the element of surprise. Once he set off the flashbang, the accompanying smoke would obscure Korso's little group for a few valuable seconds. Since Ramirez and Flores wouldn't dare fire towards Ozan's position for fear of hitting him, they'd instead concentrate their fire towards targets they could actually see: Hector and the other gunman. Who would also be thinking exactly the same thing in relation to their own employer. So with any luck those four would wipe each other out, while Korso took care of the three targets in his immediate vicinity.

That was the theory, anyway.

Meanwhile, Ozan was saying, 'Yeah, that's what I figured, but I thought I'd check anyway. Okay, forget it.' He ended the call and tucked it back in his pocket. 'Sorry, but like I said, Mr

Galicia's under heavy sedation right now. My guy says he's not expected to wake up for another couple of hours.'

'Convenient,' Sorokin said, glancing at Korso again. 'In that case, I propose we make a slight alteration to the current plan, just to make sure everyone comes away happy. Ozan, I'd like you to remain here and open that case for me. That way, we both share the risk. If nothing happens, as I'm sure it won't, then you can both retreat back to your vehicle with the asset while I inspect my emeralds. Is that agreeable to you?'

Ozan didn't look happy, but he also seemed relieved that the deal was still going ahead. 'I guess I can do that much.' He turned to Korso. 'All right, hold the case steady.'

This was it. The moment he'd been waiting for. Korso held the steel case at chest level with the locks facing outwards, using both hands underneath as support. Ozan moved in close, and with his free hand began slowly turning the dials on the left lock.

While Ozan busied himself with the dials, Korso very, very carefully slid his left hand across the underside of the case until his index finger came into contact with the small safety pin at the top of the device. Using just thumb and forefinger, he gradually detached the pin from the grenade, then poked his middle finger through the pull ring until he felt he had a good enough grip. He'd have to time this perfectly. He knew that tactical-grade flashbangs usually came with a 1.5-second timed-delay fuse, but there was no way of knowing for sure until you tested one. Since that wasn't an option, he allowed himself one second as the absolute maximum. Maybe not even that.

'Keep still, goddamn it,' Ozan said. He finished the first lock, flicked the left latch of the case and the steel U-ring snapped upwards. He moved on to the right-hand lock.

As Ozan began rotating the next series of dials, Korso positioned his right foot so it was directly underneath his right hand. He looked over towards the ruins and furrowed his brow as though he'd seen something. Then he did a number of things in quick succession.

He said, 'Hey, who's that guy over there by the church?'

As all four men were in the act of turning their heads to see what he was talking about, Korso pulled the ring free of the grenade and made a star of his hand. When the tubular device dropped onto his shoe, he punted it quickly to his right.

Korso didn't check where it fell. There was no time. Clamping his eyes shut, he let the case drop and dived in the opposite direction, hands pressed tightly to his ears.

The moment he hit the ground, the grenade went off.

FORTY-ONE

Korso could only hear a muffled *BANG*, but he felt the detonation vibrate through his bones. Almost immediately he opened his eyes again, and was glad to find his vision still fully intact, and no ringing in his ears. He turned his head and saw a cloud of smoke rising into the air all around them. Sorokin and the other gunman were in the same spots as before. Sorokin had slumped to his knees, one hand across his eyes. Korso heard bursts of automatic gunfire coming from the direction of the SUV and the church, as well as heavy coughing nearby, to his immediate right. Ozan was still in the same position, with the unopened case of gems at his feet. He was swaying slightly while holding an arm across his face.

Without wasting a second, Korso rose up, grabbed hold of Ozan's ankles and yanked both feet up towards him. Ozan gave a sharp yell of surprise as he was upended, dropping the IWI assault rifle as he toppled back to the ground. Korso was on him before he even landed, launching a right hook into his abdomen, followed by a hard elbow strike directly into his face. Ozan yelled out as the bone connected with his nose, and Korso plucked the Glock from his waistband. He jammed the barrel into Ozan's stomach and was about to pull the trigger when Ozan's right fist suddenly appeared out of nowhere. It connected with Korso's temple and the world flashed white for a brief moment. Another punch landed in his kidneys, altering the Glock's position slightly. Korso instinctively squeezed the trigger, the sound of the single gunshot muffled by the closeness of their bodies.

Korso rolled off Ozan without checking where he'd shot him, and turned to the other two assailants.

Sorokin was yelling, '*Shoot, goddammit,*' at his man. '*Fire at anything that moves.*'

Korso aimed his Glock at the man-sized shape standing before him. Centre mass. Before the other man could even raise his weapon, Korso pulled the trigger three times. Each shot hit its target, and the gunman slumped to the ground like a sack of wet cement.

Korso was just turning towards Sorokin when more automatic gunfire suddenly erupted from the direction of the BMW and the church ruins. Korso dived to the ground again, pressing his face against the grass. He could hear the pitter-patter of rounds striking concrete and metal somewhere off to his left. He couldn't tell if they were aiming at him or at each other. Probably the latter, but there was no sense in getting careless now. Any one of those bullets could kill him. Moving only his eyes, he saw the smoke from the flashbang was already dispersing in the open air. That was bad. It wouldn't be long before it drifted away entirely, and he'd be completely exposed.

He could see Sorokin still on his knees a few feet away, but he was now frantically rooting around in his gun bag. Korso watched as he pulled out the ZM-87 rifle. He inserted a fat cable into the underside of the barrel and pressed a switch on the side. When he glanced over towards Korso's position, Korso shut his eyes and played dead. Pretending he'd been hit from the gunfire behind him. After a few seconds, he opened his eyes again, and saw Sorokin in the standard kneeling position, aiming his weapon at a spot behind Korso. He squeezed the trigger. There was no gunshot, just a brief electronic hum, and a moment later Korso heard a man screaming back there. It sounded like it could be Ramirez.

One more man down. The more the merrier, as far as Korso was concerned. Just as long as he wasn't one of them.

He watched Sorokin swivel ninety degrees to his right and aim the ZM-87 again. Korso turned his head a little to see what his target was. The first thing he noticed was Ozan was no longer on the ground next to him. Instead, Korso watched as a figure jogged unsteadily towards the church ruins, one arm pressed against his side. At least Korso had gotten a good one in. Ozan was almost thirty feet away already, and had just reached the large stones that led to the huge V-shaped gap at the side of the building. As he made his way over the uneven blocks of masonry, Sorokin squeezed off several shots from the laser weapon, but none hit their target. He was too far away. Oblivious, Ozan kept moving towards the relative safety of the ruins. Within seconds, he disappeared from sight.

'*Derr'mo*,' Sorokin hissed. He turned to Korso.

Korso raised the Glock, aimed the barrel at Sorokin's chest. He pulled the trigger, the gun jerked twice, and Sorokin grunted and fell to his knees, a look of disbelief on his face. Korso put another one in his forehead, and the lifeless body collapsed to the ground.

He became aware that the sounds of automatic gunfire had died away as quickly as they'd started. Looking back towards the BMW, he saw a feverish Ramirez on his hands and knees, searching the ground for his weapon like a man possessed. He was jabbering to himself nonsensically, and showed all the signs of being completely sightless. So it seemed the prototype rifle lived up to its reputation, after all. It also meant that there were now just four more men to account for. Korso couldn't see any other bodies on the ground, but that didn't necessarily mean anything. He knew Ozan was still in one piece, but Flores and the other two gunmen could be injured, or all three could be dead. No way to tell yet.

Korso turned back to the two men he'd dropped. Both were history. There was blood everywhere. Leaning down, Korso patted the pockets of the gunman, and found the keys to the Toyota in the left jacket pocket.

As he stuffed them in his own pocket, he heard the distant sound of a man moaning in pain. It was coming from the direction of the church again. He still couldn't see any signs of movement over there.

Then he heard two gunshots in quick succession. The moans stopped.

Suspecting another player had just breathed his last, Korso decided it was time to relocate to safer quarters. Glancing at the ZM-87, he briefly considered taking it with him, before discounting it as too bulky a load to carry. But there was a far easier solution. He picked up the assault rifle lying next to the driver's body. It was a Heckler & Koch HK416 with a thirty-round magazine, containing 5.56 x 45mm NATO rounds. They'd cut through anything. He placed the ZM-87 and power cable back in the gun bag and zipped it closed. Aiming the HK416 at the bag, he gently squeezed the trigger, emptying half the magazine as he peppered the contents.

Satisfied nobody else could use the laser weapon, Korso pulled a spare magazine for the Heckler & Koch from the dead man's gun belt and stuck it in his own waistband. He also went back and grabbed the laptop case from where Ozan dropped it. He sprinted for the Toyota thirty feet away. As he ran he heard another gunshot from his left, but he felt nothing. Saw nothing. Didn't even know if he was the intended target, although he thought it likely.

He reached the Toyota and pulled open the front passenger door, hoping it was bullet-proofed like the BMW. He ducked into the front passenger seat and leaned down and tucked the laptop case under his seat. No sense in leaving it out in plain view. He'd come back for it later, assuming he was still able to.

Korso backed out of the Toyota and was about to move to the rear of the vehicle when a series of gunshots halted him in his tracks. He quickly brought his feet up as he ducked back into the vehicle, and he heard more rounds pinging against the open door. Another gunshot echoed throughout the area, and a small spider web instantly splattered against the windshield, close to where his face had been. Another gunshot, and a second spider web joined the first one. But the windshield held. So that answered his earlier question. The shooter didn't try again.

Korso now knew he couldn't simply sprint towards the church and hope for the best, as he'd planned to do. Whoever was firing at him was too good a shot for that. He needed some kind of distraction. Knowing Sorokin's men would surely have brought extra ammunition along, Korso turned and checked the rear seats. But there was nothing back there. He lowered the driver's seat and was about to crawl back and check the small cargo space at the rear when he spotted a canvas knapsack lying in the rear footwell behind him. It looked full. He pulled it out and faced front again.

Opening the flap, he saw over a dozen spare ammo magazines inside, although none matched the one in his waistband. Ignoring them, he reached underneath until his fingers came into contact with three tubular devices, each with a pull ring at one end. He carefully pulled the grenades out for a better look. The two larger ones were M84 stun grenades, while the third was an MIL-X smoke grenade.

Korso took one of each. The smoke grenade was a model he'd used before – even had some employed against him in recent months – and so he knew it had a burn time of around sixty seconds and produced smoke dense enough to conceal a small army if there wasn't too much breeze.

He looked out the windshield at the huge V shape in the church wall, just twenty feet in front of him. He still couldn't see any movement, but any survivors left over there had to be dealt with. The only way this could work was if Korso was the last man standing. Nothing else would do. He could wait for the enemy to come to him, of course, since they wanted the emeralds a lot more than he did. And in any other scenario, that might be the best tactic. But Korso was aware that locals could come along at any time to further complicate things, and the very last thing he needed were witnesses. The sooner this was finished the better.

Leaning over, Korso inserted the key into the ignition and turned it a quarter circle clockwise until the dashboard lights came on. He pressed the trunk release button next to the wheel and watched as the rear hatch slowly raised itself up. Removing the key again, he manoeuvred himself into the rear of the vehicle, bringing the Heckler & Koch with him. In the back, he pulled one of the seats forward to allow him access to the cargo area. Once he was outside again, he lowered the rear hatch and locked the vehicle.

There were no gunshots. He saw the BMW was still in the same spot as before. He couldn't see Ramirez, but he was probably still fumbling around over there. The only sounds he could hear were the ever-present bird calls, and the faint whine of a jet somewhere in the distance. The air was still, with barely even a breeze. Perfect conditions.

Pocketing the M84, he pulled the pin from the smoke grenade, keeping his fingers tight on the safety lever. Pulling his arm back, Korso lobbed the grenade fifteen feet towards the V-shaped gap. It was already starting to spew thick plumes of white smoke while in the air. The smoke only got thicker and denser once it landed on the blocks of mortar. Korso waited a few more seconds for it to spread further.

Once he felt he was safely screened from the shooter, he launched himself away from the vehicle and sprinted towards the rear of the church.

FORTY-TWO

Covering the distance in seconds, Korso pressed against the side wall as far from the V as possible, rifle in the high ready position. He hadn't heard anyone firing at him. He ducked down and peered round the corner. The whole area was fairly thick with smoke now, and he couldn't see anyone moving about back there. But he was able to make out a large open archway halfway along the rear wall, matching the one at the front. He trotted over to it, and as he got closer he noticed a body on the ground a few feet away, lying face up. Korso recognised him as the one called Hector. His upper body was covered in blood, as though he'd bathed in the stuff. Korso counted six bullet wounds in his chest. There were probably more he couldn't see. The man's eyes were open, and he wasn't breathing.

Korso approached the archway and peered round into the church 'interior', which was just a large open space with four crumbing walls. Weeds and long grass poked through the cracks in the concrete foundation. Through the gaps in the smoke, he could make out a huge stone column lying along the width of the church. It was in four uneven pieces, having probably collapsed a lifetime ago, and was almost green with mildew and rot. Dotted around here and there were large blocks of fallen masonry, all their rough edges long ago smoothed over from exposure.

Still using the smoke as cover, Korso entered the room, sweeping the gun in all directions. He walked slowly, carefully, knowing one single slip could prove fatal. The nearest piece of masonry was about fifteen feet away. It was three feet high at its tallest point, large enough to use as cover. He aimed for that. As he moved forward, he noticed something on the ground, close to the wall at his right. It was another human figure lying face down, wearing an army camo jacket and black cargo pants, like Hector. There was a huge pool of blood around the body. He wasn't moving. Maybe he'd been the source of the moaning Korso had heard.

So five down, two to go.

Korso didn't bother checking the body, but kept moving towards the block of masonry, his senses alert to the slightest sound, the smallest movement. None came. When he reached the stone block he crouched next to it, checking his six at the same time. But there was nobody coming up the rear. He was about to continue his search when he paused. He could hear the sound of rapid breathing nearby. It sounded laboured, with a faint, high-pitched wheeze accompanying each exhalation. Staying low, Korso poked his head round the slab of stone and saw a pair of outstretched legs on the other side, both boots pointing upwards. Leading with his weapon, Korso sidled around the masonry until he was able to see the rest of him.

It was Flores. He was sitting with his back against the rock. His mouth was open, but his eyes were closed. Among other things, he'd been gut-shot. He had one arm pressed against his stomach while a puddle of blood formed in a large pool underneath his body. His face was almost white. Another shot had taken him high in the chest. That wound was bleeding just as profusely, but probably not for much longer. He was clearly near the end.

Flores must have sensed a presence because his eyes suddenly opened wide. He stared up at Korso looking down at him, and opened his mouth as he took a deep, painful breath. Before he could yell out a warning, Korso quickly reversed the gun and slammed the buttstock down on Flores's face, knocking him out immediately. He watched his body slowly slide down to the side until his head made contact with the ground.

He should be grateful. At least he'd die in his sleep. Not many were that fortunate.

More importantly, that meant just Ozan was left. And his being injured only made him more dangerous. The smoke was starting to thin out now, enabling Korso to see more of the church interior. But there was no sign of the man.

Rising to his feet, Korso was about to approach the fallen column when he heard a sound that didn't belong. Without a moment's thought, he ducked back behind the rock just as a burst of gunfire erupted from somewhere to his right, past the horizontal column. He heard bullets ricocheting off stone, and saw Flores's lower body convulse violently as Ozan pumped him full of rounds meant for Korso.

Clever. Ozan must have placed the injured Flores there to divert Korso's attention just long enough for him to riddle him with bullets. It had almost worked.

Keeping his head down, Korso raised the barrel of the Heckler & Koch over the top and aimed it in Ozan's general direction. Using just one hand, he squeezed the trigger and the weapon juddered as he swept it in a small arc and then back again. Once he'd emptied the rest of the magazine, he pulled the weapon back out of sight. He quickly ejected the magazine and replaced it with a full one. His last.

There was no answering fire. Korso could have gotten lucky with one of his shots, and Ozan might now be nursing a second wound. But he couldn't afford to wait and find out.

He had to move. Now.

Pulling the M84 flashbang from his pocket, he yanked the ring free and lobbed it overhead, in the direction from which the shooting had come. He placed his hands over his ears and heard the muffled bang a moment later.

Jumping out from behind the cover of the rock, Korso ran towards the leftmost chunk of the stone column and jumped over it, weapon at the ready. He ducked down and waved his weapon in an arc, covering all angles.

No Ozan. Nothing.

Just a small cloud of smoke spiralling into the air, and already beginning to thin out.

Directly ahead was the open archway at the front of the church, where the first gunman, Hector, had greeted them. Korso made his way carefully towards it, still looking in all directions as he went. Once he'd covered the distance, he pressed his back against the wall just a few inches away from the opening.

He waited. He listened. He heard nothing out of the ordinary.

But Ozan was out there, just waiting for Korso to show himself. He knew that much. If Ozan had been fully fit he would have followed up the assault on Korso right away with a second barrage of gunfire. So maybe the wound was restricting his choices in that department. Unless Ozan just wanted Korso to think that. It was a fact that all warfare was based on deception, and Ozan was far from stupid. Korso had briefly considered waiting for the enemy to come to him, and discounted it. But that might be the best tactic for Ozan now. All he had to do was find a spot with an optimum field of view and simply wait for Korso to poke his head out. That's how Korso would play it. In which case, Ozan would most likely have positioned himself to the left or the right of the front archway, close to the corner of the building in order to cover his back.

But which corner? Was he situated to the left of the opening, or was he on the right side?

Korso almost regretted not bringing both those flashbangs from the Toyota. He felt sure he could have used the second one to draw Ozan out somehow. He began patting his pockets out of habit, and paused when he felt the cell phone in his rear pocket. Pulling it out, he frowned at the screen. It was also a fact that the most effective solutions were often the simplest. It all depended on whether Ozan had set his own phone to silent mode or not.

Korso went to his recent calls and highlighted Ozan's number. He let his thumb hover over the green Call button. In his experience, it usually took at least a couple of seconds for a call to go through. That should be enough time.

He pressed the green button, and quickly pocketed his phone. Gripping the Heckler & Koch in both hands, he stood before the opening. Ready.

One second.

Two seconds.

Three.

The silence was suddenly shattered by that same howling wolf ringtone. It was muffled, but still totally recognisable. And it was coming from the right. As soon as he was able to pinpoint the direction, Korso sprinted through the archway at full speed, veering right at the same time. He came to a rapid halt when he spotted the familiar blond thatch of hair thirty feet away. Ozan was crouched down by the corner, using the wall for support, his side blood-stained from the gunshot wound. His assault rifle was still aimed at the opening. He was looking downwards as he tried to silence the phone in his jacket pocket. But he must have spotted movement, because he raised his head up quickly. His eyes grew large when he saw Korso less than twenty feet away, his own rifle aimed directly at him.

And that was the moment he knew it was too late. Korso could see it in his eyes.

Korso squeezed the trigger and let loose a burst. The weapon shook as the half-dozen shots all found their target. Ozan slammed back to the ground from the impact, arms wide, dark red flowers already blooming on his chest and abdomen.

Korso ran over and kicked the assault rifle away from the man's reach. Stepping back again, Korso saw all of his shots had hit vital areas. Three of the large calibre rounds had taken him in the stomach, causing a real mess down there. Ozan was losing blood at a rate of knots. It was obvious his time was up, and not a moment too soon.

Ozan glared up at him, his eyelids at half mast. His breathing was already becoming shallow and hoarse. 'Piece of shit,' he hissed. 'I had you.'

'You thought you did,' Korso said. 'Just one more error to add to your long list.'

Ozan sneered. 'Was… never wrong about you, asshole. Had… your number from the start.' He took a deep breath, and grimaced from the sudden pain. It lasted awhile. 'You'll get yours.'

'Maybe. But not today.'

Ozan coughed a few times, and bloody spittle appeared at the corners of his mouth. He tried to spit some of it in Korso's direction, but the effort was too much. His head fell back to the ground, his face a picture of agony. 'Getting a kick… out of watching me die?'

'Not really. The sooner you go, the quicker I can get out of here.'

'Shoot me then… Be doing me a favour.'

Korso shook his head. 'You don't deserve favours, Ozan. Not after the things you've done. I think I'll let events play out as they will.'

'Screw you.' Another coughing fit followed, more intense and pain-wracked than before. Korso wasn't getting any pleasure out of this, but neither did he like leaving business unfinished.

It took a while for Ozan to breathe his last. Once Korso was certain the man was dead, he set to work.

FORTY-THREE

Korso turned up at the main gates of the compound at 5.23 p.m. He'd had a few last-minute errands to run in the city, which partly accounted for the long delay. He pressed the horn twice, and waited to be let through. The licence plates on the BMW had been enough to get past the guard at the outer barrier, which showed even Quezada's security had its weak spots, but he didn't expect the same level of ineptitude here.

Sure enough, two men stepped through the side gate moments later. One was Dante. The other guy Korso had never seen before. They approached the vehicle warily, hands close to their weapons. Korso opened his door and got out.

'Where's Mr Ozan?' Dante asked.

'In the back,' Korso said.

Dante went over and popped the rear hatch. Inside the cargo area was a large mass covered in a dirty, ripped bed sheet. After putting the blinded Ramirez out of his misery, Korso had searched the woods near the church and found the sheet along with some old, used syringes. Dante pulled up a section of material and stared at what was underneath for a few moments. He swore softly, glared up at Korso, then lowered the sheet and shut the rear hatch. Pulling his gun from the holster, he approached Korso and aimed the barrel at his forehead.

Korso slowly raised both hands. Nobody spoke. He tried to read Dante's eyes, but they might as well have been made of glass. The man's gun hand remained perfectly steady. Finally, Korso said, 'You really planning on using that?'

'I'm considering it,' Dante said, pulling back the hammer. 'I knew Ozan a long, long time, so I know from personal experience how good he was. Yet the first time he goes out in the field with you, he comes back in a body bag. What do you think that says to me?'

'That his luck finally ran out? Sooner or later it happens to us all. You know that.'

'I still don't buy it. What the hell happened out there?'

'What does it look like? We were double-crossed by the men we were supposed to meet. Ramirez and Flores are both dead as well. Unless you're planning to kill me too, you better call Mr Quezada and suggest he meet me in the garage. He won't want anyone else seeing this.'

Dante slowly lowered the gun, and finally reholstered it. 'Let me worry about what the boss wants. Pablo, search him.'

As the other man started patting Korso down, Dante pulled out a phone, pressed a button and raised it to his ear. He turned away as he spoke to Quezada. When he turned round again, the phone was gone. He raised an eyebrow at Pablo.

'He's clean,' Pablo said.

'We'll see about that.' Dante turned to Korso. 'The boss is heading over to the garage now, and he's seriously pissed. You drive, I'm riding with you.' He waved up at the cameras, and the gates slowly opened up. Korso got back behind the wheel, and once Dante got in the front passenger seat, he drove through the gates.

When they reached the garage annex a minute or two later, Korso saw one of the up-and-over doors was already open. He steered the vehicle under it and into the garage. The interior lights had been turned on, and he saw Quezada already in there, waiting next to an empty bay. His expression was grim. He was alone. Korso parked in the bay, killed the engine, and he and Dante both got out.

Quezada walked towards Korso while waving a remote at the door. It began to close slowly, shutting them in. Tossing the remote to Dante, he said to Korso in an icy whisper, 'Do you know how long I've been waiting for news? Over three hours. That's practically a lifetime. And now Dante tells me you've shown up with the body of Javier in the back of the vehicle? Is this some kind of joke?'

'I'm not laughing,' Korso said. 'The whole deal was a set-up from the off. I wanted to call you on the drive back, but you never gave me your number, and Ozan's cell phone was in pieces. As were the other two, along with their respective owners.'

'Yet you somehow survived intact.'

'It's what I do.'

Quezada studied him for a moment, then said, 'Show me.'

Korso went back and opened the BMW's rear hatch. He removed the old bed sheet and took a step back, while Quezada leaned in to inspect his oldest friend's bloody corpse. Dante stood nearby, his eyes on Korso, his right hand not far from his holster.

Finally, Quezada raised himself up slowly. When he turned round, Korso saw there was a tactical knife in his right hand. It looked like a slightly smaller version of the Ka-Bar Korso had used before, with a blade as black as night. Quezada's eyes were dry, his gaze emotionless. 'That man in there meant a lot to me,' he said. 'I fought a lot of battles with him at my side, and we always came out on top. In many ways, Javier was a better brother to me than my real ones.'

Quezada suddenly rushed forward, and in the blink of an eye the blade was at Korso's throat, just above the Adam's apple. Korso froze in place. He didn't blink. He barely breathed. Already, he could feel the jagged edge starting to bite into his skin. One little nudge from Quezada, that's all it would take, and he'd be bleeding out like a stuck pig within seconds.

'Do you know how long he and I have been friends?' Quezada hissed. 'Have you any idea? Answer me.'

'A lifetime,' Korso whispered back.

'Yes, a lifetime.' Quezada nodded. 'Perhaps ten lifetimes. Ever since we were both children, living on the streets and fending for ourselves. I trusted him with my life more times than I can count, and he never let me down. Not once. If it weren't for Javier, I wouldn't be where I am today. I probably wouldn't even be breathing.'

'He told me how close the two of you were. That's why I didn't want to leave him back there with the others. I figured at the very least you'd want to give him a decent burial.'

Quezada considered this for a few moments, and then finally removed the knife from Korso's throat, and stepped back. Korso let out a long breath and placed a palm to his throat, looked at it. There was no blood.

'Describe exactly what happened,' Quezada said, keeping the knife in plain view, 'and leave nothing out.'

'I can only tell you what I saw,' Korso said, pausing a moment to get his breath back and his thoughts in order. He'd been preparing for this moment for the last hour, and knew he had to be convincing or he'd end up lying next to Ozan. Dante's presence only exacerbated the danger. Depending on how much Ozan had told him of his ultimate plans, Dante could throw a huge spanner into the works at any point by openly disputing Korso's version of events. But all he could do now was wing it, and deal with each problem as it came.

'So after we left your office, Ozan explained to me that Flores was to be the designated fall guy, but that he wanted Ramirez and Flores to think *I* was to be the test subject. For that reason he wanted to issue me with just a handgun rather than an assault rifle or SMG, in order to make it more believable to those two. I thought that made sense, and since I figured you'd already agreed to the deception I went along with it.'

'I hadn't,' Quezada said, 'but it's the kind of thing Javier would think of. And so?'

'And so we arrived at the site on time, where there were already three armed men waiting. Sorokin was circling above us in a single-engine plane. We didn't know it at the time, but he was probably checking the surrounding roads and making sure we hadn't arrived with back-up. He was a skilled pilot, you know.'

Quezada waved it away. 'Go on.'

'Well, we watched him as he landed in the adjacent field, and then he got out and walked towards us, carrying a large bag over his shoulder. We fanned out in front of our vehicle while two of Sorokin's men walked over and flanked him on either side. The third man stayed near the ruins, watching us. Right away Sorokin went on the offensive and started accusing Ozan of double dealing, about how he planned to screw him over somehow, and how he'd almost decided to abandon the deal entirely. Sorokin said something smelled rotten about the whole thing, and that he wanted to talk to Galicia personally before going ahead with any exchange. That was the moment when I knew it was all going to end badly.'

'Why?'

'Because it was clear to me that Sorokin knew Galicia was dead, or at least suspected it. He could tell he was being conned, he just didn't know how exactly. But he knew Ozan wouldn't be able to get Galicia on the phone. You could see it in his eyes. Ozan made a good try of it, I'll give him that. He'd already explained to Sorokin that Galicia had nearly been grabbed a week before, mixing the truth with a few well-placed lies, and that he'd been injured in the ensuing fire fight and was now confined to his home and on heavy painkillers. So Ozan called a number and made out he wanted to speak with Galicia urgently, but soon came back with the explanation that Galicia was unconscious and would be for the next few hours, and—'

'That part's true, boss,' Dante said. 'I was the one Mr Ozan called. It was just a one-sided conversation, but I understood what he was doing so I played dumb and just let him talk. This was about a quarter after two.'

Korso managed to conceal his surprise as he looked at Dante. He hadn't counted on corroboration from such an unexpected quarter. Quezada merely nodded at this piece of news, and turned back to Korso.

'Sorokin clearly didn't believe a word of it, though, and said he still suspected there was a nasty surprise inside the laptop case that would be triggered the moment he opened it…'

'But Javier already told Sorokin we had a radioactive tripwire in the case,' Quezada said. 'Basic psychology. A lethal deterrent's no good if the other side's unaware of it.'

'Oh, Sorokin knew about the polonium-210 all right, but he just figured that was a bluff and that we'd placed a stun grenade in there instead. Just a little extra surprise that would knock him and his men off balance long enough for us to mow them all down. Like I said, he was on the offensive right from the start. So he told Ozan to come over and open it for him. Only then would he give him the bag with the ZM-87. Ozan couldn't exactly refuse at this point, so he had a brief word with Ramirez, and then he carried the laptop case over to Sorokin and began working on the combination locks.'

'And what were you doing through all this?'

'Preparing for the fireworks to come. I didn't have an assault rifle, but I'd equipped myself with a couple of smoke grenades from your armoury before we set out, so while they were talking I was pulling one out from my pocket, ready to throw at a moment's notice. At the same time, I was moving back towards the SUV here, since I knew it was bullet-proofed. If and when the shooting started, I wanted to be as close to this vehicle as possible.'

'How *did* the shooting start?'

'It kind of came out of nowhere. Ozan was about halfway through the second lock when I saw Sorokin make a weird hand gesture to the man to his left. At that point, I knew something was off so I pulled the pin on the grenade, but held on to the safety lever. Before I could do anything, the guy raised his weapon in Ozan's direction. Ozan said something I couldn't hear, and then the guy squeezed the trigger and just riddled him with bullets. As soon as Ozan fell, I immediately threw the grenade over there. White smoke started gushing out while it was still in the air. Everyone seemed to start shooting at once then, and so I lobbed the second grenade in the other direction and ducked inside the BMW.'

'You mean you wimped out?' Dante said. 'You didn't even fire off a shot?'

'He's got a point,' Quezada said. 'Why didn't you?'

'With just a Glock 17? That's the equivalent of taking a knife to a gunfight. Ramirez and Flores were the ones with the heavy artillery. Besides, you brought me in as a consultant, Mr Quezada, not as a gunman. That's not exactly my area of expertise. Anyway I couldn't see much because of the smoke, but I could hear plenty of gunfire out there. So I just stayed low and waited to see who was still breathing at the end. I planned to be one of them.'

'What a hero,' Dante said, disgustedly.

'Heroes are for the movies,' Korso said with a shrug. 'My main focus in life is self-preservation. Everything else is secondary.'

'Stick to the subject,' Quezada said.

Korso went on. 'So it was less than a minute before things quieted down outside. The smoke was dispersing in the breeze, but there was still enough to shield me as I snuck out of the car. I could only hear two voices and they were faint. They sounded like they were coming from the church ruins. So I managed to creep over there unseen, and finally saw Sorokin and one of his goons inspecting Flores's body, lying near a fallen pillar. I aimed the Glock and shot each of them in the back, and then went over and finished them off. I checked the area, and soon found the other three, all dead. So I searched the woods nearby and finally found an old ragged bed sheet to cover Ozan, and then I placed him in the back of the BMW. I would have been here sooner, but I had to take the long route back since I couldn't risk being pulled over by the cops.'

Quezada just looked at him steadily, saying nothing.

'But on the plus side,' Korso said, 'I also brought back the gems *and* the ZM-87.'

Quezada's gaze softened a fraction at this piece of news. 'And where are they?'

'The laptop case is under the driver's seat. The gun bag's lodged in the rear footwell.'

'Get them, Dante.'

Dante opened the driver's door and pulled out the laptop case and placed it on the hood. He then pulled the driver's seat forward and pulled the canvas gun bag out of the footwell. He placed the bag on the hood next to the emeralds.

Ignoring the gems, Quezada briefly studied the large bullet holes peppering the canvas bag. He unzipped it, reached in and carefully pulled out the weapon within. It closely resembled the Chinese standard-issue bullpup assault rifle, the QBZ-95, except this version also had a much fatter barrel, and instead of the usual magazine slot behind the grip and trigger guard, there was a large threaded socket for the cable that connected it to the power unit. The other main difference was that there were two large bullet holes in the breech, and another bullet hole in the stock. But it was the breech area that contained all the intricate fibre-optics, the nano circuit boards, the miniature mirrors and precision lenses that actually made the laser weapon work.

'Useless,' Quezada said, his voice barely above a whisper. His jaw was clenched tight with repressed rage. 'Completely useless. Who did this?'

'It could have been anyone,' Korso said, knowing better. Amazingly, it turned out his initial burst of rounds had completely missed the rifle itself, so he'd had to try again with a little more precision before driving back. The last thing the world needed was a psychotic crime lord in possession of a weapon that could permanently blind people. 'But I figured you'd want it anyway, even if it was only as a trophy. It's still a one-off, and I didn't want it to appear as if Ozan died for nothing.'

Quezada stayed silent, and Korso saw him mentally trying to calm himself down. After a few moments, he nodded slowly. 'I suppose you acted correctly, Graves. And you're right, it'll make a decent trophy. But in all honesty, I wish it was your body in that trunk instead of Javier's.'

'I'd probably feel the same in your shoes. If it makes any difference, I don't expect to be paid my full fee for today.'

Quezada snorted. 'Graves, I'm fully aware you could have driven straight to the airport with no one the wiser and departed this country twenty million dollars richer than when you arrived. But instead you brought my stones right back to me. Don't think I haven't taken that into consideration. I'd say you've more than earned your fee.'

'Well, it's like I said before, steady employment is worth far more to me than a quick payday.' He coughed politely. 'You mind if I stick around the estate a while, Mr Quezada? I was hoping I might pay Alex a visit, if she's back from her business in the city. That is, unless you need my help with anything else?'

'No, Dante can take care of things here for me,' Quezada said, waving him away as he turned to the laptop case. 'Go if you want.'

Korso nodded his thanks, and went.

FORTY-FOUR

Korso knocked loudly on the front door of the bungalow. When he got no answer, he let himself in. He could hear salsa music coming from somewhere, and followed it to the kitchen, where he saw Alex in front of the open refrigerator. She was carefully placing a large dish covered in tin foil onto the top shelf. He saw other fully loaded dishes already in there.

He waited by the doorway. When she finally noticed him, she smiled and came over. They kissed briefly. 'I wasn't sure you'd make it.'

'You and me both.'

Korso took a seat at the small breakfast bar, while Alex reduced the volume on her phone and returned to the fridge. She pulled out an already opened bottle of white wine and set it down on the bar counter. 'I was thinking we could eat in tonight. I persuaded Maria to prepare us some dishes that I can heat up for us. Sound good?'

'Sounds ideal.'

'That's settled then.' She tapped the bottle. 'Fancy a glass?'

'Or two.'

Alex found a pair of wine glasses in one of the overhead cupboards and set them down on the counter. Korso uncorked the bottle and did the pouring.

'So how was your day?' he asked, pushing a full glass towards her.

'About as dull as I expected,' she said, taking a sip. 'It seems my whole life is made up of one tedious business meeting after another. After a while they all kind of blend together. Oh, and your Honda's back in the garage, by the way. One of the guards picked it up this afternoon. He told me he left the keys in the ignition.'

'Thanks.'

'So what about your super-secret mission this afternoon? How did it all go?'

'Not well, or very well, depending on how you look at it. In any case, you won't have to worry about avoiding Ozan's advances anymore. He didn't make it.'

'Wait, what?' Alex stared at him as she carefully set her wine glass down. 'Did I hear that right? You're telling me Javier's... *dead*?'

'That's exactly what I'm saying. The same goes for Ramirez, and a fellow named Flores. I was the only survivor. I only just got back.'

'Wow. Just... wow.' She kept staring at him for a few more moments, then finally nodded to herself. 'I'm trying to gauge my own reaction, and I think what I feel most is relief. Does that sound callous?'

'Not in the least. I sure won't miss him. Or them.'

'Can you tell me what happened?'

'I'll give you every detail, if that's what you want.'

'I want to know everything, Ric. Please.'

So Korso told her everything, from the meeting with Quezada onwards. Or almost everything. He explained about the deal with Sorokin to purchase the ZM-87, and how Ozan revealed his own plan to use Korso as the test subject for the rifle once they arrived at the meeting site. Korso described how he'd played each side against the other to get the result he wanted, the only result that could work for him. And he also told her of the mostly fictional account he'd just given Quezada, with the crucial difference being that Sorokin now took the lion's share of the blame. But one critical part he omitted was the torture and murder of Galicia the week before. The less Alex knew about that part, the better.

Once he'd finished, Alex glanced at the darkening sky through the kitchen window, while Korso finished his glass of wine in silence. He hadn't told her all of it yet. He was still wondering just how much more he should say, and what he should leave out.

Finally, Alex turned back to him. 'That's some day you've had, Ric. I have to admit I underestimated you. I had no idea what you're really capable of.'

'I hope that's not damning with faint praise.'

'Far from it. Tell me, is your business usually this violent? I mean, is it normal for you to wake up in the morning and not know if you'll be alive by day's end?'

'Of course not. If every day were like this one, I'd have been pushing up daisies long before now. Today was very much a deviation from the norm. It would have to be.'

'But you're still in a high-risk profession, aren't you?'

'Sure, but I do as much as I can to reduce those risks down to manageable levels. Only I didn't get a chance do that this afternoon. I had to improvise on the spot, and was very lucky to come out in one piece. It's not something I want to repeat, I can tell you that.'

'I'd be worried if you did.' She looked down at her wine glass. 'So how did Miguel take the news of Javier?'

'As you'd expect, he wasn't too happy about losing his childhood friend and closest ally, but my bringing back the emeralds and the rifle, even damaged as it was, seemed to placate him a little. Or so it appeared. It's hard to know what he really thinks.'

'Reminds me of someone else I know. And what about this laser weapon, could it really do what they said? Blind people permanently?'

'More than likely. No way of telling now, of course.'

'Then you did the right thing in wrecking it. A man of Miguel's temperament shouldn't ever be allowed to possess a weapon that dangerous.'

He slowly refilled both their glasses. 'Alex, there's something else I haven't mentioned. Something Ozan told me when we were alone in the car, when he knew he was talking to a dead man. And it's particularly relevant to you.'

'Me? Why, what did he say?'

'Drink your wine first, and I'll tell you.'

'Fine.' She drank half the contents, and then put the glass down. 'Now tell me.'

'Well, when I brought your name up he said something puzzling, about how getting rid of me was just his way of doing you a favour, and how sometimes you just needed a friendly nudge to help you decide what you really wanted. Or who. And that made me think of what you'd told me last night. So I asked him straight out, "You mean like the favour you did for her four years ago, when that financier boyfriend of hers was murdered?"'

'Sander?' Alex clenched her jaw muscles tightly. 'Did you actually mention him by name?'

'I did.'

'And what did Ozan say?'

'He said it was all ancient news, and that the cops figured it was probably one of his firm's clients who was behind it. But when I flat out accused him of being the one responsible, he just smiled and said, "So what if I *was*? The man was a loser. Alex was better off without him." His exact words.'

Alex lowered her head for a few moments. Korso didn't say anything. He just let her ruminate in silence. When she finally raised her head again, her eyes were still dry. Which was understandable; she'd probably exhausted her tears long ago. 'You know, part of me always suspected Ozan had a hand in Sander's death, since he had the most to gain out of anybody. Mainly me. But whenever I brought up the subject with him, which I did quite often, he never made a single slip. Not once. He was probably secretly laughing at me every time I talked about it, though.' She shook her head. 'The bastard probably tortured Sander personally for fun, and then finished him off as soon as he got bored. That's just the kind of thing he'd do.' She paused. 'How long did it take for him to die?'

'Five or six minutes.'

'And did he suffer?'

Korso nodded. 'Gut shots are the worst, so he was in a great deal of pain. He asked me to finish him. I refused.'

'Good. I just wish I'd been there to watch it myself.'

'No, you really don't. I hope I did the right thing in telling you this.'

'You did.' She took his hand, gave it a squeeze. 'I can't begin to tell you what a weight off my mind this is, Ric. In the last four years, I don't think a single day's passed when I haven't thought about Sander, and about what I'd do if I ever discovered who was responsible for his murder. And now you come along and solve the puzzle, just like that. Amazing. I only wish I'd been the one to pull the trigger, but to be honest just knowing that animal's no longer around is satisfaction enough.' She leaned forward and kissed him again. 'You've earned your place at tonight's table, and a lot more besides.'

'I hope that means what I think it means.'

She finished off her wine, and said, 'We'll just have to see, won't we?'

FORTY-FIVE

When Korso woke up, he turned his head and saw Alex sleeping with her back to him. She was snoring lightly. Reaching for his phone on the night table, he activated the display, saw it was 02.34, and clicked it off again. Perfect.

Making as little noise as possible, he slid out from under the covers and padded naked across the room. No clothes on the floor this time. There hadn't been such a rush to get into bed as on the previous night. After a lengthy and truly delicious dinner, they'd drunk more wine while they watched a movie on the huge LCD TV in the living room. Once it was over, things got more than a little steamy. And it wasn't too long after that they both retreated, naked, to the bedroom, to continue where they left off. And then sleep.

But now it was back to work again. Hopefully, for the final time.

In the living room, Korso grabbed his clothes from the settee and quickly got dressed. Then he reached under the cushion of one of the easy chairs and felt around for the penlight he'd hidden there the previous night. It was still there. He stuffed it in his pocket. After making sure Alex was still asleep, he let himself out the front door.

Staying out of the light, Korso carefully made his way through the estate until he arrived at the garage building. The night was cool, the moon hidden under cloud cover. Other than the ubiquitous cicadas, which were particularly loud tonight, he didn't see or hear anything out of the ordinary along the way. He made his way to the side door he'd used already and tried the knob. It gave easily. He opened the door and entered the garage.

There were no windows and no night lights, so all was black inside. It was like being in a tomb. Shutting the door behind him, Korso activated the penlight and moved the beam around. He quickly found the BMW, still parked in the same spot, and went over to it. He tried the driver's door and breathed a sigh of relief when it clicked open. Had it been locked, he might have had serious problems. Once the interior light came on, he went back to the rear hatch and pulled it open. The carpeted floor in the cargo area was spotless again. Korso grabbed hold of the latch and pulled the hardboard flooring up, revealing the spare run-flat tyre. Korso unscrewed the bolts that kept it in place, and pulled the tyre out.

Underneath, everything was still where he'd left it. He leaned down and pulled out the bulging padded jiffy bag, and the micro compact S&W Bodyguard he'd originally palmed from the armoury. It now had six 9mm rounds in the magazine. He stuck it in his pocket. He also opened the flap of the jiffy bag, and checked his items were still in there. All were present and correct. Replacing the tyre, he lowered the hardboard floor and locked it into position. He shut the rear hatch, and then he shut the driver's door.

Slipping the jiffy bag in his waistband, he left the garage as silently as he arrived. Less than five minutes later, he was standing outside the annex building again. Just as he was about to pull open the entrance door, he paused. Something was nagging at him, tickling the hairs at the back of his neck. But what? He'd kept a careful eye on his surroundings as he walked back, eyes peeled for the slightest movement, ears alert to the faintest sound that didn't belong. But he'd seen nothing, heard nothing. He turned in a slow circle, looking everywhere, but there was still nothing. He stood there for a full minute, with the same result.

With a mental shrug, Korso opened the door and stepped inside the building and headed for the game room. Switching on his flashlight, he walked towards the refrigerator and bar area at the back. As before, he rolled the refrigerator away from the wall until it was at a 90-degree angle. Then he reached under the marble counter until his fingers touched the tiny switch at the back of the leftmost shelf. He flicked it to the right. There was an electronic *blip* from behind him, and he turned to see the square section of wall sliding away to reveal the keypad underneath. He waited as the automated drawer also extended itself silently out from the wall.

He just hoped his theory was correct. If that thing turned out to be anything other than a weighing scale, he was in big trouble.

He placed the flashlight on the counter and aimed it in the direction of the fridge. Opening the jiffy bag, he felt around inside and pulled out the ring he'd had made that very afternoon. It was a plain band, similar to the one he'd picked up in the evidence room back in Florida, only minus the Celtic imagery. Although it looked to be silver or platinum, it was actually made of tungsten, a cheap metal with almost exactly the same density as gold.

Korso had made some calls after Alex left this morning, and finally found a jeweller in the city with his own workshop, who'd be more than happy to make a special tungsten ring on very short notice, as long as the price was right. Korso had promised him a small fortune if he could fulfil two essential criteria: the ring would have to be made extremely quickly, and the desired weight would have to be precise to five decimal places. The only problem was Korso didn't know what that weight was going to be just yet. The jeweller had assured Korso that as soon as he texted him the correct weight, he'd get to work and have it done within an hour. So when Dog messaged Korso with the results he'd asked for on the drive to the meet, he'd immediately composed a very brief text and sent it to the jeweller:

4.23495g

The jeweller had been true to his word. Korso had paid him a visit on his way back from Vuelta Grande, where he'd been presented with the ring in question. The jeweller had two precision scales in his workshop, and Korso had tested the band on both. Each time the readout was the same: *4.2349500.* The ring even fitted on his third finger. Korso had paid the jeweller the agreed fee, along with a good tip, and left to purchase the next items on his list.

So now Korso turned to the steel tray currently protruding out of the wall. He carefully placed the tungsten band in the exact centre, and stepped back.

Nothing else happened. The room remained silent.

This second part of the combination would be the trickiest. That morning, Alex had told him Quezada disappeared every year on the same day: March 11. His infant son's birthday. And the year of his birth, and death, was 2016.

Korso approached the keypad.

He already knew the official date format for Guatemala, and for South America in general, was date-month-year. Or to be more precise: DD-MM-YYYY. But had Quezada subscribed to this format, or had he decided to add that little bit of extra security and mix things up? Maybe he'd altered it to YYYY-MM-DD. Or MM-DD-YYYY. Or, for that matter, any combination thereof.

But in Korso's experience, people tended to keep things simple where combinations were concerned. So he took a deep breath and pressed 1 on the keypad. He pressed it again. Then he pressed 0, 3, followed by 2, 0, 1 and 6.

He let out his breath.

A single red light suddenly flashed at the top of the keypad, glowing like a beacon in the darkness. It remained red.

Korso swallowed. That was both good and bad. Good, in that it confirmed he was on the right track, and he now knew what those three little holes were for. Bad, in that this looked to be a 'three strikes and out' deal. He had two more chances to get it right. Another two red lights, and it was all over. It was as simple as that.

There was no choice. He could only go onwards.

This time, he decided to reverse the order to YYYY-MM-DD. Out of the two immediate alternatives, it seemed the most likely option. He raised his index finger again, and pressed 2, 0, 1, 6, and then 0, 3, and finally 1 and 1.

Nothing.

Then a second red light joined the first.

Korso swore softly to himself. This was it. One more strike and he was out. Possibly for good. And his only defence, a compact 9mm with six rounds in the mag. Against a horde of guards armed with automatic weapons it was about as much use as a sharp stick.

So one last try. And the last remaining viable option was now MM-DD-YYYY. Unless Quezada had scrambled the numbers into a totally random order known only to him, which Korso would never guess in a hundred years. But he had to try something. And since he had no idea of what kind of time limit he had, he had to do it soon. He wiped away a globule of sweat from his hairline.

MM-DD-YYYY. 0-3-1-1-2-0-1-6. He had to chance it.

Korso raised his index finger, and let it hover over the 0 button. He didn't move. After a few moments, he slowly lowered it again. Something was tingling at the back of his mind. He was remembering his guided tour of the vault yesterday afternoon, especially those framed artworks on the wall. That Leonardo piece, in particular. He recalled Quezada saying, '*I've always loved his mirror writing, at least on an aesthetic level. It just looks right, for some reason.*' So could Quezada have literally 'mirrored' Leonardo when he came up with his own safe-room combination? By simply reversing the numbers? Not for any security reasons, but simply because it appealed to him on an aesthetic level?

Korso stood in front of the keypad without moving a muscle. He stared at the two red dots as he considered the two alternatives before him. Finally, after almost a minute, he raised his finger to the keypad.

Taking a deep breath, he pressed 6, 1, 0, 2, 3, 0, 1 and 1.

He waited.

There was no red light.

Instead, there was a solid metallic *click*, and then an electronic hum as the vault door began to open before him.

FORTY-SIX

Korso allowed himself a small grin of satisfaction as the thick steel door came to a stop, revealing the brightly lit safe room beyond. It really had been touch and go there for a moment. He knew for a fact that it wouldn't have occurred to him to reverse the date on the combination had he not discussed the particulars of that Leonardo sketch with Quezada yesterday afternoon. Fortune favours the prepared mind, as the old saying went. His continued existence was proof that it still held true.

As Korso took the ring and slipped it into his pocket, the small weighing scale silently retreated back into its slot beside the doorway. A moment later, the small section of wall slid back into its original position as well, completely concealing both keypad and slot.

Korso grabbed his flashlight and his package and stepped through the opening into the safe room. Ignoring the treasures around him, he spent a few seconds inspecting the vault door more closely. It was almost four inches thick and made of hardened steel. The rear of the door was covered in exactly the same irregular-shaped stonework as the wall surrounding it. He had no doubt that once the door was closed, it would fit perfectly flush with the rest of the wall, just as undetectable as before. But as much as he searched, he couldn't seem to find a method with which to close it. Or even open it again. There had to be a manual switch somewhere. He ran his fingers slowly up the side of the door and found nothing. He moved his fingers across the top of the door and was halfway along when he felt something touch the side of his pinkie. Like a tiny button. He pulled his hand away quickly.

Hopefully, that was the method by which Quezada had shut the door after yesterday's tour. But Korso wasn't ready to test that particular theory just yet. Not until he was done. There was still too much he didn't know about the safe room, so for safety's sake he'd have to leave the vault door open while he worked. Hardly ideal, but he couldn't take the risk.

He stepped back through the doorway and grabbed the steel handle at the rear of the fridge. He pulled the huge appliance towards him until it could go no further, and was glad to see it completely covered the opening. A certain amount of light spill could probably be seen from the outside, but it was still better than nothing.

Korso walked straight over to the work desk in the centre of the room and opened his jiffy bag. From within, he pulled out a pair of clear polythene disposable catering gloves and put them on. He reached in again and pulled out a knife and scabbard. The knife he'd picked up at a souvenir shop specialising in selling gaudy trinkets and fake Mayan antiques to the tourist trade, shortly after collecting the ring. It was a cheap piece of junk with a blade that would likely snap if you stared too hard at it. But he'd bought it mainly for the polished ceramic handle, which was a fairly decent imitation of white bone. And the shape of it wasn't too dissimilar to that of the knife handle in the display case a few feet away. The scabbard he'd purchased at a used-gun store on the same street. It was made from black wood, and looked almost the same as the one in the display case. If you didn't look too closely.

As he approached the display case in question, Korso saw the dagger was still angled over the base mount, with the wire armature holding it in place. He clamped his hands on either side of the rectangular glass display cabinet, and tried lifting it up. The whole thing came away easily. He placed it carefully on the floor.

Standing up again, Korso placed his gloved hands around the wooden scabbard, and gently detached the prized weapon from the armature. It felt extremely light, with almost no weight to it at all. Carefully placing it on the work desk, and touching only the base of the handle so as not to smudge any prints, he slowly drew the dagger from its sheath.

As it came free, he was relieved to discover the blade was clearly made out of pure jade. The shade of green was unmistakeable. He pulled the dagger out all the way, and allowed himself another smile. The lower half of the blade was completely covered in rust-coloured stains. Either dried blood, or a damn good imitation of it.

Satisfied he'd finally found what he'd come for, Korso gingerly slipped the knife back into its scabbard. From the jiffy bag, he removed three clear plastic zip-lock bags and opened them up. He also pulled out a thin, folded sheet of bubble wrap. He placed the jade dagger into the first zip-lock bag and sealed it closed. He put that into the next baggie, and then went through the same process a third time. Always better to be safe than sorry. He wrapped the sheet of bubble wrap around the whole package, inserted it back into the padded jiffy bag, and closed the flap.

He then took the fake knife and scabbard and placed it in the armature on the display case, in the exact same position as before. After enclosing it in the rectangular glass display cabinet, Korso wiped off his fingerprints and backed up a little. He gave the whole room a once over. It looked okay. Not great, but not bad. He knew the replacement knife wouldn't fool Quezada for very long, but if he only gave it a cursory glance, it might hold up. Even so, it was infinitely preferable to leaving a blank space there.

Time to leave. Grabbing the precious jiffy bag, Korso returned to the entrance and slowly pushed the refrigerator away from the doorway. As it rolled away to the left, he almost expected to see a line of guards standing there in the light, all aiming their guns at him. But there was nobody there. The game room was still empty.

Korso moved to the other side of the door and ran his fingers along the top until he felt that little button again. If that's what it was. He tapped it lightly with the tip of his finger. Nothing happened. He pressed his finger down harder, and suddenly felt a slight vibration as the door began to move back to its original position. Korso backed out of the way, and watched gratefully as the secret room was sealed up once more. He rolled the refrigerator back into its original position and was turning back to the counter when he heard a noise again.

It was a faint squeaking sound similar to last night, like a rubber sole on hard tile. It sounded as though it was coming from elsewhere in the building.

Korso's internal radar was going haywire. He might have imagined the noise the first time. But not twice. It was real. And it was close. He thought quickly. Whatever might happen next, the last thing he needed was to be caught with the dagger in his possession. He had to get rid of it. He turned back to the fridge, pulled open the door and the interior light immediately came on, showing a fridge packed with bottles and cans of sodas, as well as a large freezer compartment at the top. He reached for the light button and turned it off.

The room went dark again. Korso pulled the freezer flap open and saw it was empty except for a couple of large ice trays near the front. He placed the jiffy bag inside the compartment and pushed it all the way to the back. He positioned the two ice trays right in front of it, one on top of the other. Not much, but it was better than nothing. After a moment's pause, he also placed the little 9mm Bodyguard in there too. If it was Quezada out there, having a gun found on his person would only make things worse. Unarmed, he at least had a fair-to-evens chance of bluffing his way out.

He shut the fridge door and jogged over to the entrance to the games room. Staying close to the wall, he peered round until he could see the hallway beyond. Nothing moved out there. There were no sounds.

Korso poked part of his head out and looked to the right. As he did so, he saw a vague shadow coming right at him. Before he could move his head back out of the way, something cold and hard slammed against his right temple, and there was a momentary flash of light before everything went black.

FORTY-SEVEN

Korso's return to consciousness was painful. His skull was pounding so much he thought it might explode. He kept his eyes shut for a few more moments, hoping the intense throbbing would fade, but if anything it just grew worse. He had no idea how long he'd been out. All he remembered was a shadowy shape coming at him from the annex building hallway, and then he woke up here. Wherever *here* was.

He opened his eyes slowly and saw he was in a windowless cell, with illumination coming from a single strip light in the ceiling, just above his head. He was bound to a steel chair with legs that had been bolted to the floor. The bolts looked old. So did the chair. His hands were bound tightly behind his back with duct tape, his wrists looped around a steel column set in the back of the seat.

The room itself measured about twelve feet by ten feet, with concrete walls that looked uneven in places, almost warped. To his left was a wooden table. At one end was a cheap metal ashtray, with a thick roll of duct tape next to it. Beyond the table he spotted a single electrical socket set into the wall, just a few inches above the floor. Which didn't bode well. Directly ahead was a featureless steel door, with a steel handle and a lock underneath. There was nobody else in the room.

He tried moving his arms and shoulders around, but there was barely any give at all. And struggling would only tighten the tape further. So he stopped struggling, and waited.

As he studied the stone floor, he noticed it was heavily stained in places, especially the area around the chair. There were very old stains mixed in with more recent ones. It was hard to tell the exact colour under the harsh light, but it could only be dried blood.

Korso guessed he was currently occupying the same room where Galicia had spent his last painful hours. A fair few others had clearly met their own grisly ends here. Maybe he would too. It all depended on the identity of the next person who walked through that door. His gut feeling was that he was somewhere underground, since he could hear no sounds other than his own breathing. Possibly accessed via that trap door he'd seen in the armoury earlier. If so, that meant at least four layers of soundproofing between him and the outside world. A locked cellar, inside a locked armoury, located inside a locked garage, all of which was sealed inside a heavily protected private compound.

Not good.

But there were always options. Always, even if they might not be immediately apparent. He just had to keep his wits about him for as long as he could, and exploit any opportunity that might come along, however slight.

Korso suddenly raised his head up, listening hard. Sounds were coming from outside the room. Regular, rhythmic, but muffled. Footsteps, possibly. They continued for a few more seconds, gaining a little in volume, and then stopped. Silence. Seconds passed. Korso looked straight ahead and watched as somebody turned the handle. The door opened.

A man-shaped shadow filled the narrow opening. He was carrying a small case. The moment he stepped into the cellar, the light fell on his face.

It was Dante. And he was smiling.

'So you're awake,' he said, placing the case on the table next to Korso. He tested the duct tape holding Korso's wrists together, and nodded. 'How's your head?'

'It's been better,' Korso said. 'I don't suppose you've got an ibuprofen, by any chance? Even an aspirin would do.'

Dante patted his pockets and grimaced. 'Sorry, all out.' He came round and stood in front of Korso. 'I bet you've got a shitload of questions, am I right?'

'One or two. Such as, why am I here? Also, where is *here*?'

Dante chuckled. 'Well, the second question's easy. You're in a special little underground hideaway that very few people know exists, where nobody will bother us, or even hear us. So feel free to shout and scream as much as you want. As for what you're doing here, that's a bit more complicated.'

'All I've got is time.'

Dante raised a brow. 'Good. A sense of humour. You'll need it.' He reached into his trouser pocket and pulled out a pack of Winstons and a disposable lighter. He placed a cigarette between his lips, and said, 'You smoke?'

'Today I do.'

Dante pulled out a second cigarette and lighted them both. He stuck one between Korso's lips and backed away. Korso took a single drag of the cigarette, exhaling the smoke through his nose. The taste was rotten, but the nicotine hit was worth it. And although it was probably his imagination, it seemed the pounding in his head lessened marginally.

Speaking out the side of his mouth, he said, 'You were going to tell me why I'm here.'

'You're here because my ex-boss, Ozan, ordered me to keep a close watch on you whenever you were on the property. Right from the start, he knew there was something off about you. And even though he's not around anymore, I saw enough last night to know he was onto something. But then, he usually was.'

'Last night I was with Alejandra at her bungalow. Just like tonight. That's not exactly a secret. Even Mr Quezada knew.'

'Maybe he did. But one thing he wouldn't have known was how you sneaked out of her house in the early hours to do a little night-time exploring of your own. Unfortunately, I lost you in the trees and couldn't find you again, no matter where I looked. But I stuck with it, and luckily I spotted you an hour later as you were coming out of the gym building. Lucky for me, that is, not so lucky for you.'

Korso sucked on the cigarette again. He was remembering the glimpses he'd seen of that guard last night as he made his nightly patrol of the grounds. Or that's what he'd thought at the time. But it must have been Dante, searching for him.

'No comment? Well, that's okay. You'll have plenty to say in a short while. You won't be able to stop yourself. So, anyway, I decided to keep a closer watch on you tonight, and it's a good thing I did. Because what do I see but you sneaking out of her house again, except this time you head down to the garage for some reason, before making your way back to the utility building like before. I figure you must have hidden something in that SUV and come back for it. What was it?'

'My cell phone. I left it in the glove compartment by mistake.'

'Really? Because I searched you thoroughly before tying you up, and guess what? No cell phone. So where is it?'

'I transferred it to my Honda. I didn't need it particularly, but I didn't want someone to just drive off with it either. There are some important numbers on there.'

Dante shrugged as he took a drag of his cigarette. 'I can check on that, but we'll leave it for now. So then I followed you back to the gym building, but had to wait a few minutes before I went in myself. I couldn't find a sign of you anywhere, and I checked every room. So where were you?'

'Hiding,' Korso said. 'I was in the game room when I thought I heard someone at the main entrance, so I quickly ducked down under cover. When I finally came out, you slugged me and I woke up here.'

'More bullshit. I know every part of this compound like the back of my hand, and those entrance doors don't make a single sound. Nor did I. You couldn't have heard me.'

'If you say so.' Korso turned his head and spat the rest of the cigarette onto the floor. He'd already had enough, and the smoke was beginning to sting his eyes. 'You still haven't explained why you brought me down here.'

'Simple. With Ozan dead I've been moved up another level in the hierarchy. I may not be anywhere near Ozan's level just yet, but I'm a fast learner and I figure the best way to climb another step up the ladder is to provide Mr Quezada with concrete evidence that there's a rotten apple in his ranks. And that's where you come in.'

Dante took a last drag of his smoke and stamped the rest out onto the floor. 'See,' he continued, 'in these kinds of situations, I usually tell the poor dummy in the chair that it'll go easier for them if they just tell me everything I want to know right now, that it'll save them a lot of time and a lot of pain. Sometimes it works out, sometimes it doesn't. But in your case, I know I won't be able to just take your word for it. You're a little too slick for your own good, a little too quick with your answers, and I have to be sure that you're telling the truth. And I mean absolutely sure, beyond all reasonable doubt. You understand?'

Korso said nothing as Dante moved to the table and patted a hand against the small case. 'Which brings us to my little box of tricks here. Let's take a look inside, shall we?'

Without waiting for an answer, Dante opened the lid. As much as he hated to, Korso couldn't help but look at the contents. Inside, he saw a variety of electrical equipment, along with a large assortment of knives, scalpels, and other lethal-looking objects. His mouth went dry at the sight. His pulse was thudding in his ears, and in the back of his skull. Dante clearly knew the right approach, and understood that the torture victim's anticipation of the torment that lay ahead was an essential part of the psychological process.

From the case, Dante pulled out a small black box and placed it on the table. Korso saw a number of ports at the rear of the box. On the top was a digital display, along with a small touchpad and three large dials. Dante also pulled out a coiled cable and unwound it. Humming to himself, he plugged one end of the cable into the rear of the box, while the other end went into the wall socket. Next, he pulled out a long, thin USB cable. This he also plugged into the back of the box. The other end he left free.

'I imagine all kinds of thoughts are going on inside your head right now,' Dante said. 'You can see electricity will play a part, but which area of your body will I use it on? Maybe your balls? They're always a good reliable source of pain, but a bit too obvious. Besides, I've been doing this kind of thing for a while now, and I can tell you there are far more sensitive areas on the human body.' He rooted around in the case again, and said, 'Now where the hell is it? I'm sure I put it back in... oh, here it is.'

Korso watched him remove a thin metal skewer from the case. Unlike the usual meat skewers used in barbeques or grills, this one had a thick handle fitted at one end, instead of the usual hook. Dante held it by the handle and plugged the other end of the USB lead into a socket in the bottom. He showed it to Korso.

'They call this a picana,' Dante said. 'Want to know how it works?'

Korso already knew how it worked. He'd suffered the effects of the picana a long time ago, in a room not dissimilar to this one. He'd been a lot younger back then, of course, and the arrogance of youth enabled him to believe he could take anything thrown at him. He soon learned otherwise. 'I'm sure you'll tell me anyway.'

Dante smiled as he brought the skewer closer to Korso's face. He touched the pointed end with a finger. 'Bronze-tipped,' he said, 'for better conductivity, of course. And the rubber-coated plastic handle here is fully insulated. As for the voltage... wait, I'll show you.'

He moved the control unit around until they could both see it. Pressing a switch at the back, the box hummed into life, and the display showed a digital read-out of *000*.

'As you've probably worked out,' Dante said, 'this is a standard control unit with an inbuilt rheostat to raise and lower the voltage.' He turned the leftmost dial until the read-out changed to *25000*. 'Doesn't sound like much, does it? Here, check this out.'

Dante leaned in and tapped the tip of the picana against Korso's forehead. Korso felt a sudden electric jolt and instinctively pulled his head back as far as possible. He was surprised to discover there was almost no residual pain. Other than his headache, that is.

'See?' Dante said. 'No worse than a jolt of static electricity. But that's only part of the procedure, and I only touched it against your skin for less than a second. But the best thing about it is the low current, which means I can keep this going for hours, even days in some cases, without actually killing the victim. And it won't leave any physical marks either.

'Now this instrument's thin enough to enter any orifice in your body, but I find the really useful areas to be the nasal cavity and the ear. So that's where I'll be concentrating most. First, I'll insert this into your skull via the ear channel, but without electricity at this point. You won't feel anything at first, but then when the tip reaches the pain receptors and nerve endings in there, you'll feel it all right. That's usually when the screaming starts. It's hard to imagine the agony you'll experience at that stage. But just when you feel it can't get any worse, I'll hit you with 50,000 volts right in your eardrum. Boom. Indescribable pain. Your brain will feel like it's melting. Then after that we've still got the nasal cavity, but we can hold off on that for the moment. I don't want to give away all my surprises just yet.'

Korso looked at him. 'You enjoy your work. I can tell.'

Dante put down the skewer, lit another cigarette. 'What can I say? Once you develop a skill, you want to practise as much as you can. And I learned from a master. Ozan spent a lot of time teaching me everything he knew, until after a while I managed to teach *him* a few tricks. But let's stick to the point of the exercise, shall we? I want to know why you're really here, and since you're going to tell me sooner or later, it might as well be now. If your answer's good enough, we might even forget the pain aspect altogether. It all depends on you. Now let's keep it nice and simple. Who are you, and what are you really after?'

'My name really is Graves,' Korso said. 'And I came here to work for Mr Quezada as a trouble-shooter. That's all.'

'Exactly what I thought you'd say.' Dante blew out smoke and placed his cigarette in the ashtray. 'So let's get on with it, shall we?'

FORTY-EIGHT

Dante stepped around the table until he was positioned directly behind Korso. Without a moment's pause, he clamped his left arm around Korso's neck in a choke hold, at the same time pulling Korso's head back against his chest. Korso began thrashing violently from side to side in an effort to pull away, even though he knew it was useless. Dante quickly increased his pressure against his neck, further limiting his movements.

The moment Korso felt the cold tip of the picana probing his right ear channel, he immediately stopped struggling and became still. He still had enough sense to know he'd only cause further harm to himself if he continued thrashing about.

'Very good,' Dante whispered. 'You're a fast learner too. I like that.'

Korso just waited for the worst. It was all he could do. The seconds passed.

The pain came suddenly, like somebody turning on a switch, as violent as a lightning strike. The intense, blazing agony in his ear was worse than anything he'd ever experienced, as though somebody were using a blowtorch in his head. Actually *inside* his head. And it didn't stop. It just kept on going. Korso heard himself groaning and whimpering at the incessant pain that came in waves and seemed to go on and on and on. It came in long intense bursts, with brief pauses before it started all over again.

Korso tried to partition off a small part of his mind, create a tiny refuge where he could escape, even for just a few seconds. But it was impossible. The physical agony was all-devouring.

The torment was inexhaustible, limitless, seemingly without end. Another brief interval and then the same thing all over again. And again. And again. And again. Wave after wave after wave. Korso was unaware of the passing of time. Pain became his whole world. His universe. Nothing else but.

Then, just as Korso thought it couldn't get any worse, a sudden jolt of electricity sizzled through his ear and into his skull, and all his muscles seized and cramped up at once, and his head became a liquid ball of fire. The agony was indescribable.

That was when Korso screamed. And he kept on screaming.

At some point – there was no telling when – the pain simply ceased. It was. Then it wasn't.

Korso stopped screaming. Maybe he already had. It was hard to tell. He let his head drop forward and saw beads of sweat dripping onto the floor. It felt as though it were coming from someone other than him. No blood, though. That was good. His throat felt hoarse, and he could taste metal in his mouth. The right side of his head throbbed painfully, but he could still hear. He breathed in. He breathed out. He tried to think. It was hard, but he had to try. Had to.

There was a way out. There was always a way out.

Raising his head slowly, Korso saw Dante standing next to the table. He was smoking another cigarette. Or maybe the same one. That was a scary thought. Korso quickly put it out of his mind.

'So was it everything I promised?' Dante asked. 'One guy told me it was like being on a rollercoaster ride through hell, which I really liked. Now how was it for you?'

Korso tried to answer, but all that came out was a croak. He coughed a few times to clear his throat, and spat on the floor. Meanwhile, he was gathering his thoughts as best he could. He already saw a thin sliver of hope ahead, but he'd have to tread very carefully. He couldn't just hand it over on a plate, but neither could he afford to go through that agony again. Not if he wanted to walk out of this room the same person.

'Well?' Dante prompted.

'I've never experienced pain that intense,' Korso said. 'Not ever.'

'Sweet music to my ears.' Dante grinned. 'So you ready to talk now, or you want to move on to stage two? I'm easy either way.'

'I'll talk. Give me a moment to get my breath back, and I'll tell you whatever you want to know.'

Dante gave an irritated shake of his head. 'You've already had enough rest. Now tell me your name. Your *real* name.'

'I didn't lie about that. My real name *is* Ricardo Graves. But the rest is fiction. I didn't come here looking for steady employment. I just needed to be allowed free access to this compound, and kidnapping Galicia to gain Mr Quezada's trust was the most effective way of achieving that. There's something here that I want, and I needed time to find it.'

'Like what?'

'Like a blood diamond. It's supposed to be one of the biggest and most valuable in the world, and it's currently hidden away inside a secret trophy room Mr Quezada had built a few years back. Word is he keeps all his other treasures in there too. Since Ozan was close to Mr Quezada he would surely have known about the secret room, although he probably didn't know its exact location. But you were Ozan's right-hand man, so I imagine you at least heard rumours about it.'

Dante said nothing to that, which proved he was on the right track. Close-knit communities were invariably a hive of rumour and gossip, and there was no reason to think Quezada's private enclave was any different.

'This diamond,' Dante said. 'How big is it?'

And *that* was music to Korso's ears. The bastard was hooked. 'I don't know the exact dimensions, but it's around the size of a child's fist. I do know it's 714 carats, which translates to eighty million dollars at today's prices. And that's a minimum. It was my plan to find it, sell it on the black market, and then relocate to a remote island and live off the interest.'

'So why not just disappear with the boss's emeralds instead? They were practically handed to you on a plate.'

'I wish I had now. But at the time, I figured why settle for a slice when I can have the whole cake?'

Dante considered that. Greed was probably something he could relate to fairly easily. 'If all this is supposed to be such a big secret, how did you find out about it?'

'I learned about the blood diamond from the guy who stole it from Botswana in the first place. The rest I picked up from various sources, including a close relative of one of the workmen who helped build this room for Mr Quezada. He was killed once the safe room was finished, along with all his fellow workers, but not before he told his sister about the job he was working on. And after a certain amount of persuasion, this sister told me.'

Dante took another drag of his smoke, pursing his lips in thought. Korso let him think. He was using the time to heal. He could already feel his strength returning with each passing second.

'So this secret vault's located in the game room?' Dante said. 'Where?'

'At the back,' Korso said. 'There's a hidden opening in the wall behind the refrigerator. I found it last night. I was planning on accessing the room tonight, but then I heard noises from the hallway, so I decided to investigate. Then I woke up here.'

'Access it how?'

Korso told him about the little switch under the counter, and the keypad and weighing scale hidden in the wall. 'It's a two-part combination,' he said. 'You have to place an item of a particular weight on the scale, and then enter an eight-digit code on the keypad. Get either one wrong, and it's game over.'

'But you know the code.'

'I didn't last night, but I do now.'

'What is it?'

Korso told him the date Quezada had used for his code, and explained its special significance. He didn't mention that it had to be reversed, though.

'And what is it you have to weigh on the scale?' Dante asked.

'I had it in my pocket. You said you searched me, so it's probably in yours now.'

Dante frowned, placed his hand in his left trouser pocket, and pulled out the plain tungsten ring. 'You mean this?'

Korso nodded his head. 'I had that ring made specially today, and picked it up on the return journey. It's the same weight as the gold Mayan ring Mr Quezada always keeps on him, precise to five decimal places. I got the exact weight from the auction house he bought it from.' Korso gave a regretful sigh and shook his head. 'All I had to do was key in the code, place that ring on the scale, and I was in. Just five minutes more. I was so close.'

'Only if you're right about both parts of the combination,' he said, pocketing the ring again. 'Because I don't believe—'

Dante stopped mid-sentence, listening. Korso could hear it too. Noises were coming from outside the room. It sounded like something slamming, followed by footsteps. Loud footsteps. Dante gripped the gun in his shoulder holster and slowly backed away from the door.

Moments later, the steel door was pushed open, and Miguel Quezada stood in the opening. He was wearing a navy-blue silk dressing gown with an intricate floral design and plain black pyjama bottoms. He held a revolver in his right hand. He looked from Dante to Korso, and then back to Dante again.

'I want an explanation.'

FORTY-NINE

'Mr Quezada,' Dante stammered, clearly rattled by his boss's sudden appearance. 'Sir, I didn't want to wake—'

'I asked you a question. What is all this? Why's that man in this chair?'

Korso was already thinking two steps ahead. As soon as he'd heard the footsteps, he knew they could only belong to one man. He also knew there was only one way he could have known anyone else was down here. And if that were the case…

'I couldn't sleep, Mr Quezada,' Korso cut in. 'I was taking a late-night stroll around the grounds when I spotted Dante here entering the utility building. So I was curious and followed him in, and I saw him doing something in the games room, behind the—'

The punch landed on Korso's right temple, right at the point where it hurt most. Korso yelled out in pain as his head snapped to the left, and he heard Dante saying, 'That's bullshit, Mr Quezada. I was the one who discovered *him* in the building. In fact—'

'Dante,' Quezada said in an ominous tone, 'when I want you to speak, you'll speak. But right now I want to hear the rest of that sentence. So, Graves, you were saying, behind the *what*?'

Korso looked up at him. 'Behind the refrigerator. I was by the doorway and saw Dante placing an item on a small panel poking out of the wall. I couldn't see too much, but it looked metallic. I was about to move in for a better look when somebody decked me on the back of the head. Next thing I knew I was tied up in this chair.'

Quezada turned to his subordinate. 'Dante?'

'None of that's true, boss. Mr Ozan told me to keep a close watch on this guy, and late last night I spotted him leaving Miss Alejandra's place. I lost him for a while, but about an hour later I saw him exit the gym building and head back to her bungalow. So I made sure to keep an eye on Miss Alejandra's place tonight. And sure enough, he came out again a short while ago. I followed him to the garage first, and then back to the gym building like before. When he poked his head out of the games room, I knocked him out and brought him here. I planned on getting the whole truth out of him before waking you.' He reached into his pocket, brought out the tungsten ring and handed it over. 'I also found this on him, boss. He gave me some story about trying to access a secret vault where you've got a huge blood diamond stashed. This ring's supposed to be part of the combination to get inside.'

'Is that right?' Quezada briefly looked the ring over, and came over to the table. He pulled a smartphone from his dressing gown pocket and swiped the screen a few times. He set the phone down on the flat surface. Dante came over and stood at his boss's side. Korso saw Quezada had accessed a touchscale website, with a large blank square taking up the centre of the screen. A numeric display under the square read *0.00g*. Quezada placed the tungsten ring on the white square and the numbers rose to *4.21g*, before changing to *4.22g*.

As they all stared at the display, Korso's attention was diverted by another sound coming from outside this room. Or so he hoped. The sound was very brief, and very faint. Quezada and Dante hadn't noticed anything, and Korso couldn't be sure he'd heard it at all. His hearing wasn't exactly at its best right now. Meanwhile, Quezada took the tungsten ring off the phone and the numbers returned to zero. He pulled his gold ring from his finger and placed it on the same spot on the square. Once again, the display read *4.22g*.

Quezada stared hard at Korso as he placed the gold ring back on his finger. 'This looks bad for you. Very bad, indeed.'

Korso said nothing. He could see there was no point trying to shift the blame onto Dante any more. Quezada wasn't stupid. Besides, he'd only wanted to buy himself a few extra minutes.

Quezada put both the phone and the tungsten ring in his dressing gown pocket. Then he suddenly clamped his hand tightly around Korso's neck, trapping his windpipe and cutting off his air supply. He slowly forced Korso's head back until he was looking directly up into eyes that were as dark as space.

'I let you inside,' Quezada said, his voice barely above a whisper. 'That was my mistake, and mine alone. Nobody from the outside has ever gotten this close to me before. *Nobody*. And if that weren't bad enough, I even let you touch Alex. I'm not sure which is the worse sin. But luckily, all mistakes can be rectified.'

He squeezed even harder. Korso's head began to spin, while the pounding behind his eyeballs intensified by the power of ten. His lungs started burning as they tried to take in air that was no longer there. He could already see dark spots at the edge of his vision, while Quezada continued to stare at him with contempt.

Korso looked up at him blankly. He was powerless to do anything else. The dark spots were already growing larger as he steadily grew weaker. He waited for the darkness to take over completely, when without warning Quezada yanked his hand away. With his airway suddenly freed, Korso took in huge great gulps of oxygen, filling his lungs to the brim while coughing and spluttering at the same time. Air had never tasted so good. Once his breathing was more or less back to normal, he looked up to see Quezada still watching him.

'I still have questions,' Quezada said calmly. 'How did you find my room?'

Korso swallowed, then said, 'The quinine they use in tonic water shows up under a UV light, so I just followed the markings I'd left. The rest I figured out for myself. I never got the chance to find out if I was right, though.'

Quezada pursed his lips as he thought this over. 'And your account of today's events earlier, how much of that was true?'

'Not much,' Korso said. 'I was the one who actually killed Ozan, but it was him or me. He was planning to use me as the test subject for that laser weapon, not Flores. He told me so in the car. I had to act, so I did.'

Quezada's jaw tightened at this. Korso went on quickly, 'Since I clearly wasn't meant to last out the day, Ozan also told me something else of interest when I pressed him. He admitted to me that he was the one who wasted Alex's financier boyfriend, Sander, and he said you knew all about it.' There was a pause, and in his peripheral vision Korso saw a shadow appear on the wall in the corridor outside. But Korso kept his gaze entirely on Quezada and Dante. 'In fact, Ozan practically admitted that the order came directly from you, which kind of surprised me. That surely can't be right, can it?'

Quezada just looked at him and said nothing.

From the doorway, a voice said, 'You better answer him, Miguel.'

FIFTY

Three heads turned in unison. Korso had never seen a more welcome sight in his life. Alex stood there in jeans and t-shirt, gripping a small semi-automatic pistol in a two-handed Weaver stance. The gun was pointed at Quezada. Korso immediately recognised it as his micro compact S&W Bodyguard, which told him all he needed to know. Alex was breathing heavily, but she looked calm and composed. In control.

'Alex,' Quezada said in a soothing tone, 'I told you I'd handle this. What are you doing down here?'

'Getting the whole story at last.' Dante began to move his left hand up his body, and Alex instantly adjusted her aim to include him. 'If you even try for that gun, I'll shoot you. Don't think I won't. As for you, Miguel, throw your gun on the floor. That goes for you too, Dante. But make sure you do it very, *very* slowly.'

'With your right hand,' Korso said.

Alex nodded. 'Yes. With your right hand.'

Dante didn't move. He stayed perfectly still, and just looked at her.

'Alex,' Quezada said, 'I don't know what's come over you all of a sudden, but—'

The sudden gunshot was deafening in the enclosed space. Quezada and Dante froze as though time had stopped. Alex stood in the exact same position, gun still pointing at them. 'That was a warning. The next one won't be. Drop your weapons, both of you.'

Quezada dropped his revolver to the floor. Using just his right hand, Dante slowly removed his piece from his holster and let it fall to the concrete too.

'Now kick them towards the corner of the room,' she said. 'To my left.'

'One at a time,' Korso said.

Dante did as he was told. One by one, he slid the guns across the floor until they each clattered into the corner to Alex's left.

'You're a sight for sore eyes, Alex,' Korso said. 'Any chance of getting me out of this chair?'

'Back up first, you two,' she said. 'Up against the rear wall.'

'Alex,' Quezada said, 'you're making a huge mistake. I don't know what this man's been telling you, but it's all fiction. He's a pathological liar. He hasn't spoken a word of truth since he arrived.'

'It takes one to know one,' she said. 'I told you both to back up.'

Both men reluctantly did as they were told. Keeping her gun pointed at them, Alex came over to the table and grabbed a scalpel from the case. She stepped behind Korso, and he felt her place the handle in his right palm. 'Can you do it yourself?'

'Gladly.' Korso curled his fingers around the handle and began cutting into the tape.

Alex backed up until she was facing the other two again. 'You know, in the back of my mind I always suspected Ozan had something to do with Sander's murder, but to find out that it was *you* who arranged it... Why? What the hell did Sander ever do to you? Or was it simply that you couldn't stand the thought of me having a life apart from you? Or that I'd finally found some real happiness in my life, and that you weren't a part of it?'

'I'm telling you, Alex, *none* of it happened the way this man said it did. I was as much in the dark as you as to who kidnapped and killed Sander. You remember how I utilised all my resources to find those responsible, and we *still* couldn't find anything concrete. I'm convinced whoever was behind it used mechanics from overseas, and he most likely had them all killed after the job was done to throw off any trails. That's the only way it could have happened.'

'I remember, Miguel. And that was the part that always bothered me. That you, with all your sources and street contacts, couldn't find a single clue as to the real perpetrators. I think a part of me always knew the real reason why, but I just wouldn't admit it to myself. But now it's all as clear as day.'

'Alex, you've got it all backwards. Now put that gun down. You're not going to kill me in cold blood. I know you like my—' He stopped short.

'Like your own sister? Is that what you were going to say?'

Korso had been working as fast as he could while he listened to them talk. Finally, he cut through enough of the tape that he was able to pull his left hand partly away from the steel bar in the chair. He switched the scalpel to that hand, and moments later he had both hands free. As he finally got to his feet, he felt a sudden surge of pain in his temple and the room started to spin. He dropped the scalpel and placed a hand against the table for support.

'Ric,' Alex said, 'are you—'

Korso saw movement out the corner of his eye as Dante launched himself from the wall and rushed towards him. Acting purely on impulse, Korso grabbed the skewer from the work table and turned to face Dante, who was less than three feet away and closing. There was a single gunshot from behind them. Korso ignored it as he jabbed his arm forward, driving the skewer straight into the centre of Dante's chest. He kept pushing it further into his body, using Dante's own momentum against him. Dante halted his attack, and screamed out in shock and pain. He frantically tried to pull the object out while Korso turned back to the table and grabbed the control unit.

He placed his finger on the leftmost dial, and turned it to the right. All the way.

Dante stopped screaming, and his body began to convulse violently as he dropped to the floor, both hands curled into claws, the picana still sticking out of his chest like a vampire's stake. Korso turned away from him, and saw Quezada slumped on the floor against the rear wall, both hands clasped against his left leg. A small amount of blood seeped out between his fingers.

Alex was breathing heavily and wiping her brow as she picked her gun up off the floor. There was a red bruise on her right cheek.

'You okay?' he asked.

She turned to him. 'I'm fine. But you look like hell.'

'Funny you should say that. That's exactly where this one took me before you showed up. He's getting his own taste now.'

Dante's body was still jerking uncontrollably on the floor, his face a picture of agony as 200,000 volts of electricity surged through his heart and nervous system. Korso could already smell burning flesh. He watched for a few more moments, and then the spasms came to a sudden stop. Dante's body relaxed and his expression became blank, his eyes staring up at nothing. Whatever he had been was gone.

'Well, that's that,' Korso said, and turned off the current.

'And now you're planning on killing me too?' Quezada said.

'I didn't come here for you,' Korso said. 'I told you I'm not an assassin.'

'It wasn't you I was talking about.'

Korso turned round, and saw Alex aiming her gun at Quezada's head. 'I want to, Miguel. I really want to. You don't know how much. When you took Sander from me, you took all hope out of my life and I've practically been a shell ever since. Why shouldn't you receive the same fate as him? Tell me that.'

Quezada just glared up at her silently. Giving her nothing.

'Leave him, Alex,' Korso said. 'There's another way. A more satisfying way.'

'What are you talking about?'

‘I’ll tell you once we’re out of here. Come on, let’s go.’

He waited. Gradually, he watched the anger fade from her features and she slowly lowered the weapon. As she turned away and silently walked out of the room, Korso went over to the corner and picked up the two remaining handguns from the floor. Then he searched Dante’s body until he found a cell phone. He turned back to Quezada. ‘Yours too. Slide it over to me.’

From his dressing gown pocket, Quezada took out his cell phone and slid it across the floor. Korso stopped it with his foot, and then stamped on it, hard. More than once. He did the same with Dante’s phone.

‘So what now?’ Quezada said. ‘Or are you planning on leaving me down here to rot?’

‘That’s not my intention,’ Korso said. ‘I’ll get your wife’s phone number from Alex, and once I’m out of the country I’ll let her know where to find you. I want you alive and healthy.’

‘Why?’

‘You’ll find out.’

FIFTY-ONE

Outside in the corridor, Korso slammed the steel door shut and slid the heavy bolt across, locking Quezada inside. Alex was nowhere to be seen. He turned to his right and saw a set of concrete steps fifteen feet away, leading up to an open hatchway above. Korso climbed up the steps and wasn't surprised to find himself back in the armoury.

Alex was halfway down the narrow room, standing with her back against one of the workbenches. He lowered the hatch until it locked into place, and walked over to her. He placed the two handguns on the table.

'I heard you talking to him in there,' she said. 'Why *not* leave him to rot? It's no more than he deserves.'

'Because it's far less than he deserves. How did you even know I was down there?'

She gave him a thin smile. 'That was easy. I was hiding behind one of the arcade machines in the gaming room, so I had a front-row seat.'

'You were already in there? Why?'

'Because I'd already followed you there early yesterday morning, when you found that keypad behind the refrigerator, and so I naturally wanted to find out what you'd do today. I can be very quiet when I want to be, Ric. If that *is* your real name.'

'Not even close.' He shrugged. 'Sorry.'

'So what do I call you?'

'People know me as Korso. Although I'd prefer you keep that fact to yourself.'

'Don't worry... Korso. I know how to keep a secret. So when I heard you climb out of bed again this morning, I quickly got dressed and watched you head down towards the front of the estate, and then I simply made my way to the gaming room and waited. I figured you'd be back soon enough, and I was right. I assume that date I gave you was helpful in getting inside that hidden room?'

'More than helpful. It was essential.'

'Thought so. Anyway, when you came out shortly after, I saw you first hide that package and the gun inside the freezer, and then a few seconds later you were knocked unconscious by Dante. I followed from a distance as he carried you down to the garage and then into this armoury, but by the time I reached the door it was locked again and I don't know the access code. So I went back for the gun, and then woke Miguel up and told him to come check for himself, only this time I took note of the code he inputted.'

Korso leaned down and kissed her lightly on the lips. 'I'm very grateful you did. So if you took the gun from the freezer, you must have taken the jiffy bag too.'

'Of course. I left it in your car's glove compartment, along with your cell phone. I figured you wouldn't want to hang around here any longer than you had to.'

'You really do think of everything. Did you look inside the package?'

She nodded. 'All I saw was a Mayan dagger. It doesn't look all that valuable, although I suppose it must be.'

'You'd be surprised.' As Korso led them out of the room, he explained what made the dagger priceless to certain parties, which also explained why he wanted Quezada alive. By the time he'd finished, they were both standing next to his Honda Civic in the garage. As Alex had promised, the keys were in the ignition.

'You mean you're doing all this for a friend?' she asked.

'More or less. I don't have many, so I can't afford to lose the few I've got. But you're also on that very short list now, Alex, and I always honour my debts. So if you ever need help, any kind of help at all, just send me an email and I'll come running. I'll give you the address before I go. I check in on it every day.'

'I'll remember that.' Alex smiled up at him. 'I knew from the moment we first met that things were going to change around here. You've got that look of concealed chaos about you. I just had no idea how quickly it would all happen. How long do you think Miguel's got before they come for him?'

'Days. A week, at most. If I were you, I'd leave the country for a while, go on vacation somewhere. Believe me, you don't want to be anywhere near this place when the axe falls. Have you left anything here you can't live without?'

She thought it over for a moment, and shook her head. 'Not anymore.'

'Then let me drive you back to your apartment before I head for the airport myself. My advice is to pack a bag, and then just get yourself a ticket somewhere. Anywhere.'

'That might not be a bad idea. Okay, you're on.'

Alex went round and opened the front passenger door and got in, while Korso jogged over to the nearest garage door and raised it up manually. Returning to the Honda, he got behind the driver's seat and started the engine and steered them outside. The dashboard clock read 04.49. It was still dark. When they reached the front gates, Alex's presence was sufficient to get them through without any questions.

Once they were completely clear of the compound, Alex said, 'So where are you headed next? We could fly out together.' She turned to him. 'Couldn't we?'

He shook his head. 'I'm not what you're looking for, Alex. You can do a lot better, and you will. If that's what you ultimately want.'

She didn't answer immediately. She faced front and watched the empty road ahead of them. 'I guess time will tell, right?'

'It invariably does,' he said.

And they left it at that.

EPILOGUE

Korso was sitting on the rear terrace of his villa in Santorini, sipping a glass of red Chablis as he watched the dark blue of the Mediterranean below when the cell phone on the table began vibrating.

It had been six days since he'd left Guatemala. After dropping off Alex at her apartment building, Korso had driven straight to the central FedEx office, located west of La Aurora International Airport. He waited an hour for it to open and then arranged for his package to be couriered to Verhoeven's office in Lyon, via the First Overnight service. Once he landed in Athens, he called a very anxious Luana Quezada and told her where she could find her husband. He also advised her to bring a doctor.

Verhoeven messaged Korso the next morning to let him know she'd received the package safely. She then called that afternoon to confirm that not only was it Vice-President Dias's blood on the blade, but that seven visible prints of Quezada's had been retrieved from the bone handle. And they were beautiful examples too. Not only that, but forensics lifted three more latents belonging to the assassin, Juan Arriola. She sounded very happy.

Two days later, an army of police entered Quezada's compound by force, whereupon Quezada was charged with Conspiracy to Murder and immediately placed under arrest. To add insult to injury, the police officer who placed the handcuffs on him was none other than his newly resurrected arch-nemesis, Deputy Chief Manuel Pineda, which must have given Quezada quite the shock. But with friends in high places you could do almost anything, and it seemed Verhoeven had plenty of those. Apart from Korso, Verhoeven and Pineda, only five other people had known of the deception, and one of those was the president himself.

While Korso took care of the manual details, Verhoeven had done all the behind-the-scenes manoeuvring to ensure everything went exactly to plan. The hardest part was convincing Pineda that faking his own death would be the final nail in Quezada's coffin, but he was a smart cop. Once it was all explained to him, he eventually came round to the idea.

When Pineda arrived at the building site, the carefully disfigured corpse of a gang member who'd been killed in a police shootout that morning was already in the elevator cage, having been placed there by Pineda's sergeant, who was also in on the plan. Korso's placement of those extra cement sacks near the twenty-first-floor elevator entrance had enabled Pineda to duck down out of sight just before entering the cage, at which point he simply activated the elevator remotely.

One man goes up, another one comes down. Proving once and for all that the simplest plans were often the best.

Korso checked the phone's display. The caller was anonymous. He took the call anyway. He'd been waiting for this one. Afterwards, he'd get rid of the phone for good.

'Hey, K,' Dog said. This time it was a female voice, with a slightly husky tone.

'Hello, Dog. How are things?'

'Things are kind of amazing. Tell me, how would you feel if I erected a statue of you in Times Square, with just the words "The Man" underneath? Or maybe a personalised fireworks display would be more your thing. You know, with "Korso for King" or something, flashing over the Giza pyramids. After all, I know how you love the limelight.' Dog chuckled at his/her joke.

It was a very cute chuckle. Korso hadn't heard this particular voice on the modulator before. Then he frowned. *Or had he…?*

'You sound fairly full of yourself,' he said.

'Like someone who just got sprung from jail, you mean? Well, can you blame me? I've been on a natural high for the last two days. Right now, I'm full of love for the world and everyone in it. Seriously, how did you do it? With that cop, Pineda, I mean. I really thought you'd wasted him.'

'Killing cops is not good business, Dog. You know that. Besides, your friend Verhoeven did all the heavy lifting in setting things up with him and the other heavyweights. I just pressed a button. Actually, I didn't even get to do that.'

'Yeah, right. So who was the guy in the elevator?'

'Nobody who'll be missed. So I take it your friends from Interpol kept their word? You're a free person again?'

'That I am, K. That I am. And I see another beautiful day ahead of me.'

'And would you say I've fulfilled my end of the contract to your complete satisfaction?'

'You could very well say that, K.'

'Which leaves just one piece of unfinished business between us.'

'Yeah, I was kind of wondering when we'd get around to that.'

'Face to face, Dog. That's what we agreed. I hope you're not thinking of reneging.'

'Who, me? I always keep my word. That's why I give it so rarely.'

'Good. I approve of this voice you're using, by the way. Is it a new one?'

Dog snorted. 'Anything but. I'm really pleased you like it, though, because this just happens to be my honest-to-God real voice.'

That got Korso's attention. 'Interesting,' he said. 'Now I'm really looking forward to seeing its owner in the flesh.'

'Who says you haven't already, sugar pie?'